A seashell necklace, found in a deposit layer
in Bizmoune Cave (southwest Morocco), is
believed to be the oldest known jewelry on
Earth, dating back 142,000-150,000 years.
Source: Science Advances Journal

Also by Alfred M. Struthers:

THE THIRD FLOOR MYSTERY SERIES
The Case of Secrets
The Phantom Vale
The Curse of Halim
The Demon Tide
The Stone Ghost
The Grim Fugue
The Watchman's Keep

CHAPTER BOOKS
Did You Hear That?
(illustrated by Cathy Provoda)

PICTURE BOOKS
Pepperoni Macaroni
(illustrated by Cathy Provoda)

Available at:
Thirdfloorbooksllc.com

The Tears Of the Empress

A Third Floor Mystery

By Alfred M. Struthers

Third
Floor
Books

thirdfloorbooksllc.com

Book design by Third Floor Books

ISBN: 979-8-9870736-6-7

10 9 8 7 6 5 4 3 2 1

Published by Third Floor Books, LLC

thirdfloorbooksllc.com

Dedication

For Johnny,
the cool one

"Martin, it's all psychological. You yell
barracuda, everybody says, 'Huh? What?'.
You yell shark, we've got a panic on our
hands on the Fourth of July."

(Jaws, 1975)

Prologue

Saturday, August 7, 1858
Hammond Books
Cambridge, MA

At first, William Hammond wasn't sure what to make of the bookcase in the back office at Hammond Books. Banished to the furthest corner of the room where it was blanketed in shadows, something about the rugged wooden case was offsetting. His father Daniel never spoke of it. When asked about its origin or unusual placement in the office, he would quickly change the subject. At five years old, brimming with a seemingly endless list of questions about the world that consumes every child, William was instructed, in the most stringent terms, to never, ever, speak of the bookcase with anyone outside the family.

Five years later, at age 10, his initial curiosity about it had morphed into a low hum of suspicion. He noticed the peculiar way his father chose the books he stored on its shelves, never revealing what thread connected them, or why, unlike every other book in the shop, they needed to be sequestered in the back room, well away from the curious eyes of the bookshop's regular patrons.

At 15, with a more developed social awareness, William took greater interest in local chatter about court verdicts suddenly being overturned; whispers about innocent people, previously slandered or shamed, getting their due vindication, and tales of ruthlessness enacted upon the weak or defenseless being brought to light.

In his younger years he had no use for such gossip. The names and tribulations of those involved, as unfortunate as they were, held no relevance to his life. But that changed when he happened across one such name in a book his father left in the office, one William saw him take from the bookcase.

There was no mistaking it. The person named in the book was the same person in the news story—subjected to cruelty that had gone unpunished. Then, a month after reading the account, William learned that the offender had been identified and brought to justice.

William's suspicions were instantly confirmed with the startling realization that his father was secretly linked to each of those remarkable news stories. What's more, his questions about the bookcase had finally been answered: it was his father's personal storehouse of atrocities.

Work yet to be done.

Quietly.

For those in need.

Some months later, on a blustery Saturday morning in September, he was cleaning and categorizing books in his father's office when Vincent, one of his father's good friends, slipped into the room and quickly shut the door.

William put down the book in his hand, a newly released copy of Norse myths by Annie Keary entitled *The Heroes of Asgard: Tales from Scandinavian Mythology*, and said, "If you're looking for my dad, he's not here. But if you like, I can pass along a message."

Vincent, dressed in casual street clothes that gave no indication of his position with the recently established Cambridge Police Department, replied, "Yes, please do." There was a note of urgency in his voice. "Tell him they're going to indict Tillie Maxfield." Then, in a quieter voice, "As soon as they can find her, that is." His tone suggested it could be later that day, sometime the following week, or possibly next month. Maybe never. Tillie Maxfield had tangled with the Cambridge Police Department on more than one occasion and had shown the ability to disappear faster than a shadow on a moonless night.

"Indicted?" William asked, not wanting to believe it. "For what?"

"The robbery at Prouse Jewelers two nights ago."

No, this can't be, William thought. For the past year, Tillie had been hiring him to do odd jobs around her property, a kind gesture that had kept his pockets full of spending money. In all that time he'd come to know her as a charitable and trusting soul. Certainly not a robber. "There must be some mistake," he said.

"Could be," said Vincent, keeping his own assessment of the matter to himself. "But they're convinced she fits the crime."

"How so?" William fired back, his anger sparking to life.

"Because she's the only one small enough to get inside."

William wasn't sure what that meant, but no matter; the police had it all wrong, and someone needed to step in and prove it before they humiliated his friend by dragging her away in chains like a

9

common criminal.

When he was finished at the bookstore, he walked down Kirkland Street, past the university, and followed Mt. Auburn Street to Dunster Street. Prouse Jewelers was just beyond the bakery on the corner, a classic colonial-style building with evenly spaced nine over nine double-hung windows, a recessed eight-panel front door flanked on either side by fluted pilasters, and three dormered windows on the roof that faced the street.

He went to the front door and found it locked.

Tacked to the one of the panels was a notice from the Cambridge Police Department, meant to dissuade anyone from 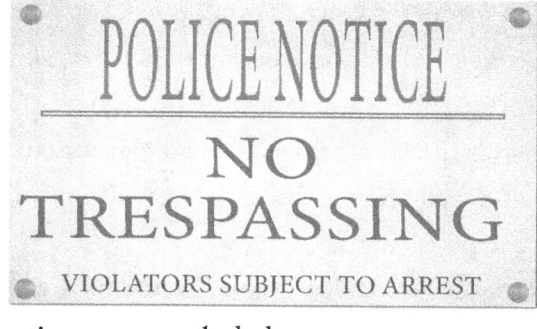 entering until their investigation was concluded.

Undaunted, he walked around to the end of the building. Near the back corner he saw a small recessed window set between the first and second-floor windows. Unlike a window with traditional glass panes, it had thin wooden louvers that had been broken apart, leaving shattered pieces of wood strewn about the lawn below.

He went over and inspected them, then looked up at the damaged opening, his mind hard at work reconstructing the crime.

"I know what you're thinking," came a voice from directly behind him. "There's no way she could've reached the window."

He spun around and saw his father standing there, gazing up at the destruction.

"Dad? W-what are you doing here?" William stammered.

"The same thing you are, son," Daniel replied.

"But…how did you know…?"

"Vincent came back into the store after you left. There was something he forgot to leave for me during his first visit."

"He told you about Tillie, didn't he?" William said, feeling his anger stirring anew.

"Yes, and now time is of the essence," Daniel replied. "To protect ourselves from the real thief, we need to proceed carefully, being ever watchful, and above all else, unseen." He looked over at the street to make sure they weren't being watched, then gestured for William to follow him. He walked as far as the back corner of the building and stopped. From that vantage point, they could see the end of the building, as well as the entire back side. "Tell me what you see," he said to William.

"Well, I see a damaged window, up there," William said, pointing. "Back here, nothing seems amiss," he added, eyeing the back of the building. "I see a downspout there on the corner, a row of windows on the second floor and another row on the first floor. The lower ones all have bars that look untouched."

"Correct," Daniel said. "That opening you see up there? The broken one? That's not a window, it's a vent. It's part of the ventilation system incorporated into the original design of the building. It allows stale air from inside to escape, as well as allowing fresh air to flow back in. Only someone very small could've passed through it to get inside, which is exactly what the robber wanted the authorities to think happened."

"Which is why they want to arrest Tillie," William grumbled, Vincent's cryptic explanation becoming clear. "Vincent said they

11

think she's the only one small enough to fit through the vent."

"Yes, but that's *not* what happened," Daniel said. He walked along the back of the house, staying well back from the foundation, all the while studying the ground. He'd gone several feet when he stopped and reversed direction, his eyes still focused downward. When he got back to where William was standing, he knelt down and patted the soil lightly with the tips of his fingers.

"What are you looking for?" William asked.

"You tell me," Daniel said. He stood, and then pointed at the ground in front of him. "What do you see here?"

"Dirt…a few weeds…some pebbles…why?"

"Do you notice anything peculiar about the dirt?"

"Not really."

"That's right," Daniel said. "Once again, that's what the robber wanted you to see—nothing unusual."

"What are you talking about?"

Daniel turned and surveyed the yard. "Over there," he said, then walked across the grass with William following close behind. In the corner of the lot was a small pile of brush. Sitting atop it was a leaf-covered branch roughly three feet long. Daniel picked it up and used both hands to bend it inward, gauging its rigidity.

"What are you doing?" asked William.

Daniel handed him the branch. "Tell me what you think of that," he said.

Like his father had done seconds earlier, William flexed the branch with both hands, then examined the end that was splintered and coarse. "This branch wasn't cut, it was snapped off," he said. "And judging by the rubbery feel of it, I'd say it wasn't that long ago."

"Very good," Daniel said, taking it back from William. "I think the robber used this before he left to brush away his tracks."

"His tracks?" William said. He considered the branch momentarily, then looked back at the building, focusing his attention on the upper windows, none of which had bars. "Of course, the downspout!" he said, realizing what his father was thinking.

"Precisely," Daniel said. "The robber used the downspout to access the second-story window. That was his way in."

"And from there, he could reach around the corner and break the vent," William said.

"And why would he do that?" Daniel asked.

"To mislead the police into thinking that whoever robbed the store used the vent to get inside."

"And...?" Daniel prompted.

"And whoever it was had to be very small to fit through the opening."

"Correct," Daniel said. "Judging by the loose soil next to the downspout, I imagine we'll find ample evidence of that theory inside the building."

"But, how do we get in?" William asked. "The front door is locked. I checked."

From his pants pocket Daniel produced a key.

"Is that what I think it is?" William asked.

Daniel nodded. "Our ticket to the truth."

"But...how did you...?" William began.

"Never underestimate the utility of a good friend," Daniel offered.

"Vincent," William said. "That's what he forgot to leave for you."

13

"Right again. Now, let's go inside and look for a dirt trail. If we're right about the downspout, I imagine we'll find the proof we need on the floor directly below that second story window."

And thus began William's indoctrination into what would become a well-kept Hammond family secret: coming to the aid of those in need by helping to right injustices done to them.

In time, William would inherit the bookcase from his father. In the years that followed, it would be passed on from family member to family member. Years would become decades, decades would become generations, and the legacy would live on, each keeper of the bookcase following the strict code defined by Daniel's three principles.

Be careful.

Ever watchful.

And above all else, unseen.

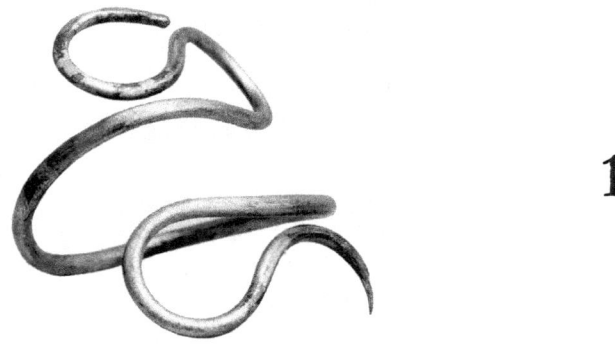

1

Cooked

Saturday, 12:45 p.m.
Willow & Vine Auctions
Brookline, MA

It was Asher. Nathan Cole was sure of it. Even from 50 feet away, seeing him was like gazing into a mirror. The man had the same hair, the color of wet beach sand and straight like uncooked pasta; the same narrow facial structure; the same slender frame. And although Asher was a few inches taller, and more muscular, he was Nathan's near body double.

Dressed in a crisp ink-blue business suit and matching blue fedora, with a classic centerdent crown, Asher appeared to be just another patron of Willow & Vine, the prestigious auction house in Brookline, MA, attending what was being billed as the auction of the year.

But Nathan knew otherwise.

Asher's presence there was purely criminal. He was the newly crowned watchman for the Covin, an international art-theft ring. His job: identify rare and extremely valuable works of art, then acquire them using whatever means or manpower necessary.

Based on what Nathan knew of him, such a high-profile auction would attract Asher like a moth to a flame. Priceless paintings, stunning jewelry, rare books—it was all here: exquisite pieces ranging in value from the high five figures to the lofty six-figure neighborhood.

And therein lay the quandary.

The Covin's worldwide operation was in the process of being shut down, thanks to the efforts of Nathan, his best friend Gina McDermott, and a legion of law enforcement officials, including Interpol and the U.S. Marshals Service. So, if the theft of priceless artwork was still an ongoing enterprise, who was Asher working for?

Himself?

Someone else?

Had some unknown kingpin taken over the reins of the centuries-old criminal organization?

Whatever the answer, Nathan knew that Asher wasn't there to bid on any of the lots. He was the set-up man, pure and simple. His task on this day was strictly research, something he'd learned from the previous watchman, Arthur Chessman. The recently retired mastermind had directed every high-profile art theft in the United States for the past 40 years, targeting, among other things, private collections, art galleries and auction houses.

Nathan pushed his hair back behind his ear and inched forward, inexplicably drawn to Chessman's young protégé whose boyish looks matched his own.

"Uh, excuse me. Where do you think you're going?" Gina said, from directly behind him. For reasons that escaped her, she had agreed to accompany him into the building. But now, every second they spent there was sheer madness. Two 12-year-olds, in one of the country's oldest and most renowned auction houses, mingling with a roomful of well-to-do art collectors? The expression "fish out of water" didn't begin to describe the awkwardness she was feeling.

Then, through the crowd, she spotted Asher. His uncanny resemblance to Nathan made her blink hard, as if she were seeing a mirage. *No, that's not possible,* she told herself.

Impervious to the clamor of voices that filled the room like a crowded subway platform, he was leaning against the back wall, flipping through a glossy catalog that highlighted the offerings of the day.

But something about him wasn't right.

It was his eyes.

They looked up every few seconds, surveying the crowd, studying each of the patrons as if committing their faces to memory. The hunter, scoping out his prey.

As his gaze swept across the room, drawing nearer, Gina grabbed Nathan by the arm and yanked him back behind a trio of gray-haired investment banker lookalikes, jabbering excitedly about one of the more coveted lots: a pair of 30-carat sapphire and diamond earrings valued at a quarter million dollars.

"What are you doing? Let go of me!" Nathan said, wrenching his arm free.

She gave him a look that would melt plastic. "You said we were just going to take a quick look around and then leave." She leaned closer and whispered, "You didn't say anything about Asher being here."

Nathan gave her a weary look. "Just relax…will you?"

"Relax?" she fired back, looking at him like he was mad. "How can I relax?"

The three gray-haired men turned and looked, each showing a look of displeasure. What parent would think to bring a child to such a formal event? And whatever happened to teaching them basic manners, like how to behave in public? Forgoing such basic instruction was beyond comprehension.

As they resumed their conversation, Nathan took Gina's arm and gently ushered her away from them. "Look," he said, keeping his voice low. "I didn't think he'd actually *be* here. It was just a hunch. But now we know he's for real, and he's still actively scoping out jobs."

"Scoping out jobs?" Gina repeated, not buying it. "The criminal organization he worked for has been shut down."

"Exactly," Nathan replied. "So why is he here? The answer is simple: there's something he wants. The question is, what?"

"You think he's here to *steal* something?"

"No. He's just here to watch the bidders, to see what they buy. Later on, he'll devise a plan to steal what he wants…just like Chessman taught him."

"And you know this, how?"

"Arthur Chessman told me."

"Yeah, well, I've got news for you," Gina said. "If Asher sees you,

you're cooked. You think he doesn't know about you? What you did to put his boss in jail?"

"You mean, what *we* did to put his boss in jail."

Gina rolled her eyes. *Fine...whatever.* "Speaking of Arthur Chessman," she said, the volume of her voice growing louder, "you think Asher hasn't heard about our meeting with him?"

"Will-you-keep-your-voice-down?" Nathan whispered, looking around nervously.

The truth was, their impromptu visit with Arthur Chessman a week earlier, at the facility in Weston where he resided, was a near fiasco. Nonetheless, it had been fruitful. Suffering from the onset of dementia, Chessman had let slip details about his understudy, someone named Asher, who, as it turned out, bore a striking resemblance to Nathan. During their conversation, Chessman had made it clear that Asher had taken over his duties as the watchman, serving as the Covin's chief architect of art thefts.

Nathan thought for a moment, then sighed as her words produced their intended result. "All right, fine," he said reluctantly. "We'll go."

"Thank you," Gina said, behind squinty eyes and a phony smile. It quickly evaporated and she shook her head in disbelief. *How is it that you've managed to live this long?*

Nathan ignored her and leaned to his right, looking through an opening in the horde of people. Asher was gone.

"Now what are you looking at?" Gina asked.

"Where did he go?" Nathan whispered as he slowly scanned the crowd. He started walking toward the back wall, his eyes darting from side to side, when Gina grabbed his arm again, this time with both hands.

"Uh-uh," she said. "We're leaving, remember?"

"Just wait," he said, holding his ground. Tucked in the far corner as a narrow archway less than 10 feet from where Asher had been standing just seconds earlier. Nathan wrenched his arm free and made his way toward it, ducking and weaving through the assembled crowd. When he reached the opening, he spotted a staircase that led down to the basement level. Forgoing Gina's earlier words of caution, he slipped through the archway and started down the stairs. He had just reached the bottom when he heard Gina call to him from the top step.

"Nathan! What are you doing?"

He ignored her and kept going.

"NATHAN!" she said, louder.

Out of nowhere a hand gripped the back of her neck, squeezing hard. She struggled to break free when another hand clapped over her mouth, making it impossible for her to scream or call out for help.

"Downstairs. Now!" a voice growled in her ear.

She was shoved forward, roughly, and stumbled awkwardly down the stairs, the hands on her neck and face the only thing keeping her from losing her balance and falling headlong down the steep incline.

The basement level was an open 10'x10' room used for the storage of extra chairs, tables, various industrial cleaners, and metal display stands of every size. The only light came from a small exit sign above a door on the far wall. As Nathan felt the wall for a light switch, he heard the sound of shuffling of feet on the stairs behind him.

Not one person, but two—coming down the steps in a hurry.

He moved forward and wedged himself between two metal shelving units. Seconds later, two figures appeared at the bottom of the stairs. One tall, one short. It was only when they crossed the room and the faint light from the exit sign painted their silhouettes that he understood what was happening.

The stranger wrangled Gina across the room, despite her attempts to break free, keeping his hands held tightly on her neck and mouth. Nathan squinted, straining to see through the darkness, as she was thrown into a broom closet in the corner. With a surge of anger welling up inside him, he sprung off the wall, lowered his shoulder and charged into the stranger's midsection, driving him sideways onto the floor.

In one smooth move, the stranger rolled over and sprung to his feet. Nathan followed a split second later, and when he turned to face his adversary, he felt two hands grab the front of his shirt and drive him backward, slamming him up against the wall. Momentarily stunned, he was helpless to escape the attacker's grip as he was dragged across the floor and flung into the closet. He landed on the floor next to Gina, who lay there, dazed, as the closet door slammed shut behind him.

Wasting no time, he staggered to his feet and threw his shoulder at the door. Too late. Something on the other side was holding it shut, and try as he might to force it open, the door wouldn't budge. Out of the darkness he heard Gina utter a painful moan.

"Are you all right?" he asked.

"No! I am *not* all right," she said angrily, as she propped herself up into a sitting position. Her shoulder was throbbing from landing hard on the cement floor, and the back of her head ached from colliding with a mop bucket.

Just then, a chorus of shouts erupted from the first floor. They were followed seconds later by a deafening metallic beeping sound that screeched through every room in the building. Next came screaming, and a stampede of feet as people raced across the floor.

"NO!" Nathan shouted, throwing his body against the door again and again.

"What is it?" Gina asked.

"The fire alarm!"

2

The Big Dog

Nathan grabbed the doorknob and twisted it, slamming his shoulder against the door over and over. When that didn't work, he balled up his fists and pounded. "HELP! SOMEONE! LET US OUT!"

Overhead, the shuffling of feet and screams continued.

Emergency strobe lights, mounted in the ceiling of the lower level, were sending staccato bursts of light through the thin opening under the door. With each sharp flash, Gina saw smoke leaking into the cramped space. "The building's on fire!" she shouted, scrambling to her feet. She stood next to Nathan and together they pounded on the door, shouting.

"HELP!"

"HELP!"

Smoke continued to seep in, slowly obscuring their feet, then their ankles, and then their shins. Suddenly, the door swung open and Kendra was standing there, obscured in a fog of smoke, holding the metal chair that had been wedged against the door to keep it shut.

"FOUND YOU!" she yelled, her voice masked by the sounds coming from the first floor. She tossed the chair aside, waved the smoke away from her face, and said, "Come on, we gotta get outta here."

Cupping their hands over their mouths to keep from gagging, they ran to the far wall and followed the stairs that led to the emergency exit. Once they pushed through it, they found themselves standing in a narrow alley that ran behind the building. In the distance, the steady whine of sirens filled the air, getting closer with each passing second.

"Are you guys okay?" Kendra asked, looking them over in search of any cuts or blood.

"Alive, thanks to you," Nathan said.

"What happened?" she asked. "I thought we agreed. You'd go in, have a quick look around, then leave." *The only reason I let you go in alone*, she didn't say.

Gina was too angry to reply as she brushed dirt and grit off her arms and legs.

"Let's talk about it later," Nathan said. He looked back at the door, afraid that their attacker might appear again at any moment. "Right now, we need to get out of here."

Kendra quickly ushered them down the alley. When they reached the sidewalk, she pushed through the assembled crowd and hurried across the street to her battered blue Volvo that was parked at the curb.

As she was pulling away, they looked over at the front of the auction house. The two large picture windows had shattered and clouds of smoke were billowing out onto the sidewalk as the last of the auction patrons pushed through the front door, coughing and hacking. She drove a short distance and then swerved down a side street just as the first two fire engines were arriving at the scene.

Nathan leaned down and checked the side mirror.

"What are you doing?" she asked.

"Making sure he's not following us."

"Who are you talking about?"

"The person who trapped us in the basement."

"Did you get a look at him?" she asked.

"No. It was too dark."

"It was him," Gina said, from the back seat.

"Him, who?" Kendra asked.

"Asher."

"We don't know that," Nathan said, sharply.

"Oh yeah?" Gina countered. "Who else would've done it?"

Kendra saw a row of empty parking spaces up ahead on the right and swerved into the first one she came to. Nathan and Gina, who were all too familiar with Kendra's unruly driving habits, braced themselves to keep from getting thrown forward like a pair of crash-test dummies.

"What's wrong?" Nathan asked her.

The car came to a grinding halt at the curb, then Kendra turned to face him. "Asher?" she said. "Are you telling me he was *there*? In the building?"

"Yes," Nathan said. *Just as I suspected.*

"And you're sure it was him?"

"Positive."

"Which means…"

"Exactly," Nathan said. "He somehow missed the news about the Covin being shut down."

"It was creepy if you ask me," Gina said.

"How so?" Kendra asked, looking back over the seat at her.

"He's the spitting image of Nathan."

"Are you serious?"

"Uh-huh," Gina said, nodding emphatically.

Kendra's expression grew darker. This was bad, very bad—for two very distinct reasons. Which of them was more disconcerting she couldn't decide. At the moment it was a 7-10 split.

"What?" Nathan asked, confused by her troubled reaction. "We knew he looked *something* like me. It's the only reason Arthur Chessman revealed everything to me when we met with him. He thought I was Asher."

"Did he see you?" Kendra asked.

"No."

"Uh, excuse me," Gina said, loudly. "Yes, he did!"

Nathan looked over at Kendra, shaking his head. "We don't know that," he whispered.

"Wanna bet?" Gina said.

Kendra looked away, thinking, then looked back. "Let's just say, for the moment, that Gina's right…"

"I *am* right," Gina said. "Not only did he see you, he recognized you. And that's when he lured you into his trap."

Nathan twisted around in his seat. "What are you talking about?"

"What am I talking about? You said it yourself: he's the set-up man. He was there scoping out the auction. Then you show up, he sees you, and he vanishes."

"Yeah? So?"

Gina shot him a pathetic look. "Do I have to spell it out for you?"

"What?"

"Asher knew you were on to him," she explained. "He hid, knowing you'd go looking for him. And what did you do? You took the bait, just like that," she said, snapping her fingers in the air. "You walked right into his trap, easy as you please." She paused, then said, "If you hadn't gone down to the basement, we would never have gotten trapped in the closet." *So, thanks a lot.*

She was right and he knew it. Asher had played him with alarming ease. The fact that he hadn't anticipated such a move sparked a wave of anger in his gut and he felt the sudden urge to scream, or kick something. *Next time, don't be so stupid!* he told himself.

"We gotta find this guy," Kendra said. There was a newfound urgency in her voice.

"And how do you propose we do that?" Nathan asked.

She straightened in her seat and stared straight ahead, thinking.

"Well?" Nathan asked, impatiently.

"We don't," she said, checking the side mirror for oncoming traffic.

"Huh?"

"We let the big dog do it."

With that, she stomped on the accelerator, chirping the tires on the pavement as the car rocketed away from the curb.

Thirty minutes later they cruised through the front gates of Birch Meadow, the sprawling retirement community on the Arlington side of Upper Mystic Lake, and followed the long snake-like driveway through a radiant forest of silver birches that lined both sides. When they pulled into the parking lot at the front of the building, they saw Kendra's father, Jameson, waiting for them beneath the striped canopy that stretched from the front door to the curb.

Kendra's call to him 20 minutes earlier had started with four short words. "I'm headed your way." When asked why, her reply was equally brief. "There's been a development."

Jameson, a long-time friend of Nathan's family, had promised Nathan's grandfather, in his dying moments, that he would watch over Nathan, the next keeper of the Hammond bookcase, which now sat in the shadows of the Cole's third-floor attic. Since that fateful day, Jameson had held true to his promise, doing his best to safeguard Nathan as he unearthed one dark secret after another buried in the ancient case. Unsolved mysteries that were long forgotten, and for good reason.

Kendra glided into a visitor's parking space and turned off the engine. She was pulling the key from the ignition when Jameson appeared at the window. His mood, already on edge, intensified when he leaned down and saw Nathan sitting in the front passenger seat, and Gina sitting directly behind him in the back.

"What happened?" he asked, as Kendra climbed out of the car.

"Not here," she said, closing the door. "Let's go inside."

Minutes later, they filed into Jameson's room. He quickly shut the door and turned to face them, studying Nathan and Gina's outward appearance with the trained eye of a trauma nurse. Nothing appeared to be physically wrong with them, so what was the big emergency? "Talk to me," he said to Kendra.

"You remember what we told you about Arthur Chessman?" she asked. "How he's been training a new recruit? Someone he refers to as the *new* watchman?"

"Yes," Jameson replied, in a guarded tone. He still harbored feelings of anger about Kendra's reckless decision to take Nathan and Gina to Weston where Chessman resided. Given the threat level at the time, not to mention the possibility of Covin operatives being present, the resulting harm that might've come to the three of them was too painful for him to imagine, especially after the savagery the Covin had inflicted on his wife, Claire, years earlier.

"Well, about an hour ago, these two spotted him," Kendra said, nodding in Nathan and Gina's direction.

"Spotted him? Where?"

"At Willow & Vine, in Brookline," Nathan said.

"The auction house," Jameson confirmed.

Nathan answered with a nod.

Then, Jameson posed obvious question #1. "What were you doing at Willow & Vine on a Saturday afternoon?"

"Based on things Chessman told me, I had a hunch that Asher might be there," Nathan replied.

"Asher?"

"That's his name," Nathan said, wondering how he'd forgotten to share that important detail with Jameson. But given the wild events that had unfolded the previous week, which had nearly cost Nathan and Kendra their lives, his memory was still teetering on emotional overload.

"Asher," Jameson repeated, trying to place the name. "Is that his first or last name?" "Couldn't tell you," Nathan said.

Jameson tucked that away, for the moment. "This hunch," he said. "It was based on what, exactly?"

"Chessman said something to me about auction houses. How I should make a habit of visiting them. Blend in. Pay special attention to the bidders to see who was buying what. He got pretty worked up about it. Said watching the buyers was key."

"A very clever strategy," Jameson noted. "Given the number of robberies from private collections every year, I'd say it's one he's employed many times."

Next came obvious question #2.

"You're positive it was him?"

"Yes."

"How can you be sure"

"We, uh, share similar features," Nathan muttered, looking down at the floor as he spoke.

"Similar features?" Gina blurted out. "Hah! Try *exact* features!"

"You're saying he looks like you?" Jameson asked.

"Yes," Nathan said, regretfully.

"Identical. Twins," Gina said, crisply. *Can you believe it?*

Jameson walked over to his antique wooden desk and sat down, to think and to plan.

"Uh…there's something else," Kendra said, reluctantly.

Jameson gave her a tired look. *Now what?*

"I'll let Nathan tell you."

"Tell me what?" Jameson asked, sitting up in the chair.

Nathan gave him the 30-second recap: how he spotted Asher standing near the back wall, watching the crowd; how he was there one minute, then gone the next; the altercation in the basement, where a mysterious attacker locked them in the closet; the ensuing fire alarm, and Kendra's timely rescue.

Jameson considered the information for several seconds, then tapped his fingertips idly on the arm of the chair, sorting out a number of scenarios. "You say his name is Asher?" he said, at last.

"Yes," Nathan replied.

"We gotta find this clown," Kendra said. She was pacing now, clenching and unclenching her fists. "If he was the one who stuck Nathan and Gina in the closet…"

"I'm telling you, he was," Gina said.

"Then he knows who you are," Kendra said, continuing her rant, "not to mention the part you played in the arrest of his boss and his evil twin of a sister."

"What's that supposed to mean?" Nathan asked. "He's going to come after *us?*"

"You should've listened to me," Gina said, in a sing-song voice.

Nathan wilted. *Here we go again.*

"I don't like that this guy looks like *you*," Kendra told Nathan, voicing the other troubling possibility. "Once the police identify his mug, what's to stop them from arresting you by mistake?"

"A valid question," Jameson said.

"Are you still in touch with the big dog?" Kendra asked.

Nathan and Gina exchanged a confused look. *Big dog?*

"I'd prefer you call him by his real name, Brett Dunlevy," Jameson said. "At this point in his storied career, the man has certainly earned that professional courtesy."

Nathan nudged Kendra with his elbow. *What's he talking about?*

Using her right hand, she signed three letters: F-B-I.

Nathan frowned. "Huh?"

"FBI," Gina whispered.

"Oh," he said, nodding slowly. Then, "Wait! You know sign language?"

She held up her fist and gestured like she was knocking on a door. *Yes.*

Jameson knew exactly what Kendra was thinking. He took his cell phone from the top of the desk and tapped an icon on the home screen. "Nathan?" he said.

"Yeah?"

"Look at me."

Elizabeth and David Cole were unloading groceries from the back of the car when Kendra's faded blue Volvo coasted into the driveway, creaking and groaning as it came to a stop next to the house. Moments earlier, Kendra had dropped Gina off at the far end of the street so her parents wouldn't see her with Nathan, the boy they believed was the king of calamity, a human danger magnet who would one day lead their daughter to a grisly end.

Nathan shuddered to think what would happen to Gina if they knew what had happened at Willow & Vine that morning.

David grabbed the last of the groceries while Elizabeth sauntered over to the Volvo. "Well, hello," she said to Kendra, as she was getting out of the car. Jameson was still sitting in the front seat, talking on the phone, and offered a quick wave. When Elizabeth saw

Nathan emerge from the back seat, she flashed a confused look and said, "Oh, Nathan was with you. We just got back from grocery shopping and he was nowhere to be seen." She turned to Nathan as he approached. "I was just about to call you," she told him. Then she noticed the long smudge of dirt and grime running up the arm of his shirt—a souvenir from the floor of the Willow & Vine basement closet. "What's this?" she said, taking his arm in her hand. She examined the fabric briefly, then leaned closer and sniffed. "Why do you smell like smoke?"

Jameson appeared at her side. "We should go inside and talk," he said.

"O-kay," Elizabeth said, eyeing Jameson and Kendra warily. Something about the looks on their faces flagged her curiosity. "Why am I getting the sense this isn't a social call?" she asked.

They assembled in the living room as they'd done many times before when there was important news to share. Jameson and Kendra sat in the large red overstuffed chairs while Elizabeth and David sat across from them on the couch. Nathan, fearing how his parents would react when they heard the news about Asher, stood at the front window, wishing it was a secret doorway to another dimension.

"What's going on?" David asked once they were all seated.

Jameson had to choose his words carefully. While there was much Elizabeth and David knew about the events of the previous week: how Nathan and Kendra had been instrumental in the capture of the Covin's current leader, Ginette Dampierre, and the recovery of the contents from the *Greenwich* bookcase, stolen from their garage, there were things they didn't know.

They hadn't been told about Arthur Chessman, or that he'd been personally responsible for art thefts totaling millions of dollars for the now-defunct Covin. They also didn't know that Nathan had visited him, and that Chessman had mistaken him for his young protégé, the heir-apparent to the crown. That information blackout ended now. It was time they knew.

Some of it, anyway.

"In addition to last week's arrest of Ginette Dampierre and her New England associates, another key member of the Covin was taken into custody," he began. "His name is Arthur Chessman, and for the better part of the past four decades he's been the pivotal figure in a staggering number of art thefts here in the continental United States."

Elizabeth sat quietly, saying nothing. She knew this was just the appetizer. The main dish was on its way.

"Unbeknownst to the law enforcement community," Jameson said, "Chessman has been secretly grooming his replacement, a young man named Asher. For some time now, Chessman has been passing on everything he knows to him in an attempt to maintain the flow of stolen artwork from a number of sources, including high-end auction houses."

"Asher?" David said. "Is that his first name or last name?"

"Unknown," Jameson answered. "Earlier today, Nathan and Gina spotted him at Willow & Vine in Brookline, prior to one of their most anticipated auctions in years. As I'm sure the media is already reporting, a fire broke out just as the auction was set to begin, and—"

"STOP!" Elizabeth blurted out, raising her hand in the air. "Nathan? Could you come over here please?" she said, in a firm voice. As she waited for him, she breathed in and out slowly, trying to quell the fury that was building inside her like a gathering storm.

Reluctantly, Nathan trudged back across the room. He went as far as the overstuffed chair where Kendra was sitting, and stopped.

"No," his mother said, pointing at the floor near her feet. "Over here."

His shoulders slumped and he slowly made his way around the back of the chair, taking a position two feet from her.

She stared at him, fire in her eyes, and spoke slowly, anger simmering beneath the surface of every word. "A professional art thief? Working for a worldwide criminal network? Please explain to me, and your father, what would compel you to pursue such a dangerous person."

"I had a hunch he might be there," Nathan said, plainly.

"A *hunch?*" she exclaimed. "Do you know what hunches can do? They can get you killed. Do you understand that? Killed!" Then, in a quieter voice that still held plenty of heat, "I should think you would've learned that by now."

He and Kendra shared a momentary glance. To date, they'd told no one how close they'd both come to their final end a week earlier on New Castle Island in Portsmouth, NH while following one of Nathan's hunches. And though he and his mother had agreed there would be no more secrets between them, he couldn't bring himself to tell her. Why subject her to such pain? What possible good could come from it? By his way of thinking, and Kendra agreed, no one else needed to know. Not his parents. Not Jameson. Not even Gina. Their brush with death was a secret, and a bond, they would share for the rest of their lives.

"I'm sure the events from earlier today will serve as an important lesson for Nathan," Jameson said, attempting to ease the tension in the room. He looked at Nathan, eyebrows raised. *Right?*

"Yes," Nathan said, humbly bowing his head. The thought of being duped by Asher, being tossed around in the dark like a rag doll, and being locked in the basement closet while the building filled with smoke, were abuses that would leave a lasting scar. From now on, things would be different.

He'd be smarter.

He'd get stronger.

And he'd learn how to protect himself from would-be attackers.

"Hold on a second," David said, copying Elizabeth's stop-right-there hand gesture. He addressed Nathan directly. "How is it that you came to know about this man, Asher?"

"David, if I may?" Jameson said, before Nathan could respond. "How Nathan came to learn about Asher isn't important. What *is* important, and most troubling, is that the two of them share a striking resemblance."

"You're saying this thief looks like my *SON?* Elizabeth exclaimed.

"He does," Kendra said. "And we're fairly sure he saw Nathan."

"He saw Nathan," Elizabeth repeated, calculating what that could mean. "And…?"

"And Gina thinks Asher recognized him."

"Recognized him? What are you talking about?" Elizabeth asked.

"There's a possibility that he knows Nathan's role in the arrest of Edouard Dampierre." She didn't mention his sister Ginette.

Alarm bells blared in Elizabeth's brain. Playtime was over. "All right," she said, "what aren't you telling me?"

Nathan's mind raced as he tried to think of how to tell her about the unknown attacker in the basement without scaring the living daylights out of her.

Elizbeth, growing impatient, looked at Nathan, then Kendra, then back to Nathan. "Let me guess," she said. "The fire had something to do with him recognizing you?"

"We don't know that," Nathan said.

"Oh really," she said. She watched him closely. If he was lying, there'd be a tell. He'd cross his arms, or avert his eyes. He did neither.

In truth, he had no answers for any of it: the fire, or being locked in the closet. But if Gina was right, if Asher *was* there to steal something, then setting fire to the building would've been a perfect distraction.

Smoke-filled rooms.

People panicking.

Running for the exits.

Utter chaos—the thief's best friend.

"We know very little about the fire," Jameson said. "And until we do, I'm going to suggest that Nathan stay under the radar, so to speak."

"Because?" Elizabeth asked.

"Well, for starters, we don't want the authorities confusing him with a known criminal."

"Because of their identical appearance," David said.

"Correct. And secondly, Asher *does* know about Nathan's involvement in the recent arrest of Edouard…"

Elizabeth flopped back, resting her head on a couch cushion as she stared up at the ceiling, stunned. *When is this going to end?* she asked herself. *First it was Edouard Dampierre, and now this: a rogue thief who looks like my son.* She took in a deep breath and pushed it out, then sat up, resigned to the job that lay ahead. "Okay, when you say 'stay under the radar', what are we talking about?" she asked. "And don't tell me you want to hide Nathan in one of the safehouses again."

At the word "safehouse," Nathan looked over at Jameson, who warned him off with a subtle shake of his head, his unspoken message abundantly clear: say nothing.

The safehouses in question had been set up by Nathan's grandfather years ago, a fact that Kendra had shared with Nathan during their recent trip to New Castle Island that ended with the arrest of Ginette Dampierre and a handful of Covin operatives. At present, Elizabeth and David weren't aware that Nathan knew that truth. As far as they were concerned, he believed the safehouses belonged to Jameson, a leftover from his previous days of intelligence work. Jameson knew they were planning on telling Nathan the rest of it, including the mystery surrounding the death of his grandfather, but now wasn't the time for that conversation. Best that it be done privately.

"There'll be no need to hide him anywhere," Jameson said. "Nathan can resume his normal lifestyle right here at home. But he needs to avoid any public appearances where someone might recognize him."

"By someone, you mean, the police," Elizabeth said.

"Yes. Once we learn Asher's true identity, it shouldn't take long for the police to track him down."

"And how do you plan on doing that?" Elizabeth asked.

"I've already sent a picture of Nathan to one of my FBI contacts. He'll run it through their NGI program to see if they can find a match."

"NGI?" David asked.

"Next Generation Identification," Jameson explained. "It includes something called IPS, which stands for Interstate Photo System. It's a massive database that contains millions of mug shots."

Before Jameson could continue, his phone rang. He pulled it from his pocket, saw who was calling, and immediately stood up to take the call. "This is Jameson," he said, walking out to the front hallway. Other than an occasional "understood" or "go on," he said nothing as he listened intently to what he was being told.

At the conclusion of the call, he slid the phone into his pocket and walked back into the living room, clearly troubled.

"What's wrong?" Kendra asked.

"It's worse than we thought."

3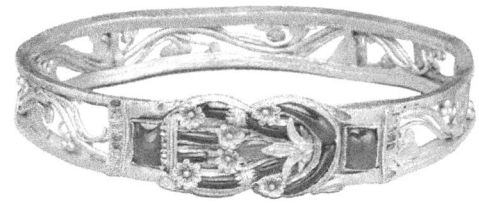

Sidney

Jameson sat down in the overstuffed chair and leaned forward with his elbows on his knees, his hands clasped together, like a man in prayer. "That was one of my contacts with the Brookline Police Department," he said. "They've completed their initial investigation at Willow & Vine and their findings are very disturbing."

"How so?" David asked.

"They discovered numerous incendiary devices placed strategically throughout the entire building. Each one had been triggered by a wireless remote. Based on the number, and their location, it's clear that the person responsible put considerable time and effort into hiding them. There was, in fact, no fire. He wanted everyone there to think there was. The smoke was intended to herd everyone out of the building in a mad dash, leaving it completely empty. In the frenzy, he made his escape through a back door."

"Him?" Elizabeth asked.

"A security camera mounted in the alley behind the building captured the image of a man ducking out the back door several minutes after the fire alarm sounded."

"And they assume this was the person responsible?" Elizabeth asked.

"At this point, they can't be sure, but it certainly appears so," Jameson said. "According to my contact, the man shown on the camera feed was wearing a hat, pulled down on his forehead to obscure his face. That, along with the timing of his departure from the building, and the fact that he used the back door instead of the front is highly suspicious."

"What kind of hat?" Nathan asked.

"A fedora."

"That's the type Indiana Jones wore, right?"

"Yes."

"It was Asher," Nathan said, matter-of-factly.

"What makes you so sure?" asked Jameson.

"When we saw him inside, he was wearing a hat just like that."

"Were any of the other men wearing hats?"

"Uh...I'm not sure," Nathan replied, trying to envision the packed room. He'd been so busy watching Asher that he hadn't paid much attention to the clothing choices of the others in the crowd.

Jameson gave him an uneasy look. "In a court of law, without more definitive proof, your assumption would be deemed coincidental at best."

"You want definitive proof?" Nathan fired back. "Show me the tape."

"Absolutely not!" Elizabeth exclaimed. "You let the authorities handle this."

"Agreed," said Jameson. "Whoever is behind this showed a complete disregard for human life. People could've been seriously injured, perhaps fatally. And if it was indeed Asher, then he's clearly ignoring whatever Chessman taught him, choosing a more aggressive method for acquiring what he wants. In other words, he's willing to sacrifice anyone who stands in his way. As much as you want to help, you need to forget about him. Like your mother said, let the authorities handle it…and they will, trust me."

"Was anything stolen?" Kendra asked, changing the subject.

"Yes," Jameson replied. "A very rare emerald and diamond necklace, valued at close to a million dollars."

"Looks like I was wrong," Nathan said.

"What do you mean?" asked Jameson. "Wrong about what?"

"I thought Asher was just there to scope out the crowd and find his next target. Stealing the necklace is altogether different. It means he's taking a bigger role in the thefts he orchestrates. From here on out, we should watch the auction houses more carefully."

"Did you hear what Jameson just said?" Elizabeth said, loudly. "You need to let this go. Is-that-clear?"

Nathan waved it off. "Fine by me. But somebody needs to tell *him* that. I don't need any more Covin goons coming after me, or Gina."

"I wouldn't worry about that," Jameson said. "Ever since your discovery at the courthouse, you've become news-media gold. The most famous 12-year-old in the country. Now that Asher has seen you in person, and knows just how similar the two of you look, he won't risk capture by being spotted anywhere near you. After today, you can bet he'll disguise his looks with something more elaborate than just a fedora."

"He'd better," Kendra warned. "Because if I catch up with him, there's no disguise in the world that will save him."

"Well then, for his sake," Jameson said, giving her a cautious look, "let's hope the authorities find him first."

Sunday morning.
North Cambridge, MA

On Sunday morning, shortly before 10 a.m., Elizabeth dropped Nathan off at Richard Abbott's home in North Cambridge. Abbott, a highly respected bookseller, trained by Henry Hammond, had employed Nathan to help process the tidal wave of books that were delivered on a daily basis to the large barn behind his house.

Nathan rolled back the heavy barn door and saw two brand new pallets waiting for him, each one loaded with boxes of books stacked in a tidy four-foot-square cube and secured with shrink wrap.

Working his usual system of sorting two stacks of books at once, he made it through the first pallet by lunchtime. He was just starting in on the second pallet when he heard a vehicle approaching, the tires making a familiar popping sound on the gravel driveway that snaked up and around Abbott's stately Victorian-style home. *Probably just Richard,* he thought.

He grabbed another box of books off the pallet and was carrying it back to the long farmer's table that ran down the center of the room when a car stopped just outside the open door of the barn. He looked over, expecting to see Richard's Subaru wagon, and saw a red BMW 3-Series sedan. "Oh no, not her again," he muttered under his breath.

The driver door opened and Jordon Prescott climbed out. She was dressed in her usual business-casual attire: platinum-grey slacks, matching vest, and powder-blue oxford shirt. She glanced at the house briefly, then strolled into the barn and stopped, sliding her round tortoise-shell Moscot sunglasses up onto her forehead. "Good day Mr. Cole," she said, when she saw him standing at the table.

"Hello," he replied, less than enthused. "Is there a book you need me to find?"

"No, but thank you for asking."

As she walked toward him, she surveyed the interior of the barn, admiring the post and beam joinery as if she'd personally cut every mortise and tenon, and then pounded in each of the wooden pegs that had held them together for nearly 160 years.

Nathan looked over at the pallet of books pushed up against the far wall, knowing this distraction would only slow his chances of getting them sorted before he left for the day. And knowing Richard's buying habits the way he did, by this same time tomorrow another pallet was sure to arrive. Maybe even two or three.

"The books can wait," Jordan said when she saw the look of futility on his face. "There's an urgent matter we need to discuss. Trust me when I tell you, it's a matter of life or death."

"For who?" Nathan asked.

"You."

Sure it is, he thought. He sat back against the edge of the table and folded his arms across his chest. "I'm listening."

44

She stepped closer and took a book off one of the stacks he had already sorted. "I understand you recently stayed overnight at Stackyard Road." As she spoke, she studied the front cover of the book briefly, then turned it over and examined the back.

"I have no idea what you're talking about," Nathan replied.

Stackyard Road, in Rowley, MA, was one of his grandfather's safehouses, a well-kept secret that wasn't open for discussion, especially with strangers.

"No?" Jordan said. "That's not what Finch told me."

Nathan's eyes went wide and his arms fell to his side. Finch was part of a select team his grandfather put together years ago, each person hand-picked for the unique skill set they possessed. Their job: to assist him, when called upon, in protecting those who came to him seeking his help: people who had been wrongly accused of a crime; confidential informants; those hopelessly entangled in a crooked legal battle. Each one innocent. Each one in need of someone who could balance the scales of justice in their favor.

"How do you know about Finch?" Nathan asked. "Or Stackyard Road for that matter?"

"How do I know?" Jordan repeated. "Who do you think *found* the Stackyard Road property for your grandfather?"

"Wait a minute!" Nathan said. "Are you saying you're...?"

"Sidney," Jordan cut in, revealing the code name Henry Hammond had given her to protect her true identity.

Nathan pushed off the table and moved away from her. Something about this was all wrong. "The first time we met, you told Richard you didn't know my grandfather."

"That's right," Jordan replied. "For our own safety, we were all told to disavow any knowledge of him."

"So…you lied."

"Lie, fib, fabrication…call it whatever you want. But it's what your grandfather instructed us to do." She paused momentarily. "Look, I don't know how much you've been told…"

"Oh, I've been told plenty," he said.

"Have you now?"

"Yeah, Kendra told me all about you guys."

"Is that a fact?" Jordan said, doubt in her voice. "Do tell."

"She said you were all waiting for me to get older. That there might come a day when I would need your help, just like my grandfather did."

"Well, that's partially true. What else?"

"She said my grandfather brought all of you together…called you 'facilitators'…and that each of you had a specific area of expertise."

"Did she say why he did that?"

"She told me that word had somehow gotten out about him, how he was secretly helping people in need. *Which all began with his bookcase, that now sits in my attic,* he didn't say. "Once that happened, strangers started showing up at his bookstore. When it became too much for him to handle on his own, he assembled the facilitators' group."

"Interesting," Jordan said. She looked down at the books on the table, the stacks of hardcover volumes unleashing memories of her time spent in Hammond Books, and the clandestine meetings she'd had with Henry. Ever since the news of his untimely passing, she'd steered clear of the bookshop. To date, she had yet to step foot in it again. *Someday,* she'd told herself countless times. *Once it's safe to do so.*

"What's wrong?" Nathan asked, when he saw the mournful look on her face.

"Everything was proceeding just as he had intended," she said, the books on the table holding her gaze. "Each member of the group did exactly as they were asked. Those who desperately needed your grandfather's help got it. Injustices were exposed. Innocent lives were spared. But after his passing, we became ghosts."

"Ghosts in waiting, you mean." *For me.*

"No. Ghosts in hiding."

"Hiding? From what?"

The image of the bookstore faded from her mind and she looked over at him, her words steeped in anger.

"From the person who killed him."

Jameson heard back from Brett Dunlevy just before lunchtime. The call came through as Jameson was on his way to the dining room, the alluring smell of chicken picatta filling the corridor like a silent invitation: come and get it.

When he saw who was calling he turned around and went back to his room. "Brett, how'd you make out?" he asked as he unlocked the door and stepped inside.

"Found your boy," Dunlevy said. His tone suggested that the search had been all too easy.

Jameson felt a charge of anticipation. "Hold on a second, Brett, let me grab something to write with. He hurried over to his desk and sat down, then took a pen from the drawer and pulled a slip of paper from his antique brass notepad holder. Not only was it a testament to art deco styling, the sides embellished with repousse floral and foliage designs, it was one of his most cherished possessions—a gift from Henry Hammond, who had unearthed it in an antiquarian bookstore somewhere in the heart of New York State. "All right, ready to copy," he said.

"The person in question is Asher Rickman," Dunlevy said, reading directly from the computer screen. "R-i-c-k-m-a-n. Born in Hartford, Connecticut."

Jameson quickly jotted down the information.

"I remember hearing about this guy," Dunlevy said. "In 2012, he was charged with first-degree larceny, which is a Class B felony. He was facing a $15,000 fine and some serious prison time, but after his court hearing, he walked."

"Excuse me?"

"He didn't serve any jail time," Dunlevy said.

"Why not?"

"He had a very good lawyer."

"I'll say," Jameson noted. "What happened?"

"Rickman was pulled over in Woodbridge, Connecticut, for a traffic violation. The officer who stopped him did a routine search of the vehicle and found a stolen painting in the trunk."

"Stolen? From where?" Jameson asked.

"An estate appraiser's shop three miles down the road in New Haven."

"Appraiser?"

"Yeah, it was called...hold on..." Dunlevy said, leaning closer to the screen as he read through the notes. "Chadbourne Appraisals and Auctions."

Auctions, Jameson thought. *Of course.*

"As I said, his lawyer was no slouch. He somehow managed to prove that the painting had been stashed in the trunk by someone else, without Rickman's knowledge. Rickman paid a fine for running the traffic light and that was that."

"When was this?" Jameson asked.

"Two years ago."

"He was practicing," Jameson muttered.

"What was that?"

"Rickman. He was practicing. The lawyer might've convinced the judge otherwise, but Rickman stole the painting, trust me. What's more, his skills have vastly improved."

"Really," said Dunlevy, confused by Jameson's analysis. "And how would you know? For that matter, where'd you get his picture?"

"I didn't."

"Excuse me?"

"That picture I sent you?" Jameson said. "That's not him."

"You lost me," Dunlevy replied.

"Are you sitting down?" Jameson asked.

"Killed?" Nathan repeated. His jaw fell open and he teetered momentarily, then his eyes drifted upward and he passed out. He dropped to the floor, landing atop a pile of flattened cardboard boxes, and when his eyes opened moments later, he saw Jordan kneeling over him. Her face was a blur and the words she was speaking had no form or meaning.

As he slowly regained his senses, his memory returned. He was in Richard Abbott's barn. It was morning. He remembered his mother dropping him off; how they negotiated the hour when she'd return to pick him up; walking up the crushed gravel driveway, the pungent aroma of a nearby rose hedge hanging in the air; rolling back the heavy barn door and seeing two recently delivered shrink-wrapped pallets of books.

"Are you hurt?" Jordan asked. Her words were clearer now. She cradled his chin in her hand and carefully turned his head, looking for any cuts or blood.

"I'm fine," he mumbled, pushing her hand away. He eased himself up into a sitting position, then struggled to stand, his head shrouded in a dense fog. It felt like someone had taken his brain apart and reassembled it, loosely, leaving a few sections on the bench. He grasped the edge of the table for support, then hobbled over to the pallet of books and plopped down on one of the stacks of un-opened boxes.

He leaned forward and placed his elbows on his knees, clamping his hands against the side of his head as he stared at the floor, over-come by a torrent of questions. *Killed? How can that be? And why am I just learning about it now? Why didn't someone tell me? My parents, Jameson, Kendra. Somebody. Anybody!*

"They didn't tell you, did they?" Jordan said.

"Huh?"

"Your family," she said. "They didn't tell you."

"Tell me what?"

She grabbed the wooden stool that Richard kept underneath the table and placed it directly across from him. "I used to do this with your grandfather," she said, sitting down.

50

Nathan broke free of his mental anguish and looked up at her. "Used to do what?"

"Sit and talk," she explained, pointing at him, then back to herself. *Like this, face to face.*

"Great," he repeated, skeptical. *Lots of people did.*

"It was always in his office at the bookstore," Jordan explained. "He'd sit at his desk. I'd sit across from him in an old Windsor armchair."

Nathan remembered that chair. It was among his earliest memories of Hammond Books. Sitting in the bow-back chair. The spines like long wooden feathers. Watching his grandfather study the pages of a book he'd pulled from the old bookcase hiding in the shadows along the back wall—the same bookcase that now sat in the back corner of the attic on the third floor of *his* house.

"Each time he needed my help, we'd meet to iron out the details," Jordan said. "They were very important conversations, ones he insisted on having face to face."

"What details?"

"Property matters."

Nathan made a face like she was speaking in some as-yet-undiscovered African dialect.

Seeing his confusion, Jordan said, "My job was to secure safe housing for those who needed to disappear because their lives were in imminent danger."

"The safehouses," Nathan mumbled.

"Yes, those," Jordan said, "which required some tricky legal work to acquire."

"Got it," Nathan mumbled. He closed his eyes and bowed his

head again, massaging his temples with the tips of his fingers, trying to calm the rising voices in his head. It was like standing in the middle of an angry mob, each person trying to scream louder than the next.

"I still remember the last time we spoke," Jordan said, breaking the silence. Her voice had grown softer, her expression somber. "He was detailing the events of that morning, and his encounter with a woman who burst through the door, out of breath and visibly shaken."

Nathan pulled his fingers from his temples and looked up. "Shaken?"

"She claimed some very bad men were chasing her. Not because of anything she'd done; it had to do with her father."

"What about him?"

"He was Walter Ballard, the noted archeologist. One month earlier, while on a dig in Naranjo, a region of Guatemala, he unearthed a generations-old treasure that, up until then, had existed as nothing more than a folk legend among the Mayan people."

"What was it?"

"Las Lágrimas de la Emperadora."

"Huh?"

"The Tears of the Empress."

Nathan shook his head, confused. "Tears?" *What kind of nonsense is that?*

"A gold necklace," Jordan explained. "And not just any gold necklace. This one was given to the empress, Lady Six Sky, in the year 740. It was strung with thick, tear-shaped wedges of solid gold, hence the name."

"So...the daughter shows up at my grandfather's bookshop, scared, and does what?" Nathan asked. "Gives him the necklace for safe keeping, to keep the 'very bad men' from getting it?"

"No," Jordan said, shaking her head. "The daughter, her name was Lía Ballard, didn't have the necklace. But she *did* have her father's field notebook from the dig. Apparently, it contained a clue that revealed the location of the necklace, which he'd hidden a week before he died."

"And these men chasing her, they wanted the field notebook?"

"Yes."

"What happened?"

"That's why I came here today to talk to you."

Nathan shrugged. *Okay, so talk.*

"After Lía gave your grandfather the field notebook, he put out a call to each of the five facilitators. We met him at the bookstore that same night, after it closed, to discuss the necessary steps needed to protect Lía Ballard. For my part, a place where her pursuers would never find her.

"And...?" Nathan prompted.

"Less than 24 hours later, your grandfather was dead."

Nathan's eyes went wide. "How?"

"Poisoned," Jordan replied.

"He was *poisoned?*" Nathan said, thunderstruck.

Jordan slowly nodded her head. *Yes.*

"But...who...?" Nathan said, too stunned to construct a complete sentence.

"Nobody knows," Jordan replied. "The police did a full investigation and found nothing, not one shred of evidence that could lead them to the killer."

"So that's *it?*" Nathan yelled. He wanted to stand up and heave one of the boxes across the room but his brain was still swimming in a fog after passing out on the floor.

"No, that's *not* it," Jordan said, pointedly. She leaned forward and looked him directly in the eye. "We need to find the killer before they find you."

4

The Rumor

The color drained from Nathan's face. "Me?" he said, pressing a finger to his chest. "Why would the killer want me? And why now? My grandfather died seven years ago."

"Hold on," Jordan said. "Just…hear me out."

"No, you hold on," he fired back. "If you know who poisoned my grandfather, why haven't you told the police?"

"If you'll let me explain…"

He buried his face in his hands like they were playing a game of hide-and-seek and it was his turn to count. *This isn't happening,* he told himself. *My grandfather gets poisoned. Nobody tells me. And now the killer might come after ME?*

"When we learned about your grandfather's sudden passing, we all went into hiding," Jordan said.

Nathan pulled his hands from his face. "We?"

"All five facilitators: Finch, Wroth, Pennyman, Fane, and myself."

He made a mental note of each code name, which according to Kendra, his grandfather had chosen from 17th century theologians and writers—a logical choice, given his profound knowledge of literature. Still, they sounded like partners in a big New York City law firm: Sidney, Finch, Wroth, Pennyman & Fane. In his mind he could envision the sign.

"Because of our close affiliation with your grandfather, we feared that we might be next," Jordan said.

Nathan shook his head, confused. "Why would you be next?"

"Because, in helping those in need, your grandfather came up against some very dangerous characters. Any one of them might've sought retribution for his actions. From what Lía Ballard told your grandfather, the men chasing her fit that very description."

"You still could've gone to the police," Nathan mumbled.

"No, we couldn't," Jordan countered. "The work we did for your grandfather was bound by an oath of secrecy. If we *had* gone to the police, we would've been breaking that oath. Not only that, we would've run the risk of destroying all the good work he did by putting the lives of those people he helped in danger."

Nathan had no rebuttal. This was about belief and respect.

"There's something else," Jordan said. "And it's at the very center of this whole thing. You remember what I said about Walter Ballard's field notebook? How Lía gave it to your grandfather?"

"Yeah?"

"It vanished."

"What do you mean, it vanished?"

"The day after our meeting with your grandfather, I stopped by the bookstore to give him the location of the safehouse I'd secured for Lía." She paused, shaking her head sadly. "I'll never forget that day. When I got to the bookstore in the late afternoon, Jameson had just gotten back from the hospital and he gave me the tragic news. I immediately suspected that the poisoning of your grandfather was linked to Walter Ballard's notebook, which I distinctly remember Henry putting in his desk drawer for safekeeping. While Jameson was busy with a customer, I went into the office and checked the drawer. The notebook was gone."

"So? It was gone. Big deal," Nathan said. "You saved the daughter from the men chasing her. Wasn't that the whole point? Protect a human life, not some ancient relic?"

"The notebook is a *very* big deal," Jordan replied. "If my suspicion is correct, it's the only thing that can link the killer to the crime."

"How do you figure?"

"Other than your grandfather, there were only five people who knew about it."

"You mean, the five of you," Nathan confirmed.

"Yes... but I don't count."

"Oh really," Nathan said. He gave her a look like he wasn't ready to tear her wanted poster off the wall just yet.

Jordan frowned. "What? You don't believe me?"

"I don't know, Nathan replied. "Can you prove it?"

"Yes, as a matter of fact, I can. After we met with your grandfather, I drove north to Camden, Maine, to find safe housing for Lía Ballard. When I returned the next afternoon, your grandfather had already died. You can call the Grand Harbor Inn if you like. They keep very detailed records of their guests."

Satisfied, Nathan moved on. "So, you suspect one of the remaining four stole the notebook for the clue it contained about the necklace."

"Yes," Jordan said, matter-of-factly. "It's the only thing that makes sense. They stole the notebook and poisoned him to keep him from trying to get it back. And knowing your grandfather, that's *exactly* what he would've done."

"My grandfather died because of a stupid *NOTEBOOK?*" Nathan shouted.

"Sadly, yes. But there's more."

"Of course, there's more," he said, throwing his hands in the air. "When isn't there?"

"Not only was the notebook never recovered, neither was the gold necklace."

"How could you possibly know that?" Nathan asked.

"Simple. If the killer managed to find it, it's not the kind of thing he would've put on a shelf like a trophy. The necklace is a rare, not to mention legendary, artifact. Because of its enormous value, which runs into the millions of dollar, the killer would've sold it on the black market, or tried to fence it through some other criminal channel. But in the seven years since the notebook vanished, I've heard of no such attempt."

"How *would* you?" Nathan asked. "It's not like there's a daily black-market news report."

"Let's just say, I have my sources," Jordan said, leaving it at that.

A brief silence followed as Nathan digested everything she'd told him. "I still don't understand how this involves me," he said.

"Really," she said, surprised that she had to explain it to him. "For starters, you're the famous grandson of Henry Hammond. That's connection #1. Connection #2: you're the most recognized 12-year-old on the planet. Ever since you and your friend made that discovery in the basement of the courthouse, the whole world knows about you and your uncanny knack for finding things. Lost things. Things that have mysteriously disappeared."

They don't know everything, Nathan thought. There was a stolen boxcar he and Gina found, missing for 150 years; a collection of priceless star rubies; millions of dollars in pirated gold coins hidden on an island in Casco Bay. With some quick thinking, and help from various members of law enforcement, those were discoveries that would never be linked to him or Gina. It was part of an ongoing effort, one that followed three key principles uttered by each keeper of the bookcase.

Careful.

Watchful.

Unseen.

"You think the *killer* doesn't know about you?" Jordan asked, raising an eyebrow. "Think again. Whoever it is not only knows who you are, they have every reason to fear you."

"Fear *me?*" Nathan said, with a smirk. "Yeah, right."

"You don't believe me?" she said. "Maybe you're not as smart as everyone claims."

Nathan waved off the notion and looked away, disgusted. *Let them think what they want.*

"Your detective skills are well documented," she explained, softening her tone. "Which means you could very well figure out who poisoned your grandfather and stole the notebook. With Ballard's notebook in hand, you'd be able to implicate the killer." She paused a beat. "And who knows," she said, "you might even find the necklace."

Nathan was speechless. He stood, legs shaky, and shuffled over to the next pallet of books, leaning on it for support as he stared at the shadows that draped the back wall of the barn like a thin black curtain. As if Arthur Chessman's replacement wasn't enough, now a phantom killer was coming after him?

He pushed the thought away and turned his attention back to the matter at hand. His grandfather hadn't withered away, old age plucking him from the life and the people he loved. He hadn't fallen and hit his head, or been the unfortunate victim of a drunk driver. He'd been betrayed—by someone he trusted.

From the yard next door, the sound of a lawn mower echoed across the driveway, chugging a few times, coughing and spitting, then roaring to life. As it slowly faded into the distance, Nathan turned and faced Jordan. "So, what now?" he asked.

"Now we talk to Jameson. See about getting you some protection."

"I already have someone for that," Nathan said, referring to Beck, Jameson's ex-military contact. He had helped with the raid on the Hamilton Mill and the subsequent arrest of Edouard Dampierre. Currently, he was acting as Nathan's private self-defense instructor.

"What about your friend? What's her name, Gina?"

"Gina McDermott."

"Right."

"I'll talk to her," Nathan said, imagining how that conversation would go. *Not good*, he told himself.

Not good at all.

After that, Nathan got back to sorting books. His head felt like it was stuffed with cotton, and he had to sit on the stool to keep from falling down as he slowly worked through the mountain of books on the table. With Jordan's revelation searing his every thought, his anger grew, and it was everything he could do to keep from heaving a book across the room. Maybe all of them.

As his rage continued to burn, he never saw Jordan step outside. She walked to the front of her car and leaned on the hood, keeping her back to the open barn door as she placed a call to Jameson. It was their first conversation in years and it got off to a rocky start.

"You *told* him his grandfather was poisoned?" he exclaimed, when she revealed where she was and what she'd done. "Why did you do that?"

"Because I'm hearing some chatter," she said. "There's a rumor going around that it was a 12-year-old kid who brought down Edouard Dampierre and his sister, beginning a worldwide manhunt for members of the Covin."

Jameson, who'd been standing when he took the call, walked over to his desk chair and sat down, feeling like he'd been punched in the gut. Adding to his dread was the fact that Jordan had somehow linked Nathan to the Dampierre saga, especially since the U.S. Marshals Service had gone to great lengths to ensure that Nathan's name was nowhere near the story.

"What makes you think it was Nathan?" he asked.

"Please," she said, offended by the question. "It wasn't that hard to figure out."

"Oh?"

"You've been chasing the Covin for how many years now?" she asked.

"Too many."

"Exactly. And you're the trusted friend of Henry Hammond, who, as it turns out, has a 12-year-old grandson with the nose of a bloodhound when it comes to tracking down lost people."

Jameson said nothing.

"Did you put him up to it?" Jordan asked.

"No, that was all his doing," Jameson said quietly, his admission stoking the anxiety that was scorching his senses.

"Well, if I can figure it out, what's to keep Henry's killer from doing the same?" she asked. "You know what I'm getting at, right?"

"Yes," Jameson said. He stood and began to pace. "Did you tell Nathan about this rumor?"

"No," Jordan said. "He's upset enough as it is, learning how his grandfather died."

"I'm sure," Jameson noted. "Are you still there with him?"

"I am."

"Do me a favor and stay put until I can get someone over there. Will you do that?"

"Of course."

The sound of a car coming up the driveway made her turn and look. When she saw who was driving, she pressed the phone to her ear again. "Jameson? Change of plans. Elizabeth just arrived."

"Of course," he said. "I forgot she's been driving him there and back each day."

"I need to leave," Jordan said urgently.

"Yes, right away," Jameson told her. "She doesn't know who you are and now isn't the time to tell her."

She was climbing back in her car just as Elizabeth's Subaru crept past.

No wave.

No introduction. *"Hi I'm Elizabeth, what's your name?*

Elizabeth just drove past the BMW and made a U-turn in the large gravel parking area that separated the house and the barn. Moments later, Nathan climbed in and slammed the door, his face tight with anger.

"What's wrong?" Elizabeth asked.

"Nothing."

"Come on, you can tell me," she said, in a jovial voice.

No, I can't, he said. Talking to her about how her father died was the express lane to grief and misery.

For her.

And for him.

After Jordan left Abbot's barn she drove as far as the O'Neill branch of the Cambridge Public Library. She turned into the small lot next to the building and slid into an empty parking space that faced Rindge Avenue. With the car still running, she pulled out her cell phone and thumbed one of her preset numbers. As was often the case whenever she dialed this particular number, the call was answered on the first ring.

"How'd it go?" said the voice on the other end of the line.

"Just as we expected," Jordan replied.

"You told him about the notebook?"

"Yes," Jordan said.

A mid-size SUV pulled into the next parking space and she looked over, her brain subconsciously taking a mental inventory as a young family emerged. *Mom. Two young kids. Boy and a girl. Books in hand. Excited.*

"What was his reaction?"

Jordan shifted her gaze back to the traffic passing by on Rindge Avenue. "Let's just say he was none too pleased to learn that it was the cause of his grandfather's death."

"Good, good. You gave him the names?"

"Yes."

"Nothing more?"

"No."

"Perfect."

"What now?" Jordan asked.

"Now we wait."

On the way home, Nathan stared down at the footwell, trying to corral his rage. If Lía Ballard hadn't walked into Hammond Books seven years ago, his grandfather would still be alive today. How many conversations would they have had, he wondered? How many stories would his grandfather have shared, about their family, and more importantly, about the bookcase? What critical, possibly life-saving advice would he have offered?

He'd never know, because all those moments had been snatched away by an unknown assassin. In his grandfather's absence, the information he wanted to know, *needed* to know, was being spoon-fed to him by Jameson, Kendra, his parents, and now, a complete stranger code-named for a British noble from the 17th century.

The loud blast of a truck horn jarred him from his reverie and he looked up. They were in a line of slow-moving traffic approaching Alewife Station. He'd been so engrossed in thought that he didn't notice his mother pulling out of Richard's driveway, or slogging through the seemingly endless line of Sunday afternoon traffic.

"You know you can talk to me and your father about anything, right?" his mother said.

"Yeah, sure, Mom." *If only that were true*, he thought.

In his mind, he couldn't let go of what Jordan had said about the police investigation: how they couldn't find a single shred of evidence that would lead them to the killer. *Nothing?* he wondered. *Not one single thing? How could that be? Did they interview everyone?*

The thought stayed with him the whole way home.

When they pulled into the driveway several minutes later, he saw his father and Beck standing next to Beck's Dodge Ram pickup truck that was parked in front of the garage. Looped over Beck's shoulder was black canvas duffel bag.

When David saw Elizabeth's car come to a stop next to the house, he said something to Beck and then hurried over to the car. Like a hotel valet, he opened the door for her, then closed it once she had gotten out. "Jameson called," he said.

"Oh? What did he want?"

"I'll tell you inside. What's eating him?" he asked, nodding in Nathan's direction.

Nathan was out of the car, looking like someone who had just taken a rolling tumble down a steep incline. His clothes still carried bits of dust and grit from the barn floor.

"Couldn't tell you," Elizabeth said, keeping her voice low. "I don't think he uttered three words the whole way home."

"I'll talk to him," David said. He gave her a reassuring pat on the arm, then made his way around the front of the car. "Hey, what's up pal? Are you all right?"

"You know? I wish people would stop asking me that!" Nathan snapped.

"Is this about that Asher character?"

Nathan held up a hand...*don't start with that*...then pushed past him.

"Where are you going?" David asked.

"To talk to Beck."

Across the street, and one house up, a pewter-gray Lincoln MKZ sat parked at the curb. Through the side mirror, the driver watched as Elizabeth turned into the driveway. When he saw Nathan climb out of the car, he lowered the window several inches for a clearer view, studying the face of the boy he knew all too well. *Not here, not now,* he told himself.

He raised the window and pulled away from the curb, his thoughts shifting to other options, any one of which would require careful planning and precise execution.

Nathan pushed through the side door of the garage and saw Beck in the far corner. He was standing on a stepladder, screwing a thick eye bolt into one of the rafters.

"What are you doing?" Nathan asked.

Beck gave the eye bolt one last turn and climbed down from the ladder. "Installing this," he said, standing up the heavy bag that was leaning against the wall. It was nearly four feet tall, slate black, with four ring tabs on the top. Attached to each one was a length of chain, which were held together at the ends by a large carabiner.

From where Nathan stood it looked like a hanging garment bag, round not square, that was stuffed to capacity with stale-smelling clothes. "What is it?" he asked.

"It's called a heavy bag," Beck replied. He bent down and wrapped his right arm around the lower half of it, then hoisted it up off the floor with ease, as if it were a small child. In one fluid move he stepped up on the ladder and hooked the carabiner to the eye bolt, allowing the bag to swing freely.

"What am I supposed to do with it?" Nathan asked.

"Punch it."

"Punch it," Nathan repeated. "And why would I do that?"

"To get stronger."

"O-kay," Nathan said, struggling to understand how simply hitting something could make him stronger.

"A heavy bag helps you strengthen your core," Beck told him. "It improves your focus, relieves stress, and boosts your self-confidence." *All of which you desperately need to work on.*

"Punching does all that?"

"Yes, but you don't flail," Beck said. "You punch, like this." He balled his fists, brought them in tight to his chest, then leaned forward and unleashed a series of straightaway jabs. Right-left, right-left. Each one landed with a heavy thud that made the bag shiver.

"Go ahead, you try," Beck said.

Nathan eyed the bag from top to bottom. *How hard can this be?* he thought, then stepped up to it, tightened both fists into a ball, and punched the bag. "Oww!" he said, flexing his fingers.

"Hold on," Beck said. He dug into the canvas duffel bag, sitting next to the wall, and pulled out a brand new pair of neoprene training gloves. "These have a gel insert in the knuckle," he said. "They'll help cushion your fists."

He showed Nathan how to put them on, then stepped back. "Try it again."

Nathan brought both fists in to his chest, like Beck had done, then threw a right jab. Then a left. "I like *these*," he said, admiring each of the gloves.

He was about to continue when Beck stepped in front of the bag. "That's enough for now," he said. "We'll get back to this when you're ready."

Nathan peeled off the gloves and slipped them back in the duffel bag. "What's this?" he asked, pulling a hand weight from the bag. It had a contoured chrome handle, and the hexagonal head was encased in thick black rubber and embossed with the number three.

"It's a hand weight, or dumbbell," said Beck. "It'll help you build muscle mass in your shoulders, your forearms, and your biceps."

Nathan pulled a second one from the bag. "You're not serious," he said with a smirk, lifting one, then the other. "They weigh nothing."

"Is that so?" Beck said. "Let's try this. Hold them down by your side, palms forward."

Nathan gave him a tired look, then complied.

"Now, keep your elbows against your body and slowly lift the weights upward."

Again, Nathan did as he was told.

"Okay, hold right there," Beck said, when the dumbbells were nearly touching Nathan's shoulders. "Now, lower them...slowly."

Nathan rolled his eyes...*this is ridiculous*...then eased his arms back down. When the dumbbells were hanging by his side once again, he said, "That's it? That's supposed to make me stronger?"

"Twenty times," Beck said.

"Excuse me?"

"Do it 20 times."

Nathan slumped both shoulders. "Seriously?"

"Let's go," Beck said, motioning with his hand. "I don't have all day."

Fine, Nathan thought, then repeated the process.

Lift, pause, slowly lower.

Lift, pause, slowly lower.

He was on his eighth repetition when the muscles in his arms began to ache. By number 12, they began to burn. When he got to 15, he clenched his teeth, grimacing, as he struggled to raise the dumbbells as far as his waist.

"You still want to make jokes?" Beck asked.

Nathan dropped the dumbbells to his side, exhausted. "No," he said softly.

"Okay then. When you can do 20 repetitions without breaking a sweat, we'll increase the weight."

"What about that?" Nathan asked, pointing at the heavy bag.

"Twenty repetitions," Beck repeated, jabbing a finger at the dumbbells. "Then we'll see about the heavy bag."

After Beck went into the house to talk with David and Elizabeth, Nathan set the dumbbells on the floor and approached the heavy bag. "Relieves stress, huh?" *We'll see about that.* He took the training gloves from the duffel bag, slipped them on, then punched the bag.

It barely moved.

He took a deep breath and blew it out, recalling what Jordan had told him about Lía Ballard's sudden appearance at Hammond Books, her father's field notebook, and how she left it with Henry for safe-keeping—an act of desperation, but one that would ultimately spell the end of his days. The cruelty of such a deadly outcome made Nathan's emotions boil over and he hit the bag again, harder.

Thud.

This time it moved, but only slightly.

He thought about the facilitators, assembled by his grandfather to aid his cause of helping those in need—a noble pursuit—only to have one of them deceive him. And for what? A gold necklace worth millions? "This was all about *money?*" he shouted. His anger surged again and he launched a volley of punches, shouting as each one struck the bag.

"He *trusted* you!"

Thud.

"And you *betrayed* him!"

70

Thud.

"Now he's *gone!*"

Thud.

He paused long enough to wipe the sweat from his brow with his sleeve, then continued, this time using a series of right-left combinations.

"I'm gonna hunt you down..."

Thud-thud.

"No matter how long it takes..."

Thud-thud.

"And when I find you..."

Thud-thud.

"You're gonna pay!"

Thud-thud.

Thud-thud.

Thud-thud.

5

Wild Stallion

Nathan left the garage and went into the house, exhausted, but renewed. Beck was right. Punching the heavy bag really did help relieve stress. Gone was his earlier fog, and the dark images of a phantom killer that had stabbed at his every thought like a French dagger. And while his arm muscles were sore, it was a reminder of the perilous road that lay ahead, should he initiate the plan that was forming in the back of his mind.

He knew this wouldn't be like any of the other mysteries he'd solved. This one was personal, and that made all the difference in the world.

He walked up the back stairway into the kitchen and saw his mother and father huddled together with Beck, deep in conversation.

"Oh, there you are," Elizabeth said, when she saw Nathan step

72

into the room.

"Here I am," he replied, in a flat tone.

"Can we talk to you for a moment?" David said.

"Right now?" he said. *I don't smell that great.*

"Yes, right now," his mother fired back.

"I got a call from Jameson today," David said. "He spoke with someone at the FBI…"

"The big dog," Nathan said.

"Excuse me?"

"They call him the big dog."

"The-big-dog?" his father repeated, slowly.

"Yeah. Don't ask me why."

"Okay, well, Jameson said his contact…dog man…"

"The big dog, Dad! Maybe you should just call him by his first name. It's Brett."

"Fine. *Brett* identified Asher. His full name is Asher Rickman."

Oh joy, now we know his last name, Nathan thought.

"I know you had a concern about members of the Covin coming after you, but I don't want you to worry about that," Elizabeth said. "Now that the police have Rickman's full name, it'll make finding him that much easier."

Nathan shook his head, mumbling to himself, "They should work on finding the name of—"

"What was that?" his mother said, before he could finish.

"Nothing," he muttered.

"No, tell me what you said. They should work on finding the name of who?"

Nathan and his father looked at one another, busted.

Elizabeth saw the exchange and said, "What's going on between you two?"

"Nathan asked me how your father died," David said, gently.

She closed her eyes, shaking her head. *No, no, no.*

"He was going to find out sooner or later," David reasoned.

Yes, but I wanted to be the one to tell him, she thought. She was still baffled that, after all this time, the police still hadn't found anything substantial. Not a single lead. As she had done every day since her father's passing, she fought desperately to blot out the image of him lying in the hospital bed, his body convulsing as the poison stole the final moments of his life.

"Did the police question everyone?" Nathan asked.

Beck looked over at him, a bad feeling washing over him.

"Yes," David answered. "Their investigation was very extensive."

"What about his regular customers? The people who came into his shop every day? Nathan asked. *Like Lía Ballard?* "Did they talk to them?"

I don't believe this kid, Beck thought, his initial suspicion confirmed.

"I'm sure they did," David said.

Nathan saw Beck staring at him. When their eyes met, Beck didn't look away. Nathan cinched his shoulders, confused. *What?*

Beck just shook his head, confounded. *You are unbelievable!*

Nathan got the sudden sensation of being trapped under a heat lamp.

"Can we not talk about this anymore?" Elizabeth said. "Whoever was responsible for my father's death is still out there and there's nothing we can do about. We just need to forget about it and move on!"

"Sorry, Mom. I won't mention it again," Nathan said. *But I'm going to find whoever did it, if it's the last thing I do.*

"I think what your mother means is that you should be on the lookout for anything or anyone suspicious," David said.

"Did I not make myself clear?" Elizabeth snapped.

Nathan waved his hand back and forth in the air. "Phew! I need to change out of these clothes," he said, breaking the tension in the room. He pushed past the three of them, making momentary eye contact with Beck, who eyed him with the same steely look as before. Nathan ignored it and went upstairs to his bedroom. Once there, he closed the door and took his flip phone from his pocket to call Gina. Three rings later, she answered.

"Hello?"

"It's me," he said. "Have you got a minute?"

"Hold on," she replied. There was a brief pause as she walked over to the window directly above the sink and parted the curtains with her finger. Her parents were in the backyard, tending to the vegetables in the raised beds that lined the back edge of the property. "Yeah, we're good," she said. "What's up?"

"We need to talk."

"O-kay," she said slowly. "Can you be more specific?"

A sharp knock on the door made Nathan turn and look. It opened halfway and Beck stuck his head in the room.

"Gina, I gotta go," Nathan said quickly. "I'll call you back."

Click!

He closed the phone and shoved it back into his pocket. "Can I help you?" he said.

Beck walked in and closed the door behind him. "What is it with you?" he asked. "Do you have a death wish?"

"What are you talking about?" Nathan asked.

"You know exactly what I'm talking about."

"Actually, I don't," Nathan said, trying to sound convincing.

"Is that so? Why were you pressing your parents about the police investigation?"

"Uh…no reason," Nathan said, fishing for an answer. "Just curious, that's all."

"Curious?" Beck said, not buying it. "Fine, have it your way. But don't forget what happened to you at Whitehall."

"Huh?"

"On the boat?" Beck said.

Nathan's eyes darted down and to the left.

"Yeah, I know all about it," Beck said.

Impossible, Nathan thought. He and Kendra had made a pact not to tell anyone how they'd been ambushed by Sato's men in the woods that overlooked the dock, and how they were subsequently tied up aboard the Covin's yacht as it was being loaded with stolen artwork. Before its rendezvous with the container ship waiting a mile off-shore, Sato's plan was to serve them both up as shark food in the waters off Portsmouth, NH.

"You think I didn't speak to the U.S. Marshals?" Beck asked, when he saw the look of confusion on Nathan's face. "They told me all about their search of the boat, and the severed zip ties they found on the floor of the main cabin."

Nathan's body sagged. In their haste to escape, neither he nor Kendra had thought to pick up the ties that had them bound to the deck chairs. At the time, they were more concerned with escaping before their captors returned. "Please don't tell my parents about that," he said. "Or Jameson."

"How about this?" Beck countered. "You stop charging into dangerous situations like a wild stallion. One of these days, there might not be someone there to save you. It's about time you realized that."

"We didn't charge," Nathan mumbled.

"What was that?"

"We didn't charge! We were very careful."

"Obviously not careful enough," Beck said. He opened the door, stepped halfway out, then paused to look back. "I promised I'd help protect you, and I will. But you have to be smarter next time. Understood?"

"Yes," Nathan said, nodding his head sadly.

"In the meantime, if you need me, you know how to get a hold of me," Beck said. He held Nathan's eye for several seconds, as if conveying an unspoken message, then ducked out into the hallway and pulled the door shut.

Nathan contemplated what that could mean, then pulled out his flip phone and called Gina.

"Hello," she said, deadpan. "Let me guess. You're going to say another 15 words then hang up again?"

"It was more than 15 words," he joked.

"Yeah, right," she replied. *Let me know when you learn how to count.*

In his mind, he could see her shaking her head and rolling her eyes. "We need to talk," he said. "There's been a development."

"Does it involve your identical twin, Asher?"

"No. We can forget about him. He's long gone."

"Another crime lord, perhaps?" she asked. *Please say no.*

"Nope."

"A hired killer?"

"Hired? Uh…no…definitely not hired." *As far as I know.*

"What's that supposed to mean?"

"It's kind of a long story."

Oh brother, she thought. She pulled the phone from her ear and stared at it momentarily, debating whether to listen to more of his nonsense or simply hang up and be done with him. But one word he'd said had her curiosity crackling and she pressed the phone to her ear again.

"Okay, I'm listening."

Beck was backing out of the driveway when his cell phone pinged. When he saw who was calling, he pulled to the curb and took the call. "Jameson," he said, his voice free of emotion.

"Can you talk?" Jameson asked.

"Yes."

"We may have a problem," Jameson explained. "I heard from a trusted source that word has leaked about the arrest of Edouard and Ginette Dampierre. More precisely, that it was a 12-year-old boy who was responsible for their capture."

"So, what you're saying is, we have a weak link in the chain," said Beck.

"It would appear so," Jameson replied.

"Do we know if a connection has been made to Nathan?"

"From what I was told, no, although that could change at any moment."

"Agreed."

"Until we can figure this out, we need someone to stay close to Nathan," Jameson said. "But he can't know we're guarding him. He doesn't respond well to the idea of being babysat."

"Say no more," Beck said. "I'll take care of it."

"Good," Jameson told him. "You'll let me know if you need any help?"

"I won't need help," Beck replied.

"Are you sure?"

"Yeah, I got this."

Monday, 9:30 a.m.

Gina waited until her parents left for work, then grabbed her leather notepad from the desk drawer in her bedroom and went over to Nathan's house. As she was walking across his driveway, headed for the back door, she heard the unmistakable sound of someone jump roping in the garage, the rope keeping a steady rhythm as it hit the concrete floor.

Whap-whap-whap-whap

Whap-whap-whap-whap

For reasons she still couldn't fathom, jump roping had become Nathan's daily obsession, something he referred to as his "training." *Training for what?* she wondered. And unlike his initial attempts with the rope, when he had the coordination of a newborn calf taking its first wobbly steps, he was actually getting better at it.

He had his back to the door when she walked in, and it wasn't until she slammed the door shut that he stopped and turned around.

"Oh, hey," he said, out of breath, his face glowing a soft shade of crimson.

She looked past him and pointed at the heavy bag hanging in the corner. "What's *that* doing here?"

"It's called a heavy bag."

"Yes, I know what it's called," she said, annoyed. "What's it *doing* here?"

He walked over and brushed the side of it with his hand like he was patting a champion thoroughbred. "Beck lent it to me. He said it'll help me get stronger."

"Is that a fact?"

"Yup. Go ahead, punch it."

"Uh, no thank you," she said. *I don't punch.*

"Come on, just one time," he said, egging her on. *What are you, chicken?*

She tilted her head, lips pursed, and gave him a bored look… *really?*… then walked over to the bag and poked it with her finger. "There," she said. "Are you happy now?"

"You call that a punch?"

She gave him another weary look, then closed her fist and gave the bag a quick jab, high and tight, her fist making a sharp *smack* on the bag.

"Nice!" he said, nodding his head. "That felt good, right?"

"Delightful. Now, can we get to the matter at hand?" she said, waving her notepad in the air.

He hung the jump rope on the 10-penny nail he'd pounded into a nearby stud. When he turned back around, she had the notepad open and was reviewing her notes.

"I still can't believe you want to pursue this," she said, referring to what he'd told her on the phone. "Someone poisons your grandfather and you want to go after him? In case you didn't know, that's a job for the police."

"Yes, I know," he countered. "But like I told you, their investigation turned up nothing."

"And you think yours will?" she asked, looking up from her notepad. "You have nothing of substance to go on. I checked into Lía Ballard like you asked me to. All I could find was that she used to be an adjunct professor at Boston College. That was seven years ago. After that, nothing."

"Yeah, I figured as much. After she showed up at my grandfather's bookstore, he helped her disappear."

Gina gave him an exasperated look. *Then why ask me to investigate her?*

"What about her father?" Nathan asked.

"He was a professor in the Department of Earth and Planetary Sciences at Harvard University. He died…" she said, pausing to flip to another page, "a week before your grandfather was…you know…"

"Anything else?"

"Nope," she replied. "As far as the group your grandfather put together…"

"Facilitators," he said.

"Whatever," she said, with a shrug. "Without their actual names, we're never going to find them. You said their code names are from the 17th century? Well, I did some digging," she said, reading directly from her notes, "and the name Sidney is probably Mary Herbert Sidney, an English author and poet. Finch, I'm assuming, is Anne

Finch, the Countess of Winchilsea, also a poet and courtier."

"A what?"

"Courtier," she repeated. "It's like, an assistant to a member of the royal family."

"Okay."

"Wroth has to be Lady Mary Wroth, an English noblewoman and poet. Pennyman, if I'm not mistaken, refers to Mary Pennyman, English writer and polemicist."

"Pole-*what?*"

"Po-*lem*-i-cist," she said, enunciating each syllable. "It's someone who's very skilled at arguing controversial beliefs." She flashed both eyebrows and turned the page. "Sounds like someone I know," she mumbled under her breath.

"I heard that," he said.

"The last one, Fane," she said, continuing, "is Mary Fane, the Countess of Westmoreland, another author."

"That's it?" he asked.

"Uh-huh," she said.

He bit the inside of his cheek and began to pace, refusing to admit defeat. "We need to find those names."

"Does Jameson know them?" Gina asked.

"No."

"Are you sure? From what you've told me, he and your grandfather seemed pretty tight."

"That's true, but if Jameson knew their real names, he would've questioned them, or had the police do it."

"Agreed," Gina said. She looked away. *I hate it when he's right.*

"It's safe to assume that my grandfather didn't write them down.

I mean, why would he? Still..." He stopped pacing and looked past her, lost in thought.

"I know that face," she said. "What are you thinking?"

"He still would've wanted me to know how to contact them."

"What are you talking about?"

He blinked the idea away and looked at her. "When I first met Jameson, he told me that my grandfather had chosen *me* to be the next guardian of the bookcase."

"Yeah? What about it?"

"Think about it," he said. "If he assembled the facilitator group to help him with things he couldn't arrange on his own, things like creating a new identity for someone, or finding a safe place to hide them, or getting them legal help, wouldn't he want them to help *me* too?"

"Sure," she said. "If he thought you were going to do all those things." She gave him a hard stare. "Is that your plan? Find people new names? Hide them? Sort out their legal problems?"

"No...well...I don't know...maybe."

She shook her head, dizzy. "What is *that* supposed to mean?"

"Ever since my ancestor Daniel Hammond came to America with the bookcase, each person in my family who guarded the book-case has helped those who have somehow been wronged or shamed, and has worked to bring criminals to justice."

"Yes, I know. You've only told me that, like, 50 times. What's your point?"

"My point is...that's exactly what *we've* done. We revealed the truth about Alastair Raven. We cleared Wynn Barrett's name. We found Stanley Kendall's killer. We exposed Edouard Dampierre and his sister, Ginette, along with Arthur Chessman and his replacement. And with each mystery, things got more difficult."

"Uh, you mean, life-threatening," she muttered.

"Exactly!" he said, jabbing a finger in her direction. "And if that trend continues, we're going to need help, the kind that the facilitators group can provide. Face it, the bookcase is a mine field. Jameson pretty much told me that. He also warned me that some mysteries are better left unsolved, and that there are people out there who will go to great lengths to keep them hidden."

"You mean, people like Edouard and Ginette Dampierre."

"Yes, and *that's* why my grandfather would've wanted me to have the facilitators at my disposal." He paused a beat, then said, "Actually, one of them already helped me."

"One of them already *helped* you?" Gina exclaimed.

"It was Finch. Kendra set it up when we were going to Stackyard Road. Apparently, Finch is the one who stocks all the safehouses with supplies."

Gina leaned forward, eyebrows raised. "*All* the safehouses?"

"Uh-huh."

"There's more than one?"

Nathan nodded his head. *Yup.*

She stared at him in disbelief. Apparently, Henry Hammond's efforts on behalf of the innocent and oppressed extended much further than she initially thought. "Maybe he had every intention of telling you their names and how to contact them," she said, "but then…"

"Yeah, then Lía Ballard walked into his shop changed everything," he said, Gina's comment confirming the idea that his grandfather would've wanted him to have access to his team of specialized collaborators.

"So, we're right back to square one again," she said.

"No, not yet," he replied, the idea in his mind running at full bore. The question was, how would the information come to him? Would it be like before, the answer sitting right before his eyes? There was only one way to find out.

"What do you mean, not yet?" Gina asked.

"I'll show you," he said, brushing past her. "Follow me."

He left the garage and went into the house. His mother had already left for work, and on the way past the basement door, he heard his father downstairs in his office, talking to a client on the phone.

"What are you doing?" Gina asked, as Nathan continued down the hallway toward the front hall.

"You'll see."

He hurried up the stairs, and when he reached the second floor he walked past his bedroom and headed for the attic stairs. He was opening the door to the third floor when Gina pressed her hand against it and pushed it shut.

"Hey! What are you doing?" he asked.

"You're going up to the attic?" she said.

"Yeah?" he said, defensively

"To do what?" she asked. "Search the bookcase for the names?"

"Uh…you could say that."

"But *you* said your grandfather didn't write them down."

"That's right."

"So then, why go up there?"

Then it hit her, and she backed away from him, gesturing with both hands. "Oh, no," she said. "I'm not doing this again."

"Relax, will you?" he said.

She stood her ground, her head shaking slowly from side to side. *No way.* The spiders in the attic were fine. Cute, even. But the old bookcase hiding in the shadows, and all the supernatural things it did, were downright creepy. For a short stretch of time she thought she had overcome her fear of it, but deep in her gut she believed they hadn't seen the strangest or the worst of it yet—and she had no intention of finding out what that could be.

"Tell you what," he said. "You don't have to go in. You can stand in the doorway."

"And do what?"

"Watch."

She stared at him, tight-lipped. *Why do you always do this to me?* "Fine," she said, at last. "I'll stand in the doorway, but I am NOT going in."

"Suit yourself," he said, then pulled the attic door open and made his way up the creaky stairs.

At the attic door, Gina stopped and watched him weave his way through the crooked piles of cardboard boxes, stacks of plastic tubs, and tangled heaps of outdated toys and furniture. A single lightbulb hung from the ceiling by means of thick black electrical cord. Another outdated third-floor original. In the feeble light it threw, Nathan's body was like a phantom drifting through the murky gloom.

He made it to the bookcase and stopped. For several long seconds he stood before it, overcome with the same feeling of awe.

Elegant in design, it was remarkably intact after being smuggled out of England five generations earlier—a perilous journey that began at the West India Docks on the Isle of Dogs in London, followed by a treacherous voyage across the open ocean in the hull of a brigantine ship.

"I need your help," he said softly.

"What did you say?" Gina asked, playing with a nickel-sized spider she found crawling up the inside of the doorframe.

He ignored her and continued, his eyes scanning the shelves up and down and side-to-side as he spoke. "I need the names of the team you put together. The facilitators."

"Uh...if you're talking to me, you need to speak up," Gina said. She placed the spider on her wrist and watched it race up her forearm. When it reached her elbow, she used her finger to gently lift it up and bring it back down to her wrist, where it started its upward climb in earnest once again.

Just then, the light bulb in the middle of the room cut out, throwing the room into total darkness. The only light filtered in through the far window that was blanketed with a thick layer of spider webs.

"Oh, great," Gina muttered. The spider jumped off her arm and disappeared in the dark.

Nathan stood perfectly still, waiting and watching, his heart racing in anticipation.

And that's when he saw it. Centered in the middle of the bookcase was a patch of light no bigger than a pie plate. At first it looked like a tiny cloud, or a vapor trapped in the still air of the attic.

It had no apparent source; it just appeared in the dark, and he watched as it slowly began to inch its way upward, pulling his gaze with it as it climbed higher.

When it reached the next shelf, it stopped.

6

W. Heffron

The light paused, hovering inches in front of the books on the shelf. Through the thin haze, a single letter on one of the spines flashed a fiery gold color, as if touched by the sun. Nathan watched, spellbound, as it faded and then continued on, washing slowly over the titles. As it moved, random letters flashed, but only for a split second.

When it reached the end of the shelf, the light faded. But just as quickly, it reappeared where it had started and began another slow crawl across the shelf.

"What are you telling me?" he said.

"Uh…you're doing it again," Gina crabbed.

The light moved like it had before, stopping and starting, letters glowing momentarily before going dark.

"The letters? You want me to see the letters?" he asked.

Gina rolled her eyes. *I give up.*

"Gina!" he called out.

"Yes? I'm still here," she groaned. *Where else would I be?*

"Get out your notepad."

"What?"

"Your notepad," he repeated, louder.

"What about it?"

"Get it out!"

"And do what?" she asked. "It's pitch black."

"JUST DO IT!" he shouted. "HURRY!"

"All right, all right, calm down," she said as she fished it out of her back pocket.

"I'm going to call out a series of letters," he said. "I need you to write them down."

"In the dark? You can't be serious."

"Are you ready?"

"Hold on!" she said. She opened the notepad, felt for the small pencil she kept tucked inside it, then flipped through the pages, stopping at one she hoped was blank. *This is nuts,* she thought. "Okay, ready."

Nathan waited until the light reached the end of the shelf. When it reappeared on the left side and began another pass, he called out each letter as it burned through the thin veil of light.

"D!"

"D," Gina repeated. She pictured the letter in her mind as she wrote it on the page, hoping she'd be able to read it in the full light of day. For all she knew, she was writing over the notes she'd already jotted down.

"E!"

"E," she replied, writing it directly below the D.

"V!"

"V?" she asked.

"Yes, like Victor."

"Right." Again, she moved the pencil lower and wrote the letter.

"E!"

"E," she called back.

"R!"

"R," she repeated. She had reached the bottom of the page and quickly turned to the next.

"E!"

"E," she confirmed.

"U!"

"Got it," she said.

"X!"

The light reached the end of the shelf and evaporated into the dark. "Did you get all that?" Nathan shouted.

"Yes," she called back. Then, to herself, "Whether we'll be able to read it is another thing."

He turned from the bookcase and started back down the narrow pathway toward the door when the bulb hanging from the ceiling suddenly flicked back on.

"Okay, that's not normal!" Gina said.

Moments later, when they reached the bottom of the attic stairs, she stepped out into the hallway and stopped to read what she had written. The letters were remarkably neat, despite the fact that they'd been written in complete darkness. "D-e-v-e-r-e-u-x?" she said, stringing the letters together. "Does that name mean anything to you?"

"No," Nathan said, running the name through his memory. "Do me a favor," he said. "Work your magic and see what you can find."

"It's hardly magic," she said with a smirk. "But I'll do some digging."

Just then, Nathan's father called from the front hallway. "NATHAN?"

Nathan put a finger to his lips…*shhhh*…then shouted, "YEAH?"

"You have a visitor," his father said.

"Be right down," Nathan called back. "Wait here," he told Gina, then hurried down the hallway. When he reached the top of the stairs, the front hallway was empty. Very slowly, he eased down the stairs, stopping to look over the bannister. From that vantage point, he saw his father walking through the kitchen, headed for the back door. Moving quickly, he raced back up the stairs and motioned to Gina with his hand. "Come on," he said. "Hurry."

He waited until she slipped out the front door, then he walked into the kitchen and down the back stairway. When he stepped outside, he saw his father and Beck standing near the garage. Their conversation came to an abrupt halt when they turned and saw him approaching.

"What's going on?" he asked, eyeing both of them suspiciously.

"What are you doing right now?" asked Beck, ignoring Nathan's question.

"Nothing special. I don't have to be at work until one o'clock."

"Good," said Beck. "That'll give us plenty of time."

"For what?" Nathan asked.

"The next phase of your training."

Asher Rickman stepped through the front doors of the posh downtown hotel, happy to be free of the midday Boston tourists who were clogging the sidewalks like an army of ants as they made their way to Quincy Market. To ensure his anonymity, he was dressed in a silver business suit, a light brown wig, and dark green aviator sunglasses. In one hand he carried an exquisitely crafted brown-leather Bennet Winch folio. In the other hand was a plain white box, a cube roughly five inches square, held shut by a fancy gold ribbon that was tied in a neat bow at the top. Tucked inside the box was the emerald and diamond necklace he'd pilfered from the Willow & Vine auction two days earlier.

He surveyed the lobby, checked his watch, then scanned the lobby again, giving the outward appearance of a man who was meeting someone who had yet to arrive. When he saw the reservation supervisor appear behind the front desk, he walked over at once, the two men making eye contact well before Asher stepped up to the marble counter.

The supervisor, whose nametag identified him as Mr. Ellison, was clean shaven, in his mid 50s, and exuded a butler-like air of efficiency and proper social comportment. He'd been secretly recruited by Asher a year earlier and was an important cog in the processing of the new watchman's ongoing acquisition of stolen goods. Ellison knew exactly why Asher was there at the desk, and their conversation, as always, followed the same course.

"Good afternoon, sir" Ellison said, as if speaking to a complete stranger. "How may I help you?"

"I'd like to store this in one of your safe deposit boxes," Asher said, sliding the box across the counter.

Ellison took the package without question. "Why, of course, sir," he said.

At that, each man turned away from the counter: Asher walking casually toward the front entrance, Ellison taking the box to the bank of safety deposit boxes that were located in a secure room in the back.

Within the hour, a courier would retrieve the package and process it through a number of trusted channels. By week's end, it would be safely out of the country, on its way to a well-guarded Covin storehouse in Europe.

As Asher stepped back outside onto the busy street, he turned his attention to the troubling matter that had been gnawing at his every waking thought since Saturday, after he ducked out the back door of Willow & Vine.

During his last visit with his mentor, Arthur Chessman, the old man had babbled on and on about Asher's visit the day before: how he had voiced his uncertainty about his new duties; the two women he'd brought with him, who Asher claimed were helping him; and the melee that ensued when a complete stranger entered the room and began grilling Chessman about the items he'd accumulated during his many years of service to the Covin as its original watch-man—a position he created, and worked to perfection.

But Asher hadn't visited that day. In fact, he was nowhere near Weston, MA, where Chessman resided. His most recent meeting with the old man had taken place a week earlier. What's more, he had never, ever, voiced a single doubt about his duties. And while there were women in key roles across his criminal network, there were no two that he brought with him to "help" with whatever task was at hand.

So, who was this charlatan who had duped Chessman? How much did he know about the Covin? About Asher himself? And why did he show up at Willow & Vine? Was this mysterious imposter hunting him? If so, why?

As he was swept along the sidewalk, held captive by the endless throng of pedestrian traffic, he decided it was time to put a name to his pursuer. Once that was done, a decision would have to be made on how best to proceed.

"Are you working on the things we discussed?" Beck asked Nathan. They were standing alone in the backyard after David had gone back into the house to resume working.

"Yes," Nathan answered.

"You're speed and agility? Your evasive techniques?"

Nathan nodded. "I started jump roping like you suggested—"

"Show me," Beck cut in.

"Huh?"

"Your evasive techniques."

"O-kay," Nathan said, giving Beck a quizzical look. *How do suggest I do that?*

With no warning whatsoever, and with lightning speed, Beck's fist flew up from his side, aimed directly at Nathan's head. Nathan, in turn, dropped to the ground and watched Beck's fist fly over his head, completely missing his scalp. Grinning, he began to get up when Beck reached down and grabbed him by the shoulders, his fingertips like the claws of a giant prehistoric bird, digging into his trapezius muscle, forcing him back down onto the lawn.

Nathan struggled to break free, but Beck kept him pinned to the ground with his knee. "Evasion is more than just ducking down," he said. He stood, then grabbed Nathan by the bicep and pulled him to his feet as easy as picking up a dried stick. "You can slip the jab, but that's not enough," Beck told him. "Try to keep at least six feet between you and your attacker, and always have an escape route."

"Escape route?" Nathan asked, rubbing his aching shoulder.

"That's right. It's part of something called free running. It starts with being aware of your surroundings at all times. Once you plot your angle of escape, you can dodge, vault, or roll your way to safety."

"Roll?" Nathan asked, looking skeptical.

"Yes," Beck replied. "Here, I'll show you." He stepped back, putting several feet between them. "Come at me, swinging, like you really want to hurt me."

"You're not serious," Nathan said.

"I'm very serious," Beck said. "But if you'd rather, we can just forget the whole thing and you can spend the rest of your life being roughed up and bloodied, or worse, by people who want to hurt you." He paused briefly, then said, "Is that what you want?"

"No, of course not," Nathan scoffed. *What kind of question is that?*

"Did you enjoy getting manhandled by Edouard Dampierre's goons? Or Ginette Dampierre's hired assassin?"

"What do *you* think? Nathan shot back, the mention of those events sparking his anger.

Beck saw the rage in Nathan's face and kept on. "What if you're confronted by the person who killed your grandfather?" he asked, knowing he was hitting a central nerve. "What's your plan? Are you just going to stand there and—"

"AAAAHHHHH," Nathan shouted, exploding at Beck in a blinding rage, his fist cocked and ready to strike.

Beck waited until the last second, then dove to the ground, tucking and rolling on the grass past Nathan's right side.

Nathan's momentum carried him forward and his fist sailed harmlessly into empty air, causing him to stumble, nearly falling to the ground. When he regained his balance and turned around, he saw Beck standing six feet away, arms up, his fists clenched and ready for another attack.

"See what I did there?" Beck asked. "It was a basic drop and roll. You need to practice it. Practice it a *lot*."

Nathan gave him a wary look. *Drop and roll. What am I, five years old?*

"Come on," Beck said, gesturing with both hands. "Let's see you try it."

"Right now?"

"Yes. Right now. Drop and roll."

This is silly, Nathan thought, looking around to make sure no one was watching. He let out a nervous breath, set his body, then dove forward, planting both palms on the ground as he summersaulted on the grass. But instead of tucking his body into a ball, he flopped over and landed hard on his back.

Beck stifled a laugh.

"Don't say it!" Nathan barked as he climbed to his feet.

"See it in your mind," Beck said. "Identify point A, the spot where you want to land, then point B, where you want to end up.

97

And don't roll on your back, unless you want to hurt yourself. Roll on your shoulders, making sure your head and neck never touch the ground."

Nathan returned to his original position, crouched down, and eyed a patch of grass three feet to the left of Beck. Point A. Six feet beyond that was a section of lawn dotted with clover. Point B. Once again, he set, then dove forward like he was diving off a cliff into the water below. When his hands met the ground, he tucked his body into a tight ball and rolled past Beck, coming to a stop in a sitting position atop the clover.

"Very good," said Beck. "Now try it again, but this time, as you roll, use your momentum to propel yourself back up into a standing position."

Nathan climbed to his feet and stumbled back to his starting point. After a deep breath, he dove again, tucking and rolling like before, and using his forward motion to spring back up onto his feet.

"Perfect," said Beck. "Once more. And this time, when you stand up...run."

"Run where?" Nathan asked.

"Someplace where I can't get you."

Gina sat at the computer in the living room muttering under her breath. Following Nathan's directive, she'd begun a hard search for the name Devereux. Unsure of what significance it had to Nathan's grandfather, or the facilitator group he assembled, she checked every listing, every link, that had that name. Each one turned out to be a dead end.

She found Devereux, a national non-profit behavioral healthcare organization. Next, Devereux Beach in Marblehead. There were two schools: The Devereux School, a private boarding school north of Worcester, and another with the same name on the North Shore. There were few, if any, personal listings. The only one north of New York City was a woman working at a charter school in Newton. Other than that, she found nothing.

She turned off the computer and closed her notepad, feeling even more confused than when she started. Normally, when she was researching something for Nathan, she could find *something*. Frustrated, she got up from the chair and went next door to give Nathan the bad news.

She ducked out the back door and started across the lawn when she saw him come racing around the front corner of his house. He clipped the rhododendron bushes that lined the front porch, nearly falling in the process, then sprinted up the driveway.

Seconds later, Beck appeared, chasing after him and closing fast. Nathan made it as far as the back corner of the house when Beck caught up with him and tackled him, the two of them landing hard on the grass.

"Aren't you a little old to be playing tag?" she called out as she crossed the driveway.

Beck got to his feet and pulled Nathan up off the ground. "Remember what I said about being aware of your surroundings?" he said. "It's part of something called free running where you identify obstacles that you can use to help you escape."

"Obstacles," Nathan repeated, out of breath, his face covered with sweat.

"Yes," said Beck. "They could be anything from a bush to a

dumpster to a crowd of people waiting for the bus on a street corner."

Gina listened from several feet away, baffled. *What are they talking about?*

Nathan surveyed the yard, imagining what obstacles he could've used to aid his escape just minutes earlier. Other than the picnic table, and the row of lilacs that lined the side yard, his choices were pretty slim.

Beck checked his watch. "You said you had to be at work at what time? One o'clock?"

"Yeah."

"Then we'd better call it a day. I'll be back tomorrow and we can pick up where we left off. In the meantime, keeping practicing the drop and roll."

Gina waited until Beck was backing down the driveway, his mammoth pickup truck growling like a caged tiger, then said, "Drop and roll?"

"Never mind that," Nathan said. "What'd you find?"

"Nothing good," she said, with an uneasy look. She pulled the notepad from her back pocket and thumbed through the pages until she came to her Devereux notes. "I found a behavioral healthcare organization, a beach, and two schools. Oh, and a woman who works at a charter school in Newton."

"That's it?" Nathan asked. This was very un-Gina like.

Frustrated, she just nodded. *Yup.*

"You think maybe it's the woman?" he asked, going with the most logical choice.

"I don't see how. I mean, her job at the charter school is…" she said, pausing to check her notes, "a speech and language pathologist." She closed her notepad and looked up at him, eyebrows raised. "You want to tell me why someone like that would be working with your grandfather?"

"Let's not take any chances," he said. "See what you can find out about her. If she's the Devereux we're looking for, you might find something, no matter how minor, that could link her to my grandfather."

This attention to detail was part of his new three-point plan: assume nothing, read every word, and leave no stone unturned. He'd been honing it after he and Gina had missed critical details during a recent search for clues; details that were right before their eyes, yet, somehow, they'd overlooked them.

"O-kay, I'll do it," Gina said, unconvinced. "But if I were you I wouldn't hold my breath."

Nathan's father dropped him off at Richard Abbott's barn just before one o'clock. Nathan pulled back the massive barn door and got right to work sorting the next pallet of books. He was standing at the long farmer's table in the center of the room, removing books from the first box when Richard appeared in the doorway. He was dressed in his usual camel-colored khaki pants and blue button-down oxford. His tortoiseshell eyeglasses hung from a thin leather cord that was draped around his neck. In one hand he was holding his car keys.

"Ah, already hard at work I see," he said. "We have an errand to run, one that I think you'll find most interesting."

Nathan set down the books he was holding and followed Richard out to his car. As he slid into the front seat, he felt a twinge in his lower back, the result of being tackled by Beck. It reminded him that he needed to work harder on his agility, his speed, and most of all, his cunning.

"Are you familiar with a section of Boston called the Leather District?" Richard asked when he came to a stop at the bottom of the driveway.

"Doesn't sound familiar," Nathan replied.

Richard watched the line of oncoming cars, saw an opening, and darted out into the street. "Fascinating neighborhood," he explained. "Of course, it didn't come to be until the 1830s, when they filled in the South Cove. In the years that followed, it became the center of Boston's leather industry."

"Huh," Nathan said, only half listening. He was staring straight ahead, preoccupied with what Gina had told him about the woman named Devereux, wondering how she could've been associated with his grandfather. Was she a friend? Did she help him assemble the facilitators group?

Several cars back, the driver of the gray Lincoln MKZ mimicked Richard's every turn, taking great care to maintain a safe distance, not that the old man was watching his rearview mirror. Nonetheless, stealth was a mandatory principle the driver of the Lincoln strictly adhered to, as suited his profession.

Richard drove through Porter Square, followed Beacon Street to Inman Square, and continued on to Broadway. As they crossed the Longfellow Bridge, the surface of the water was cornflower blue and as smooth as a pane of glass.

They had just passed the Tufts University School of Medicine when Richard turned left onto Lincoln Street, lined with 19th century brick buildings that had once been thriving factories and warehouses. Some of them had retained their original architecture, while the lower sections of others had been retrofitted with large windows set in modern steel-gray facades.

Richard drove slowly, scanning the street ahead, when he saw an open spot up ahead on the left. He slid into the space, killed the engine, and directed Nathan's attention to a small storefront across the street. The front door, set back from the sidewalk in a deep alcove, was solid hardwood, the color of acorns. In the center was a thick beveled-glass panel. Directly above the door was a rectangular fanlight, dusted with a thin layer of grit from years of city smog. Despite the hazy coating, Nathan was still able to read the coal-black lettering printed on the glass.

W. HEFFRON
ANTIQUARIAN BOOKS

"William runs one of the oldest bookstores in the city, and by far one of the finest," Richard explained. He paused a beat, then added, "He calls me whenever he acquires an unusual find, just as he did with your grandfather."

"He knew my grandfather?" Nathan asked, turning from the window.

"Oh, my, yes," Richard gushed. "Your grandfather was the one who introduced us."

They climbed out of the car, and as they crossed the street Richard explained the phone call he'd gotten from Heffron earlier that morning, boasting of a rare find that he was saving for Richard's consideration. He made it clear that should Richard pass on it, one of the shop's regulars would snap it up without a moment's hesitation. It was that special.

When they reached the front door, Richard pulled it open, stepped back, and gestured for Nathan to enter. With their backs to the street, neither one saw the gray Lincoln MKZ drive past.

Perfect, the driver thought, when he saw the name above the door. He watched Nathan and Richard step into the store, then drove on in search of a place to park.

Nathan walked into the bookstore and got the immediate sensation of entering the private home of a well-travelled antiques collector. Exquisite pieces of vintage furniture were placed strategically throughout the entire shop, an amazing collection that included a late 1800s Davenport desk, a matching set of Pembroke tables, set on either end of a plush leather couch, an antique Hamilton oak map cabinet, and a stunning 16th century French draw table, heavily carved in solid walnut.

The entire space had a decidedly open feel. Despite the absence of separate rooms, the few walls that existed featured original architectural drawings of some of Boston's oldest buildings. Gone was the grinding din of the city. In its place, a Mozart flute and harp concerto played softly from small speakers positioned in the ceiling. Rows of track lighting created pleasing pockets of tempered light that accentuated the rows of oak shelves, each one filled with a tantalizing assortment of rare books and periodicals.

As he continued on, the wooden floor creaked softly beneath his feet. He stopped to study an early drawing of the Boston Public Library, an eerie reminder of the Alastair Raven blueprint he and

Gina had found in the basement of the courthouse.

Richard checked each of the aisles and found Heffron, dust cloth in hand, cleaning and straightening books. When he saw Richard, he quickly made his way back up the aisle.

"Richard, thank you for coming so promptly," he said. He placed his hand on Richard's shoulder and flashed a devious grin. "Once you see what I have to show you, I think you'll understand why I was compelled to call you. Come, let's go to my office…right this way…"

They cut across the shop and disappeared around a corner, leaving Nathan on his own. As he began to explore the aisles of vintage books, their pages filling the air with the unmistakable scent of age, he soon found himself in the back corner of the store. There, he discovered a small room roughly eight feet square. When he stepped through the open doorway, his attention was drawn to an antique mahogany bookcase pushed up against the opposite wall. The craftsmanship was stunning, with elaborate carvings and four glazed doors, the center two of which featured curved glass panes.

As he stood there admiring it, he became aware of someone standing behind him. He turned at once and saw a man well over six feet tall looming in the doorway.

The floorboards never creaked.

No shadow crossed the floor.

The man simply appeared there.

Unseen.

Unheard.

As was his plan all along.

He glanced over one shoulder, then the other, checking the main sales floor. Then, satisfied that there were no witnesses, he stepped forward to complete the job he'd been hired to do.

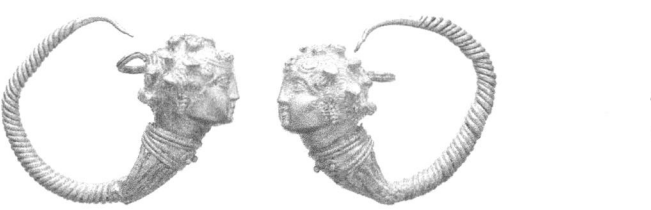

7

Things That Must Not Be Found

Heffron walked through the arched doorway to his office and went straight to his desk: a magnificent Napoleon III parquetry pedestal design from the mid 19th century with a dark green leather top and finely cast gilt-bronze scrolls and floral garland accents. It was placed strategically in the middle of the cramped room, and from one of the side drawers he pulled out a thick hardcover volume housed in a cloth slipcase. As he came back around the desk, he removed the aged cloth cover and handed the book to Richard.

"Oh, my!" Richard murmured, as he examined the front and back. "*A Week on the Concord and Merrimack Rivers,* Thoreau's first published book, and certainly one of his most intriguing."

"Indeed," remarked Heffron.

Richard admired its features, voicing them aloud like an auctioneer announcing the next lot of the day. "Publisher's black cloth cover, gilt lettering on the spine." He opened to the publisher's page. "First edition, first issue." He looked up at Heffron, smiling. "How could I refuse it?"

Heffron smiled approvingly. "It's curious, this book business," he said, handing Richard the slipcase. "After failing to find a publisher, Thoreau printed 1,000 copies at his own expense, only to buy them back years later due to poor sales."

"Just over 700 copies if I remember correctly," Richard added.

"That's right. And now, nearly 170 years later, a first edition, such as the one you're holding, has immense value."

"May I ask how it came to be in your possession?" Richard asked.

"It came from a private collector in Ithaca, New York," Heffron replied. "A retired English literature professor at Cornell." He walked over to the front corner of the room, to a stack of cardboard boxes piled neatly against the wall. "This is the rest of the lot," he said, patting the top box. "Feel free to examine them. There are quite a few treasures that I'm sure you'll want to add to your collection."

When the stranger stepped forward, Nathan instinctively took a step back, keeping a six-foot buffer between them, just as Beck had taught him. At the same time, his eyes darted from left to right in search of an escape route. Point A and point B.

The man brushed past Nathan and walked over to the bookcase. He leaned close, examining the carved figure of a draped figure that adorned the front corner. The bushy hair and long beard gave it a remarkable Zeus-like appearance. An identical carving was set on the left side. "R.J. Horner," he said.

"Excuse me?" Nathan blurted out.

"This bookcase," the man explained. "It was made by R.J. Horner, the famed New York City designer. I've seen others like this, but none as elaborate. If I had to guess, I'd say it dates back to the mid 1800s." As he spoke, he ran his fingertips over the frieze, the dentil molding carved with elegant foliate scrolls. He pulled open one of the curved center doors, inspected the books on the shelves inside, then closed the door and stepped back. "It's quite a thing of beauty," he said. "Not unlike the one your grandfather had."

Heffron left Richard alone in the office to peruse the Ithaca collection, then went back out on the sales floor to assist customers. Richard, energized from the Thoreau title, wasted little time digging into the stack of boxes. He took the top one off the pile and set it on a nearby sorting table. One by one he pulled out the books, checking their year of publication while marveling at their excellent condition. It was as if the previous owner had travelled back through time and purchased each book fresh off the press from the printer. By the time he was halfway through the box, he'd already accumulated a dozen "keepers."

"My grandfather?" Nathan asked suspiciously. Something about the stranger didn't add up. He had neatly groomed salt and pepper hair and a closely cropped beard and moustache. His attire consisted of a white Irish grandfather shirt with a line of small buttons running up the front to the neck, a gray tweed vest, and blue jeans. At first glance he appeared to be a college professor, but he had the athletic build of an NFL linebacker or British rugby player, willing to charge through the nearest wall at the slightest provocation.

Hardly the gentlemanly type.

"What do you know about my grandfather, or his bookcase for that matter?" Nathan demanded.

The stranger went back to the doorway and scanned the shop, checking to make sure no customers had wandered close enough to hear what he was about to say. Seeing no one, he turned back to Nathan. "Your grandfather employed me for the special service I offer," he said.

"Special service?" Nathan repeated. "And what might that be?"

"I'm the keeper of things that must not be found."

Nathan gave him a skeptical look. "Keeper of things that must not be found? What's *that* supposed to mean?" It sounded like something straight out of the wizarding world of Harry Potter. What else did he do? Nathan wondered. Sell magic wands? Teach enchantments?

"Lockboxes, vaults, safes…they can be all be broken into," the man explained. "Household hiding places are even less secure, and, sadly, many people make the mistake of thinking those spaces can't be found. Truth to tell, they can and *will* be found, by someone trained to look for them. Quite easily as a matter of fact. What I offer is guaranteed security, with the assurance that whatever my clients need hidden will never be found, by anyone. Ever."

"And you say my grandfather employed you for such a service?"

"Yes. The most recent time was a year before he died."

Nathan considered him cautiously for several seconds. "Why should I believe you?" he asked.

"Edouard Dampierre," the man said.

"What was that?" Nathan asked, turning his ear toward the man, pretending he hadn't heard.

"Edouard…Dampierre," the man said again, slower, putting emphasis on each word.

"Never heard of him," Nathan said, feigning ignorance. "And what does he have to do with anything?"

"I suspect you already know the answer to that question, Mr. Cole," the stranger said, grinning at Nathan's attempted deception.

"Well, you're mistaken," Nathan replied. Currently, no one knew of his connection to Dampierre, his sister Ginette, or what he'd done to bring down their criminal empire, landing the two of them in prison, their home away from home for many years to come.

"Mistaken?" the stranger repeated. "If that's the case, then perhaps you can tell me why your grandfather insisted I mention that name should we happen to meet."

Nathan's jaw fell open in shock. "My g-grandfather gave you that n-name?" he stuttered.

"Yes," the stranger said, nodding. "That was the sign."

"Sign? What are you talking about?"

"Your grandfather told me to watch for a sign. He didn't say when or even if it would come to light. But if it did, then and only then would it be time."

"Time?" Nathan said, his mind reeling. "Time for what?"

"Time to seek you out."

From his vest pocket he produced an old-style calling card. He handed to Nathan, who took one look at it and blinked hard, as if his eyes were playing tricks on him.

"It's you," he said, struggling to comprehend his grandfather's actions. *How did he know about Edouard Dampierre? Or that one day our paths would cross?*

He turned his attention back to Devereux, reworking the time-line that had brought him to the bookstore. "You saw the news stories about Edouard Dampierre..." he said.

"Yes," Devereux replied.

"That's where you heard his name..."

"Correct. As I said, that was the sign."

"And after that, you did what?"

"I watched you, from afar," Devereux said casually, like surveillance was a routine part of his job.

"You *watched* me?" Nathan said, put off.

"I had to find the right time and place to make contact with you."

"Why here?" Nathan asked.

"It seemed like an appropriate place to meet, given your family history."

"You could've just come to my house."

"No," Devereux said, shaking his head. "The service I provide is highly secretive. The goods I handle, by virtue of the fact that the owner wants them hidden, are very sensitive."

"Sensitive?"

"Potentially dangerous in ways that I can't fathom," Devereux explained. "Why else would my clients want them hidden? For that reason, it's imperative that I maintain complete anonymity, not only for my safety but also for the security of the items I receive."

"Because there might be people who want the things your clients give you," Nathan offered.

"It's not a question of might," Devereux explained. "There are any *number* of people who want what my clients entrust to me—very bad, very desperate people, a few of whom I've had the misfortune of meeting."

Nathan gave him a knowing look. *Yeah, tell me about it.* He was all too familiar with secrets that are best left unrevealed, and the criminals who will do anything to keep them that way. After discovering the bookcase in the attic, he and Gina had encountered a number of such people, and had barely survived more than one life-threatening incident. He often wondered what other explosive, potentially deadly secrets awaited him in the bookcase, and if he should just leave them alone, lost and forgotten, forever. By doing so, it was a safe bet that he'd live a lot longer.

"Now you understand why we needed to meet in private," Devereux said.

Nathan nodded his head. "So, what is it?" he asked.

"What is *what?*"

"The thing my grandfather gave you."

"I have no idea," Devereux said, like it was a silly question.

"He didn't tell you?"

"No. My clients don't tell me what they want hidden, and I don't ask. Call it a professional courtesy."

Nathan considered that momentarily. "All right," he said, at last. "So, what now?"

"I've apprised you of the situation. Now I need you to either agree to, or decline, receipt of the package. It's completely up to you. Despite your grandfather's instructions, you're under no obligation to take possession of it."

"It's a *package?*" Nathan asked, surprised.

"You could call it that," Devereux said.

"Then why not just bring it with you?"

"That's not how I work."

Nathan leaned in eyebrows raised. *How you work?*

"Your grandfather's request was very unusual," Devereux said, by way of explanation.

"Unusual, how?" Nathan asked.

"My job is to secure items in such a way that they'll never be found. I don't examine them, I don't photograph them, I hide them. And I *don't* deliver them to a third party—that's what FedEx is for."

"Yet, here you are," Nathan countered.

"Yes," Devereux said, matter-of-factly. "Your grandfather was not only a friend, he was a valued customer. When he explained what he wanted me to do with the package, I made an exception to my standard arrangement—a personal favor, if you will."

Nathan said nothing. He still couldn't shake the fact that years earlier, his grandfather had anticipated him becoming entangled with Edouard Dampierre, global criminal and mastermind behind the Covin. It was beyond comprehension. *When he died, I was six years old,* he told himself. *So if he gave Devereux the package a year earlier, that means I was only five. That's crazy!*

"I need to hear you say it," Devereux said, his voice snapping Nathan's mental quandary.

"Huh? Oh, right," Nathan said. "Yes, by all means. I want what my grandfather gave you."

"Very well. You'll have it tomorrow," Devereux said. With that, he backed out of the room as quietly as he had entered and vanished like a wisp of steam among the aisles of books.

Richard placed the second box on the sorting table and pulled open the flaps. There were over 20 books packed inside, all early works by Samuel Clemens, known throughout the world as Mark Twain.

He pulled out an 1859 edition of *The Celebrated Jumping Frog of Calaveras County, and Other Sketches.* After that, a copy of *Pudd'nhead Wilson,* published in 1894. He was examining a copy of *Tom Sawyer,* from 1936, illustrated by Norman Rockwell, when Nathan poked his head through the open doorway.

"Find anything good?" he asked.

"Come, come!" Richard said, waving him closer. "We've hit the jackpot."

Nathan stepped through the doorway and did a quick sweep of the room with his eyes. His first impression was that someone was either moving in and hadn't finished unpacking their things, or that they were moving out and had yet to start. Open boxes of books littered the floor. Random stacks of books were piled here and there. A full-length bookcase stretched along one wall, crammed with a haphazard assortment of periodicals that were threatening to spill onto the floor at any moment.

115

Most notable was the tall display case pushed up against the back wall, home to an impressive collection of antique bookbinding tools. There were clamps, grattoirs and frattoirs, creasers, polishing irons, and a Victorian bookbinders' plough. Sitting atop the case was an antique French bookbinding press.

"Look at this," Richard said, picking up one of his keepers. "*Round the Moon*, by Jules Verne. This is an author's copyright edition published in 1873." He set it down and picked up another. "*The Song of Hiawatha*, by Henry Wadsworth Longfellow. A signed first edition, first printing, dated 1855." He opened it and began gently turning the pages. "Look at these marvelous engravings and illustrations!"

"Very nice," Nathan said, meaning it.

"Wait, here's another…also by Longfellow," Richard said. From the pile he took a copy of *Voices in the Night: Ballads and Other Poems* and handed it to Nathan. "What you're holding in your hands is Longfellow's first book of poetry. It includes nine original poems plus another seven he wrote as a teenager."

"First edition, published in 1839," Nathan said, reading the copyright page.

"Yes," Richard said, excitedly. "Very rare and *highly* collectible."

Nathan was studying the gold gilt harp on the front cover when Richard said, "Did I ever tell you about Longfellow?"

"Uh…no, I don't think so," Nathan replied, sheepishly. *Should you have?*

"He was one of five members of the Fireside Poets, a group of American writers closely associated with New England. They adhered to conventional forms of meter and rhyming stanzas—

something we call 'poetic convention'. In the second half of the 19th century, they gained great popularity. Families would gather around the fire at home to read their work, which gave way to the name Fireside."

"Cool," Nathan said, handing him back the book. "Do you want me box those up?" he asked, pointing at Richard's pile of keepers.

Richard considered them briefly, chin in hand, tapping his lips with his index finger. "No, don't bother," he said. "We're going to need a dolly."

"Excuse me?" Nathan said.

Richard pointed at the stack of remaining boxes. "We'll be taking the entire lot."

On the drive back to Abbott's barn, Nathan stared out the side window, the startling truth about his grandfather's affiliation with Devereux cycling through his mind. As they meandered through traffic, Richard recited a protracted summary of his findings in Heffron's office, his words fading in and out of Nathan's consciousness like the erratic signal of a late-night radio station.

"…A nearly perfect copy of *The Birds of America,* by John James Audubon," he heard Richard say. "It's simply stunning, which makes it one of the most sought-after books of all time." He looked over at Nathan and said, "Audobon's goal was to paint every bird in North America. Did you know that?"

"Every bird?" Nathan replied, appearing to be interested. "Really?"

"Yes. And since the publication of the book, six of the birds he painted have become extinct."

"Huh," Nathan said, his thoughts shifting back to something Devereux told him.

"Your grandfather was not only a friend, he was a valued customer."

Valued customer? Nathan thought. Did that mean what he thought it did? That his grand-father had given Devereux *other* things to hide as well?

"…An outstanding copy of Steinbeck's *Cannery Row*," Richard was saying, the words slicing into Nathan's thoughts. "What I find fascinating is that the location Steinbeck was writing about, Ocean View Avenue in Monterey, was later named 'Cannery Row,' in honor of the book."

"Interesting," Nathan said, only half listening as he wrestled with Devereux's curious revelation. It was a foregone conclusion that whatever his grandfather had given him was somehow related to the bookcase.

"…Ghost stories…" he heard Richard say moments later, the word 'ghost' pulling his attention from the window. "I'm sorry, what was that?" he asked.

"Black Spirits and White – A Book of Ghost Stories," Richard said, repeating the title of another book he'd found in the first box. "Written by Ralph Adams Cram and published in 1895. It's a very rare book about the supernatural, and possibly one of the most astounding books of terror tales ever written."

That one I'd like to read, Nathan thought.

They pulled up to the barn and Nathan hopped out. As he rolled back the massive wooden door, another question emerged, this one prompted by the very last thing Devereux had said to him.

"You'll have it tomorrow."

Have it how? he wondered. *Will it be tucked inside the mailbox? Sitting on the front door mat like an Amazon delivery? No,* he told himself, *Devereux wouldn't do that; someone might steal it.* It was also safe to assume that Devereux wouldn't entrust delivery of the package to anyone else, which left only one option—Devereux would deliver it himself.

Tuesday, 8:45 a.m.

Nathan waited until he heard his mother leave for work, her car's muffler making its usual groaning sound as she drove away from the house. The moment he heard it he climbed out of bed and got dressed. He went downstairs and checked the front porch, eying the area directly in front of the door, then went to the back door and did the same. No package. Not that he really expected to find one. Still, he had to look.

He slipped out the back door and walked down the driveway to the mailbox. As expected, it was empty. He went to the garage for his daily training routine, which now began with 100 skips of the jump rope, followed by 50 curls with the three-pound dumbbells. That part of his regimen was getting ridiculously easy and the next time he saw Beck he'd let him know it was time to increase the weight.

He stepped into the garage and walked over to the far wall. Just as he was reaching for the jump rope, hanging on the nail where he'd left it the day before, he noticed a small metal box resting on the fireblock directly behind it. In the shadows, it was nearly invisible.

It was charcoal black, roughly eight inches long, three inches wide, and a little over an inch thick. But unlike any other box he'd ever seen, this one had a four-digit combination lock centered on one of the long sides.

He picked it up and turned it over in his hand, examining the top and bottom. He tried to pry it open with his thumbnail but the lock was holding it shut. *This is it,* he told himself, his heart beating faster. *It has to be.* He looked from the box to the fireblock, then back at the box, remembering what Devereux had said about watching him from afar, waiting for the right time and place to make contact. *He saw me jump roping in the driveway…every morning… at the same time.*

In his mind he envisioned Devereux ducking into the garage in the early hours before dawn, leaving the box on the fireblock right behind the jump rope where he knew Nathan would be the first one to find it.

The vision melted away when he heard a soft knock on the door. He turned to look when it opened and Gina stepped inside. "I checked into that woman like you asked me to," she said, waving her notepad in the air.

"Oh, that's right," he said, suddenly remembering their last conversation. As he walked over to where she was standing she noticed the box in his hand.

"What's that, a birthday present?" she joked. "If it is, you're way too early. Nice thought, though."

"Very funny," he said.

"Seriously, what is it?"

"I don't know, but I'm about to find out," he replied. "And, oh, by the way, you can forget about that woman. I found Devereux."

"You, *what?*" she exclaimed.

"I found Devereux," he repeated. "Actually, he found me."

"Are you serious?" Gina exclaimed. "*Our* Devereux? The one from…you know…the attic?"

Nathan nodded slowly. *Yup, same one.*

"But…how?"

Jordan Prescott came into the office early that morning to review some real estate transaction paperwork that involved a bothersome law firm from Connecticut. She was paging through the contract, shaggy with orange Post-it flags, when her cell phone rang, playing Schubert's composition, *The Trout Quintet*. It was music she had assigned to one caller, and one caller only, and when she heard it she slid the phone closer, tapped the green phone icon at the bottom of the screen, then the speakerphone symbol. "Good morning," she said, turning her attention back to the contract.

"Anything yet?" the caller asked.

"No," she replied. She reached the bottom of the page and flipped to the next.

"Maybe you should pay him another visit."

Jordan read a clause that made her shake her head in disgust. *We agreed on that already!* she thought, angrily plucking the orange flag from the page.

"You still there?" the caller asked.

"Sorry," Jordan said. "What were you saying?"

"I said, perhaps it's time to pay Mr. Cole another visit."

"I was going to wait another few days," Jordan said, scanning the list of exclusions in the agreement. "Best not to arouse suspicion."

"Agreed, but let's take his temperature anyway," the caller suggested, encouraging more than demanding. "See if he's fully engaged."

"Oh, he's engaged, trust me," Jordan said, coming to the list of contingencies. "He's very passionate about his grandfather."

"Nonetheless, a quick visit wouldn't hurt. You might even throw a little more chum in the water, so to speak, just for good measure."

"Not a bad idea," Jordan said, skipping down through the list.

"You'll go see him then?"

"Will do," Jordan said. She ended the call, then cursed out loud and tore off another orange flag.

Nathan recounted his trip to Heffron's bookstore with Richard: how Devereux had followed them there; the unusual service he provided; his affiliation with Henry Hammond, and the odd request Henry had made regarding the small black box. He explained the "sign" Henry had told Devereux to watch for, a green light for Devereux to deliver the box, and how he had observed Nathan for nearly a month, waiting for the right moment and the right place to make contact.

"He *followed* you?" Gina blurted out. "That is so creepy!"

"He was just doing what my grandfather hired him to do," Nathan said, making it sound less disturbing than it really was.

"And Edouard Dampierre was the sign?" Gina asked, stunned.

"Insane, right?" Nathan said.

"Uh, you *THINK?*"

For several seconds, neither one spoke. Then, her curiosity reached a full boil and she took the box from him, held it to her ear, and gave it a shake.

"What are you doing?" he asked.

"SHHH," she whispered, trying to hear if anything rattled around inside the box. She tried again, and when she heard nothing she gave it back. "It's empty," she said.

He held the box next to his ear and repeated what she had done, giving it a vigorous shake while listening for any movement inside. When it emitted no sound, he held it in his hands and stared at it without speaking. *Why would my grandfather give Devereux an empty box?* he thought. *Go to all that trouble, for nothing?* The answer was simple: he wouldn't.

"If you think staring at it is going to make it open, I've got news for you," Gina said.

"SHUSH!"

She looked at him, dumbfounded. "You're *shushing* me?" *Since when was that allowed?*

He tuned her out and used his thumbs to spin each cylinder to the same number, starting with the lowest one.

0-0-0-0.

Once they were set, he tried opening the box with his thumbnail. No good. He thought for a moment, then tried again, turning each cylinder to a different number.

1-2-3-4.

When that didn't work, he tried it in reverse.

4-3-2-1.

"Here, let me try," Gina said, snatching the box out of his hands. She tried several different number combinations, none of which worked. "I give up," she said, then gave it back to him.

He considered the lock momentarily, nibbling the inside of his cheek, then tried again with a random grouping of numbers.

1-1-2-2
2-2-3-3
2-2-2-2
4-4-4-4
2-4-2-4

"Hold on," Gina said. "You said your grandfather instructed Devereux to give this to you, and only you, right?"

"Yes."

"Try this number," she said. "Four, eight, zero, one."

"Four…eight…zero…one," Nathan repeated, making sure he'd heard her right. Something about the number was familiar. "I know that number," he said, trying to place it. Then it came to him. "Of course… April 8th, 2001…that's my birthday."

"Very good," she said, patting his shoulder like he was a three-year-old who had just tied his sneakers for the first time.

"What?" he asked, pushing her hand away.

"If your grandfather intended this package to go to you, doesn't it make sense that he'd use a combination that was somehow related to you—one that you were sure to know?"

"Uh…" Nathan said, drawing the word out for a full three seconds. "Yeah, I guess."

"Good. Now that we have that settled, shall we continue?" she said, pointing at the box.

He thumbed in the combination, wondering why *he* hadn't thought of it, and just as he set the final number, the box popped open.

"You're welcome," she said.

He lifted the lid and looked inside, a grin creasing his face.

"What is it?" Gina asked.

"You were wrong," he said.

"About what?"

"It's not empty."

8

Handsome Dividends

Tucked inside the box was a piece of rolled-up paper. The diameter was such that the box had pressed down on it, holding it securely in place. Nathan turned it so she could see it, then removed the paper, closed the box, and set it on the workbench.

Julie Nichols
Jordan Prescott
Connie Freeman
Donald Brandt
Frank Sobol
Perseus

The paper was a heavy stock, the color of dense fog. Six names were written on it and when Nathan saw them he looked over at Gina, speechless.

"What is it?" she said.

When he didn't answer, she grabbed his wrist and pulled his hand closer so she could read what was on the paper.

"Is that what I think it is?" she asked.

Jordan Prescott's name was the giveaway, and the second Nathan saw it, it confirmed his initial belief about his grandfather's intention that he have access to the facilitators' group.

"It's just as I thought," he said. "He wanted me to…have these names…just in case…"

His words fell away and he stared at the paper saying nothing.

What's wrong?" Gina asked.

He flashed back to his discussion with Kendra, on the ride to Stackyard Road, when she explained the facilitators group. Five in total. Jordan Prescott had told him the same thing. *Did Kendra forget one?* he wondered. *Or was there a sixth person no one knew about? One that my grandfather never revealed? If so, why?*

"There's only supposed to be five," he mumbled.

"Five what?" Gina asked.

"Facilitators."

"Excuse me but I see six names," Gina said.

The sudden roar of a truck chugging up the driveway snapped him out of his funk. "Beck's here. Quick, take this," he said, handing her the paper. "You know what to do."

She opened her notepad and laid the list carefully inside just as Beck's truck came to a stop in front of the garage, the growl of the engine making the door rattle. "The usual?" she asked.

"Anything-and-everything," he replied.

Just then, Beck appeared at the side door. He peered through the glass, then pushed the door open, ducked down, and stepped inside. "You ready?" he asked.

"Uh, yeah," Nathan said, debating whether he should explain Gina's presence in the garage at that hour of the morning.

In the awkward silence that followed, Gina waved her notepad in the air and said, "Well, okay then, thank you for that information. I'll go and leave you guys to…whatever." As she walked toward the door, she offered Beck a weak smile as she passed him then stepped outside and hurried back to her house to start researching the list of names—a six-part puzzle that was already tugging at her curiosity.

"Information?" asked Beck, eyeing Nathan suspiciously.

"Oh, that?" Nathan said, waving it off. "It was nothing."

Beck gave him a hard stare. *You want to try that again?*

"What?" Nathan asked, shrugging.

Beck crossed his arms, saying nothing, as he continued to stare. *Well?*

Nathan was debating what to say when he remembered something Beck had told him the day before. "*I promised I'd help protect you, and I will.*"

Promised.

That one word was enough to convince Nathan that the truth was his best option. If they were going to track down the facilitators, they'd need a driver. And if they happened to run into trouble along the way, who better to have with them than Beck? The man was a mountain—a walking, talking, living, breathing Mt. Everest.

"What if I told you I know who killed my grandfather?" he said.

"Impossible," Beck replied.

"Uh-uh," Nathan said. "Not impossible."

"How do you figure?"

"I have an eyewitness," Nathan replied. He thought for a second, then said, "Actually, I take that back. I have four of them."

By 9:30 that morning, the Home Depot in Everett was already doing a robust business. As Asher Rickman cruised past the lot, which was already half full, he spotted a white Bickford Electric van parked in one of the center rows, very close to the front entrance. The driver, Bobby Campbell, had purposefully chosen that spot, creating the false illusion that he was a busy electrician who needed to get in and out of the store as quickly as possible. After all, time was money.

But Campbell wasn't an electrician. At least, not in the traditional sense. Working with his cousin Danny Mack, known to his friends as "D-Mack," he was a key member of Asher's crew: an expert at disabling security alarms, jamming phone systems, and cutting power to whatever home or business was being targeted. From time to time, he and D-Mack performed special jobs. They were the ones who had planted the radio-controlled smoke bombs throughout Willow & Vine in preparation for Asher's visit on Saturday.

As work vehicles went, the van was a six-cylinder chameleon. Today, it was an electrician's van. Other days it was plumbing, or HVAC, or pest control. Campbell's collection of magnetic signs allowed him to disguise the van as whichever type of service provider best fit the job.

Asher pulled into the facing parking space, bringing the grille of his Audi A6 nose to nose with the van. When Campbell saw that, he and D-Mack got out and slipped into the back seat of the Audi, the tinted windows providing them complete privacy from the outside world.

"Nice job at the auction house," Asher said, eyeing them in the rearview mirror.

"Don't mention it," Campbell replied. "I wasn't sure we'd hear from you again after we saw the recent news reports."

"Don't believe everything you hear, or see," Asher said, referring to the intense media coverage of Edouard and Ginette Dampierre's arrest. "The authorities can do as they please, but I have no intention of stopping, or slowing down for that matter. Consider our arrangement secure and actively ongoing." With that, he reached over the seat and handed Campbell an inch-thick cash envelope stuffed with crisp $100 bills.

Campbell was tucking it into his shirt pocket when Asher's hand appeared again, this time with a folded note. On it was the address of a private residence in Manchester-by-the-Sea, the affluent town north of Boston on Cape Ann.

"On Saturday night there's going to be a party at that home," Asher explained, seeing it in his mind as he gazed across the parking lot. "Invitation only... star-studded guest list... a gourmet feast prepared by Elio Biaggi, the world-renowned Italian chef..." His tone suggested that such affairs were so engrained in his social schedule that they'd become mundane.

Campbell read the address, committing it to memory, and waited to hear the rest.

Asher turned in the seat to face him and D-Mack. "As luck would have it," he said, grinning, "the hosts are very close friends with Damien Grün."

Campbell shook his head and shrugged. *Never heard of him.*

"You've never heard of Damien Grün?" Asher asked, surprised.

Again, Campbell shook his head. *Sorry.*

"Isn't he that whacko artist from New York City?" D-Mack said. "Uses bird feathers to create weird overpriced artwork?"

"Weird, maybe. Overpriced, yes," Asher replied. "But his artwork is highly sought-after and exceedingly collectible. We're talking upwards of the high six-figures to start."

For feathers? D-Mack thought, shaking his head in disbelief. What some people chose to spend their money on was mind boggling.

"According to my source, a dozen or so of Grün's works will be on display at the party, including one he calls 'The Subway Swan', a rendering of Marilyn Monroe in her famed subway dress, done completely in swan feathers."

"Freak," Campbell muttered under his breath.

"I'm inclined to agree," Asher said calmly, "but the word is, it's his favorite and he refuses to sell it despite countless offers from some of the art-world's wealthiest collectors. Its current value is estimated to be close to two million dollars."

Campbell and D-Mack let out an audible gasp.

"I've also learned that the artwork will be delivered by a private courier on Friday, the day before the party."

Campbell knew what Asher was going to say even before he voiced it. "You want us to intercept the...*swan*...before it gets to the house?"

"Exactly."

"We can do that," Campbell said confidently. "You say it's being delivered on Friday?"

"Yes."

"Do you have the name of the courier?"

"Funny you should ask," Asher said, smiling. He reached into his pocket and took out another note, which he handed over the seat.

Campbell glanced at it briefly, grinned, then tucked it into his shirt pocket behind the money envelope. "Anything else?" he asked.

"No, that should do it," Asher replied, confident that the job would be handled without any hiccups. To date, Campbell and D-Mack had never let him down.

"Okay then," Campbell said. "We'll talk to you on Friday." He elbowed D-Mack…*come on, let's go*…then pushed the door open and stepped out into the mid-morning heat, which had already climbed five degrees since they'd arrived.

"What's up with the courier?" D-Mack asked, after they climbed back into the van.

Campbell pushed the key into the ignition and looked over. "What do you mean?"

"I saw you make a face when you read the name."

Campbell pulled the note from his pocket. "See for yourself."

D-Mack took it, read the name, and smiled. "Seriously?" he said. "How perfect is that?"

"Tell me about it," Campbell replied. He twisted the key and the engine roared to life.

"Do you think she still works there?" asked D-Mack.

"I know for a fact that she does," Campbell said, letting the implication hang in the air.

"Do you now?" D-Mack joked, giving Campbell a sly look. "I guess it's safe to say that you'll be seeing her again very soon?"

"To quote my kid's Magic Eight Ball…'Signs point to yes'."

Beck listened quietly as Nathan explained his theory about the facilitators group.

"One of them killed my grandfather..." he began.

"How could you possibly know that?" Beck asked.

He told him about Jordan Prescott, the only facilitator he'd met, and everything she'd told him, starting with Lía Ballard, the men who were pursuing her, the field notebook her father had given her just before he died, and the coded entry it contained that identified the whereabouts of an ancient gold necklace worth untold millions. Lastly, he revealed something else Jordan Prescott had told him: a key clue that no one else knew.

Not his parents.

Not Jameson.

Not even the police who had investigated the case.

"That night, my grandfather called an emergency meeting of the facilitator group. They met in his office after the bookstore closed and..." His words fell away as he was reminded of a critical detail he had yet to explain: the fact that there were six names on the list, not five.

"What's wrong?" Beck asked.

"Uh...nothing," Nathan said, tucking the thought away for the time being. "Where was I?"

"The emergency meeting...after the store closed..."

"Oh, right. My grandfather told them about Lía Ballard's visit, then showed them her father's field notebook. One by one, he told each of them what he needed them to do to help Lía disappear. The next day, my grandfather was dead...poisoned...and Ballard's notebook was nowhere to be found."

"And that's why you think one of these…*facilitators*…killed him?"

"It's the only logical conclusion," Nathan said.

"How do you figure?"

"Because, other than my grandfather, they were the only other people who knew about the notebook."

"You said there are five of them?" Beck asked.

"Uh, yeah," Nathan said, trying not to think about the sixth name. "That's what Kendra told me."

"So, who are these eyewitnesses you claim to have?"

"The four members of the group who didn't do it," Nathan replied.

"What about the fifth one?"

"We can rule her out. She's innocent."

"Oh really? And how do you know that?"

"She's the one who came to see me at Abbott's barn yesterday. Not only does she have an airtight alibi, she's the one who told me about the meeting in the bookstore. If she was the killer, do you really think she'd share that critical piece of information with me?"

Beck nodded his head, seeing the logic in Nathan's thinking. "So, what's your plan here?" he asked. "Are you going to hunt them down and question them? You have no idea who they are."

"Guess again," Nathan said. He took the black box from the workbench and held it up for Beck to see. "A gift…from my grandfather."

Beck considered the box with a dubious expression. "Your grandfather *gave* that to you?" he said. "How is that possible? The man's been dead for years."

"Yes, I know that," Nathan said, annoyed. "And thank you very much for reminding me of that painful fact." He took in a calming breath, then said, "He sent it through, what do you call it, an inter-something?"

"Intermediary?"

"Yeah, that," Nathan said. "My grandfather hired him to give me this box when the time was right."

"When the time was right?" Beck repeated, more confused than before. "What does that even mean?"

"It means that my grandfather was much wiser than anyone realized."

There was an explanation buried in there somewhere, but Beck had no interest in sparring for another three rounds to find out what it was. Instead, he spoke as one friend to another.

"Is this guy legit?" he asked.

"Absolutely," Nathan said. "There's no way this could be a trick or a scam."

"And the names," said Beck. "They're in that box?"

"They were. I gave them to Gina. She's looking for any information she can dig up on each one of them."

"Fine, in the meantime you and I have work to do," Beck said. "What time do you need to be at work?"

"Pretty much anytime I want."

"Good," Beck said. He pulled his truck keys from his pocket and jingled them in the air. "Let's go for a ride."

"Where to?" Nathan asked.

"You'll see," Beck said. He made it as far as the door when he stopped and looked back, staring at Nathan's feet.

"What?" Nathan asked, checking the floor to his left and right.

"Just checking," said Beck.

"Checking what?"

"To make sure you're wearing sneakers."

"Why?"

"Because you're going to need them."

Gina's fingers flew over the keyboard, filling the living room with a steady clicking sound that resembled a row of birds perched on the window sash pecking on the glass. She only stopped to make an entry in her notepad, then she pushed on, doing Google searches, checking social media pages, and stumbling across more than a few press releases.

Anything and everything.

Just as Nathan had requested.

By the time she was done, each of the names on the list had produced a bounty of information—except for the last one: Perseus.

She had started by trying Perseus as a first name. Then, Perseus as a last name. She tried companies named Perseus: Perseus Cleaning, Perseus Construction, Perseus Financial Planning. Next, she tried state parks, historic landmarks, and conservation areas. Each search produced the same message.

No Reply Found

Other than its prominent place in Greek mythology, the only other mention of the name was a constellation and a meteor shower.

She sat back in the chair and reviewed her notes, which filled over 10 pages. Satisfied that she'd found all there was to find, she closed her notepad and went in search of Nathan.

Beck turned left at the end of Nathan's street, then took a series of rights and lefts that ultimately put him on Harvard Avenue headed for West Medford.

"Are you going to tell me where we're going?" Nathan asked.

"Can't," Beck replied.

"Why not?"

"Because I'm not sure yet."

Nathan gave him a look. *Seriously?* What he wanted more than anything was to be back at home, doing his daily workout routine while he waited for Gina to finish researching the list of names. He was still awed by the discovery of the black box, and the steps his grandfather had taken years earlier to ensure he'd get it. The fact that his grandfather had anticipated what would happen in the future was astonishing: trusting that his grandson would find the bookcase; that he'd start investigating the mystery buried in each book it held, thereby furthering a generational Hammond-family legacy.

He could've quit after the first one, following his adventure in the courthouse with Gina that had very nearly taken their lives. Just walk away and never give it a second thought.

Nope, sorry, can't do it…

Family legacy or not, this is too weird…

And way too dangerous.

They came to the Boston Avenue intersection and Beck drove straight, following Harvard Avenue briefly before pulling over in front of the Medford Fire Department. Across the street was St. Raphael Church, the Parish school, and Convent, forming a make-shift triangle of buildings positioned around a large central parking lot. He considered it for several seconds, then shook his head, checked the side mirror for oncoming traffic and pulled away from the curb. He maneuvered through a quick right, then left, eventually ending up on Rt. 38 north. "You ever been to Woburn?" he asked.

"Woburn? Uh…no…I don't think so," Nathan said, trying to place it.

"Good."

"Good?" Nathan asked. "Why is that good?"

"You'll see."

"You know? You've been telling me that a lot lately," Nathan grumbled.

Beck drove on without comment, straight through Winchester to the Woburn Common. He veered right onto Main Street and hadn't gone far when the long line of traffic came to an abrupt stop. As he waited for it to clear, he looked to his right and saw Everett Street stretching to the east, past a large bank building, to a mix of apartment houses and residential homes that lined either side of the road It was the middle of the morning and most if not all of the residents would be at work. *Perfect*, he told himself.

When the knot of traffic finally began to move, he drove past the bank and turned into the parking lot. At the far end of the building he found a vacant parking space separated from Everett Street by a low guardrail. He pulled the keys from the ignition and said, "Get out of the truck."

"Huh?" Nathan grunted.

"Get out," Beck repeated, louder.

"Why? What are we doing?" Nathan asked.

"OUT!" Beck shouted.

Nathan flinched at the sudden outburst, then opened the door and jumped down onto the pavement. Beck did the same, then leaned on the side of the truck bed and eyed Nathan with a contemptuous look. "You brought the feds down on Edouard Dampierre," he said.

"Uh, *yeah*, hello, I know that," Nathan replied.

Beck began to creep slowly around the back of the truck, his eyes never leaving Nathan. "Do you know what that did to his operation?" he asked.

"What is this, a joke?" Nathan asked.

"You ratted out his sister too," said Beck. He was at the tailgate now.

"I didn't rat her out," Nathan said, defiantly. "I discovered her illegal operation and...why are you asking me these questions?" he demanded. "You know what happened!"

Beck kept coming, slow and steady, with the look of a predator stalking its prey. "I guess you never considered just how far the Covin's reach extends."

"What's that supposed to mean?" Nathan asked. He took a step back.

"Did you think your actions would go unpunished?" Beck said. There was an eerie calm in his voice, and as he came around the back bumper, he crouched down, hands open at his side, his fingers curled like the talons of a hawk. "It's payback time," he said. "Courtesy of Edouard and Ginette."

The color drained from Nathan's face. He jumped the guardrail and ran as fast as he could across Everett Street, toward a small tenement house with a long patch of lawn that hadn't been mowed in weeks. Maybe months. It was dotted with tall shade trees and surrounded by a four-foot chain link fence with sections that were either sagging or crooked, or both.

To the left of that was a parking lot that fronted an old two-story brick factory building. The top half had been converted into apartments while the bottom floor was home to a handful of small retail shops. Twenty feet back, he heard Beck's boots scuffing the pavement as he gave chase, drawer closer with every step.

When he reached the tenement house, Nathan faked right then ran up the steps that led to a long porch that skirted the left side of the first-floor apartment. Seconds later, Beck reached the steps and leapt over them, his boots slamming down on the porch's weather-beaten floorboards with a thunderous boom.

When Nathan heard that he vaulted over the railing and landed in the stringy grass below. He cut through the matrix of shade trees, picking up speed with every step. When he reached the chain-link fence, he placed both hands on it and swung his legs up and over like an Olympic gymnast performing a pommel horse routine.

In the parking lot, he looked to his right and spotted a small four-yard dumpster set between two of the retail shops. The angled plastic cover was closed, and directly above it, bolted to the brick, a rusted fire escape ladder stretched all the way up to the roof.

Dumpster – ladder – roof, he told himself, seeing the route in his mind.

Point A, B, *and* C.

He ran to the dumpster just as Beck lumbered over the fence, the links rattling under his considerable weight. By the time the giant reached the dumpster, Nathan was already halfway up the ladder. He made it to the roof before Beck laid a hand on the first rung.

The roof was flat and covered by a synthetic rubber membrane. Nathan stepped off the ladder, his heart racing, but with plenty of energy to spare—his daily regimen of jump roping and muscle toning paying handsome dividends.

He ran to the front of the building and peered cautiously over the parapet. A line of overgrown shrubs hugged the front wall. Directly in front of them was a row of half-filled parking spaces. He looked left and saw an abutting building—same brick construction, but smaller, with a traditional gabled roof. Beyond it was a wide band of tall maple trees.

Building – trees – ground, he thought, once again envisioning his next series of moves. He glanced over his shoulder and saw Beck's head crest the roofline. In a matter of seconds, he'd step off the ladder and...

And what? Nathan wondered, trying desperately to understand how a person he trusted, a person *everyone* trusted, could've so easily slipped into their lives, fooling them all. He forced the thought aside and ran to the far side of the roof. In one smooth move he sat down, swung his legs over the edge, and pushed off with both hands. He landed on the roof below and crawled along the ridge on all fours, the asphalt shingles warm to the touch.

When he reached the end, he stood and looked up at the tree branches towering over his head. Several were within reach, and forgetting all else, he pushed his hair back behind his ear and jumped, grabbing the closest branch with both hands. It bowed under his weight but it didn't break as it dropped him down several feet. Hand-over-hand he shimmied his way along the limb. When he reached the trunk, he used the lower branches to climb down.

His sneakers had just touched the ground when Beck stepped out from behind a nearby tree. With surprising speed he charged, his massive frame closing in with the bearing of an oncoming locomotive.

Startled, Nathan stumbled backward and tripped, collapsing into the base of the tree.

Trapped with nowhere to run.

His entire world closing in on him.

9

Promises

Beck clamped onto Nathan's shoulders and pulled him up off the ground.

"LET *GO* OF ME!" Nathan shouted, struggling to break free.

Beck held him firmly with both hands, refusing to ease his grip. Then, slowly, his menacing expression melted into a wide smile and he released his hands. "That was awesome!" he said. "The dumpster to the ladder to the roof? And the second roof to the tree to the ground?" he added, his finger tracking the roofline and the tree branch overhead as he spoke.

"Okay, now I'm confused," Nathan said. "I thought Edouard and Ginette sent you to dish out some sort of payback."

"That was a test."

"What?" Nathan exclaimed.

"It was an act; I had to make you believe I was going to hurt you, *bad*."

"WHY WOULD YOU DO THAT?" Nathan shouted.

"I wanted you to feel afraid," said Beck. "More importantly, I wanted to see what you would do with that fear. Would you shrink or would you run? If you ran, would you seek out obstacles to slow me down, like I taught you, or would it be like before?"

Nathan had no comment about their last training session in his backyard. Memories of Beck dropping him to the ground like a rodeo calf were still painfully fresh in his mind. "So, you're telling me this was just *training?*" he said.

"That's right. It's called mindset training, which forces you to apply what you've learned in a real-life situation while considering all possible outcomes."

Well isn't that wonderful? Nathan thought. "Is that why you told me you didn't know where we were going?" he asked. "You were searching for the right place?"

"Yes," Beck replied. "Learning escape tactics isn't just something you talk about. If you want to get good at it, if you want to survive, you'll practice it regularly. Don't practice it and you'll fail. The choice is yours."

"Survive what?" Nathan asked.

Beck hesitated for a split second, then said, "Anyone that comes for you."

It was the momentary pause that caught Nathan's attention. "There something you're not telling me," he said.

Before Beck could answer, Nathan's flip phone rang. He pulled it from his pocket, saw Gina's name on the call screen, and tapped the talk button. "How'd you make out?" he asked.

"And hello to you too," she said. "Sorry. I'm kinda busy here." *Being chased by a pretend killer.*

"Busy where?" she asked. "I went over to your house and you were gone."

"I'm with Beck, in Woburn."

"You're in *Woburn?*" she repeated, stunned.

"Yeah, why? Is something wrong?"

"Hold on," she said.

Several seconds passed.

"Gina?"

"Just wait," she said.

More seconds passed.

"Where in Woburn?" she asked, at last.

Nathan pulled the phone from his ear. "Where are we?"

"You know where we are," Beck said, frowning. "We're in Woburn."

"Yes, I know we're in *Woburn*," Nathan said, in a tired voice. "Where, exactly?"

"Everett Street."

Nathan pressed the phone to his ear again. "We're on Everett Street."

"Everett Street," Gina confirmed.

"Yes."

"You're on Everett Street," she said again, like she couldn't believe it.

"Yes, that's what I said."

"E-v-e-r-e-t-t?"

145

"Oh for crying out loud. YES! For the third time, we're on Everett Street."

"What number?"

Asher was sitting at the desk in his basement office, lights dimmed, staring at a pair of side-by-side, dual-mounted 32" monitors while a "data scraping" bot searched the internet's massive public photo database, estimated to be in the tens of trillions. Considering the fact that people uploaded nearly two billion photos a day, he had no doubt he'd find what he was looking for: the image of the imposter whose looks mirrored his own—the one who, for reasons unknown, had visited Arthur Chessman and then subsequently appeared at the Willow & Vine auction.

His search began with a photo of his own face, taken with his camera. Once he entered it in the program, the computer began a systematic sweep of social media posts, comments, likes, shares, and more, from Facebook, Instagram, Twitter, YouTube, LinkedIn, and other popular applications.

Within minutes, information began pouring in at lighting speed, including pictures of his face—only it wasn't him. The resemblance was jarring, and when he fed the data into a state-of-the-art facial recognition program, he discovered that the person in question was a boy named Nathan Cole. The name was vaguely familiar but he couldn't place it.

He continued scouring the bot data and unearthed more of Nathan's information, including his home address the name of his school. But it was the video clips from news stations around the country that finally jolted his memory.

Nathan Cole was the 12-year-old wunderkind who had made an amazing discovery in the basement of an old courthouse in his home town, earning him countless accolades—fame that continued to follow him to this very day. Many were calling him "the most famous kid detective in the country...possibly the world."

Asher compiled the information, including Nathan's picture, in a file he simply labelled "Cole." When he was done, he stared at the screen, pinching his lower lip between his thumb and forefinger as he pondered how best to proceed. In the back of his mind he could hear his mentor, Arthur Chessman, grilling him repeatedly in a stern voice: *Do your homework, learn everything there is to know, and by doing so you'll be able to determine the best course of action.*

He grabbed his phone from the desktop and dialed an associate he used for gathering background data on potential targets: wealthy art collectors, museum curators, gallery owners, and employees of those institutions who might be persuaded to reveal sensitive information. Collecting information, after all, was Asher's specialty and the prelude to every theft he orchestrated.

The call connected and rang several times before a young woman's voice answered.

"Well hello," she said. "I thought you'd forgotten about me."

"Priya, how could I ever forget *you?*" he told her.

"Oh, *that* was smooth," she said, dismissing his usual attempt to charm her—part of an ongoing game they'd been playing for years. "What's up?"

"I have a job for you," he said. "You interested?"

"Could be. How soon do you need me?"

"The sooner the better." He clamped the phone to his ear while he opened a new email thread and attached the Cole file.

"Not a problem," she said. "Send me the particulars and I'll get right on it."

"On their way," he said, a mischievous grin crossing his face as he clicked the send button. Young Mr. Cole had no idea that he was about to gain an all-seeing, all-hearing, shadow—an information-gathering phantom whose value to Asher was immeasurable. As she'd done numerous times before, Priya would provide him with critical details that would allow him to assess the threat level posed by this barnacle of a lookalike. Then, with his "homework" done, as Arthur would call it, he'd devise a course of action and remove the problem with speed and precision.

He had people for that, too.

Nathan turned and eyed Everett Street through the trees. "Hold on, Gina," he said. He walked past the end of the gabled building and then cut back into the parking lot. When he reached the street he stopped. On the opposite side was a row of evenly numbered duplexes, set less than 20 feet apart. "You still there?" he said into the phone.

"Uh, *yeah!*" she said, annoyed. "I'm not like *some people* who just up and disappear."

Nathan ignored the dig. "I'm standing across from 22 Everett Street," he said.

"Turn around."

"Excuse me?"

"Turn. Around," she said.

O-kay, he thought, as he turned and faced the parking lot.

Beck watched from several feet away, unsure what was happening.

"Did you turn around?" Gina asked.

"Yes."

"What do you see?"

"Uh…a parking lot, a long brick building with a bunch of small businesses…"

"Good. Can you see any street numbers?"

He took several steps forward, scanning the storefronts. "No, it doesn't look like they're numbered, but…hold on." Parked in the back corner of the lot, facing the ragged chain link fence, was a white service van. A business name and address were painted on the side in crisp black letters, along with a mnemonic phone number.

Northeast Lock & Key
24-Hour Dependable Service
23 Everett Street • Woburn, MA
1-800-GET-KEYS

He walked as far as the back bumper and stopped. Just beyond the van, near the end of the building, was the lock shop. Attached to the brick right above the doorframe were two adhesive numbers that matched the ones on the van. "Got a number," he told Gina.

"What is it?"

"Twenty-three."

"Twenty-three?" she repeated. "This is nuts."

"What are you talking about?" he asked.

"There should be a business right next to it. Number 23-A."

"Hold on," he said, walking toward the lock shop. "Yeah, I see it. It looks closed. The lights are off and…wait a minute," he said, reading the number above the door. "Number 23-A, how did you know?"

"Oh, I know a lot more than that," she said. "It's a stereo repair shop, right?"

He walked up to the window and read the name stenciled on the glass.

Wired Electronics, Inc.
Equipment & Repair

"All right," he said. "What's going on?"

"I researched those names like you asked me to," she said. "The fourth name on the list, Donald Brandt? He owns a small electronics repair shop at 23-A Everett Street in Woburn."

"What were the chances?" Nathan mumbled, shaking his head in disbelief.

"Right?" Gina said. "First you disappear, then you show up at a store owned by one of the facilitators. That's pretty freaky if you ask me."

He leaned closer and cupped his free hand against the window, blocking out his reflection as he peered through the glass. With no lights on, the entire shop was blanketed in shadows. The only thing visible was a low shelf that ran the width of the front window. It was home to an odd assortment of vintage radios, stereo receivers, and not-so-old gaming equipment.

From somewhere behind him came a voice he didn't recognize.

"Hey! What are you doing? Get your hands off the glass!"

He and Beck turned around and saw a man in his mid 30s walking toward them. His dark brown hair hadn't been washed or combed in days, making him look like a mad scientist who spent all his time in a secret underground laboratory. He was wearing an unbuttoned plaid shirt over a gray tee that read, "Don't Know. Don't Care. Now Go Away!"

In one hand he was carrying a large styrofoam coffee cup. In the other was a flat box filled with fresh pastries from Hot Breads on Main Street.

"Uh, Gina, I'll have to call you back," Nathan said, then flipped the phone shut and shoved it in his pocket. He still hadn't taken his other hand off the glass. *This is Donald Brandt?* he thought. *No, that's impossible.*

"Hey kid! What did I say about the glass?" Brandt yelled, like he was teetering on the edge of a nervous breakdown. He charged toward Nathan when Beck stepped directly into his path.

"That's far enough, pal."

Brandt stopped short, causing hot coffee to spill out of the cup's sip hole. He looked down to see if any of it had landed on his favorite shirt, then cast a menacing look at Beck. "Who are you?" he demanded. "And what are you doing hanging around in front of my shop? Did you see the sign? It's right back there," he said, nodding toward the street. "Plain English. It says no loitering! If your plan was to break in, you should know: I have security cameras recording your every move, as we speak!" He put extra emphasis on the words 'as we speak'.

What? Beck was tempted to say. *They don't work when we're not talking?*

151

Nathan pulled his hand from the window and wiped it on the side of his jeans as if the glass was coated with some kind of deadly tropical germ spore. "We're not loitering," he explained. "And we're not trying to break in. The fact is, we didn't even realize your shop was here until just now."

"Well, I don't open until 11," Brandt replied. "So, if you don't mind…" He jerked his head toward the street…*get lost*…then stepped around Beck, tucked the pastry box under his arm, and pulled the front door key from his pants pocket.

Nathan didn't move. He stood there sizing up Brandt, wondering why his grandfather would recruit such a crazed hothead. More importantly, what skill could this man possibly possess that would be of any need?

Brandt shoved the key in the lock, paused, and looked over at Nathan. "What are *you* looking at? I thought I told you to scram."

"You're Donald Brandt," Nathan said.

"Yeah? What of it?"

"You worked with my grandfather, Henry Hammond."

"Henry who?" Brandt said, annoyed that he was being forced to use his brain, and for some annoying kid no less.

"Hammond," Nathan said. "He owned a bookstore in Cambridge."

"Never heard of him," Brandt muttered. He unlocked the door and pushed it open with his hip, then tucked the key back in his pocket and pulled the mangled pastry box from under his armpit. "Don't let me see you touching my window again," he said, letting go of the door.

"Not so fast," Nathan said, grabbing it as it was closing.

Brandt exhaled angrily. "Kid, you are *really* trying my patience. Keep pushing me and I'll—"

"And you'll what?" Beck cut in. "Hit him with a doughnut?" He eased Nathan aside and stepped into the doorway, coming face to face with Brandt. "Come on, let's see what you got."

Brandt said nothing, his mouth stuck halfway open as he looked up at Beck who had at least six inches on him. The man was the human incarnation of Paul Bunyan.

Nathan patted Beck's arm. "It's okay, I got this."

Beck held his ground for several more seconds, daring Brandt to make a move, then took a step back.

"Look, I know my grandfather swore you to an oath of secrecy," Nathan said. "But there are things I need to ask you. Important things."

"Sorry kid, you got the wrong guy. I never helped your grandfather, and I never heard of his bookstore." He looked past Nathan, scanning the parking lot, then pushed the door shut and turned the deadbolt. His eyes met Nathans for a split second, then he stepped away from the door, his body dissolving into the darkness like an apparition.

"What a jerk," Beck said, as they walked back across the parking lot.

"Tell me about it," Nathan said. He glanced over his shoulder and saw Brandt standing at the door, watching them, his body ghost-like behind the thick glass.

"You really think he was one of the facilitators?" Beck asked.

"Oh, he's one of them all right," Nathan said.

"What makes you say that?"

153

"I said, 'you worked with my grandfather'. He said he never 'helped' him."

"Is there a difference?"

"Sure," Nathan replied. "The facilitators were all about helping. That's why my grandfather recruited them. He needed the kind of help only they could provide."

"Specialized help," Beck offered.

"Exactly."

"And this secret oath. You think that's why Brandt denied knowing your grandfather?"

"That's part of it, but there's more."

"What do you mean?" asked Beck.

Nathan stopped and looked back a second time.

Brandt's silhouette was still visible in the doorway.

"He's scared."

Beck treated Nathan to lunch. As they were waiting in the drive-through line, Nathan said, "I need you to promise me something."

"Oh yeah? What's that?" asked Beck.

"I need you to promise that you won't tell anyone about the box my grandfather gave me, or the list of names that was inside it."

Beck shot him a curious look. "Why?"

"If certain people find out I have the names, and that I'm planning to track them down and question them, it's not going to go over very well. We're talking, major fireworks here."

"Certain people?" Beck said.

"You know who I mean."

"Okay," Beck said, nodding. "I'll promise not to say anything, but

154

you have to promise *me* something in return."

"Which is…?" Nathan asked.

"I'll say nothing to anyone, but only if you promise not to pursue any of the facilitators on your own. I want to be with you each time. That means no trickery. No ducking out. No ditching me."

"Deal."

As they drove home, questions about Donald Brandt peppered Nathan's thoughts like corn kernels popping in a microwave. *Why did he lie? Does he know something about Walter Ballard's field notebook? Or the killer? Is HE the killer?*

When Beck turned onto Nathan's street, they saw Kendra's battered blue Volvo sitting at curb in front of his house. "Kendra's taking you to work today?" he asked.

"Looks that way," Nathan said as they passed the Volvo. He looked over and saw her sitting behind the wheel, staring straight ahead with her phone to her ear, caught up in what appeared to be a heated conversation. Without looking at them, she offered a token wave and kept talking.

Beck pulled up next to the house and stopped, letting the engine run. "Okay, good work today," he said. "You showed me some really good stuff. I'm thinking you may actually live to see your 20th birthday."

There it is again, Nathan thought. It was the hint of impending danger, masquerading as a wisecrack.

"Now, about your promise," Beck said.

"Yeah? What about it?" Nathan asked.

"You're not going to go slinking off in the night with Gina, or skip out of work without telling anyone so you can chase down one of the names on your list, right?"

"Right."

"Good. Just checking."

"What about you?" Nathan asked. "You're not going to accidentally tell my folks that I have the list, or casually mention to Jameson what I'm doing over coffee, *right*?"

"Nope. You have my word. And for the record, Jameson and I don't meet for coffee. I'm pretty sure he's an Earl Gray tea guy."

"Okay then, we're good," Nathan said. He pushed the door open and climbed down from the truck, the growl of the engine much louder outside than it was inside the cab. He stood in the driveway and watched as Beck backed out into the street. The truck was thundering out of sight when he heard Gina call to him from her back porch. He turned in time to see her push through the screen door and come running across the lawn.

"What happened?" she asked, coming to a stop beside him, out of breath.

"What do you mean?"

"When we were talking…on the phone…I heard shouting."

"Oh, that," he said. "We met Donald Brandt." At the curb, he saw Kendra getting out of her car. She still had her phone pressed to her ear.

"And?" Gina asked.

"I'll tell you later," he said, watching Kendra walk up the driveway. "Listen, do me a favor," he said. "Don't say anything about the list to Kendra, okay?"

"Why not?"

"I don't want word getting back to Jameson…or my parents."

"Yeah, that would be…oh, I don't know…calamitous, catastrophic, cataclysmic. And those are just the words that begin with C."

Ever since their second adventure, deep inside a remote mine in Crawford, NH, Gina's parents were on permanent information lockdown. Not need-to-know; theirs was full scale communication blackout. They had no idea she was still collaborating with Nathan on a regular basis. To hear Gina tell it, if they somehow learned that she was actively solving mysteries with him, they'd pack up everything they owned, sell the house, and move as far away as possible: the Pacific Northwest; maybe an island in the Florida Keys; a foreign country might not be far enough away.

Nathan saw Kendra walk halfway up the driveway and stop, still actively engaged in conversation. Sensing he had more time, he said, "Quick, tell me what you found."

"I've got everything we need to track them down," she said. "All of them except the sixth one, Perseus."

"You couldn't find anything?" he asked, shocked.

"Oh, I found out plenty, if you like Greek mythology."

"I've been wondering about that name," he said. "Kendra never mentioned it. Neither did Jordan Prescott, which is curious." He threw a glance over his shoulder and saw Kendra pacing back and forth, still embroiled in conversation. "Whatever it is," he said, turning back to Gina, "we can't let it slow us down."

"Agreed," Gina said. "Maybe one of the others will know who—"

"HEY! LET'S GO!" Kendra shouted.

Nathan motioned to her with his index finger. *Just a sec.* "Let's talk when I get home. I want to tell you about my meeting with Brandt."

"And I need to show you what I found out about each of the people on that list."

"Facilitators."

"Whatever," she shot back.

"UH…STILL WAITING!" Kendra yelled.

"Go! Before she blows a gasket," Gina said, pushing him gently toward the street.

"I think that time has already come and gone."

"Rough day?" Nathan asked, after they'd gotten into the Volvo.

"Rough would be a huge improvement," Kendra growled.

Nathan said nothing. Why shake the hornets' nest?" he reasoned.

"What about you?" she asked. "What diabolical plot are you two hatching now?"

"We were just talking," he said, casually. Because he'd driven with Kendra on numerous occasions, he buckled his seatbelt, then grabbed hold of the armrest with one hand and the center console with the other. *Houston: we're ready for lift-off.*

"Just talking?" she said, as she checked the side mirror. "Yeah, right. You guys are never 'just talking'."

Nathan held on tight.

…T-minus 10…

Kendra saw a UPS truck coming up the street.

…9…

"That's not true," he said.

…8…

"No?" she replied, watching the truck approach.

…7…

The truck was 10 feet away when it came to a full stop in the middle of the street.

...6...

"What are you, *lost?*" Kendra snarled.

...5...

The truck just sat there.

...4...

"Oh, for crying out loud!"

...3...

"Are you talking to me?" Nathan asked.

...2...

"No," Kendra said. "I'm talking to that...aw the heck with it!"

...1...

She punched the gas and the Volvo shot out into the street, leaving behind a cloud of silvery gray exhaust.

Nathan held on tight. *Houston: we have lift-off.*

"You're probably wondering why I'm taking you to work and not your mom," Kendra said, as she raced down the street.

"The thought did cross my mind," Nathan replied.

Kendra came to a grinding halt at the stop sign and looked left, then right. "Your mom was pulled into a last-minute meeting," she said. "She called me and asked if I could take you." As she waited to pull out, her hands were white-knuckled on the steering wheel.

Nathan knew what was coming and kept his hands clamped tightly on the armrest and the center console. *Houston: preparing for second-stage ignition.*

"I'm glad she called," Kendra said. "With the day I've been having, a nice relaxing drive was *just* what I needed."

Nathan gave her a dubious look. *Relaxing? Is that what you call this?*

She saw a break in the line of traffic and stomped on the gas pedal. The Volvo leapt forward, just ahead of an oncoming box truck. As she sped away, Nathan peeled himself off the door and sat back up in the seat. *Houston: second-stage ignition complete.*

After that, Kendra flew through town like she was being chased by the police—weaving around FedEx and UPS trucks that had stopped to make a delivery, blasting past vehicles that were slowing to turn, and passing drivers who, in her estimation, were simply driving too slow for the good of mankind. Each one got a loud rebuke as she tore past them.

They came to a busy four-way intersection and she veered into the left-turning lane, the Volvo's brakes groaning as she came to a stop just inches behind the next car in line.

As they waited for the light to change, Priya pulled up next to them on her silver and black Yamaha SR400. She was clad in a black touring jacket, and a matching full-face helmet with a tinted visor. She could be a member of the royal family and no one would be the wiser.

She looked over at Nathan, captured his face in her photographic memory, then revved the motor and roared through the intersection.

Target identified.

10

4:55

Tuesday, 1:55 p.m.
North Cambridge, MA

Nathan walked into Abbott's barn and saw Richard standing at the long farmer's table, rifling through a box of books.

"Oh good, you're here," Richard said. "I'm looking for that copy of *Twice Told Tales,* by Nathaniel Hawthorne. I could've sworn in was in this box but it seems to have vanished."

"*Twice Told Tales?*" Nathan asked. The title rang a bell, a very small bell.

"Yes, it was part of the Lenox delivery?" Richard said, referring to the purchase he'd made from the wife of a recently deceased and highly eccentric book collector in the small Western Massachusetts

161

town.

"Oh, right, the Lenox delivery," Nathan quipped. "How could I forget?"

Three pallets.

Thirty two boxes stacked on each one.

Encased in an intricate web of bailer twine.

At first glance it looked like they'd been captured by a spider the size of a 1949 Buick Roadmaster.

"It's back here," Nathan said, snatching his clipboard off the table. He walked deeper into the barn, to a pile of boxed books he had finished sorting days earlier. He flipped through the pages on his clipboard until he found the title in question. "Box #7," he said, reading the number he'd scribbled in the margin.

Working quickly, he dug down through the stack and pulled out box #7, then carried it over to the table and removed the Hawthorne title. "*Twice Told Tales*," he announced as he handed it to Richard.

"*This* is a rare treasure," Richard declared, gazing at it with utter fascination.

"Rare, indeed," came a voice from several feet away.

They both turned to see Jordan Prescott standing in the doorway, her slender body casting a long shadow that stretched well into the barn.

She walked up to Richard and held out her hand. "May I?"

"Why, certainly," Richard said, passing it to her without hesitation.

She pulled it close and inspected the front, the spine, and the back. "I'm impressed," she said. "This was a breakthrough book for Hawthorne. Copies in such excellent condition are extremely hard to come by."

'Yes they are," Richard said, flashing both eyebrows. "Now, if you'll excuse me," he said, gently prying the book from her hands, "I've got to get this wrapped for a very good client, whom I expect will be arriving within the hour." He stepped away from the table and offered Jordan a curt bow. "Ms. Prescott, as always, a pleasure to see you. I'll leave you in Mr. Cole's capable hands. If you need me, I'll be in the house."

Jordan watched him scurry past, then turned to Nathan. "So, here we are," she said. "You and me, just like before."

"Yeah, just like before," Nathan muttered in a flat voice. *Joy.*

She moved closer to the table and began poking through box #7, using one finger to flip idly through the books. "I came here today to offer you an apology," she said, following the script she'd rehearsed on the ride over.

"What are you talking about?" Nathan asked.

"During my last visit, it was wrong of me to tell you how your grandfather died. I realize now that information of that magnitude should've come from your parents."

No kidding, Nathan thought.

"Your safety notwithstanding, it's just..." she said, pausing for effect, "*baffling* that the police still haven't found his killer."

"How could they?" Nathan blurted out, anger in his voice. "The people who knew critical details...I'm talking about *YOU* and the other four facilitators...simply up and vanished. And to make matters worse, none of you have come forth to help with the investigation!"

Jordan opened her mouth to respond when Nathan continued.

163

"Which reminds me," he said. "You know how you told me each of the code names?"

"Yes?"

"You never explained why my grandfather chose you."

"Why he *chose* us?"

"Yeah, what skill did each of you have that he so desperately needed?"

It was a curious question, one that confirmed her belief that the detective in him wouldn't sit idly by, now that he knew the truth. "Well, let's see," she said, pretending she had to think about it. "Finch was the cleaner. She maintained the safehouses…"

"That one I know," Nathan said, having been told by Kendra.

"I handled real estate matters, things like finding the safehouse properties, processing the necessary sale documents and such. I also set up the dummy corporation."

"Dummy corporation? What's that?"

"For the property transactions, your grandfather couldn't use his name or the name of the bookstore."

"Why? Because the bad guys might trace ownership back to him?"

"The bad guys. I like that," she said, smiling. "Yes, to shield his identity, and to ensure the safety of those people he was helping, he created what they call a dummy corporation."

"Is it legal?"

"Technically, yes. They tend to get a bad name because they've been used by unscrupulous people to avoid paying taxes. In your grandfather's case, it was just a protective layer to safeguard everyone involved."

"Okay, what about Fane?"

"Fane was the legal expert."

"Legal?"

"Not everyone your grandfather helped had access to legal representation," Jordan explained. "If the court system was somehow involved in their plight, they were at a clear disadvantage. So, your grandfather recruited Fane, a legal secretary, whose job it was to arrange proper counsel."

Fane: legal, Nathan noted.

"Wroth handled electronics," Jordan said, continuing.

The word 'electronics' jolted Nathan as one of the puzzle pieces snapped into place. *Donald Brandt is Wroth*, he told himself. That explained Brandt's lie about not knowing Henry Hammond. But electronics? *How is that important?* he wondered.

"What's wrong?" Jordan asked.

"Uh…nothing… I was just wondering why my grandfather needed an electronics expert."

"Evidence," Jordan said.

"Huh?"

"Wroth provided digital, electronic, and sometimes video information to help your grandfather prove someone's innocence."

"Sounds like he was a valuable member of the team," Nathan said, immediately realizing his slip. "Uh…I don't mean…'he' as in…a guy," he stammered. "I was just using it in …you know…a *general* sense."

I don't believe it! she told herself. *He found Wroth.* She didn't bother asking him how he'd managed to do it because she figured he'd just deny it. Besides, she already had what she'd come for so she moved on. "The last one was Pennyman," she said, "who was responsible for transportation to and from the safehouses, or, if someone needed to be relocated."

"So, he was a driver," Nathan said, like it was more of an indulgence than a need.

"Yes," Jordan said, matter-of-factly. "But it wasn't like calling for a cab. He followed a strict routine, set up by your grandfather."

"What do mean, 'routine'?" *Isn't something gymnasts do on a balance beam?*

"Pennyman always met the 'rider', as your grandfather called them, at a prearranged location, and always after dark. Even the vehicle he used was designed for the utmost safety: Cadillac Escalade with bulletproof doors; beefed-up engine; tinted windows, you name it. Remember, these were people who needed protection, so safety was everything."

Pennyman: transportation, Nathan thought, making a note of it on his mental checklist.

"Now, I want to address something you said earlier," Jordan said, "about how we vanished after your grandfather died, and how none of us has come forward to help the police."

"You don't have to explain," Nathan said. "I already know; you're all scared." *Not that it justifies anything.*

"That's right," she said. "Someone in our group is a killer. And while we never called each other by our real names, our faces are easily recognizable."

"I know how *that* goes," Nathan muttered, picturing Asher Rickman's face.

"When your grandfather was poisoned, we didn't know who we

could trust, so of course we all went into hiding."

"Including the killer," Nathan said.

"Yes."

"Who may or may not know your real name."

"Correct," Jordan said. "Your grandfather insisted we keep them a secret."

Then it was time for the last hook.

"I just…" she began. She paused and closed her eyes as if fighting back tears. "What happened to your grandfather was the act of a monster!" she said, raising her voice loud enough to send it echoing across the room. Then, through clenched teeth, "I just pray that someday, someone finds that traitor and, well, I'd rather not say what punishment I'd dish out, if it were up to me."

Nathan had any number of suitable punishments in mind. His gaze drifted down to the open box of books as he debated who in the group had the capacity to take a life. *Finch, the safehouse cleaner? Sidney, the real estate lawyer? Fane, a legal secretary? Could Brandt, the electronics expert do it? Pennyman, the driver? And what about the sixth name on the list, Perseus?* Why didn't Jordan mention *that* person? As much as he wanted to ask her, he didn't want her to know he had the list. As it was, he still didn't know if he could trust her.

She saw the pensive look on his face and knew that her words were having their intended effect. And to think, it had been *so* easy. She fought back a smile as she watched him trying to work it out in his mind: digesting her words; sifting through the facts as she had presented them, and very likely plotting his next move.

Time to go, she told herself. *My work here is done.*

Nathan's father picked him up just before five o'clock. On the ride home, he tried repeatedly to engage Nathan in conversation, but Nathan had no interest in chit-chat. His mind was absorbed with the facilitators, the skill they each possessed, how that skill might've put them in a position to poison his grandfather, and how they were able to do it without being seen.

There was an after-hours meeting at the bookstore, he thought, re-calling the things Jordan had told him. *Each member of the team was there and they were given an assignment. Then they left. Or did they? Did one of them stay behind? Did the killer leave and then return later? Somehow, someone administered a lethal poison in such a way that...*

He furrowed his eyebrows, realizing that there was one key detail he hadn't considered. "Can I ask you a question?" he said, breaking the dreary silence.

"Sure. Fire away," his dad said, excited at the prospect of having an actual conversation with his son.

"It's about grandpa."

"All right. What is it you want to know?"

"How did he die?" Nathan said, pretending he didn't already know.

David's eyebrows flared. "Wow," he said, surprised. "I didn't see *that* coming. Are you sure you want to know?"

"Why? Was it bad?"

"He was poisoned."

"Did you say...poisoned?"

"Are you sure you want to hear this?" David asked.

"I think I deserve to know, don't you?" Nathan asked.

"Yes," David said, resigned to telling him. He took a breath, then said, "The detectives working the case determined that a poison had been added to the bottle of water your grandfather had on the desk in his office."

"A bottle of water," Nathan confirmed. "On his desk."

"Yes. According to the medical examiner, he ingested the poison, or the water I should say, sometime the previous day."

"The previous day? Did the medical examiner say when, exactly?"

"No," David said. "He could only give an approximate time."

Nathan leaned in, eyebrows raised. "Which was?" he asked, impatiently.

"He said it was 20-24 hours before your grandfather died."

"And grandpa died when?" Nathan asked.

David stared absently at the traffic ahead, flashing back to that day: standing with Elizabeth in the corridor outside Henry's room; the door opening and the doctor stepping out, his eyes meeting Elizabeth's; shaking his head, sadly.

It was a moment that would haunt David for all time, remembering how Elizabeth had wilted into his arms, trembling, as the devastating news rocked her body, and how he had hugged her tightly, his eyes drifting up to the clock on the wall, seeing the hour and minute hand seemingly frozen in time. It was a number that would be burned into his memory forever.

"Four fifty-five," he said.

"Four fifty-five?" Nathan repeated. *Four fifty-five minus 18-20 hours would be...* he thought, counting backwards...*somewhere between five and nine o'clock the previous evening...which was after the bookstore closed.*

"Why all these questions about your grandfather?" David asked, his words jarring Nathan's thought process.

"No reason," he said, trying to casually sweep the question aside. "Just curious, that's all."

His father gave him a dubious look. "Just curious, huh? Need I remind you, curiosity is what nearly got you killed in the basement of the courthouse? And at the Whitney Mine? Would you like me to continue?"

"Don't bother," Nathan muttered. He looked at the side mirror and saw a long line of traffic behind them. Several cars back was a silver and black motorcycle. The rider had full-face helmet with a black visor that obscured his face, and he was wearing a matching black touring jacket. The combination seemed eerily familiar, but he couldn't recall where he'd seen it before.

"All I'm saying," David told him, "is that you of all people need to be extremely careful when it comes to the things that peak your curiosity. You understand what I'm telling you, right?"

"Uh-huh," Nathan replied. In the mirror he saw that the motorcycle was now two car lengths closer.

"And don't ever think you can't come to me with questions," David added.

"What about Mom?"

"Uh, it's probably best to ask me first, just in case…you know…"

"Oh, I know," Nathan said. "Trust me."

As his father slowed to turn onto their street, Nathan checked the mirror again. The motorcycle was gone.

They came to a stop in the driveway and Nathan hopped out, then headed straight for the garage. The events of the day had robbed him of his daily workout, but with another 45 minutes until dinner he figured he had plenty of time to go through his progression: jump rope, hand weights, then the heavy bag, in that order.

Despite the fact that Beck had told him the heavy bag would wait until later, after he'd built up more muscle mass, Nathan had been secretly working it, taking out his frustration and anger with two-hand volleys. He had just started jump roping when the side door opened and Gina ducked inside.

"I thought you'd never get home," she said, out of breath from running.

Nathan stopped jump roping. "What's wrong?" he asked.

"Nothing's wrong. I was going to show you the information I found, remember?" She waved her notepad in the air as a reminder.

"Right!" he said, excitedly. He hung the jump rope on the wall and hurried over to where she was standing.

For the next 10 minutes she worked through her notes, name by name, explaining in detail what she'd learned about each facilitator. Her research had unearthed their occupation, the company they worked for, and where it was located. She also explained the social media postings, press releases and new stories she'd found, mostly related to the law firms where Jordan Prescott and Julie Nichols were employed. It was like a tell-all book, *The Facilitators: The True Story*, condensed into 10 handwritten pages.

"Can I look at that?" he asked, pointing at the notepad.

"Be my guest," she said, handing it to him.

He removed his grandfather's list from inside the front cover and slipped it in his back pocket, then combed through Gina's notes, reading each person's name aloud, along with their job, linking it to the skill they brought to the group.

"Julie Nichols works for... (pulling the notepad closer) ... Daglan, Flaherty & Pratt, as a legal secretary. She's Fane, the one who arranged legal counsel for anyone who needed it."

Next name.

"Jordan Prescott works for a real estate law firm. I already know she's Sidney. She handled all the—"

"Hold on," Gina cut in. "You already know she's Sidney? How is that possible?"

"She came to see me at Abbott's barn."

"She *what?*"

"She came to see me at work. Uh...actually," he said, "she stopped by a few times."

"And you didn't think that was something I should know?" Gina said, nearly shouting.

"I was going to tell you...but..."

Oh boy, here it comes, Gina thought. "But what?" she asked.

"I...uh...didn't want you to worry about me," he said, saying the first thing that came to mind.

"Worry about you? Why would I do that?"

"Uh, hello!" he said, waving the notepad at her. "Five potential killers? One of them comes to see me not once but two...no, wait... *three* times?"

"All right, all right, I get it," she groused. "You didn't want me to freak out."

"May we continue?" Nathan asked.

She gave him a backhanded wave, like she was brushing away a fly. *Go on!*

"All right, where was I?" He opened the notepad and began flipping pages.

"You still should've told me," she muttered, just loud enough for him to hear.

"Enough," he said, when he found Jordan Prescott's name.

She glared at him. "Are you serious? First it was 'shush', now it's 'enough'?"

"As-I-was-saying..."

She gave him an evil stare, but he was busy reading her notes and didn't notice.

"Sidney handled all the real estate transactions," he explained.

"What real estate transactions?"

"The safehouses."

"Oh, those," Gina replied, remembering that Henry Hammond had more than one.

"She also set up a dummy corporation to hide my grandfather's involvement, but that's not important right now." He flipped to the next page, and then the next, skimming the press release headlines Gina had listed, all highly publicized real estate deals that Jordan's firm had handled, and controversial cases litigated by Daglan, Flaherty & Pratt.

Next page.

"Connie Freeman is a professional house cleaner. Makes sense. She's Finch, the one who cleaned and stocked the safehouses."

Gina shook her head, dizzy, from the complexity of the organization Henry Hammond had assembled. This was clearly no Saturday night poker group; old friends getting together weekly for cards, cognac, and cigars.

"Donald Brandt, we know, owns Wired Electronics in Woburn," Nathan said quickly, not bothering to read Gina's notes. "He's Wroth, the one who provided electronic evidence."

"Wait. What?"

Nathan gave her a 15 second recap of what Jordan had told him about the digital evidence that Wroth would gather, when needed, to help prove someone's innocence.

Last page.

"Frank Sobol is a car salesman in Saugus?" he asked. "Figures."

"Why do you say that?"

"Because he was the driver. His code name was Pennyman."

"The driver?" Gina asked.

"When my grandfather hid someone in a safehouse, he needed a driver he could trust to take them there. And it wasn't just around the corner. The one I stayed at is in Rowley. According to Jordan Prescott, transportation was a highly regimented process."

"Of course," Gina said. She pictured an innocent person, fearing for their life, being whisked away by a stranger in the back of a car, to an unknown destination, all the while questioning what the future had in store for them, and for the family they left behind.

Nathan closed the notepad and said, "All five of these people were at the meeting in my grandfather's bookshop. Somehow, one of them managed to slip poison into his water bottle without being seen."

"Uh, I hate to be the bearer of bad news," Gina said, "but there's one problem with that theory. It's a little thing called proof?"

"The timeline is the proof," he said. "According to the medical examiner, the poison entered my grandfather's bloodstream approximately 20-24 hours before it took his life."

"O-kay," Gina said slowly. "And…?"

"Do the math," he said. "The meeting took place after the bookstore closed. Let's assume that was five o'clock, which was 24 hours before he died. If they met at six o'clock, that's 23 hours. Seven o'clock would've been 22 hours. Eight o'clock…21 hours."

"Okay, okay, I get it," Gina said, waving her hand in the air for him to stop. "We know he was at the bookstore; the five of *them* were at the bookstore; the store was closed, so, obviously, there were no customers. Was there anyone else there? Someone we're forgetting?"

"No. According to Jordan Prescott, the only ones at the meeting were my grandfather and the five facilitators. Jameson had the day off. What we need to figure out is which one did it, and how they managed to put the poison in his water bottle without anyone else noticing."

"I think the answer is pretty obvious," Gina said. "We need to talk to each one of them and see how they react. How we do *that* is another question altogether."

"Actually," Nathan said, "it's already been taken care of."

"What are you talking about?"

"Beck agreed to drive us wherever we need to go."

"You *told* him what we're doing?"

"Uh-huh. I told him everything."

"Because…?"

"He made a promise to protect me. He also promised not to tell anyone what we're doing. Plus, if we're going to talk to each of the facilitators, I figured we're going to need a ride. And, having a bodyguard won't hurt."

"A bodyguard?" she repeated.

"Yeah, for any… *unpleasantness*."

Great, she thought, slumping her shoulders. *More unpleasantness.*

He started to pace, strategizing aloud. "The first thing we need to do is figure out where to start. Jordan Prescott claims to have an airtight alibi. She said she left the meeting and drove straight to Maine where she stayed until the next day. But based on what the medical examiner reported, that alibi doesn't hold up. She could've poisoned the water before she left. As far as Donald Brandt goes, the way he acted when I spoke to him makes him suspect #1 in my book."

"Why? How did he act?"

He came to a stop in front of her. "Well, let's see," he said, taking a moment to choose his words. "Spooked? Skittish? Shifty? Definitely scared. See how I did that, with all 'S' words? Pretty clever, right?"

"Copycat!" she said, grabbing her notepad from his hand.

"Brandt lied," he said, turning serious. "We'll definitely go talk to him again, but first, let's weed out the others." He pulled his grandfather's list from his back pocket and considered each of the people he hadn't spoken to yet. "Connie Freeman, Julie Nichols, Frank Sobol. Which one should we talk to first?"

"Well, Connie Freeman cleans houses for a living. That means we won't be able to talk to her until the end of the day. Julie Nichols? She works for a busy law firm. The best time to catch her would be during her lunch break. And Frank Sobol? He's a car salesman. I'm guessing we could talk to him any time, as long as he's not out on a test drive or busy working a deal."

"Okay then. Frank Sobol it is."

Wednesday, 9:30 a.m.
The Auto Barn
Saugus, MA

The Auto Barn, where Frank Sobol worked, was located on Rt. 1, halfway between the Square One Mall and the Lynn Falls Parkway exit. Beck pulled in, paused momentarily to survey the lot, then turned right and looped around a long double-row of new cars that were parked back to back, one side facing the highway, the other side facing the showroom.

Now you see me.

Now you see me again.

He came to the main building and pulled into a visitor's space several feet from the showroom entrance. "The Auto Barn," he said, in a tired voice. "Whose bright idea was this?" He leaned forward and gazed up at the front of the building, which, in keeping with the name had vertical siding painted brick red and a black-shingled roof that angled downward from the center peak. Unmistakably barn-like. All that was missing was a rolling pasture, some cows, and a John Deere tractor. He grimaced, then looked at Nathan and said, "All right, what's the plan?"

"Same as before, at the electronics shop," Nathan told him. "I'll mention my grandfather and see what he says."

"And if he plays dumb, like Brandt?" Beck asked.

"Oh, I'm counting on that," Nathan replied. On the way over he'd studied Gina's notes on Frank Sobol and found some valuable ammunition he could use if Frank got squirrely—which Nathan assumed would be the case. Squirrely Sobol. It had certain ring to it.

From the back seat, Gina asked, "What about me?"

"Once we're inside, I need you to stay out of sight," Nathan said. "After we leave, stick around for a few minutes and watch him. See what he does, then meet us outside."

"See what he *does?*" Gina repeated.

"Yeah, you know, does he call anyone? Does he look nervous or tense? Whatever you do, don't let him see you."

"Oh, sure, no problem, I'll just slip into my invisibility suit. Hey! Where is it?" she said, frantically pawing the seat next to her. "I just had it. Do you see it anywhere? Oh no, that's right, you can't…it's *invisible!*"

Oh brother, Nathan thought as he pushed the door open.

Beck walked into the showroom first, followed by Nathan, then Gina. They hadn't gone far when they were greeted by a young woman standing behind the front counter. It was raised off the ground several inches, giving her a commanding view of the showroom.

"Well, good morning!" she said loudly as she stepped down onto the sales floor. She clasped her hands together as she approached. "Welcome to the Auto Barn." She eyed Beck for a split second, then addressed Nathan and Gina with wide eyes. "Did your dad bring you in here to pick out a new car?" she gushed, talking to them like they were toddlers.

I'm going to be sick, Gina thought.

"Uh, no," Nathan said, reading her nametag. "Chelsea is it? We're here to see Frank Sobol."

"Frank? Why certainly!" Chelsea said. She leaned down and

spoke in a near whisper, like she was sharing top secret and highly classified government information. "I think he's out back in the service department. You wait here and I'll page him."

As she hurried back to the front counter, Nathan turned to Gina and said, "He's in the service department. She's going to page him."

"You are *such* a jerk sometimes. Did you know that?" she said.

"Yeah, I know," Nathan said, grinning. "I like seeing you get all worked up."

"Is that a fact? You know who does that?"

"Who?"

"A *jerk*!" she snapped, then turned and walked over to a bright yellow Ford Mustang GT convertible, one of several vehicles parked on the sales floor. She was admiring the interior when Chelsea's voice erupted from the speaker high above and echoed throughout the showroom.

"Frank Sobol to the showroom. Frank, showroom please."

When Nathan heard that, he turned to Beck and said, "You're the only one old enough to buy a vehicle, so he's going to zero in on you. String him along and make him feel like you're ready to buy. Once he's fully engaged, I'll jump in."

"Will do," Beck said.

Seconds later Sobol pushed through a set of swinging doors that led to the service garage. He was in his mid 50s and projected the image of a man who couldn't drive past a donut shop without pulling in. He had a square face and receding sandy brown hair that was shaved to within a half inch of his scalp. His drab brown and white-striped tie did little to help his polyester suit, the color of a coffee bean.

When he saw Beck standing in the middle of the showroom, he walked right over, smiling, his eyes bright. "Good morning," he said, shaking Beck's hand with a squishy grip. "I'm Frank Sobol. How can I help you today?"

Beck hitched his thumb in the direction of the front window. "Been thinking about trading in my truck," he said.

Frank leaned to the side slightly, gazing at Beck's immaculately maintained Dodge Ram. In the blazing sunlight, the midnight finish sparkled like black onyx. "Very nice," he said, imagining the hefty commission he'd make when he sold it.

"That, it is," Beck replied. "But I'm ready for something new. Something sleeker, with enough power to make it hard to catch, if you know what I mean."

Sobol nodded his head confidently. "Oh, I certainly do," he said. "Let's go over to my desk and I'll check our inventory. I've got several vehicles in mind, but with three locations, I'm sure we'll find several more."

He led Beck over to a row of desks set at intervals along the front windows. They were angled in such a way as to allow customers a clear view of the front lot. "Why don't you have a seat right here," he said, patting the back of a bonded black-leather guest chair. "And I take it this is your son?" he asked, smiling at Nathan.

"Friend," Nathan replied.

"Well okay, friend," Frank said. "You're welcome to join us."

"Sure," Nathan said as he slid into the matching guest chair.

Halfway across the showroom floor, Gina eased open the back door of a shiny Chevrolet Silverado crew-cab pickup and climbed inside. She pulled the door shut and slid across to the other door, giving her a clear view of Nathan and Beck through the tinted windows.

"Hmm...something fast and sleek," Frank said, staring at his computer monitor as he navigated his way to the inventory screen. "Me? I prefer the foreign makes. Don't get me wrong, there are many *fine* American-made vehicles, but there's nothing quite like the feel of a Jaguar V6 Coupe. Know what I mean?"

"Do I ever. If you have one in stock, this might be the quickest sale you ever made," Beck answered. He threw Nathan a glance. *How's that?*

Nathan nodded his approval. *Perfect!*

"Well, as luck would have it, we just took one in on trade at our Belmont dealership," Frank said. "Give me... just... one second... while I...check...our inventory," he added, his words coming out in short burst as he scanned the list of vehicles.

Doing two things at once, Nathan thought, like he was filling out an employee evaluation. *Improvement needed.* He looked to his left and saw a narrow section of wall that separated two of the enormous plate-glass windows. Running down the middle of it was a collection of laser-engraved sales awards, platinum gray with silver writing.

"All right, here we go," Frank said, when he found the Jaguar listing. He spun the monitor so Beck could see photos of the outside and the interior of the vehicle.

"Oh yeah!" Beck said, sliding his chair closer to the desk. "That's what *I'm* talking about."

At that, Frank launched into a detailed explanation of the car, citing each of its features in technical terms as if he'd personally designed the vehicle himself.

While he was doing that, Nathan got up from the chair and walked over to the wall of plaques. Each one featured the Auto Barn logo, the year of the award set prominently in a circle of stars, Frank's name, and the words, "Salesman of The Year."

Frank was clearly on a roll, having won the award for six consecutive years. And that gave Nathan an idea. He waited for Frank to finish his soft-sell pitch and then said, "Wow, you sure have a lot of awards."

Frank looked over and frowned. "Oh, those," he said, pretending to be annoyed. "The owner insists that we hang them up where our customers can see them. If it were up to me, they'd be stashed in a drawer somewhere out back."

"No, they're cool," Nathan said, like Frank was his buddy. "You're obviously very good at what you do."

"Well, for me, this job isn't about flashy awards," he said, sliding right back into salesman mode. "It's about helping hard-working folks, like your friend here, find the vehicle of their dreams."

"You like helping people, that's nice," Nathan said, as he walked back to the desk and sat down.

"Yup," Frank replied, nodding. "It's more than just a job, it's a passion."

"Really?" Nathan said. "Is that what you told my grandfather?"

11

Stirring Things Up

"I'm sorry, what was that?" Frank asked.

"My grandfather," Nathan replied. "You worked with him. Excuse me, you *helped* him."

"I don't follow…"

"His name was Henry Hammond. He owned a bookstore in Cambridge. You know the one: Hammond Books?"

Frank sucked in air through his teeth. "I don't know," he said, shaking his head. "The name does sound *vaguely* familiar, but I don't remember working with anyone named Hammond. Is it possible you have me confused with someone else? I'm sorry, I didn't get your name."

"Nathan."

"Nathan…?" Frank said, prompting him for a last name.

"Cole," Nathan said, anger stirring in his gut after hearing Frank's blatant lie. "Henry Hammond was my grandfather."

"Right," Frank said, nodding thoughtfully. "You mentioned that."

"This would've been seven or eight years ago," Nathan said. *Remember?*

Again, Frank just shrugged. "Sorry, it doesn't ring a bell."

Fine, you want to play? Let's play, Nathan thought, his anger burning hotter. "You were working at the Cadillac dealership in Medfield back then, weren't you? General Manager if I'm not mistaken"

"Yes," Frank said, baffled at how a kid he'd never seen before could possibly know that. "But I don't see how that has any bearing on —"

"Escalade," Nathan said, cutting him off.

"Excuse me?"

"A Cadillac Escalade. That's the vehicle you drove, right?"

"Well, yes, as a matter of fact I *did* drive an Escalade, once upon a time."

"But not just any Escalade," Nathan said, pressing.

Frank offered yet another shrug. "You lost me."

The lie only served to stoke Nathan's anger and he doubled down. "You know, I'm curious," he said, like he'd been giving it a lot of thought. "Where does one get a vehicle with bulletproof doors? It's not like they just roll off the production line every day. Did you find it at government-surplus auction, or did you have one of the body shop guys install them?"

"Look," Frank said, pushing back from the desk. "I don't know what this is about, but I think it's time for both of you to leave."

"Come on," Beck said. "Let's go."

As they stood, Nathan's anger surged and he fired one last salvo. Staring down at Frank he said, "My grandfather was a modern-day hero. He saved the lives of many innocent people, and you were helping him. I know it and you know it. So, why all the lies? Have you forgotten all the 'riders' you drove to safety? Don't bother replying, I already know the answer."

He walked away from the desk and left Frank sitting there, speechless.

Gina watched as Nathan followed Beck out the front door, then shifted her gaze back to Frank. He had turned his chair and was watching them through the plate-glass window. He waited until they backed out of the parking space and then spun his chair back around and began typing furiously on his computer keypad. When the results of his search appeared, he scrolled through the links, his eyes glued to the screen. One in particular made him stop and lean closer as he devoured every word.

Overhead, a tired male voice boomed from the intercom. "Frank to the Service Department please."

Frank closed the page he was reading and made his way across the showroom floor. Gina waited until he was out of sight, then slipped out of the truck. She was zig-zagging her way toward the front door when her curiosity spiked. She paused, looked around to make sure no one was watching, then hurried over to Frank's desk. His screensaver was charcoal black with an endless stream of multi-colored bubbles, bumping and careening across the screen.

When she tapped the keyboard's spacebar, the bubbles disappeared and were instantly replaced by the home page of the Auto Barn's website. Working quickly, she clicked on the Google Search icon in the toolbar, then checked the history tab at the top. The first listing made her eyes go wide.

G Nathan Cole - Google Search

Across the showroom, the double doors swung open and Frank emerged. Panicked, she ducked down behind the desk and then scurried to her right, staying low, until she came to the yellow Mustang. She hid behind the front bumper and watched as Frank walked toward his desk. He was almost there when he stopped, muttered something under his breath, then turned around and retraced his steps, remembering something he'd forgotten to tell the mechanic.

Gina waited until she heard the *whoomph* of the double doors, then stood and walked quickly in the opposite direction, making a bee line for the side entrance. Once outside, she looked left and saw Beck's truck sitting 50 feet away, idling next to the side of the building.

As they roared out of the lot and merged into the long line of traffic cruising up Rt. 1, Beck said, "Was all that stuff true? The Escalade and the bulletproof doors?"

"Yup," Nathan said. "Jordan Prescott told me about it." Nathan said. His arms were crossed and he was staring out the side window, his anger still boiling hot. Donald Brandt was no longer Suspect #1. That title now belonged to Frank Sobol. *They should hang another plaque on the wall,* Nathan thought. *Frank Sobol, Liar of the Year.*

The ease with which he'd done it told Nathan one of two things: either the man was still fiercely loyal to Henry Hammond, holding true to the oath of secrecy he took, which kept him from revealing the work they'd done together, or he was hiding something.

Nathan's money was on the latter.

"Escalade? Bulletproof doors? What are you talking about?" Gina asked.

"The vehicle Sobol used was a Cadillac Escalade," Nathan explained. "It had bulletproof doors and tinted glass, probably a bunch of other stuff too."

"Seriously?"

"Uh-huh. It was designed to help protect the person he was driving to a safehouse."

"That is *crazy*," she muttered. "So, what happened in there? You guys sure left in a hurry."

"We were having a very nice conversation," Nathan said sarcastically. "Until he started lying."

Gina let out an exasperated breath. "All right, what did you do?"

"Nothing bad," Nathan said.

Beck cleared his throat.

"Okay, I *may* have mentioned some particulars about his work history."

"*May* have?" Beck said. "Come on, you were laying it on pretty thick." He checked the side mirror again, saw an opening, and powered into the left lane.

Several cars back, Priya did the same.

"Was that wrong?" Nathan said, defensively. "The guy was lying to my face!"

Beck made eye contact with Gina in the rearview mirror. "What did he do after we left?"

"He watched you leave, then he did a Google search…on *you*, Nathan."

187

"On me? How do you know that?"

"I may have accidentally checked his computer as I was leaving."

He turned in the seat, grinning from ear to ear. "You are so bad," he joked.

"Yeah, well, I wouldn't get too giddy about it," she said. "You should be asking yourself why he was searching the internet trying to find information about you."

"Maybe he wanted to see if I was really the grandson of Henry Hammond."

"Yes, that's possible," she said, humoring him. "But what if he has another motive in mind?"

"She's right," Beck said. "You're stirring things up, and now we all need to be extra careful." He checked the rearview mirror and saw a long line of cars trailing behind them for a solid half mile, their rooftops, like a row of diamonds in a tennis bracelet, reflecting the midday sun. The only variation was a motorcycle five cars back. The driver, outfitted in a black jacket and matching helmet was leaning forward to cut the wind.

"We'll be careful, but we're not done stirring," Nathan said. "Not by a longshot." He looked over the seat again. "Where to next?"

"Let's go to Newton and talk to Fane," Gina said. "It's early, but that may actually work in our favor."

Jordan Prescott was overjoyed when her client meeting ended early. With lunch just over an hour away, and her stomach was gurgling like a water cooler, she left the office and walked down the street to a small café near St. Elizabeth's Medical Center. She took a table near the front window and ordered a large chef salad. As she was waiting for it to arrive, her cell phone started playing *The Trout Quintet* by Schubert.

She answered the call at once, apologetic. "Hi, I'm so sorry I didn't call you."

"Is everything all right?" the caller asked.

"Everything's fine. After I left Abbott's barn I got blindsided at work putting out one fire after another. It was brutal." As she spoke she shifted in her seat to face the window. Directly across the street was the Brighton/Allston Police District building. Five round shrubs, over eight feet wide and shaped like French berets, sat in a cluster at the near side of the building. She wasn't sure what variety they were; to her they looked like giant space pods from another planet, masquerading as ordinary bushes but secretly filled with alien spores that would soon hatch and infiltrate the neighborhood.

"Speaking of Abbott's barn, how was your visit? Is everything on track with our friend?"

"Very much so," Jordan said. "I don't know how he managed to do it, but he found Wroth."

"He found Wroth?" the caller exclaimed.

"Yes. He didn't say it in so many words, but it definitely happened."

"How do you like that?" the caller mused. "This kid is either very clever, or exceedingly lucky."

"I'd say he's both," Jordan replied.

"Either way," the caller said, "I'd feel better if we had a sentinel in place, someone to keep a close eye on him so we know exactly what he's up to."

"You know? I may have the perfect person for that."

189

"Are you sure?"

"Absolutely! It's perfect."

"Okay then, I'll let you set it up. Let me know how it goes."

"Will do." She glanced over her shoulder and saw the waitress approaching with her chef salad. "Hey, I have to go, but I'll be in touch."

The waitress set the salad down in front of her and said, "Can I get you anything else?"

"No, I think I'm all set for now," Jordan said, eyeing the salad with hungry eyes. She watched the waitress walk away, then picked up her phone and used both thumbs to compose a short text.

interested in earning some quick cash?

Seconds later came a reply.

you know it

Jordan smiled, then sent a follow up.

job starts immediately – I'll send details

Which prompted a one-word response.

sweet

Daglan, Flaherty & Pratt was located in a modern brick and glass building on Wells Avenue, right down the street from the Newton-Wellesley Hospital Rehabilitation Center. The flat roof and large tinted windows gave it an ominous, almost government-agency appearance. Beck turned into the parking lot and drove slowly past the front door. The temperature had soared into the low 90s for a second straight day, so he parked in a shady spot at the back corner of the lot, right next to a row of towering pines. "Same plan?" he asked, as he turned off the engine and pulled the key from the ignition.

"Yup," Nathan said.

"Uh, maybe you should let me do the talking," Gina suggested.

"Why?" Nathan asked, without turning around.

"Well, it seems to me that during our visit with Frank Sobol, you were…let's see… bad-tempered? Blunt? Belligerent? Perhaps a little *brusque?*" She leaned forward and reached over the seat. "How do you like that?" she said, drilling the tip of her finger into his shoulder. "All words starting with B!" *No one messes with the Puzzle Master!*

"I think she's got you there, buddy," Beck said.

Nathan looked at him, speechless. *Really? You're agreeing with her?*

"Sorry," said Beck. "But she's right."

Nathan muttered something under his breath and looked away.

"Here's an idea," Beck said, as a peace offering. "We let Gina start, and if she leaves anything out, that's when you speak up."

Gina frowned. *Leave anything out? As if.*

"Fine," Nathan grumbled. He pushed the door open, then stopped to look over the seat at Gina. "Come along now," he said. "You wouldn't want to fall *behind*. See how I used a word beginning with B?"

"Jerk!" she muttered.

"Got 'cha again!" he said, grinning, then hopped down out of the truck.

"He's *walking* home," she told Beck.

"Come on," he told her, trying not to laugh. "Let's do this."

The front lobby was an homage to silver, gray and black. It was like the paint store had run out of every other color except those three. A long curved counter with a midnight-black facade was positioned on the right. Directly behind it was a shark-skin gray wall that stretched all the way up to the ceiling. Centered in the middle of it was the name "DAGALAN, FLAHERTY & PRATT." Below it, in smaller caps, the words "LAW OFFICES." The soft lighting overhead gave the silver letters an iridescent quality, adding an eerie, futuristic feel to the room.

The floor was equally drab. It was a mosaic of large rectangular tiles, dark gray frames with a lighter gray center, each with a pattern that resembled roughly combed concrete. Directly across from the counter, pushed up against a pale gray wall, was a modern black-leather couch with block-like cushions set in a retro-style chrome frame. Sitting next to it at a 90-degree angle was a matching chair. Mama bear and baby bear.

The centerpiece of the room, one that commanded the attention of all who entered, was an enormous Brice Marden abstract that hung on the wall behind the couch. It featured an erratic series of black lines on a starched-white canvas that could be interpreted in any number of ways.

A woman in her early 40s sat behind the counter, busily answering the phone that seemed to ring without pause. "Good morning, Daglan, Flaherty & Pratt. How may I direct your call?" she said. "Yes, I'll put you right through." Five seconds later: "Good morning, Daglan, Flaherty & Pratt. How may I direct your call? No, I'm sorry, Mr. Flaherty is in court this morning."

The white blouse and black blazer she wore set off her smooth complexion, the color of roasted almonds, and her jet black hair was pulled back into a tight ponytail that made her sterling silver hoop earrings even more prominent.

Beck and Gina took a seat on the couch, while Nathan plopped down in the chair. They had waited nearly 10 minutes when the receptionist looked across the room and said, "Thank you for waiting. How may I help you?"

Gina stood up at once and walked over to the counter. "Hello, my name is Gina McDermott," she said. "We're here to speak with Julie Nichols."

"I'm Julie Nichols," the woman said, speaking quickly. "What is it you'd like to discuss?"

"Actually," Gina said, showing unease, "it's a personal matter that's extremely sensitive. I can see that you're very busy, but if you could spare a few minutes we would really appreciate it. Like I said, it's a very sensitive matter, but once you hear what we have to say, I know you'll understand why we needed to talk to you."

Intrigued, Julie eyed Gina for several seconds then checked the time on her watch. "Well, your timing is good, I'll say that much. I was just about to go to lunch."

"Perhaps we could chat while you eat?" Gina suggested. "It won't take long."

The phone rang again but Julie let it go to a prerecorded message. "Sure, why not?" she said. "We can go outside."

"Perfect," Gina said. She turned and looked at Nathan. *See how easy that was?*

He was actually impressed. He held his fist against his stomach and gave her a thumbs up.

Nicely done.

Julie pulled a square plastic container from her purse, along with a fork wrapped in a paper napkin, then led Gina, Nathan and Beck outside to a grassy area behind the building. Situated in the middle of it, bathed in the shade of a tall maple tree, was a wooden picnic table.

Beck waited for Julie to sit, then slid onto the bench next to her. Nathan and Gina took a seat on the opposite side.

"I come out here every day for lunch," Julie said, "when the weather cooperates, that is." She pried the top off the plastic container and poked through her Greek salad, mixing the chopped cucumbers, cherry tomatoes, Kalamata olives, bits of bell pepper and chunks of feta cheese until they were evenly blended.

Fifty feet away, not far from Beck's truck, Priya watched from behind a huge boulder left in place by the land developer years earlier to give the property a more authentic, more natural look. She had followed Beck after he left the Auto Barn, and when he pulled into the law office parking lot, she slipped into the adjacent lot, parked the motorcycle where Beck and the others wouldn't see it, then took a surveillance position behind the boulder.

Option #1: change out of her riding gear and go inside the law office, hoping to learn why Nathan was there. Neither he nor the two people with him had ever seen her face before. To them, she'd be a total stranger. Risk factor: zero. Intel-gathering potential: high.

Option #2: sit tight and observe. Then, see where they went next. Report each of their stops to Asher and let him sort it out. Risk factor: zero. Intel-gathering potential: marginal.

She chose option one and began removing her touring jacket. When she saw Nathan and his two friends come around the far corner of the building along with what she assumed was one of the law firm's employees, she pivoted to Option #2 and ducked back down behind the rock.

"Thank you again for meeting with us," Gina said. "This is Nathan Cole and that's our friend Beck."

"Hello Nathan, hello Beck," Julie said, as she speared a piece of cucumber with her fork. "What is it you'd like to discuss?"

"It might be better if I let Nathan explain," Gina replied.

"Very well. Nathan, what's on your mind?"

Nathan didn't sugarcoat it. "My grandfather was Henry Hammond," he said. "We know you worked with him and that you were part of a special team he assembled, a group he called his 'facilitators'."

"I see," Julie said. "This, Henry Hammond…you say he was your grandfather?"

"Yes," Nathan replied. *Here we go again.*

"And what makes you think I was part of this *facilitators* group?"

Nathan pulled the list of names from his back pocket and laid it flat on the table. "My grandfather gave me this note through…let's just say…a back channel. It has the names of all five facilitators. *Your* name is at the top of the list. There's another name here, but we haven't been able to find him," Nathan said. "We thought you might know who it is. Perseus? Does that name mean anything to you?"

Julie's eyes widened, like she'd seen a ghost. "Only someone who utters that word could be related to Henry Hammond," she said.

"So, you did know my grandfather."

"Yes," Julie confessed, setting her fork down. "And devastated doesn't begin to describe the grief I felt when he died. The reason you can't find Perseus is because it's not a he or a she. It's a code word. It was created by your grandfather and used exclusively with the five facilitators. Had you said that word when you entered the office, I would've known at once that you were somehow connected to Henry Hammond, and more importantly, that I could trust you."

"Because of that one word?"

"Yes. Your grandfather used it to summon us. It was, among other things, a call-to-arms."

"You mean, like the bat signal?"

"Nothing quite that dramatic, but, yes, I suppose you could view it that way. Because there was always someone trying to thwart the work we were doing, your grandfather instituted a number of precautions to ensure secrecy and the safety of everyone involved, most importantly the people we were helping. The code word Perseus is one such precaution. If he called us, it was the first thing he'd say, letting us know it was really him and that he needed our help. One time, he slipped me a note in passing. It contained no details about who he was helping or what he needed me to do—only the name Perseus."

"And then you met with him?"

"Yes, in his office at the bookstore."

Nathan sat momentarily stunned. His initial belief about his grandfather wanting him to have access to the facilitators had been confirmed yet again. The fact that he'd included the all-important code word on the list was undeniable proof of that.

Julie reached across the table and picked up the note. She examined the names briefly, then folded the paper into a neat square. "Destroy this immediately," she said as she handed it back. "And from now on, never mention the facilitators or the work we did with your grandfather to anyone. Is that clear?"

"But...?"

"But nothing," she said. "That piece of paper is a death warrant. Every second you possess it, you're putting yourself and those around you in grave danger."

Nathan stared at the note, struggling to rationalize what she was saying.

I know he wanted me to have the list...

He hired Devereux to keep it safely hidden...

Then deliver it to me when the time was right...

Why go to such lengths...?

Unless...

12

Blood Money

Astiff breeze swept through the parking lot, making the maple tree bristle and sway, its leafy branches waving in the wind as if painting the sky.

"You may be right about this," Nathan said, holding up the folded note. "But I think there's another reason my grandfather wanted me to have it."

"And that is?" Julie asked.

"There's someone in the group he didn't trust. He gave me the names, and the code word, so I could determine who that person is and steer clear of them." *Or find them and expose them.*

"Interesting theory," Julie said. "But let me ask you this Mr. Cole. Do you value your life? Do you Ms. McDermott? And what about you Beck? Do you value *your* life?"

"I value my life very much," Beck replied.

"We all do," Nathan said, frowning. *What kind of question is that?*

"Then do as I say," Julie told him. "Destroy the list and forget you ever saw it. If you fail to do this, I fear that your life is going to come to a very sudden and tragic end."

"I can't do that," Nathan said. "Someone poisoned my grandfather and I intend to find out who it was. From what information we've been able to gather, and from what I've been told, all signs point to someone in the facilitators' group."

"What you've been told? By whom, if you don't mind me asking?"

Nathan looked at Gina, uncertain.

"Tell her," Gina said.

"I first heard about the facilitators from my friend Kendra."

"Really. How *is* Kendra?"

Nathan blinked hard. "You know her?"

"I do. And Jameson? Is he still alive?"

"Uh...yeah..." Nathan said slowly, looking confused. "Why wouldn't he be?"

"That's not important," Julie replied, her tone suggesting there would be no further discussion on the topic. "Who else have you been talking to?"

"Just one other person. She's another member of the five."

Julie's expression grew troubled. "Which one? It's alright, you can tell me."

"Sidney."

"I see," Julie said. "And what did she tell you?"

"She said I was in danger."

"She's right. You *are* in danger. All three of you are, especially if

199

the killer knows you have that," she said, pointing at the folded note in his hand.

"So then, you agree that the killer was someone in the group."

"Given certain developments at the time, yes, I do," Julie said, pushing bits of salad around in the open container with her fork.

"You're referring to Lía Ballard, and her father's field notebook— the one she gave my grandfather."

Julie's head snapped up. "You *know* about that?"

"I do," Nathan said.

She sat stunned for several seconds, then stood and began to pace with her head down and her arms crossed tightly against her chest. "This is far worse than I thought," she muttered. She stopped pacing and came back to the table. "Who told you about Lía Ballard?" she demanded. "And have you told anyone else about the notebook?"

"Sidney told me about Lía Ballard, and no, I haven't told anyone else about the notebook."

"Good," Julie said, relieved. "Keep it that way. Not a word about it to anyone." She paused briefly, then said, "Did Sidney mention anything about a gold necklace?"

"She did."

"No," Julie said, correcting him. "She didn't."

"Huh?"

"As of today, you never heard of it. The conversation with Sidney never happened. There is no necklace." She thought for a moment, wondering if she'd left anything out. "You're going to need protection," she said.

"That's my job," said Beck.

Julie considered his bulky frame, then said, "Don't get me wrong. You look plenty capable…"

"But?" Beck asked.

"You may not be enough."

"All the more reason to find the killer," Nathan said.

"You really think you'll find the killer before he finds you?" Julie asked.

"That's my plan," Nathan said. He stood, tucked the list in his back pocket, then said to Gina and Beck, "Let's go."

Beck wrenched himself free of the picnic table and stood. "Thanks," he told Julie.

"For what?" she asked.

"For hearing him out."

"No thanks needed," she said, waving it off. "Henry Hammond was like the father I never had. Unfortunately, the person who killed him might very well come after Nathan. You need to watch him like a hawk. And keep me posted, will you? I may be of some use to you before this is over."

"Will do," said Beck.

Nathan and Gina had stopped halfway back to the truck, waiting for Beck to catch up.

"What was that about?" Nathan asked, as Beck approached.

"I was just thanking her for her time, although I'm not sure what we learned."

"What we learned is, she's not the one."

"Oh really?" said Beck. "Why do you say that? Because she showed genuine concern? Because she urged you to drop the whole thing before something bad happens to you?"

"He's got a point, Nathan," Gina said. She lowered her voice and said, "What if she *is* the one? Her concern for your safety might've just been an act, designed to make you quit searching. Think about it. If she did it, and she thinks you'll succeed in tracking down the killer, she's toast."

"But she said it herself. She thinks it was someone in the group."

"Of course she did. It was all part of the act," Gina said.

Nathan looked at each of them, baffled. "Why am I the only one who thinks this woman is innocent?"

"Hey, I'm just sayin'," Gina replied.

"That thing she said about the necklace…?" Beck asked.

"Las Lágrimas de la Emperadora," Nathan said, pronouncing each word crisply.

"Is that the same one you told me about yesterday?"

"The very same," Nathan said.

"You can tell me about it over lunch. I don't know about you two but I'm starving."

Julie watched them pile into Beck's truck and drive out of the lot. Once they were gone, she sat back down at the table and continued eating, all the while wondering if her act had worked.

From somewhere nearby came the sudden growl of a motorcycle engine. It snarled like the scream of a mountain lion, once, twice, three times, as the rider revved the engine, then raced down the street, quickly shifting through the gears.

As the whine of the engine gradually faded in the distance, she snapped the lid on the plastic container and walked back inside the building. When she got to her desk, she slid the plastic container and fork into her purse and sat perfectly still for a moment, contemplating her next course of action. She reached for the phone, but pulled her hand back. *No, not yet,* she told herself. *Let's see how this plays out.*

Beck drove into Newton Centre and parked in the Beacon Street Parking Lot, directly across from Johnny's Luncheonette. The popular local diner served lunch and dinner, but what made it one of Beck's favorite eateries was their all-day breakfast.

They walked in as the lunch crowd was thinning and grabbed a table along the side wall. Within minutes the waitress had taken their order, and as she walked back to the kitchen, Beck sat back in the chair and crossed his arms. "Okay," tell me about these tears."

"What tears?" Nathan asked.

"Las Lágrimas de la Emperadora? The tears of the empress?" Beck said.

"Oh, yeah, right. Wait, you speak Spanish?"

"Apparently."

Gina clapped her hand over her mouth to smother a laugh, which earned her an icy stare from Nathan.

"You think this is funny?" he asked her.

"Sorry," she muttered, averting her eyes. "Please continue."

"Like I told you before," he said. "The day before my grandfather died, a woman named Lía Ballard came into his shop seeking his help." It took him several minutes, but he explained the events of that fateful day: Lía's anxiety when she burst through the shop door; her desperate plea to his grandfather, seeking his protection from the thugs who were chasing her; the field notebook she'd found among her father's effects, which, contained a hidden code that revealed the whereabouts of an ancient Mayan necklace he had unearthed while on an archeological dig in Guatemala a month earlier. According to local legend, the necklace was a gift to Lady Six Sky, the Mayan warrior queen, in the year 740, and was strung with thick tear-shaped wedges of pure gold.

"Tears of the empress," Beck said, nodding.

"Yes, and it's worth millions," Nathan said, "which was obviously too tempting for one of the facilitators to pass up, so they poisoned my grandfather and stole the field notebook."

"Which they used to find the necklace," Beck said.

"Well, they might've tried, but they never succeeded."

"How do you know that?"

"Jordan, or Sidney, whatever you want to call her, told me that no necklace matching that description has ever surfaced."

"What do you mean, surfaced?" Gina asked.

"It's never been recovered by the police. It's never been fenced. There's no proof that it was ever sold on the black market, or through any other criminal network. To this day it remains hidden wherever Lía's father stashed it."

"And Jordan knows this, how?" Beck asked suspiciously.

"She claims to have access to criminal *channels*," he said, framing the last word with air quotes.

"Interesting," Beck said, making a mental note of that tidbit of information.

Their food arrived and they attacked it like a pack of ravenous wolves: Beck, devouring a triple-stack of pancakes with two fried eggs and an extra order of bacon; Gina, a chicken breast sandwich and a small mountain of French fries; Nathan, a cheeseburger and onion rings.

"So, Fane thinks the killer will come after you if he, or she, learns that you're trying to find your grandfather's killer," Beck said, peeling apart two strips of bacon.

"Mm-hmm," Nathan said, with a mouthful of food.

"Maybe it's not that at all," Gina said. "What if she's the one who poisoned your grandfather? Now *you* show up trying to find his killer. Maybe she's afraid that you'll get your hands on the notebook, you'll find the hidden clue, solve it, and then locate the necklace, robbing her of a massive payday."

"I could care less about the necklace," Nathan said. "The only thing I want is to find the traitor—the one who took my grandfather from me."

"Of course," Gina said. "But still, you have to admit, a few million dollars would be *pretty* nice."

"A few hundred, a few thousand, a few million," Nathan said. "I don't want it, and I wouldn't take it if it was offered it to me. It's blood money." He jammed his fork into the remains of his cheeseburger bun with enough force to shake the table, rattling everything on top of it, then stormed out of the restaurant.

"I'd better go talk to him," Gina said.

"You do that," Beck told her. "I'll get the check."

"Wish me luck," she muttered, then left the table and went outside.

Two doors down, she spotted Nathan leaning against a narrow slab of gray marble that separated the bank from the small leather shop next door. He was looking down at the sidewalk, kicking angrily at the concrete as if trying to dig a hole in it with his sneaker.

"Nathan, look, I'm sorry," she said, as she walked up to him. "I shouldn't have said that thing about the money."

He ignored her and continued abusing the concrete with his foot.

"I know you're not trying to find some ancient piece of jewelry so you can cash it in," she said. "Your grandfather, and all of your family members who had the bookcase before you—I know they weren't a bunch of money hungry treasure seekers. The same goes for you. If there's one thing you've shown me, it's that the legacy of the bookcase is about coming to the aid of people who have somehow been wronged, helping them restore their dignity..."

"Save their lives," he muttered.

"Yes!" she said. "And save their lives when no one else will."

He looked up and stared at the parking lot across the street, a trance-like expression on his face. "I'm going to find him, Gina. I'm going to make him pay for what he did."

"I know you will," she said. "And I'm going to help you. Beck's going to help you. We all will."

He turned to her, eyes moist, and then, for the first time in all the years he'd known her, he wrapped his arms around her and hugged her.

"Uh, you said *talk* to him, not make out with him," Beck called out as he came walking up the sidewalk.

"SHUT UP!" they yelled.

Just then, a police cruiser came to a sudden stop in the middle of the street directly in front of them. The light bar came on, and two uniformed officers stepped out of the vehicle. As they approached,

Beck gently swept Nathan and Gina back, creating a human wall between them and the police.

The lead officer, Hale, stepped up on the sidewalk with his hand resting on his taser. "Sir, can I see some identification?"

"What's this about?" Beck asked.

"Identification?" Hale repeated.

Beck raised both hands in a conciliatory gesture...*okay, relax...* then pulled out his wallet and removed his driver's license.

Hale took it from him and compared the license photo to Beck's face, his eyes jumping back and forth from one to the other. Satisfied, he nodded at Nathan and Gina. "Are these your children?"

"No," Beck replied. "But they're in my charge."

Hale handed Beck his license. "Okay sir, I need you to wait right over there," he said, pointing to a section of the sidewalk several feet away.

Beck slipped his license back into his wallet, then complied.

That's when Hale turned his attention to Nathan and Gina, who were standing frozen in place, unsure what was happening.

A young mother with her teenage daughter came walking up the sidewalk. When Mom saw the two officers, she grabbed hold of her daughter's arm and steered her out into the street, cutting a wide birth around the two juvenile offenders. "You see what happens when you break the law?" she said. "Let that be a lesson to you."

The daughter stopped walking and yanked her arm free. "You don't know that they broke the law, *Mom!*" she said, angrily. "You don't know anything," she muttered, then stormed away.

"You watch your mouth young lady," the mother said, chasing after her.

The second officer, Lowrey, said to Gina, "Miss, I need you step away." As he spoke he waved his hand sideways through the air like he was parting two business suits on a department-store clothing rack.

Gina immediately moved to her left, stopping five feet away. "Here?"

"That's fine," Lowrey said.

Hale's focus was on Nathan. "Son?" he said. "What's your name?"

"Nathan Cole."

"Would you spell that please?"

"C-o-l-e."

"Do you have identification?"

"No," Nathan said, like it was a stupid question. "I'm only 12 years old."

"Officer, I can vouch for both kids," said Beck.

Hale studied Nathan's face, then turned to Lowrey. "I don't think this is him."

"I think you're right," Lowry replied. "He's too short."

"Let me guess," Nathan said. "You think I'm Asher Rickman."

Hale spun his head back in Nathan's direction. "How do you know that name?"

"Officer, if I may?" Beck said. "This is a simple misunderstanding. We have a good friend who's connected with the Brookline Police Department. He warned us that this might happen, that Nathan might be mistaken for some guy named Asher Rickman. Apparently, the resemblance is…"

"Uncanny," Lowrey said, before Beck could finish.

Hale pulled a small notepad and pencil from his pocket. "They are *not* going to believe this back at the station," he said. He took down each of their names, their home address, and their phone number. Then, convinced that Nathan wasn't Asher Rickman, who was currently wanted for questioning in connection with the theft at Willow & Vine, he thanked them for their cooperation and let them go on their way.

Once they were back in Beck's truck, no one spoke for nearly a minute. Beck had one arm draped over the top of the steering wheel as he stared absently at the far side of the parking lot, knowing the incident on the sidewalk was going to happen again and again until Rickman was caught. Nathan, already in a sour mood, was slumped back in the seat, arms crossed, burning a hole in the glove box with his eyes. In the back seat, Gina was sitting forward, her head cradled in her hands. "I am in SO much trouble," she said. If she thought that tearing her hair out would fix the problem, she'd do it.

"Why is that?" asked Beck.

"If those officers call my house, I am finished!"

"I wouldn't worry about it," Beck told her. "Cops are required to keep a daily log. The only reason they'd call your parents is if they arrested you." He paused, then asked, "You're not planning on breaking the law any time soon are you?"

"NO!" Gina said, the words exploding out of her mouth.

"Then you're in the clear. *You*, on the other hand," he said to Nathan. "We need to get you some kind of disguise, maybe a hat, to hide your face…at least until they catch your evil twin."

"Very funny," Nathan grumbled. "And I'm not wearing a hat. Let them arrest me."

"Uh, I'd be careful what I wished for if I were you," warned Beck.

"Have you ever seen the inside of a jail cell? It's not pleasant, trust me." He slid the key in the ignition and started the truck. "What time am I dropping you off at Abbott's barn?"

"You're not."

"Why is that?" Beck asked.

"I'm not going to work today. I'm not in the mood."

Beck said nothing.

"Hey, how far is Jamaica Plain?" Gina asked, trying to lighten the mood.

"From here?" Beck said. "Not far. Maybe 15 or 20 minutes. Why?"

"We should drive by Connie Freeman's house and see if she's there."

"Do you have the address?"

"Of course I do," Gina replied.

"Let's do it."

Connie Freeman lived in a small, one-story dormered cape on Lila Road, a stone's throw from Brigham and Women's Faulkner Hospital and the Arnold Arboretum. A three-foot white picket fence enclosed the front yard that was overrun with a variety of flowering shrubs. In several sections, large pink rose bushes were creeping over the top of the fence as if trying to escape.

Beck stopped at the mouth of the driveway that ran along the side of the house. "Looks like nobody's home," he said, seeing no vehicle there.

"Maybe," Gina said. "There's only one way to find out."

She opened the door and hopped down onto the pavement, then

followed the driveway to the side door. She knocked softly on the rectangular glass window, then waited. Ten seconds later she knocked again. Nothing. No shuffling feet scraping the floor. No barking dog. No parting of the curtain behind the window. She was about to knock again when she heard someone call to her from the next yard.

"Honey, if you're looking for Connie, she's not home."

Gina spun around and saw an older woman standing behind a rose hedge that was loaded with deep burgundy blooms. She was dressed in work clothes and a gardener's apron. In one of her gloved hands was a pair of pruning shears.

"Do you know when she'll be back?" Gina asked.

"Yup," the woman snapped. "Just as we're sitting down to dinner. How I know is 'cause when she pulls into the driveway, Pepper pitches a fit."

"Pepper?" Gina asked. *Please tell me that's not your husband.*

"Pepper's my little baby," the woman gushed.

Gina's eyes went wide. "You named your child *Pepper?*"

"No, honey, Pepper is a Papillon."

"A what?" Gina asked.

"A toy spaniel."

"Oh, yes, of course," Gina said. *Next time just say dog.*

"The best time to catch Connie is in the morning," the woman said. "She doesn't leave for work until about 10 o'clock…sometimes later." She snipped a dead bloom off the hedge and muttered, "How that woman makes a living is beyond me."

"Okay, well, thank you," Gina said. "And by the way, your roses are spectacular."

"Thank you. If you want 'em to look this good, you gotta give 'em plenty of water. Anyone tells you otherwise should grow something else, like a brain!"

Gina gave her a short wave…*good to know*…then ran back down the driveway and climbed up into the truck. "The neighbor said she doesn't get home until dinnertime, but she'll be here tomorrow morning."

Nathan was now sitting up in the seat, his face pressed to the window, surveying the front of the property: the louvered shutters, lipstick red; the grapevine wreath hanging on the front door, interlaced with a plastic strand of bright yellow forsythia; the hand-painted mailbox with, appropriately, an artist's rendering of a white picket fence with pink roses spilling over the top.

"Looks like an elf's cottage if you ask me," said Beck.

"Yeah," Nathan mumbled. "The perfect cover for a killer in hiding."

After Beck dropped them off at home, Nathan went straight to the garage. The emotional events of the day were weighing on his every thought like a 20-ton cruise ship anchor, and he needed to work it off.

Lift something.

Hit something.

In keeping with his regular routine, he started with the jump rope.

One hundred jumps. Pause. Count to 10. Then, 100 more.

Next, it was the hand weights.

Right hand: 20 reps, deep breath…20 reps, deep breath…20 reps, deep breath.

Left hand: 20 reps, deep breath…20 reps, deep breath…20 reps, deep breath.

Last up: the heavy bag.

He didn't time it, or count his punches. He just slammed his fists into the bag, over and over until he lacked the strength to lift his arms. With each punch, he envisioned the killer's face. And despite the fact that he'd only spoken to four of the five facilitators, he'd already figured out who betrayed his grandfather. Now he just needed to prove it.

How to do it wasn't an issue; he'd already formulated the perfect scheme. What he needed was someone who could help make it happen.

An expert by trade.

And for that, only one person came to mind.

13

Guilt

Thursday, 9:30 a.m.
Lila Road
Jamaica Plain, MA

Beck pulled into Connie Freeman's driveway and came to a stop behind a white Subaru wagon parked next to the side door. The decal on the back window advertised the business she ran out of her home.

Home Sweet Home

SPOTLESS CLEANING SERVICES
www.BeautifulHome.com
1-800-GET-TIDY

They piled out of the truck, and as Nathan walked past the car he looked in the back and saw an assortment of cleaning supplies and paper goods housed in series of low plastic tubs.

From the house next door came the muffled sound of a barking dog.

"Oh, Pepper, you poor tormented soul," Gina said.

"Who are you talking to?" Nathan asked.

"I'll tell you later."

He stepped up to the door, inspected the rectangular window briefly, then balled up his fist and knocked on the wood partition right below it.

Pepper barked louder.

A shadow fell across the curtain that covered the window, and seconds later the door opened and there stood Connie Freeman, dressed in a thick pink terrycloth bathrobe. Her hair was unbrushed and ragged, like she'd been dusting the furniture with it, and her eyes had yet to decide if they were going to open for the day.

"Yes? How can I help you?" she asked, groggy.

"Connie Freeman?" Nathan asked.

"Yes, that's me. And you are…?"

"Nathan Cole. These are my friends, Gina McDermott and Beck."

"Beck who?" Connie rasped, squinting as she peered through the doorway at his monstrous frame.

"Just Beck, ma'am," he said.

"Okay just Beck, what can I…? Wait a minute," she said. Her eyes opened another fraction of an inch. "Did you say Nathan *Cole?*"

"That's right," Nathan said. "You worked with my grandfather,

Henry Hammond. You were the one responsible for—"

"NATHAN?" she exclaimed, finding her voice.

Pepper started in again with the frantic barking. Gina pictured him standing at the window, springing up and down like a cartoon dog. *Oooh, oooh, can I come too? Can I? Can I?*

Connie motioned all three of them inside. Nathan had just stepped through the doorway, into a spotless mud room, when she smothered him with a bear hug. "You're safe!" she said. "All this time, I've been so worried."

It took some doing, but he wrenched himself free and said, "Worried about me? Why?"

She held up her index finger...*hold that thought*...then stepped around Beck, which was like circling an ancient Greek statue, and pushed the door shut. "Follow me," she said.

She led them through an open doorway, into a long narrow kitchen that ran along the back wall of the house. At the far end was a square table with a bleached maple top and white legs. "Please, sit," she said, gesturing at the chairs that were neatly pushed in on each side.

The morning fog that previously embraced her had lifted, and once they were seated she clapped her hands together and said, "Okay, who would like something to drink? Water? Juice? Coffee?"

"Nothing for me, thanks," Gina said.

"I'm all set," Nathan added.

"Coffee sounds good," Beck told her.

"Coffee it is," she said. "But first, if you'll excuse me..."

She exited the room, leaving them sitting at the table in silence, their eyes wandering around the room. Moments later she reappeared a new woman, hair brushed, wearing a flowery tee shirt and blue jeans. "Okay, *now* I'm ready for the day. You said coffee, is that right Mr. Beck?"

"Just Beck," he said.

"Oh, excuse me," Connie said, embarrassed. "Just, Beck. I won't make that mistake again." She went to the counter and turned on a Mr. Coffee machine that looked like she'd taken it out of the box that morning. "Nathan, before I answer your question," she said, "I need to know if we can speak freely, in front of your friends, that is." She opened a drawer beneath the counter and pulled out a paper coffee filter.

"Yes," Nathan replied. "Gina and Beck are as good as family. Whatever you have to say to me, you can say to them."

"Very well," Connie said. She pressed the filter into the removable filter basket and then went to the refrigerator for the coffee. "After Kendra called me, requesting provisions for two at Stackyard Road, I immediately began to worry about you." She peered into the refrigerator briefly, then grabbed a large can of Maxwell House coffee from the top shelf.

"I'm confused," Nathan said. "How did you link me with Kendra's call?"

"You don't remember?" Connie asked as she walked back to the coffee machine.

"Remember what?"

"Her call? I just assumed you were with her at the time." She peeled the lid off the can and began scooping ground coffee into the filter.

"I was," Nathan confirmed.

"As part of her request, she asked for a set of clothes for a 12-year-old boy."

"And you assumed that boy was me?"

"Yes, which made me wonder what had happened that would require Kendra to hide you in a safehouse of all places."

"Hold on," Nathan said. "Why would you assume I was the one she was with?"

"Oh, I hear things," she said, in a dreamy voice. "But let's not get bogged down in the past. You're here. You're alive and well. And I must say, you've grown into quite the young man since I last saw you."

Since you last saw me? he thought. *When was that?*

She snapped the lid back on the coffee can and then added water to the reservoir, using a large glass measuring cup from the drying rack next to the sink.

"The coffee will take just a minute," she said to Beck as she padded back to the refrigerator. "In the meantime, can I get anyone something to eat?" She slid the coffee back on the top shelf and then took a quick inventory of the items in the fridge. "Let's see…I've got fruit, bagels, yogurt. Ooh, how about some cinnamon rolls?"

Back at the counter, the coffee machine began to gurgle. Slow at first, then faster and louder.

"No thanks," Nathan and Gina said in unison.

"You be sure to let me know if you change your mind," Connie said. She closed the refrigerator and took a seat at the table. "Well then," she said. "To what do I owe this unexpected visit?"

Sticking to the plan they'd discussed on the ride over, Nathan spoke first.

"Perseus."

At the mention of the word, Connie flinched as if touched by a live electric wire. Then, slowly, her eyes narrowed, and she looked across the table at him. When she spoke, her words were slow and menacing. "I don't know where you came across that word, but I suggest that you never utter it again."

She stood, unsteadily, and hobbled over to the counter. The coffee maker was gurgling madly now as it neared the end of the brewing cycle. She leaned on the counter with both hands, bracing herself for how Nathan would respond to what she was about to say. "Tell me what you know. Leave nothing out."

"I know everything," he said. "You were part of a group my grandfather called 'facilitators'. Your job was to keep the safehouses stocked and cleaned. I also know about Lía Ballard, the notebook she gave my grandfather, the meeting at the bookstore, and the poison that was found in my grandfather's water bottle."

At the word 'poison,' her body buckled. With surprising speed for a man his size, Beck launched himself out of the chair and grabbed her as she was falling to the floor.

"I'm all right," she said, pushing his hands away. She stood on her own and shuffled back over to the table, clutching the edge of it as she lowered herself onto the chair.

"Are you alright?" Gina asked. "Would you like me to get you a glass of water?"

"No, that won't be necessary," Connie replied, "but thank you." She closed her eyes and took in a slow, deep breath, then spoke with heartfelt conviction. "Lía Ballard? The notebook? The poison? Those are things I believe you *should* know. After all, Henry Hammond was your grandfather, not to mention, a great, great man…"

"But," Nathan said, sensing she wasn't done.

"There's something you *don't* know."

Priya was sitting in her gray Honda Civic, parked on Louders Lane, directly across the street from Lila Road. From where she was situated, she had an unobstructed view of Connie Freeman's house, although she hadn't yet run the house number so she had no idea who lived there. What she did know was that Nathan, and the girl she assumed was his best friend, since they were always together, had once again been picked up by "Gargantuan Man," as she was calling Beck, shortly before 9 o'clock that morning. From there, they'd driven to Jamaica Plain, to this funny little house that looked like it belonged on the set of The Wizard of Oz. All that was missing was an army of oh-so-jolly Munchkins, singing and dancing on a curly ribbon of yellow bricks.

She'd been watching the house for 30 minutes when her cell phone beeped. She checked the call screen, then tapped the talk button with her thumb and held the phone to her ear.

"You were thinking of me, weren't you?" she said. "Come on, admit it."

"When am I *not* thinking of you?" Asher replied.

And the game continued.

"Touché," she said. "What's up?"

"Just wondering how it's going."

"Well, I'll say this: for a 12-year-old kid, Nathan Cole sure does get around."

"Oh?"

"Yesterday morning he was in Saugus. By lunchtime he was in Newton. In the afternoon he was in Jamaica Plain, which is where he is now."

"Huh," Asher said. "Do you think those locations are related somehow?"

"You tell me. In Saugus he visited a car dealership. In Newton, a law firm. Here in Jamaica Plain he's at a personal residence that's crying out for a clip-clip here and a clip-clip there."

"Did you just make a Wizard of Oz reference?"

"Bravo," Priya said. "I wasn't sure you'd get that."

"Surveillance is definitely wearing on you," Asher quipped. "Keep at it and let me know if you see or hear anything suspicious, okay?"

"Actually, now that you mention it, I did hear something peculiar yesterday. The kid said it as they were leaving the law firm. Lágrimas de la Emperadora. Does that mean anything to you?"

"Say it again? Lágrimas…*what?*"

"Lágrimas-de-la-Emperadora," Priya said slowly.

"Lágrimas de la Emperadora," Asher repeated. "Are you sure that's what he said?"

"Positive."

"Okay, I'll look into it and see what I can find out."

"You do that," Priya said. "And remember, all you have to do is… follow the—"

"*Don't* say it!" Asher blurted out, before she could finish.

"Aw, you're no fun."

"Good-*bye* Priya."

Nathan sat forward, resting both arms on the tabletop, hands clasped together. "What don't I know?" he asked.

"That day, when Lía Ballard came to the bookstore?" Connie began. "Your grandfather contacted us and asked us to meet him there after he closed for the day."

"Yes, I'm aware of that," Nathan said. "He called the five of you together to discuss how you were going to protect her."

"That's right. In that meeting we were each given a task, which included finding her a safehouse..."

"Sidney's job," Nathan interjected.

"Correct. Obviously, the safehouse in question needed to be *stocked* with food and other supplies..."

"Your job."

"Yes. Then, someone had to *drive* her there..."

"Pennyman."

"Right again. But it didn't end there. Your grandfather was intent on catching the men who were pursuing her, and delivering them to the police. To do that, he needed proof of their aggressive actions against Lía, along with any threats they may have made."

"Wroth," Nathan said.

Connie nodded. "He and your grandfather discussed setting a trap for them. First, they'd lure them in. Then, Wroth would record everything they said. Once that was done, a legal case could be developed..."

"Fane."

"You appear to be very well informed," Connie said. "But what you don't know is this: once the tasks were assigned, your grandfather showed us the field notebook that Lía had given him. He recounted what she had told him about the cryptic code hidden on one of its pages, and how that code divulged the whereabouts of an ancient necklace her father had discovered—"

"During a dig in South America," Nathan said, cutting her off. "Yes, I know all of this."

Gina glared at him. "Will you let her *finish?*"

"Sorry," Nathan said. "Go on."

"When he was done, your grandfather put the notebook in his desk for safekeeping. We were leaving the bookstore when I realized I'd left my jacket in his office. When I went back to get it, one of the group members was there, standing at his desk, paging through a book your grandfather had set aside for a customer."

Nathan's heart began to race.

"At the time, I thought nothing of it. I just grabbed my jacket and left. But the next day, after I learned that your grandfather had died from a poison they found in the water bottle he kept on his desk, I knew who was responsible."

"The person you saw in the office," Gina said.

"Yes, it had to be. At no other time before, during, or after the meeting was anyone else alone there."

"And even though you knew this, you've never shared it with the police," Nathan said, anger simmering in his tone.

"You're no dummy, Nathan," Connie said. "I'm sure you know why that information couldn't be 'shared,' as you so politely put it. Certainly not with the police, or with anyone else for that matter."

"Yeah," Nathan said, disgusted. Protecting the network his grandfather had established, safeguarding each of the people he had helped, and most of all, fear of retribution from the killer, were all logical reasons to say nothing. Still, just thinking about them was enough to send him into a blind fury.

"Anyway," Connie said, continuing. "The image of that person standing at his desk has haunted me to this very day."

"That person…" Nathan said.

"Pennyman," Connie said.

Nathan ground his teeth together. *Frank Sobol, I knew it!* he thought, closing each fist into a tight ball.

Connie saw his reaction and said, "I know that information is troubling…"

"No, I'm fine," Nathan assured her, his thoughts already shifting to what needed to be done next.

"Nonetheless," she said, "for your own safety, and for the safety of you, Gina, and you, Beck, I insist that you take no action. Let this go. And whatever you do, *never* say the word Perseus to anyone ever again. You could be opening yourself up to unimaginable danger at the hands of a cold-blooded killer."

"You mean Frank Sobol…or Pennyman…" Nathan said.

"Most certainly him, yes. But who's to say he hasn't recruited others? After all, he's got the notebook. You think he's not searching for the necklace?"

"I'm sure he is," Nathan said. *And failing miserably.* "So I guess we'll just have to be careful," he mumbled under his breath.

"What was that?" Connie asked.

"Nothing," Nathan replied. He stood and pushed in the chair. "Getting late," he said, eyeing the clock on the near wall. "We should go."

Priya was growing bored. She desperately needed to get out of the car and walk. A block and back would do wonders for her circulation, but professional protocol demanded that she stay out of sight. She was twiddling her fingers on the armrest when she saw Beck's truck back out of Connie's driveway. "Finally!" she said. She watched as the truck drove away, then started her car and followed after it. At the end of the street she paused long enough to allow Beck to get a sizeable head start. Then she pulled out and shadowed his every turn.

"I knew it was Sobol," Nathan growled, as Beck cruised down Westchester Road, bound for Centre Street.

"So, what now?" Gina asked.

"We need to pay Donald Brandt another visit," Nathan said. "I have a job for him."

"Oh really," Beck said. "You think he'll talk to you?"

"I know he'll talk to me."

"How's that?" asked Beck.

"Perseus."

"Seems logical," Beck said. "It worked with Julie Nichols and Connie Freeman, but logic can be a fickle friend."

"What's the job?" Gina asked.

"It's genius, if I do say so myself," Nathan said.

"Am I going to approve?"

"Uh-huh."

Then he told them.

"Wow," Gina said, after he finished. "You thought that up all by yourself?"

"Yup."

"I think it's good," said Beck. "In fact, I think it's very good. Do you have a backup plan, in case he refuses?"

"He won't," Nathan said. "I mean, he can *try*, but I've got something that's sure to change his mind."

Donald Brandt was in the back room, nose-deep in an old Harman Kardon tube amplifier, when he heard the ring of the shopkeeper's bell, alerting him that someone had entered the shop. "Be right there!" he shouted, his voice carrying through the arched doorway that connected his workshop to the sales floor.

Beck, Nathan and Gina walked up to the sales counter that ran along the back wall. It was pasty yellow Formica, made to look like strips of laminated hardwood, set atop a wooden frame sheathed in mud-brown peg board.

After nearly a minute, Brandt pulled his hands from the amplifier. "Sorry for the wait," he said as he stepped through the arched doorway. "Some of these old amplifiers can be…oh for crying out loud, not you again," he said, when he saw Nathan standing at the counter. Next to him was a girl he didn't recognize, and towering over the two of them was the Paul Bunyan guy.

"Yup, me again," Nathan replied, upbeat. "We didn't have a chance to talk last time, so I thought we'd come back and give it another try."

"Listen," Brandt said, sounding like a guy who was having a real bad day, "I don't know who that guy is, the one you were talking about. Hammer? Hammel?"

"Perseus," Nathan said.

Brandt blinked hard, stunned, like he'd just gotten sprayed in the face with vinegar. He stared at Nathan for a full five-count, his mind spinning. "Who are you?" he asked, confusion and fear clouding his eyes.

"I told you who I am the last time I was here," Nathan said, bothered that Brandt couldn't remember a simple name. "My name is Nathan Cole. These are my friends, Gina and Beck."

Beck, Bunyan…I was close, Brandt thought.

"Like I told you before," Nathan said. "I know you helped my grandfather. What's more, I know you gathered digital and video information for him, designed to prove the innocence of the people he was helping."

"Guilt," Brandt mumbled.

"Excuse me?"

"Guilt," Brandt repeated. "Most of the time the information I provided was used to prove someone's *guilt*, not their innocence."

"I'm glad to hear that," Nathan said. "Because you're going to help us do just that."

"What are you talking about?" Brandt asked. He looked past the three of them, nervously watching the front window as if expecting to see someone appear there at any moment.

"You're going to use your infinite knowledge of electronics to help us prove someone's guilt," Beck said. His tone indicated there would be no negotiation on the matter.

"And who might that be?" Brandt asked.

"The person who poisoned my grandfather," Nathan said.

"Well, I can't help you there," Brandt said.

"Why is that?"

"Because no one knows who did it."

227

"You're wrong," Nathan said. "It was Pennyman. Or are the two of you on a first name basis now?"

"Hey, look," Brandt said, pushing both palms at him. "I had nothing to do with what happened."

"*We* know that," Nathan said. "But the police don't."

At the word 'police,' a look of dread washed over Brandt's face.

Nathan saw the fear in his eyes and said, "If you want to prove to them that you didn't spike my grandfather's water with poison, then help us nail Sobol."

"I can't believe it," Brandt said, dazed. "Sobol did it?"

"Yes," Nathan said. "And we're going to prove it."

"I don't know," Brandt said, nibbling his lower lip. "What if he finds out I'm helping you? What then? I'll tell you what then—I'm gonna end up dead just like your grandfather!"

"All the more reason to help us," Nathan explained. "You get us what we need, and we'll make sure Sobol never comes after you. It's as simple as that. Do we have a deal?"

It wasn't like Brandt had a choice. If he refused, Nathan would simply shift to Plan B: twist what Connie Freeman told them and name Brandt as the one standing alone at Henry Hammond's desk that night. Once he told Brandt there was an eyewitness, how could he say no?

"I think I'm gonna be sick," Brandt muttered. He leaned on the counter, wobbly, looking like his arm might give out at any moment and send him crashing to the floor. "All this time," he said weakly, "we had no idea who poisoned your grandfather. Each of us feared we'd be next."

"Why would you be next?" Gina asked, speaking for the first

228

time.

Brandt looked at her like she was daft. "Why? Because he's a ruthless killer, that's why!"

"Donald, you need to calm down," Nathan said. "My grandfather was killed seven years ago. If Sobol was going to come after you, don't you think he would've done it by now?"

"What kind of question is that?" Brandt fired back. "We have no idea how the man thinks, or if he thinks at all. He could be driven by sheer madness. To just snuff out your grandfather's life the way he did? What compels a person to do something like that?" He lowered his head and closed his eyes as if reciting a silent prayer. If only that would work. "I just want this whole nightmare to go away," he said. "Forever."

"Me too," Nathan said. "So here's what you're going to do."

14

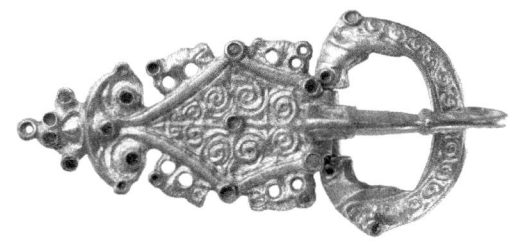

Zee

C amped out in his basement office, it took Asher Rickman less than an hour to learn everything about "Lágrimas de la Emperadora." It actually amazed him how easy it was. There was an abundance of information on the internet from The National Geographic Society, PBS, The History Channel, as well as countless links to Mayan experts worldwide. One in particular directed him to a Mayan archeologist from the Institute of Archaeology at the University College London. That one was especially insightful.

But the thing that made him lean in, heart racing, was an editorial dated seven years earlier, in *Prensa Libre*, Guatemala's newspaper of record. According to the story, Walter Ballard, an archeologist from Harvard University, had unearthed a gold necklace gifted to Lady Six Sky, the Maya queen who ruled Naranjo beginning in the year 682. While there was no official documentation of the discovery, at least two workers at the sight claim to have seen Ballard pull the necklace from the hooked fingers of Lady Six Sky's skeletal hand.

Asher tried relentlessly, and failed, to find one shred of information about the current whereabouts of the necklace. At first, he assumed Ballard still had it. But the *ladrón de tumbas*, or grave robber, as the two witnesses were calling him, had died a month after returning to the United States. That was seven years ago. So what happened to the necklace?

With an estimated value that ran into the millions, not to mention the additional premium at least three of his preferred customers would pay to possess such a rare treasure, Asher moved "Lágrimas de la Emperadora" to the top of his acquisitions list.

Next, he turned his attention to Nathan Cole. Why would a 12-year-old boy utter the name of an ancient Mayan necklace? *Is he looking for it?* Asher wondered. *Why would he do that? Did someone put him up to it? Who would use a child to locate a piece of jewelry worth millions?* It made no sense. On the other hand, if Cole's whirlwind tour of suburban Boston was somehow tied to the necklace, that meant he wasn't hunting *him*, the person whose looks he shared, which put Asher in the clear.

Still, the necklace called to him. He had to have it. And not just for the riches it would earn him—it was the story behind it.

Buried in the ground for over a thousand years.

Unearthed by a Harvard archeologist.

Only to have it vanish after his death.

It was just too good to pass up, and just like each of the other items on his acquisitions list, he was prepared to take whatever steps necessary to acquire it.

At 12:30 p.m., Campbell and D-Mack were at their storage unit just off of Rt. 1 in Malden, preparing what they'd need to "capture the swan," as they were calling the following day's grab-and-go job.

"You haven't said much about last night," D-Mack said, smirking. He was referring to Campbell's date the night before with his on-again, off-again, girlfriend. Six months earlier, she'd taken a bookkeeping job with the courier who would be delivering Damien Grün's artwork to the party.

"What's to tell?" Campbell replied. "We met for dinner. We talked. We left."

"But during dinner you got her to reveal the departure time of the truck and the route they'll be taking."

"Among other things," Campbell said.

"And just how did you manage that?"

Before Campbell could respond, his cell phone rang. He checked to see who was calling, then tossed the black duffel bag he was holding in the back of the van and took the call.

"This is Campbell," he said.

"Are we on track for tomorrow?" Asher said.

"We are," Campbell answered. "I was going to call and thank you for that information about the courier. We have the route and the time the artwork will be delivered. By this time tomorrow, I'll have the item in question for you."

"Excellent," Asher said. "When you deliver it, there's another job we need to discuss. I'm not sure of the timing, due to the nature of the item, but we can discuss that when we meet."

"The nature of the item?" Campbell asked.

"It's a very unusual piece," Asher said. "I can't say for sure when it'll be ready for pick up."

"I see," said Campbell. "Just say the word. We'll be ready to go, whenever."

"Nothing could make me happier," Asher quipped. "And when you see the item in question, you'll understand why I want it."

"Now you've got me curious."

"I'll explain everything tomorrow," Asher said. "In the meantime, good luck with the other thing." He clicked off the call and did a quick assessment of the manpower he'd need to acquire the necklace. If Nathan Cole was, in fact, searching for the priceless Mayan artifact, Priya's continued surveillance would be essential in tracking his exact whereabouts. Should he find it, that's where her participation would end. Enter Campbell and D-Mack.

Giddy at the prospect of acquiring the necklace, a crowning achievement that would stand well above all his previous acquisitions, he dialed Priya, who picked up on the first ring.

"You just love the sound of my voice, don't you?" she said.

"How could I not? It's…angelic."

"Oh, come on, you can do better than that," she said, returning the tease. Then she turned serious. "Something must be up," she said. "We spoke, what, an hour ago?"

"I need to amend our initial arrangement," he said. "Actually, *extend* would be a better word."

"Sounds ominous. What are you having me do now?" she asked.

"More of the same. Keep up the surveillance and report back to me immediately if you see or hear anything suspicious."

"Define suspicious."

"I can't go into specifics over the phone. Suffice to say that the target is searching for a certain item. Should he find it, I need to know immediately."

"This 'something'," Priya said. "Is it related to our previous conversation?"

"Yes."

"You researched the name I gave you?"

"I did," Asher replied. "By the way, where are you?"

"Believe it or not, I'm sitting in a bank parking lot across from a stereo repair shop in Woburn."

"Is that where—?"

"Yes," she said before he could finish. "Don't ask me why."

"So, let me get this straight," he said. "In the past 24 hours, or thereabouts, he's been to an auto dealership, a law office, a personal residence, and now a stereo repair shop?"

"That's correct."

"It makes no sense to me," Asher said, "but we need to keep watching him. Sooner or later something is going to happen. And when it does, we need to be there."

"We will be," Priya said. "I guarantee it."

Brandt listened quietly while Nathan explained what he needed him to do. By the time he finished, Brandt's mind was already hard at work, plotting. "I know how we can do this," he said. "It'll take me no more than an hour to gather the equipment and test it. I'm guessing you want to do this right away?"

"As soon as humanly possible," Nathan said. Payback was long overdue. "If we need to, how should we communicate with you?" he asked.

"Cell phone is fine. But if you call, make sure to use that word."

"Perseus?"

"Yes. That way, I'll know it's really you."

"Just like with my grandfather."

"Right." He took a business card from beneath the counter and handed it to Nathan. "My number is on this card."

"Okay, good," Nathan said. "You'll let me know when everything is in place?"

"I'll have the tracker up and running by midnight."

"Perfect," Nathan said. He checked his watch, then said to Beck, "We need to get moving. I want to be at work by one o'clock."

"And we need to eat lunch," Gina reminded them.

"Do you like roast beef?" asked Beck.

"I love roast beef."

"Good. There's a great place not too far from here. It's right on the way."

Less than 10 minutes later, Beck pulled into Bill & Bob's Roast Beef on Main Street and fell in behind the string of cars waiting in the drive-through lane.

"Bill & Bob's?" Nathan said, in a skeptical voice. *This is the great place?* He stared at the letters on the sign, the bold slab-serif font eliciting memories of the building blocks he'd had as a child.

"Home of the three-way roast beef sandwich," Beck announced. "It's a classic."

They were on a tight schedule and there was no time to fuss over menu choices. "Okay, I'll take one of those," Nathan said. "Gina?"

"Same."

He pulled a brushed-chrome money clip from his pocket and removed three crisp $10 bills. "This should cover it," he said, handing them to Beck.

Twenty minutes later they were back on the road, the car heavy with the smell of roast beef sandwiches and onion rings.

Beck had one hand on the steering wheel. In his other hand was possibly the biggest cup of soda Nathan had ever seen. "So, explain this to me again," Beck said. "Brandt puts a GPS tracker on Sobol's car, which allows him to track Frank's every move…"

"Correct," Nathan said. "Which in turn lets *us* track Frank as he leads us straight to Walter Ballard's notebook."

"And why will he do that?" Gina asked.

"Because we're going to force his hand."

"You said something about that after we left Connie Freeman's house," Beck said. "What did you mean?"

"It's simple," Nathan said, as he crumpled up his sandwich wrapper and tossed it in the to-go bag. "We know Frank stole Ballard's field notebook from my grandfather's desk. The question is: where did he hide it? The man would be stupid to keep it at his house because it ties him to the tainted water bottle."

"Well," Beck said, uneasily. "Any lawyer worth his salt will tear that assumption to shreds. Don't get me wrong; I think you're right. Having the notebook in his possession gets him a lifetime stay in a federal prison. It proves he was in the back room, at your grandfather's desk, the night of the meeting."

"After my grandfather showed everyone the notebook."

"Doesn't that prove he had added incentive to steal it?" Gina asked.

"Yes," Beck said. "It's called intent."

"All the more reason to find out where he hid it," Nathan said. "And to do that, we're going to *make* him take us there."

"That's what you meant by 'force his hand'?"

"Yes. We let him know that I'm trying to find the notebook. Better yet, we let it slip that I've already located it. When he hears that, he'll jump in his car and go get it before I have a chance to grab it."

"I like it," Beck said. "But I see one potential problem. Sobol is sure to question why you, Nathan Cole of all people, are interested in the notebook. It's not like a 12-year-old kid gives a hoot about an ancient gold necklace."

"A hoot?" Gina asked.

"It's an expression," said Beck.

"I don't have to give him a reason," Nathan insisted. "If he's been searching the internet, like Gina said, trying to find information about me, he's going to come across the courthouse story and how we discovered Alastair Raven's secret chambers. The way the media blew it up? How could he miss it?"

"What you're saying is, if he knows you're capable of *that*..." Beck began.

"Then he'll have no doubt that I can find the notebook."

"You mean, we," said Gina.

"Yes, of course."

"Let's back up a second," Beck said. "You said we'll let him know that you're trying to find the notebook. How exactly do you plan on doing that?"

Nathan twisted around in the seat and looked at Gina. "Do you have the phone number for the Auto Barn?"

"What do you think?" she said. *This is me, remember?*

"Do me a favor and call the dealership. Find out what day Frank has off."

"Okay. Then what?"

"Then, I go in, on his day off, and talk to Chelsea."

"Oh, great! Good old cheery Chelsea," Gina droned. "Try saying *that* three times fast. Cheery Chelsea, Cheery Chelsea, Cheery Chelsea."

Nathan gave her a look. *Are you done?*

Gina made a face, then looked out the side window, dreading the prospect of having to talk to the phony baloney, over-caffeinated receptionist again.

"All right, so you go in and you talk to Chelsea," Beck said. "What are you going to say?"

"I'll go up the counter, nice as can be, and ask if she could give Frank a message. It'll be something like: I'm very sorry about the way I acted the other day; I've been super busy tracking down a notebook someone stole from my grandfather's office. It belonged to a famous archeologist and I've been working day and night trying to find it. The good news is, I figured out where it is and I just have to go get it."

Beck began to chuckle. "When Sobol gets that message, his head is going to *explode!*"

"Right?" Nathan said. "He'll be in his car, and out of the parking lot before you can say Cheery Chelsea, Cheery Chelsea, Cheery Chelsea."

They got to Richard Abbott's barn with 10 minutes to spare. After Beck and Gina left, Nathan got right to work sorting the next pallet of books. He had just finished the first box when Richard came strolling into the barn.

"Nathan, there's someone I'd like you to meet," he said excitedly.

Nathan set down the two books he was holding and turned around. Standing next to Richard was a man most people would call a "beanpole." He was just over six feet tall with a frame that showed no discernible shape. No bulging arm muscles. No beer belly. He looked like a wooden tongue depressor with arms and legs. His wheat-colored hair was tied back in a ponytail that fell below the neckline of his mustard-yellow tee shirt. Silkscreened on the front was the face of reggae legend Bob Marley, along with the words "One Love."

"This young man is going to rid us of our rather unsightly pile of cardboard," Richard said. "Zee, this is my able-bodied assistant Nathan Cole. Nathan, this is Zee."

"Hey, dude," Zee said, raising his hand in the air for a high five.

Really? We're going to do this? Nathan thought. He reached up, reluctantly, and gave Zee's hand it a slap. "Hey."

"Zee works for a company that recycles cardboard," Richard explained. "You can imagine my elation when he contacted me. As I told him on the phone, we have a rather *abundant* collection of cardboard. I fear that once he sees it, he may leave and never return."

"No worries, man," Zee said, waving off the notion.

"I'll leave that evaluation up to your professional scrutiny," Richard said. "Right now, I'm off to a meeting with a potential client, an appointment we've already postponed twice." He faced Zee and said, "It was a pleasure to meet you in person. I leave you to your daunting task."

He offered his trademark nod, and then made a hasty exit.

"Your name is really Zee?" Nathan asked, breaking the momentary silence.

"It's short for Zeppelin."

Nathan looked at him, astonished. "Your parents named you after a *blimp?*"

"You're thinking of the German airship."

That's even worse! Nathan thought.

"My folks were big into music," Zee explained. "They named me Zeppelin, after the band. Pretty cool, right?"

"The band?" Nathan said.

"Led Zeppelin? You know, Robert Plant? Jimmy Page? John Bonham? John Paul Jones?"

"Oh, right," Nathan said slowly. *Never heard of them.*

Zee looked up, admiring the barn's hand-hewn rafters, and the original post and beam construction. "Man, this place is cool," he said. "I love old stuff. Don't you?"

"Uh, yeah," Nathan said, following his gaze. "Old stuff is all right."

Zee's focus shifted to the farmer's table. "So, what's the deal here?" he asked, pointing to the double stack of books Nathan had positioned next to his clipboard.

"I call it rapid sorting," Nathan explained. "First, I read the titles." He picked up the top book from each pile and showed them to Zee. One was *The Rains Came*, by Louis Bromfield. The other was *A Tree Grows in Brooklyn*, by Betty Smith. "Then," he said, setting the books down, "I look for them on th:s this list of customer requests."

Zee watched as Nathan ran his finger down the first page, which took less than five seconds. When he reached the bottom, he turned to the next page and did it again.

He made it as far as the fourth page when he found the Bromfield title.

"Dude, you are, like, a *machine*," said Zee.

"Well, I don't know about that," Nathan said. "I've just been doing it for a while." He set *The Rains Came* on his 'keepers' stack and then continued searching for the Betty Smith title.

"No, seriously, man, it's impressive. Two books at once?"

"Well, it helps if you like books," Nathan said, scanning the remaining pages as he talked.

"*Like* books? Are you kidding?" Zee said. "I *love* books."

"Do you now?" Nathan said. *Imagine my surprise.*

"Oh, yeah," Zee said. "I just started reading this one book called *Point Blank*, by Catherine Coulter. It has this treasure-hunting FBI agent who's trying to find stolen Confederate gold that's hidden in a cave in western Virginia." He shook his head, amazed. "Seriously intense, man. Seriously. Intense."

"Yeah, it sounds pretty...wild," Nathan said, for lack of a better word.

"Do you like mysteries?" Zee asked.

Funny you should ask, Nathan thought. "As a matter of fact I do,"

241

he said, as he came to the bottom of the last page. He put *A Tree Grows in Brooklyn* in an open cardboard box to his left and moved on to the next two books. Once filled, the box would live with dozens like it atop pallets in the back of the barn, waiting to be sold to one of Richard's many bookstore contacts.

"How about lost treasure stories?" Zee asked.

"Lost treasure? Sure," Nathan said. *Got a whole bookcase of them in my attic.*

"I think, like, how cool would it be, right?" Zee said. "To be a treasure hunter? Reading old manuscripts for clues, or how about this: an old diary?"

"Yeah, that would be something," Nathan replied. He picked up his clipboard and flipped through the pages, checking to see how many more unfilled orders remained.

"I know," Zee said. "Instead of lost gold, you're trying to find a skeleton key that can open a chest full of precious gems? Or, even better, you find a secret code that leads you to a treasure left behind by an ancient civilization."

Nathan heard 'code' and stared straight ahead as thoughts of Walter Ballard's field notebook churning in his mind. They had the perfect plan to find it, but what if it didn't work? What if Sobol didn't take the bait. What then? The notebook was the only thing that would link him to the poison. Without it, they had nothing.

"Come on, man…admit it," Zee said, nudging Nathan's arm. "You'd love to do that."

"I'm sorry. Do what?" Nathan said, setting the bait question aside.

"Search for hidden treasures, man!"

"Oh, right," Nathan said, still a bit fuzzy. "Who wouldn't love that?"

"Dude, this is what I'm saying! Just think of all the lost treasures out there, just waiting to be found." He looked around the room, dreamy eyed. "There could be hidden treasure *right here*, in this old barn. Did you ever think of that?"

"Uh, no...can't say I have," Nathan said.

"Anyway," Zee said, letting the thought drift off to a remote corner of his imagination. "Where is this legendary pile of cardboard the boss man was talking about?"

"Pile?" Nathan said, smirking. "Oh, it's more than a pile."

The workspace at Wired Electronics was a cramped 8' x 8' room. Aside from the staggering collection of hand tools, measuring instruments, and power supplies that littered each of the counters, the most noticeable feature in the room was the rectangular metal shelving unit that occupied the middle of the floor. Commanding in its presence, Brandt had positioned it there for quick and easy access to the open shelves on each side, each one lined with plastic tubs.

After Nathan, Gina, and Beck left the shop, he removed one of the tubs, carried it over to the counter, and he dug through the tangle of wires and electronic components piled inside. Near the bottom he found what he was looking for: a small battery operated GPS tracker no bigger than a bar of soap. It was a standard "slap and track" device, designed to be hidden practically anywhere on a vehicle, providing real-time tracking capabilities by way of a small internal antenna. To help conserve the battery, it would 'sleep' when the vehicle wasn't moving, and 'wake up' once it sensed movement.

He returned the tub to the shelf and then replaced the batteries in the tracker. All that remained now was installing it, which he would do sometime after 11 o'clock that night. In a matter of days, if all went according to plan, he'd be able to sleep through the night again. He'd be able to come and go as he wished, free of the fear that, at any moment, the killer might suddenly appear and take his life. At long last the guilt he'd carried with him for years would melt away.

Zee left Richard Abbott's barn, drove a mile down the road, then pulled to the curb and texted Jordan.

call me

Jordan was working at her desk when her phone dinged, alerting her that she'd received a new text. The second she read it her heart raced and she sent a reply.

is something happening?

Zee was persistent.

call me

Jordan got up from the desk and closed her office door. She found his number and hit the call button, and by the time she sat back down again the call was already connecting. She heard it ring once, then Zee picked up.

"That was fast," he said.

She was too curious for idle chit chat. "What's going on?" she asked, "First contact complete," he told her, speaking like a communications officer aboard a futuristic starship cruising the furthest reaches of the galaxy. Just one of his many fantasies.

244

"Anything to report?" Jordan asked, assuming there was. Otherwise, why the urgent text?

"That dude definitely has somethin' cookin'."

"How can you tell?"

"I dropped a few key words like you suggested. He was totally affected."

"You mean, it affected him in an unusual way?"

"Yeah, that."

"Can you be more specific?"

"We were talking about lost treasure. You know...searching for it?"

"And...?"

"I said something about a book with a code that leads to ancient treasure and he just froze up. I'm talking, statue city, man. Something about the word 'code' and 'treasure' rocked his world. I mean, totally."

"Interesting," Jordan said. *Why would those two words cause a reaction like that? Unless...*

"This is good news," she told Zee. "How soon can you go back, without arousing suspicion?"

"Oh, I'm going back tomorrow. They've got, like, 20 or 30 loads of cardboard to get rid of. You should see it. It's wild."

Jordan recalled seeing the mountains of cardboard in the back of the barn. It was the reason she'd thought of Zee in the first place. "Here's what I want you to do," she said. "Take your time removing it. Tell Richard that your truck can only hold so much weight. Explain gross vehicle weight restrictions, even if you have to make them up. Keep the loads small. That way you can make multiple visits."

"Works for me," Zee replied, who was getting paid by the truck load.

"Good. Now there are two more key words I need you to drop the next time you talk to him."

15

Latitude and Longitude

Friday, 4:20 a.m.
School Street
Manchester-by-the-Sea, MA

C ampbell and D-Mack were in place by 4:00 a.m. For the plan they'd devised, they needed a very specific vehicle, one that would stand up to the rigors of the job. D-Mack came through with a jet-black Ford F-350 Super Duty pick up, purchased from an associate who owned a junkyard in Worcester. In the gloomy pre-dawn darkness, parked in a residential driveway across from the Essex Country Club, they were as good as invisible.

Campbell checked his watch. Based on the information he'd been able to pry from his on-again, off-again girlfriend, the small plane carrying Damien Grün's artwork for the party on Saturday would've landed at Beverley Regional Airport 20 minutes ago. Calculating the time it would take for the plane to taxi to the prearranged location on the tarmac and then offload the cargo into the courier's vehicle, Campbell knew with reasonable certainty that they'd see the shipment drive past them sometime in the next 5-10 minutes. The vehicle in question, he'd learned, was one of the company's standard fleet vans: a slate-gray Mercedes Sprinter.

He looked to his left. School Street was deserted and probably would stay that way for another hour, when the first commuters of the day left for work to avoid the flood of traffic that would eventually bring Rt. 128 to a mind-numbing standstill.

"So, what was their plan here?" D-Mack asked, baffled by the timing of the delivery. "Truck the artwork to the house in the wee hours of the morning to avoid getting caught in traffic? Look around. Do you see any traffic?"

"Traffic was the last thing they were worried about," said Campbell, keeping his eyes on the far end of School Street. "They were more concerned about people like you and me."

"That's laughable," D-Mack snorted. "I'm sorry, but Grün's work is nothing special. I don't care what anyone says. It's just not."

A pair of headlights appeared at the far end of the street.

"Here we go," Campbell said. *Right on time.* He started the truck and slipped it into neutral. To pull this off with the least amount of damage to the truck, or themselves, he needed to slow the Sprinter's speed down to at least 20 miles per hour. Slower would be even better. "That's it, buddy, keep coming," he said, watching the van approach.

The Sprinter was 50 feet away when Campbell turned on the

headlights, yanked the gearshift down one notch, and pulled out of the driveway. He went as far as the middle of the road and stopped. The Sprinter's tail lights flared and the driver came to a screeching stop 15 feet from the truck, painting the early dawn in an ethereal red glow.

Campbell immediately backed up into the driveway. *Sorry pal. My bad.*

Seeing that, the driver started forward again. As he passed by the driveway, he raised his hand in the air to shield his eyes from the intense glare of Campbell's headlights.

Campbell watched him pass, then stomped on the gas pedal and pulled out again, bringing the F-350 up along the right side of the Sprinter. He inched over until they were touching, then cut the wheel hard left and used all 13,000 pounds of the truck's weight to force the lighter van across the oncoming lane. It sailed over the shoulder and smashed into a three-foot stone wall, built by an early New England settler over 350 years earlier.

The collision catapulted the driver over the steering wheel and into the windshield. As he lay slumped over, dazed and bleeding, Campbell and D-Mack jumped out of the truck and opened the Sprinter's rear doors.

"Which one?" D-Mack asked, staring at the collection of wooden crates that lay scattered across the floor of the van, jarred loose by the collision.

"Who knows?" Campbell said. "Take it all."

By 9:15a.m., Nathan had finished the jump roping and hand weights portion of his daily workout routine and was directing his pent-up anger on the heavy bag with a flurry of right-left combinations. Why he ever questioned Beck's assertion that hitting it would produce beneficial results seemed ludicrous to him now. Punching the bag helped erase his anger. And there was no doubt that it was producing the results Beck had said it would. He was adding bulk, getting stronger, and his body was more toned than it had ever been.

He was punishing the heavy bag when the side door opened and Gina stepped inside. She saw his mushroom-gray sweatsuit, and the short towel draped around his neck, and exclaimed, "I don't believe it! Rocky Balboa! What are *you* doing here?"

Nathan paused and glanced over his shoulder. "Hey," he said, then continued pummeling the bag.

"You know, if you like, I can hum the theme song to *Rocky*," she said as she walked toward him.

He stopped punching, exhaled, then dropped his arms to his side. "No thanks," he said, out of breath, and too spent to fire back a clever response.

"I have news," she said.

"Oh?"

He pulled the towel from around his neck and buried his face in it.

"I called the Auto Barn," she said. "Frank Sobol has the morning off. He won't be in until just after lunchtime."

Nathan pulled the towel from his face. "I say we don't wait. Let's go there as soon as Beck shows up."

Just then, they heard the rumble of a truck chugging up the driveway.

"Speaking of Beck," Gina said.

250

Nathan peeled off the training gloves and set them atop the heavy bag. When he and Gina got outside, Beck's Dodge Ram was rolling to a stop in front of the garage door. He killed the engine and swung the door open, then grabbed two six-pound hand weights from the passenger seat. "Brought you something," he said, as he climbed down out of the truck.

Nathan walked toward him, eyeing the weights.

"Thought you might be ready for an upgrade," said Beck.

Nathan took one of the weights from him, twisted it one way, then the other, gauging the feel of it. "Got anything bigger?"

"How about you walk before you run?" Beck said, in the way of an answer.

"This is too light," Nathan said.

"Oh yeah? Prove it."

Nathan gave him a tired look, then took the other weight and grasped one in each hand. "Like this?" he asked, alternately flexing each arm.

Up. Down. Up. Down.

Up. Down. Up. Down.

"Or like this?" he asked, flexing both arms at the same time.

Up. Down. Up. Down.

Up. Down. Up. Down.

Beck said nothing, waiting for Nathan to tire.

He didn't.

"Check this out," he said. He held both weights in his right hand.

Up. Down. Up. Down.

Up. Down. Up. Down.

Then, he switched hands.

Up. Down. Up. Down.

Up. Down. Up. Down.

"All right, all right, you sold me," Beck said.

Nathan handed him the weights and then started walking toward the back door. "I have to change my clothes," he called over his shoulder. "I'll be right back."

"Make it quick," Gina shouted.

"Are we going somewhere?" asked Beck.

"The Auto Barn," she replied.

"Sobol's off today?"

"He comes in at noon."

Beck nodded his understanding, then went back to the truck and set the weights behind the driver's seat. Several minutes later, Nathan emerged from the house dressed in a clean tee shirt and blue jeans.

"You ready to do this?" Beck asked him after he'd gotten in the truck.

"Yup," Nathan said as he buckled his seat belt. "Today we're going to lure a killer out of hiding and pull him right into our trap."

Zee backed the 22-foot box truck up to the door of Richard Abbott's barn but didn't get out. The heavy wooden door was closed and the sun had already climbed halfway up the morning sky, threatening to send temperatures well into the mid 90s before lunchtime.

He checked his watch. "Geez, people, it's almost 10 o'clock. Where are you?"

As he sat in the air conditioned cab, debating whether to stay or leave, Richard came bustling out of the house and made a beeline for the barn door. As he passed the cab, he gave Zee an apologetic quick wave for making him wait.

Zee climbed out into the sweltering heat and walked to the back of the truck as Richard was rolling back the barn door. "My apologies," Richard said. "I never heard you pull in." He stepped back and wiped his brow with a cloth handkerchief.

"No worries, man," Zee replied. He flipped the locking mechanism on the truck's rolling back door and pushed it up, the echo of the one-inch rollers making the empty cargo area sound 10 times bigger than it actually was. "Where's Nathan?" he asked. "I figured he'd be here by now, hard at work. That system he has is crazy, man."

"Oh, he's become quite good at sorting books, I must say," Richard noted. He walked into the barn and flicked a switch on the wall, filling the space with a silky white light. "Truth be told," he said, "I don't know how I'd keep up with all my orders without him."

"He taking the day off today?" asked Zee.

"Not exactly. He called and said he had an important errand to run. Apparently, it came up at the last minute. The way he spoke, it sounded pretty important. He said he wasn't sure what time he'd be coming in, if at all."

Zee shrugged...*oh well*...then walked to the back of the barn to start removing cardboard. *Important errand that came up at the last minute?* he thought. *What could that possibly be?* He grabbed a handful of flattened boxes and carried them back out to the truck. After Richard went back in the house, he took out his phone and called Jordan.

"What's up?" she asked. Her head was tilted, pressing the phone against her shoulder as she rifled through a file cabinet in her office.

253

"Got a weird feeling," Zee said.

"A weird feeling," Jordan repeated, distracted, as she pulled out a file folder and began paging through its contents.

"Yeah, the bird has flown the proverbial coop," Zee said.

Jordan stopped what she was doing. "Bird? What are you talking about?"

"I'm at the barn," Zee said, knowing she'd understand what that meant. "The kid didn't come to work today. Told the boss man he had an important errand to run. Wasn't sure if or when he'd be coming to work."

"And you think that's suspicious?" Jordan said.

"Well, yeah. What 12-year-old has an all-day errand? If he had a dentist appointment or a birthday party, I'd understand. But this sounds like something else."

"Maybe he's helping his parents with something."

"No, he didn't say he was helping someone. He said *he* had an errand to run. I'm telling you, man, I have a sixth sense about this kind of stuff. People say I'm like a hound dog."

"Stuff like what?" Jordan asked, ignoring the hound dog reference.

"Things that don't smell right."

"I see. Well, thank you for letting me know," Jordan said. *I can't believe I'm about to say this,* she thought. "Get back to me if you catch another whiff."

Beck pulled up to the front of the Auto Barn showroom and parked in the exact same spot as before. "You want me to come in with you?" he asked.

"No, I won't be that long," Nathan replied. "But here's what I need you to do. If you see me scratch the side of my head, honk your horn."

Beck looked at him like it was a joke. "Honk my horn?"

"Yeah, one time, short."

"Short?"

"Yeah, you know, not *beeeeeep*...just *beep*."

"Just beep, got it."

"Now, if I scratch my head a *second* time, then you lay on the horn."

"Long beep?" Beck asked.

"Yes. Long beep."

"All right. If you say so."

Nathan got out of the truck and went into the showroom, walking slowly, shoulders hunched, like a kid who'd been summoned to the principal's office at school.

"You're back!" Chelsea exclaimed. She glanced past him, at Beck's truck idling just beyond the front window. "Is your dad coming in?" she asked, a little too excitedly.

"No. I asked him to wait outside," Nathan told her in a miserable tone. "I need to talk to Frank Sobol."

"Oh, Frank isn't here, hon," Chelsea said. "He's got the morning off. Perhaps you'd like to come back after lunch?"

Nathan gave her another sad look, like he just couldn't catch a break. "I can't," he said. "Would it be possible for me to leave him a message?"

"Well, of *course* you can," she said, like he was the saddest thing she'd ever seen. "Would you like a piece of paper and a pen?"

"No, that's okay," Nathan said, like he was ready to drop the whole thing. He reached up and scratched the side of his head, like he was trying to decide what to do.

Muffled by the thick plate glass, but still audible, came the blare of Beck's horn.

Nathan turned and extended both palms outward, beseeching him. *WHAT?*

Beck honked again.

Nathan made a calming motion. *All right, all right…calm down, already.*

"How about this?" Chelsea offered. "You give *me* the message and I'll make sure he gets it the second he arrives."

"You would do that?" Nathan asked, hope in his voice.

"I'd be happy to," she said. Her bubbly demeanor was gone now, replaced by a look of pity.

"Okay, well, I just wanted to tell him that I'm sorry for the way I acted on Wednesday. I've been going crazy trying to find something that was stolen from the desk in my grandfather's office. Actually, it belonged to a famous archeologist and I really want to find it. I know that doesn't excuses my behavior, but, the good news is," he said, relieved, "I figured out where it is. Now I just need to go get it." He scratched the side of his head a second time.

Beck honked again. Two times. Long beeps.

Nathan spun around and shouted, "I SAID, JUST WAIT!" He growled in frustration, for effect, then turned back to Chelsea. "Sorry about that."

"No apology needed, but I think you'd better go. Your dad seems very, uh, anxious." She stepped down from the counter, put her arm around his shoulder, and gently ushered him toward the door. "Now, I don't want you to worry one teentsy bit," she said. "I'll give Frank your message. You can count on it."

"Thank you," Nathan said, reassured. "I feel really bad about the way I acted. I hope he can forgive me."

"Oh, I'm sure he will."

He pushed the door open and paused. "You won't forget to tell him?"

"You have my word," she said.

Campbell sent Asher a coded text at 5 a.m., once he and D-mack arrived back at the storage unit in Malden.

your order has arrived

Asher had been awake since 4 a.m. working in his basement office and sent back an immediate reply.

USXI

Campbell knew the coded location, US, was an abbreviation for Union Station in Somerville. Specifically, the alley behind Warehouse XI, the brick mill turned trendy event space. He and Asher had met there on several occasions to transfer product, well away from the prying eyes of the general public.

At 10:55, he pulled his white van, still outfitted with the magnetic Bickford Electric signs, into the alley and spotted Asher's Audi A6 up ahead on the right, parked next to a large rolling door across from The Jungle music club. The driver's window was down and Asher's hand was resting on the side mirror.

D-Mack lowered his window as Campbell came to a stop alongside the car.

"How'd it go?" Asher inquired.

"They should all be so easy," D-Mack replied. The plan had worked to perfection, with minimal damage to the truck, which would get a new paint job in the coming days and be put into storage for future use.

D-Mack pushed the door open, taking great care not to clip the Audi, then slid open the side door of the van and took out a thin plywood box that measured approximately 30" x 36". By the time he reached the back of the Audi, Asher had already opened the trunk using the switch on the driver's door.

D-Mack carefully laid the box in the cargo space, closed the trunk, and climbed back in the van. "What about the rest of it?" he asked Campbell.

"Don't ask me, ask *him*," Campbell replied.

D-Mack leaned out the window and said, "What about the rest of it?"

"The rest of what?" Asher replied.

"The rest of the artwork. We didn't have time to sort through it so we grabbed everything."

"Did you now?" Asher said, a smile forming on his face. It wasn't often that these two surprised him. "I'll tell you what," he said. "Keep it as a token of my appreciation for a job well done. And...I know you're not a fan...but there's an active market for his work. You're looking at a handsome return if you process it through the right people. Would you like me to set that up for you?"

D-Mack looked over at Campbell, who nodded. *That's fine.*

"Sure, that'd be great," D-Mack told Asher. "You mentioned

another job?"

In the side mirror, Asher saw a large refrigerated food-delivery truck pull into the alley. "Let's go around the corner and I'll explain," he said.

Campbell pulled ahead and turned into the small parking lot that sat directly behind Warehouse XI. He had just pulled into a shady spot facing Stone Place Park when Asher slid the Audi in next to him. He and D-Mack took their usual places in the back, the plush leather and the air conditioning a welcome relief from the stuffy van's worn cloth seats.

"As I mentioned previously," Asher said. "I'm awaiting news about a very unique item that, for lack of a better term, is unequalled in value. The person who will deliver it, so to speak, is currently under surveillance. Once I have confirmation that he has it, I'll call you immediately and have you retrieve it. There's bound to be resistance but I'm sure it's nothing you can't handle. *How* you get the item is of no matter to me; use whatever methods you deem necessary. Should you succeed, I'm prepared to triple your usual fee."

Campbell and D-Mack exchanged a look of surprise.

Triple our fee?

This must be some item.

"You said something about the timing?" asked Campbell.

"Yes. The timing is the biggest unknown," Asher replied. "We're looking at a window of anywhere from a week to a month, possibly longer. There's simply no way to know. My advice to the both of you? Keep your phone handy at all times and be ready to move at a moment's notice."

For triple our fee, thought D-Mack, *I'll tape it to my head.*

259

After Nathan, Gina, and Beck left the Auto Barn, all they could do was go somewhere and wait. If Frank took the bait and panicked, as they assumed he would, Brandt would know immediately and he'd call them at once. Nathan had instructed him to pay close attention to the GPS tracker shortly after noontime.

As it turned out, Brandt called them at 12:10 p.m., while they were camped out in Beck's truck in a small parking lot off of Central Street, devouring roast beef sliders from Nick's Place.

"I don't know what you said to the receptionist," Brandt said, "but Frank came into work, stayed for five minutes, then left."

Nathan lowered the phone and whispered to Beck, "He took the bait!"

Beck checked the time. "That was five minutes ago. Where is he now?" *Hopefully not driving to Nick's Place for lunch,* he thought.

"Brandt, where is he now?" Nathan said into the phone.

"He just stopped. Let's see, the coordinates are… 42.470440° N, -71.006830° W."

"Huh?" Nathan said.

"GPS coordinates are shown in latitude and longitude."

"Oh great," Nathan muttered.

"What's wrong?" asked Beck.

Nathan lowered the phone again. "The tracker gave the location in latitude and longitude."

"Yeah? You didn't know that?"

Nathan gave him a look. "In what *world* would I know that?"

"Hold on," Beck said. He wrapped the slider he was eating in the foil it came in, then grabbed his phone from the spare cup holder in the center console. "Read me the coordinates."

Nathan pressed the speakerphone button and turned the screen upward. "Brandt, what are those coordinates again?"

Brandt read them off slowly and Beck entered them in his Google Maps app. "Uh, guys," he said, cautiously, when he was done. "He's a half mile from here."

"*What?*" Nathan exclaimed.

"Maybe they sent him out to get lunch," Gina said.

"No," Beck said, working the map feature on his phone. "He's at a storage facility."

"Hmm, what do you know?" Nathan said. "He gets my message, then leaves and goes to a storage facility? Are you thinking what I'm thinking?"

"Relax," Beck warned. "It could mean anything."

"Or nothing," Gina chimed in.

"Exactly."

"All right, he's on the move again," Brandt reported.

"That was quick," Nathan said, giving Beck a knowing look.

Beck motioned with his hand. *Calm down.*

Nathan rested the phone on the center console, awaiting Brandt's next update. In his mind he pictured Frank, panicky, driving like a madman through traffic. Seconds later, Brandt's voice erupted from the phone's speaker and snapped him out of his reverie.

"He just turned onto Rt. 1 heading north."

"Is he going back to the dealership?" Nathan asked.

"Hold on."

A minute passed. Then another.

"Are you still there?" Nathan asked.

"Still here," Brandt replied.

More silence.

"Okay, he just passed the exit for the dealership."

Nathan and Beck exchanged a suspicious look but said nothing. In the background they could hear the faint sound of Brandt puttering around the shop, or fidgeting with something. It was impossible to tell.

Another minute passed.

"He just turned off Rt. 1," Brandt said.

As more time elapsed, an anxious silence filled the truck.

"He turned left," Brandt said. Another pause. "Now he's going straight…"

Nathan gestured impatiently with his hand. *And…and…?*

"Huh, that's strange," Brandt said. "Why is he going *there?*"

16

Breakheart Reservation

"Brandt! What's happening?" Nathan asked, leaning closer to the phone.

"He just pulled into Breakheart Reservation. The coordinates are 42.4926284° N, -71.0207832° W."

"Where?"

"It's a public recreation area. I think it's about 600 acres. People go there to hike, swim, fish...stuff like that."

Nathan looked over at Beck, confused. *This makes no sense.*

Beck raised his hand in a calming gesture. *Just wait.*

"Well, okay, now that's curious," Brandt said.

"What's curious?" Nathan asked.

"He's leaving."

"He's *leaving?*" Nathan repeated. *He just got there!*

"Uh-huh, and it looks like, yup, he's headed back to Rt. 1."

Nathan stared at the phone in his hand, envisioning Sobol's erratic trek. *He goes to work, leaves, drives to a storage facility, stays there for all of five minutes, leaves, drives to a recreation area, stays for a minute, then leaves.* It had all the markings of a person in full-out panic mode.

"He's headed south, now, on Rt. 1," Brandt said.

Nathan didn't have to ask for an update—he already knew where Frank was going.

Priya was parked 100 yards away. With the way her car was angled at the curb, she had a direct view of the parking lot. On the seat next to her was the small spiral notepad she carried with her to record important information that she'd pass on to the client. Today's entry began with another trip to the Auto Barn in Saugus, a short stay that defied explanation, and now, lunch in town.

The visit to the dealership would've made perfect sense if Gargantuan Man had gotten out of the truck and gone inside. She would've assumed he was buying a vehicle and had returned to pick up his new wheels. But when Nathan got out of the truck, alone, and ventured inside, all logic and reasoning flew out the window.

With each passing day it was becoming apparent that she was on a wild goose chase.

A very well-paying wild goose chase at that.

If Nathan Cole was, in fact, searching for something, she was hard-pressed to say what it could be.

Thirty seconds after his previous update, Brandt's voice sounded once again. "He just pulled into the dealership."

Nathan had heard enough. He nudged Beck and said, "Let's go."

"Go where?" Beck asked.

"Breakheart Reservation."

Beck made an uneasy face. Before he could voice his objection, Nathan raised his index finger. *Wait.* He turned off the speakerphone setting and pressed the phone to his ear. "Brandt, thanks for the updates. Call me right away if he does anything suspicious."

"I will," Brandt said, then disconnected.

Nathan closed the phone and stared at Beck, eyes wide. "Don't you see what just happened?" he asked, knowing Beck hadn't come to any hard and fast conclusions about Frank's behavior. "It played out just as we suspected it would. My message spooked him, he went and got the notebook from where he'd been hiding it, in a storage unit, apparently, then took it to another location to keep me from getting it."

Beck was still evaluating the situation and said nothing.

"Explain to me any other way you could interpret his actions," Nathan said. He turned in the seat and faced Gina. "How about you? What do *you* think?"

"I think we're wasting time sitting here," Gina said.

Nathan looked at Beck again. "Well?"

Beck nodded his head, then started the truck.

Breakheart Reservation was a short 10 minutes away. Beck followed the entry road to the upper parking area, situated in front of a large visitor's center building surrounded by a waist-high chain of flowering shrubs. To the immediate right was a small wooden ranger's shack, and at the far end of the lot was brick maintenance building.

"Well this is interesting," Gina said, as Beck pulled into a vacant parking space.

The parking lot was a beehive of activity. Families were offloading bikes from the back of their cars. Young couples clad in hiking gear were making their way to one of two entrances to the Outer Loop Trail. Others were strolling the tracts of lawn that abutted the woods on either side of the visitor's center.

"If Sobol stashed the notebook here, it could be anywhere," Beck said, scanning the grounds from left to right.

"True," Nathan said. "But he wasn't here that long. How far could he have gone?"

"Not far," said Beck.

"Come on," Nathan said, pushing the door open. "This should be easy."

They got out of the truck and assembled in the middle of the parking lot. "Based on Brandt's updates," Nathan said, "we can assume that Sobol pulled in, got out of his car, ran to a specific area and stashed the notebook, then ran back to his car and left. All of this he did in roughly one minute. That's 30 seconds out and 30 seconds back. Or, this has nothing to do with the notebook and we're just wasting our time."

"Okay, so we split up," Gina said. "Each person take a direction. Walk, or rather, *run*, for 30 seconds, then stop and look around. Do we know what the notebook looks like? How big it is? The color?"

"No, but I'm guessing we'll know it when we see it."

"And I'm guessing you're right." She pointed to the left, where the Outer Loop Trail broke off into the woods. "I'll go that way."

"And I'll go that way," Beck said, pointing to his right, where the second trail entrance began.

Nathan turned and looked behind him. Other than a large rock and an information bulletin board, there was only a scattering of trees. "I got middle," he said, pointing at the visitor's center.

"Ready?" Gina said. "Remember, 30 seconds, then stop."

"Ready," said Beck.

Nathan nodded. *I'm ready.*

"On the count of three," Gina said. "One, two, three, GO!"

They each took off in their chosen direction. Gina sprinted down the parking lot and then veered right and ran up the trail. While she ran, she counted off the seconds in her head.

Beck ran at a moderate pace, taking less than full strides. Given his length, as compared to Sobol's shorter build, running at full speed and extending his legs fully would put him well past the spot where Sobol would've stopped.

Nathan followed the curved sidewalk to a wooden walkway that led up to the front porch of the visitor's center. He was about to go inside when he stopped. *No, he wouldn't have gone inside,* he told himself. *There was no time, and there'd be too many witnesses.* He checked his watch. Fifteen seconds to go.

Gina got to 30 seconds and stopped running. As she bent over, her hands on her knees, she looked left, then right. She was completely surrounded by woods. Other than trees and low shrubs, there was nothing. Certainly no place to stash a notebook where it wouldn't be ruined by the rain, or carried off by a woodland creature.

Beck pulled up at 30 seconds, his breathing normal. It felt good to run, especially after sitting in the truck all morning. A young couple on bikes approached and he stepped back to let them pass. Overhead, the sun was skewering the branches, casting irregular shadows on the trail. He surveyed the forest on either side and saw nothing that looked like a notebook. If Frank Sobol had stashed it anywhere nearby, he was either a fool, or exceedingly desperate to be rid of it; a park attendant or a passing hiker would've spotted it and taken it back to the visitor's center. He made a mental note to check with a staff member in case that had happened.

Nathan ran back down the wooden walkway to the cement sidewalk. To his right was an open section of lawn with a large wooden gazebo set at the far end. Beyond it, the forest. To his left was a sidewalk that skirted the front of the building and led to an open picnic area. He went right. Just beyond the end of the building was a much smaller wooden structure. He stopped and checked the time. Five seconds to go. "No, this is all wrong," he said. He eyed the small wooden building, then the gazebo, then looked back at the parking lot. Time to try again.

He returned to his original starting spot, checked his watch, then took off running again. This time, he ran past the wooden walkway and cut across the lawn to the gazebo. He stepped inside it and stopped to check the time. Ten seconds to go. Plenty of time.

Gina and Beck arrived back at his truck at the same time. "I take it you had the same luck I did," she said.

Beck nodded. "I saw a lot of nice places to pitch a tent," he quipped. "By the way, we need to check in there," he said, nodding at the visitor's center. "Someone may have found the notebook and turned it in."

"That's brilliant," Gina said. "Why didn't I think of that?"

"Don't beat yourself up," Beck told her. "You can't think of everything."

Wanna bet? she thought.

They went into the visitor's center and Beck asked a very nice intern named Autumn if anyone had found a notebook. Gina stood at his side and put on her best sad face, implying that the notebook belonged to her and that she had accidentally left it behind while hiking.

Autumn pulled a square cardboard box from beneath the counter and let them examine the contents. In it they found a hooded sweatshirt, several pairs of reading glasses, two plastic water bottles, a baseball cap, and a cellphone. No notebook.

Beck thanked Autumn and they walked back outside.

"What happened to Nathan?" Gina asked, as they walked back to the parking lot.

"Beats me," Beck replied.

Gina stopped and did a full turn. "There he is," she said, pointing at the gazebo.

"What is he doing?" Beck asked.

Nathan was standing on the railing that separated each of the columns, gripping one of the diagonal braces with his left hand. Everything from his shoulders up was obscured by the angled roof.

"I think he found it," Gina said excitedly, then took off running across the pavement. When she came to the cement sidewalk, she took a hard right and ran across the lawn with Beck following close behind. They reached the gazebo just as Nathan was climbing down.

Priya stood on the front porch of the visitor's center, trail map brochure in hand, and watched the girl and Gargantuan Man race across the lawn toward the gazebo.

After following Beck's truck up the entry road, appropriately named Forest Street, she pulled over and parked along the grass behind a line of other vehicles. From the trunk of her car she took out a pair of hiking boots and a backpack. When she strode into the parking lot minutes later, a water bottle clipped to her backpack and an orange bandana draped around her neck, she blended in perfectly with the crowd.

Yup, just another avid hiker.

Here to stretch my legs and enjoy all that nature has to offer.

Once inside the building, she watched through a window as Beck, Nathan, and Gina huddled together in the middle of the parking lot. Then, for reasons that escaped her, they suddenly took off running in different directions, as if being chased by a swarm of angry bees. The second they were out of sight, she grabbed a brochure from one of the racks and went back outside. When Beck and Gina returned a short time later and went into the visitor's center, she buried her nose in the brochure and they walked past her without so much as a glance.

Gina's jaw dropped open when she saw the notebook in his hand. It was roughly 5" x 7", with a bright yellow cover dotted with faint smudges of dirt. Other than that, it was in remarkable condition. "Where was it?" she asked, as they walked back to the truck.

"It was on one of the crosspieces that run between the columns," Nathan said, eyeing the notebook as he walked. "He pushed it back so no one would notice it. Well, no one who wasn't looking for it, that is."

"Can I see it?" Gina asked.

Nathan stopped and looked around, eyeing the various park visitors, then handed her the notebook. As she paged through it, he kept a steady vigil.

"I can't believe you found it," she murmured.

"You mean, we," he said.

"Right," she said softly, totally engrossed by the notes and diagrams that filled each page.

"Come on, we need to keep moving," Beck said, herding them gently toward the parking lot.

Gina handed Nathan the notebook and said, "We're going to find it, you know."

"I already told you, I don't care about the necklace" he said.

"Oh really," she said, not buying it. "We'll see about that."

Priya walked casually down the wooden walkway and stopped at the concrete sidewalk just as Beck, Nathan and Gina were approaching. The bright yellow notebook in Nathan's hand stood out like a traffic flare, and the moment she saw it, and heard him mention the necklace, she abandoned her wild-goose-chase notion. The first thing she did when she got back to her car was call Asher.

"Well, well," he said. "It looks like *you're* the one who can't—"

"Is it a necklace?" she said, cutting him off.

"Excuse me?"

"The thing the kid is trying to find. Is it a necklace?"

"Yes," he said, sitting up in his chair. "Why do you ask?"

"You said when something happens, we need to be there."

"That's right. Did something happen?" he asked, his heart starting to beat faster.

"I'm at Breakheart Reservation in Saugus. They came here, stayed for 15 minutes, and now they're leaving. I'm watching them drive out as we speak."

"Go on," Asher said. He grabbed a pen and wrote the name Breakheart Reservation on a slip of note paper.

"When they arrived, the kid was emptyhanded. When he left, he was carrying a small yellow notebook, maybe five or six inches by about seven inches. Bright yellow."

Asher was scribbling furiously. "Yellow notebook, got it."

"And I heard him say something about a necklace."

"Are you sure? He actually used the word?"

"Yup."

Asher pounded his fist on the desk. *YES!* "This changes everything," he said. "Here's what I need you to do. Stick to this kid like glue. I'm talking, Super Glue. Wherever he goes, you go. I want to know every move he makes, the second he makes it."

"Got it," she said. "One tube of Super Glue coming right up."

On the way out of the park, Nathan paged through the notebook, scanning each page for anything that might be a clue. Ballard had compiled copious daily notes, maps and scale drawings, a textual description of the excavation process, a catalog of objects found at the various sites, and his overall impressions of the dig. Nowhere did he mention the gold necklace.

Gina couldn't stand the suspense any longer. "Hey! Let me see it," she said impatiently.

"Just wait," he told her.

"You're not going to find it, so you might as well let me look."

He knew she wouldn't stop until he gave it to her, so he passed it over the seat and considered their next move. "We need to go to the police," he said. "The sooner the better. Once Sobol learns the notebook is gone, he's going to come after us. Come after *me*, that is."

"No," Beck said.

"What do you mean, no?"

"No police. Not yet."

Rt. 1 was heavy with traffic, and as he drove, his eyes jumped from the rearview mirror, to the side mirror, to the road ahead. Over and over. One repetitive motion, like a robotic spot welder.

"What do you mean, no police?" Nathan asked. "That was the whole point of getting the notebook, remember? It's the only way we can nail Sobol."

"All right," Beck said calmly. "You go to the police. What are you going to tell them? I have this notebook that Frank Sobol stole from my grandfather's desk seven years ago? Then, he poisoned him? By the way, how those two things are connected I still don't understand, but anyway, you show them the notebook and that's that, right?"

"Right."

"Wrong."

"I think you're forgetting something," Nathan said. "His fingerprints are on the notebook."

"Yes, they are," Beck said. "Along with yours, and Gina's, as well as who knows how many others?"

Nathan said nothing.

"The fingerprints prove nothing," Beck said. "Actually, I take that back—they prove that Sobol held the notebook in his hand. And that's exactly what he'll say in court. Yes, your honor, I found the book and I looked through it, then I put it back in the desk. And you know what the prosecution will say? Nothing. That's because they'll have no proof to dispute his claim."

"But we have an eyewitness, remember?"

"Ah, yes, the eyewitness, Connie Freeman. I forgot about her. What do you think she'll say? That she walked into the office and found Frank Sobol standing at the desk, reading some book your grandfather had set aside?"

"Well, *yeah!*"

"Frank's lawyer will feast on that. First, he'll say, 'Other than yourself, Ms. Freeman, did anyone else see my client in the back room?'. When she says no, he'll release the hounds."

"The hounds?" Gina asked. "Is that another expression?"

"Yes. It's a hunting term. In this case, it means he'll launch his primary defense, claiming there's no definitive proof that Frank stole the notebook or touched the water bottle."

"Whatever," Nathan muttered. "I still say we go to the police."

Thirty seconds of strained silence followed, both of them like steeled generals camped out on facing hilltops refusing to surrender their position.

Beck watched the road ahead, convinced he was right.

Nathan stared out the side window, convinced Beck was wrong.

"What if we catch him with the necklace? Gina asked, breaking the stalemate.

"That would be game, set, and match," Beck said.

"Then we need to set another trap," she said, "only this time we use the necklace as bait."

"Sure, but there's only one problem," Nathan replied. "We don't have the necklace."

"Hmm…I guess that means we'll just have to find it."

"And how do you propose we do that?" Nathan asked. "Sobol's had the notebook for seven years and *he* couldn't find it."

"Frank Sobol couldn't find his car keys if they were in his back pocket."

Beck gave Nathan a knowing look. *The girl has a point.*

Nathan had Beck drive him directly to Richard Abbott's house. He needed time to cool off and think things through, and sorting books in the peace and quiet of the old barn would allow him to do just that.

Beck had just come to a stop in front of the barn door when Gina passed the notebook over the seat to Nathan.

He pushed it away.

"What are you doing?" she asked.

"Keep it," he said.

"You don't want to take it with you?"

No. Apparently, it's of no use to us and we wasted our time looking for it, he wanted to say. Instead, he told her, "No. I'll look at it when I get home." Part of him wanted to take it and toss it out the window.

"Okay," she said, pulling it back. *If you insist.* She fanned the pages with her thumb. "If there's a clue in here, I'll find it."

"Call me if you do," he said, then opened the door and jumped out.

"I don't think he liked what I had to say," Beck said, as he drove back down the driveway.

Gina had set the notebook in her lap and was busy scrutinizing each entry. "He'll get over it," she said without looking up.

"You think?"

"Yeah, he always does."

Nathan pushed open the barn door and was greeted by a pleasing rush of cool air. That, and the smell of the aged timbers soothed his senses, knocking his anger down several notches. An hour later he had finished off one pallet and was ready to start on another. The whole time he worked, Beck's words continued to simmer on a low boil in the back of his mind. Gradually, he began to accept the fact that Beck was right. For every charge the prosecution could bring against Frank Sobol, his lawyer would mount a bulletproof defense. The only chance they had of exposing Sobol for his crimes was with the necklace. But could they even find it? If they did, would Gina's plan work? Could they use it to trick Sobol into admitting what he'd done?

He was peeling the shrink wrap off the next pallet when he heard Zee's box truck back up to the open door. The driver door slammed shut and then Zee walked into the barn, holding a pair of work gloves in his hand.

"Hey, how's it going, man," he said. "Missed you yesterday."

"Yeah, I had a thing to do," Nathan replied in a flat tone. He balled up the shrink wrap and tossed it into an open cardboard box sitting several feet away, then grabbed a box of books from the top tier and carried it over to the table.

"Been thinking about our last conversation," Zee said. "Lost treasure buried right under our feet. I see myself in a desert, digging in the sand, when I find a lost gold necklace." He watched Nathan closely, waiting to see if his words elicited a reaction. But Nathan was already pulling books out of the box two at a time, piling them up in twin stacks for another lightning round of sorting.

Zee kept on about treasure hunters and the amount of wealth sitting on the ocean floor, which was there for the taking, but Nathan had already tuned him out. He was searching for his first two titles on the clipboard when his flip phone rang. Without taking his eyes from the clipboard, he took his phone from his pocket, pried it open with his thumb and pressed the talk button. "This is Nathan."

"Hey, it's me," Gina said. "You want to hear something crazy?"

"Yeah?"

"I think I found something."

17

Right in the Rain

"You found it?" Nathan said, the words exploding out of his mouth.

Zee was walking to the back of the barn to start hauling cardboard. When he heard Nathan's outburst, he froze.

"Yes and no," Gina said.

"Oh, come on," Nathan moaned. "Tell me what you found."

"It would be better if I showed you," Gina explained.

"Hold on a second," Nathan said. He tossed the clipboard on the table and walked to the door. Zee's truck was parked so close that he had to squeeze between the door frame and the back bumper to get outside. "Okay," he said to Gina, "I had to go outside."

"Outside? Why?"

"There's a guy here hauling away all the old cardboard boxes. It's a weird story. I'll tell you later. But enough about me, tell me what you found!"

Zee hurried back to the door and peeked around the side of the truck. Nathan was standing next to the driver's door, his phone to his ear.

"I *told* you, I have to show it to you," Gina said.

"Can you give me a hint?"

"A hint? Okay, how's this? Sobol never found the clue because he's a moron."

"You call that a hint? For crying out loud, are we going to find the necklace or not?"

"Hold on," she said.

Through the phone he heard her shout, "I'M ON THE PHONE!"

Several seconds passed, then she shouted again.

"DO I HAVE TO?"

Another pause.

"Unbelievable," she grumbled.

"What's wrong?"

"I have to go," she said. "*Someone* is making me go to the grocery store with her."

"Let's talk when I get home," he said.

There was no answer.

She had already hung up.

When Zee saw Nathan close his phone and walk toward the door, he rushed to the back of the barn and began ferrying armloads of cardboard out to the truck. In keeping with the guidelines he'd been given from Jordan, he didn't inquire about Nathan's phone call or comment on his reaction to what the caller had told him. His job was to monitor Nathan's overall demeanor and, if the situation warranted, drop a key word or two then gauge his reaction.

Observe and report.

Nothing more.

He wasn't to push too hard or ask too much for fear that Nathan might become suspicious.

He loaded a token amount of cardboard into the truck, well under the maximum capacity of its legal weight limit, then left. He hadn't gone far when he pulled into a gas station parking lot and texted Jordan.

Jordan was in the conference room, meeting with a trio of investors who were facing fierce neighborhood opposition to a planned multi-million-dollar condominium project. Her phone was on the table next to her yellow legal notepad and when she saw a message notification appear on the screen, she glanced at it briefly, then did a double take.

"Uh, gentlemen, my apologies," she said, sliding her phone off the table. "I need to take a short break." She pushed her chair away from the table, and stood up. "When I return, we should talk about an outreach strategy that addresses each of the concerns being voiced by the community."

The investors nodded in agreement and then began a conversation in earnest as she walked to the far end of the room and stepped out into the hallway.

Zee was sitting in the truck, waiting for a reply text, when she called. He answered on the first ring. "Hey."

Jordan walked up the hallway slowly, keeping to the side of the corridor. "You texted me?"

"Yeah, something is definitely going down."

"Why, what happened?"

"Dude got a phone call," Zee explained. "Whoever called him found something."

"How do you know that?"

"He said it. Actually, it was more like a shout...you know, like he was super excited."

"Okay, so someone he knows called him and told him they found something," Jordan said, summarizing his words.

"Yeah, man, he was pretty worked up about it."

"In your message you mentioned a necklace."

"The necklace, right. He said something about it. I mean, it wasn't much..."

"Tell me what he said, word for word." Her breathing had accelerated and she leaned on the wall as she awaited his reply.

"I think he was getting frustrated with whoever called him. He said something like, 'What about the necklace?'...no, wait, that wasn't it. Let me think...oh yeah, he said, 'Are we going to find the necklace or not?'"

Jordan felt her knees weaken, as if the building had shifted. She took in a deep breath to steady herself, then said, "Are you still at the barn?"

"No, I grabbed some cardboard and got out of there so I could call you without him knowing."

"Good," Jordan said. "Here's the plan. I want you to go there every day, whether he's working or not. You never know, Richard might reveal some information that we can use. Call me with anything you learn."

"This is like one of those Nicolas Cage treasure movies," Zee said, picturing himself in a leading role.

"Zee, listen to me," Jordan said, attempting to wrestle his attention away from the big screen. "I want you to focus on the way he acts and the things he says. Nothing else. And I want you to call me right away if you hear anything more about the necklace."

"Way he acts, things he says, necklace," Zee said, like he was reciting a grocery list. "Got it."

Jordan ended the call and dialed another number. It rang several times, and she was just about to hang up when the call was answered.

"Hi, I only have a minute. What's up?" came the voice from the other end of the line.

"Good news," Jordan said. "I think he found the notebook."

"Are you sure?"

"He's talking about the necklace," Jordan said.

There was no reply.

"Hello?" Jordan said, afraid that the call had cut out.

"I'm here. I'm just at a loss for words."

"If he was able to find the notebook, how long do you think it'll take him to find the necklace?"

"Based on what we've read about him, not long at all."

"Exactly!" Jordan said. "Now, once we have it, we're going to have to move it quickly and quietly."

"I agree. Let me work on that. It's not like either of us has any experience in such matters but I'll poke around and see what I can find."

"Promise me you'll be careful."

"I will."

At 5:00 p.m. Nathan turned off the lights and rolled the barn door shut. Knowing that Gina had found something in the notebook, and having to wait until the end of the day to find out what it was, had made the afternoon unbearable. At one point, he considered walking home. But now, the answer to the question burning inside him was a short 15 minute car ride away.

At 5:10, he was still waiting.

At 5:20, he walked down the driveway to the street.

At 5:27, his father turned into the driveway.

"Sorry I'm late," David said, after Nathan got in the car. "How was your day? Come across any good books?"

"My day was remarkably good," Nathan said, upbeat. "And some would say that every book is a good book."

"Well, yes, that's…uh…very prophetic," David said, blindsided. As late as he'd arrived, he was fully expecting an all-out explosion. But for Nathan, the thought of what awaited him at home was too significant to be tainted by loud voices and anger. It was everything he could do not to tell his father everything—that after seven long years he was about to lure his grandfather's killer into a trap.

He hadn't thought about it before that precise moment, but he wondered how much his parents knew about Lía Ballard, the field notebook, and the gold necklace. For that matter, did Jameson know? Sooner or later they would need to be told, and how that conversation would go was anybody's guess.

After a slow ride through sluggish traffic, it was almost six o'clock by the time they arrived home. Nathan knew Gina was probably sitting down at the dinner table and it would be at least seven or eight o'clock before she'd be able to sneak out of the house. Maybe even later.

He got out of the car and headed straight for the garage, the heavy bag calling to him like a whisper in the wind. A solid 20-minute session would help him burn off his anticipation and contemplate the tricky turns in the road ahead.

When he got to the side door, he was reaching for the doorknob when he looked through the glass and saw Gina pacing from the back of the garage to the front. In her hand was Walter Ballard's yellow field notebook.

"Well, it's about time!" she said, when he walked through the door.

"You're *here?*" he said, confused. "But…how…?"

"I snuck over here an hour ago, expecting you'd pull in at any moment. Then my dad got home and I was pretty much trapped. If he saw me coming out of your garage, let alone setting foot on your property…"

"Yes, I know, he'd call in the National Guard," Nathan said quickly. This wasn't the time to talk about her neurotic father. "What did you find?" he asked.

She opened the notebook and began turning pages, pointing out various sections as she went. "This whole notebook is one continuous diary," she said. "I'm not sure how much of it you looked at, but it's pretty detailed. Walter Ballard kept daily logs about the dig, including descriptions of what they found, and where, drawings of the excavation site, you name it."

"I only glanced at it briefly," Nathan said, taking a closer look. "I'll say this much, for something that's been kicking around for seven years, it's in pretty good shape."

"That's what I thought too, so I checked it out. This is a "Right in the Rain" notebook. The whole thing, cover, pages, even the binding, are designed to withstand the worst weather."

"That's good for us, right?"

"Yes, and I'll show you why." She flipped to the middle, to a map that stretched across both pages. "See this line right here?" she said, tracing it across the page with her finger. "That's the Usumacinta River."

"The what?"

"Yoo-sah-mah-*cinta*," she said, enunciating each syllable.

"O-kay," Nathan said slowly. *If you say so.*

"These little black diamonds scattered along it are different archeological digs. She turned the page. "He listed them right here: Uaxactún, Tikal, Lolmul, La Sufricaya, Machaquilá, Naranjo, Nakum, Piedras Negras, and Altar de Sacrificios."

"Are those important?" Nathan asked.

"The names? No." She turned back to the map. "But those are," she said, pointing at each of the dig sites.

He took the notebook from her and held it inches from his face. None of the black marks were named. Instead, next to each one was a pair of numbers, written so small they were almost unreadable.

"Look familiar?" Gina asked.

"Are those latitude and longitude coordinates?"

"Yes. Archeologists use different methods to mark the exact location of excavation sites, where they unearthed a specific item, a room, a wall, whatever they deem important."

"Makes sense," he said. "So how does that help us find the necklace?"

"Look again," Gina said, pointing at the map.

He pulled it close again. "What am I looking for?"

"Just look. You'll see it."

He pulled it so close it was almost touching his nose, then eyed each of the excavation sites from left to right, working his way across and down the map. "It would help if I knew what I was—"

"And then he found it," Gina said, like she was narrating a documentary.

"This location in the lower corner," he said. "The numbers are different."

"Do you recognize the first two digits?"

"Forty two," he said, reading them aloud. Something about them was familiar. "This morning," he said, thinking back. "When Brandt was reading us the coordinates, they all began with 42."

"That's right," Gina said. "I'll bet you anything those coordinates are a location in Massachusetts. Ballard wrote them so small, they look just like the others."

Nathan looked at her, awestruck. "Frank Sobol never looked close. That's why he never recovered the necklace."

"Uh-huh"

"Hold that thought," Nathan said. He pulled out his phone and dialed Beck.

"Hey," Beck said, answering right away. "Are we good?"

"We're very good," Nathan said. "Gina found the hidden clue in the notebook."

"Already?" he exclaimed. "She's only had it for…(checking his watch)…five hours."

"Can you check a set of coordinates for us?"

"Coordinate? Sure, hold on," Beck replied. He hit the speaker-phone button so he could talk and work the GPS app at the same time. "All right," he said. "What are they?"

Nathan pulled the notebook closer so he could read the numbers. "The first one is 42.4274271 N."

"Got it, and the other one?"

"-71.2313248 W."

Several seconds passed, then Beck came back on the line.

"Okay," Nathan said, flashing Gina a thumbs up.

She poked his arm. "What did he say?" she whispered.

Nathan pulled the phone away from his face. "It's in Lexington."

"Massachusetts, I knew it!" Gina said.

"Wait, what was that?" Nathan asked Beck.

Gina flicked his shoulder. *Tell me!*

"Okay, thanks. You're stopping by tomorrow morning, right? Yes, I know it's Saturday. Just get here as soon as you can." He closed the phone and shook his head in disbelief. "You're not going to believe this," he said. "That location?"

"What about it?"

"It's a farm."

18

Everett

Saturday, 6:05 a.m.

Nathan woke up earlier than normal for a Saturday. It was going to be a great day and his excitement refused to let him to sleep for another second. On this day, longstanding questions were going to be answered. Long overdue justice would be served. And his family would finally be able to move on from one of the darkest chapters in their history.

With 6:05 showing on his alarm clock, he sprung out of bed and got dressed, then went downstairs to the kitchen and devoured two bowls of cereal. Then it was out to the garage for 200 jumps of rope. After that, he skipped the 3lb. hand weights and moved on to the heavy bag where he practiced a variety of three-minute drills, pausing for a three count between each series of punches.

He started with a basic jab/cross.

Thud, thud.

One-two-three.

Thud, thud.

One-two-three.

Thud, thud.

One-two-three.

Next came a jab, cross, hook. He kept the same tempo for all three punches, moving in and out of range between each repetition.

Thud, thud, thud.

One-two-three.

Thud, thud, thud.

One-two-three.

That was followed by a jab/cross, jab/cross combination, slowly at first, then faster as he became accustomed to the motion.

Thud-thud, thud-thud.

One-two-three.

Thud-thud, thud-thud.

One-two-three.

Thud-thud, thud-thud.

One-two-three.

When he was finished, he went outside where the chill of the early morning air cooled his face like a cold compress. As he walked to the house, he glanced over at Gina's driveway. Her parents' cars were parked in front of the garage and the sight of them made him stop short.

They're not going to work today, it's Saturday.

There's no way she can sneak out of the house without them knowing.

Even if she does, if they can't find her they'll go crazy.

He went into the house and found both of his parents sitting at the kitchen table, enjoying their first cup of coffee of the day. They didn't appear to be in a hurry to go anywhere, or get an early jump on a Saturday house project, and that's when he got an idea.

"How'd it go?" his father asked.

"My work out? It was good," he said, nonchalantly. He pulled out a chair and sat down, then stared at the tabletop gathering his nerve.

"Is something wrong?" his mother asked.

"I need to ask the two of you a favor," he said. "Two favors, actually."

"*Two* favors?" Elizabeth said, surprised. She looked over at David. "What do you think?"

"Oh, I don't know," he replied, doubtfully. "Doesn't that exceed our one-favor-per-week rule?"

"Dad, this is serious."

David and Elizabeth exchanged a look, eyebrows raised. *Serious, he says.*

"Before I tell you what they are," Nathan said. "Are you guys doing anything today?"

"Today? No," his mother said. "Your father and I were planning on spending a relaxing day doing nothing for a change."

"Good," Nathan said. "Because I need you to distract Gina's parents for an hour or two while we run an errand. That's favor #1."

"An errand?"

"We need to go check something out."

"I see. And what's favor #2?" his mother asked.

"Don't ask me to explain why."

"Well, you see, that's going to be a problem. When you and Gina check something out, it tends to result in a near catastrophe. And when I say 'tends to' I mean every time."

"Beck's going to be with us," Nathan said. "In fact, he's driving us."

"Beck is going to be with you?" David repeated. "The whole time?"

"Yes. But Gina's parents can't see her climb into Beck's truck."

"With you," his mother added.

"Yes, especially with me."

"I get it," David said. "You want us to distract her parents so she can go with you and Beck."

"That's right," Nathan said. "We should only be gone for about two hours, maybe less. I promise you, when I get back, I'll explain everything."

Elizabeth eyed him suspiciously, weighing everything he'd told them.

"It's just..." he began.

"It's just what?" Elizabeth asked.

That's when the significance of what was going to happen in the next two hours came crashing down on him: recovering the necklace, which no one else had been able to find; using it to lure his grandfather's killer into a trap; ending a nightmare that had haunted his family for seven years.

He closed his eyes and calmed his breathing.

Elizabeth placed her hand on his forearm. "What's wrong?" she asked.

He wanted to tell them so badly. But now wasn't the time. "This is…" he said, pausing. "The most important thing I've ever done. It may be the most important thing I *ever* do. For that reason, I need you both to trust me like never before."

David looked over at Elizabeth and nodded. *It's fine.*

"If Beck wasn't going with you, I'd say no," his mother told him. "But since he'll be there to keep you out of any… (clearing her throat) …entanglements…then, yes, we'll do as you ask. Truth be told, we haven't seen Bill and Laura for quite some time, and there's a new restaurant in Cambridge that your father and I have been wanting to check out."

"Thank you," Nathan said. He stood and gave each of them a long hug, knowing the next time they spoke, the emotions meter would be pushed to the very limit.

For all of them.

At 10:45, Nathan stood at the screen door and watched his father back the car out of the driveway, then pull into Gina's driveway. When he saw Gina's parents come out the front door and climb into the car, he shut the door and called Gina.

"You ready to go to Lexington?" he asked her.

"Sure…but…what just happened? My folks going to lunch with *your* folks? When does that ever happen?"

"I called in a favor," he told her. "I bought us a couple of hours."

That must've been some favor, she thought.

"I called Beck and told him to wait at the far end of the street until our folks left."

"Sounds like you have this all planned out."

"We're so close to finishing this," he said. "I'm not going to let anything stop us. And I do mean us." He heard Beck's truck pull into the driveway and said, "Beck's here. Let's go find a gold necklace!"

He grabbed his backpack from the front hallway and raced out to the truck. "Thanks for doing this," he told Beck, as he climbed up into the front seat.

"No thanks necessary," Beck replied. "How are we set for time?"

"My folks are taking Gina's parents to a new restaurant in Cambridge. With Saturday traffic, I figure we have at least two hours."

"A new restaurant in Cambridge?" Beck asked. "There's sure to be a line."

"Okay," Nathan said. "Make it three hours."

"We'll be back long before that," said Beck. "Where we're going is less than seven miles away."

The back door opened and Gina climbed up into the seat.

"Nice job with the notebook," Beck told her.

"Thanks," she said. "Anyone with a brain could've figured it out. I mean, Walter Ballard was an archeologist. You want to find his hidden code? Think like an archeologist!"

Nathan looked over at Beck, the hint of a grin on his face. *She's good, right?*

Beck nodded emphatically. *Oh yeah!*

Traffic on Rt. 2 was heavy but Beck made it to the Waltham Street exit in Lexington in less than 10 minutes. He drove for a mile and then slowed as he approached the address that corresponded with the coordinates from his GPS app.

"Are you sure this is the place?" Gina asked. "I thought you said it was a farm."

A white 1950s era house sat on the right of a large square parking area. Directly across from it was a long barn, also white, and in pristine condition. Positioned at the front corner of it was a smaller structure with a greenhouse on the front and another running down the side.

Parked in front of the barn was a lime-green 1970s Chevy C10 pickup truck with a white roof, looking as new as the day it rolled off the assembly line in Flint, Michigan. Beck pulled in behind it and turned off the engine.

"I don't know," Gina said doubtfully, as she studied the greenhouse through the side window. "This doesn't feel quite right."

"No, this is the place," Nathan said, his eyes fixed on the back window of the old truck. "And I know how we can prove it." He pushed the door open and jumped down onto the pavement just as an older man emerged from the screen porch attached to the back of the house. His thick gray hair was brushed back, as if windblown, and his moustache and beard were neatly trimmed. Despite the fact that it was Saturday, his window-pane oxford and blue jeans conveyed a decidedly business-casual look.

"Good morning," he called out, as he crossed the pavement. "How can I help you?" Nathan stepped forward, closing the distance between them. "Hi, my name Nathan Cole." Gina and Beck walked up behind him and he motioned to each of them with his hand. "This is Gina McDermott, and this is our friend, Beck."

"Nathan, Gina, Beck," the man said, offering each of them a polite nod. "It's a pleasure to meet you. I'm Everett Sayers."

"I noticed the Harvard University decal on your truck," Nathan said.

"Oh, that," Everett said, shaking his head. "That was my daughter's doing. She believes that since I taught at Harvard University for 36 years, the least I could do was display the school's crest. Truth be told, I think the fact that I'm retired but still managing this tree farm sends a much louder statement than a window decal."

"This is a tree farm?" Nathan said. He looked to his left. Between the house and the barn he could see down into a large field with row after row of small saplings. Set in the back corner was another barn, older than the main barn and not nearly as well kept.

"The official designation is 'demonstration tree farm,'" Everett explained. "It was created for the students and faculty of the university, to enable experimentation and research for growing, harvesting, and the replacement of trees for timberland. Now, to me that sounds like something you'd read in a brochure. I prefer to call it an outdoor classroom."

"Can I ask you a question?" Nathan said.

"Please do."

"When you were at Harvard University, did you, by chance, happen to know Walter Ballard?"

"Walter? Why of course," Everett exclaimed, with a look of delight. "We were in different departments, but we had many spirited conversations about geography, ancient cultures, land forms, and, not surprisingly, the curious things one can find buried deep in the soil."

"Do you remember the last time you spoke with him?"

"Well, let's see," Everett said, scratching the back of his head as he searched his memory. "It would've been about a week before he died. Yes, I'm quite sure that's when it was." A smile formed on his lips as he recalled the day. "He had just returned from a dig in Mexico. It was Guatemala if memory serves me right. It was just like old times. He stopped by to say hello and we ended up chatting for quite some time. He was quite intrigued by what we do here so I gave him a tour of the property."

Nathan looked at Gina and Beck but said nothing.

"Did you know Walter?" Everett asked.

"No," Nathan replied. "Someone in his family knew my grandfather."

"Uh, Mr. Sayers," Gina said, before the conversation went off the rails. "Would you mind if we looked around? I'd love to see the different things you grow."

"Why, certainly," Everett said. He swept his hand in the direction of the field. "Learning is what we do here."

Nathan and Gina looked at Beck. *You coming?*

"You guys go ahead. I'll wait here," he told them. Then, as a way of telling them to be careful, he said, "If you come across anything you think I should see, give me a shout."

"Beck was it?" Everett said. "I was brewing a pot of coffee when you pulled in. Perhaps you'd like to join me for a cup? We can sit on the back porch and enjoy this beautiful day." "By all means," Beck replied. "I never refuse a cup of fresh-brewed coffee."

As Everett escorted him back to the house, Nathan went to the truck for his backpack. "Where do you want to start?" he asked Gina, as he looped the strap over his shoulder.

"Well, I think we can rule out the house," Gina replied. "That leaves the barn, this smaller building, and the greenhouses."

"Don't forget the other barn."

"There's another barn? Where?"

"Follow me."

He walked over to the opening between the house and the main barn and pointed to the old structure in the corner of the field. "That one."

"Oh, okay," Gina said. "I didn't see that."

Nathan eyed the old barn, then the new barn, then the green-houses. "Are you thinking what I'm thinking?"

"I don't know. What are you thinking?"

"He said this property is an educational facility for the students and faculty of Harvard University."

"Yeah?"

"So, if you're Walter Ballard, and you know that, and you're trying to hide something where no one will find it, which of these buildings seems like the most logical choice?"

"That's easy. The one with the least amount of foot traffic."

"Exactly."

In unison, they glanced at the barn across the field.

"What are we waiting for?" Gina asked.

The driveway snaked past the house then angled downward and came to an end at the edge of the field. From there, they followed a rough dirt road that ran along the tree line to their left. The soil was marked with ruts and washboards, and a set of fat tire tracks were visible in the dirt, made by some kind of farm machinery or very large truck. As they walked, they looked to their right and saw the field extending to the north for another two acres, lined with an assortment of tree species.

The barn was nothing like the one next to the house. It was smaller and unpainted, and years of harsh New England winters had weathered the outer boards to a bleached gray color. Unlike Richard Abbott's barn, with its single rolling door, this one had had a pair of large hinged doors made with reverse "K" bracing. From afar, it resembled a giant snowflake.

Nathan wrestled with the rusty hasp holding them closed, then swung both doors open, casting light onto a large green farm tractor parked inside. Directly behind it was a flat hay wagon.

They stepped inside, keeping to the left of the tractor, and saw a small tool room that occupied the front corner of the first floor. It was cluttered with shovels and spades, digging bars, fence post drivers, and more than one crooked stack of watering buckets. Hanging on the walls were a variety of loppers, pruners, and saws.

They continued on, past a row of old horse stalls, each one outfitted with a heavy 4' wooden gate, held in place by long cast iron hinges.

As they walked deeper into the barn, the natural light gradually began to fade. Nathan slipped the backpack off his shoulder, dug out two flashlights, one for him and one for Gina, and they moved on, past the hay wagon to the back wall. There, they saw another set of hinged doors. To the right of them, in the back corner, was a small workshop.

Nathan shone his light through the open doorway and saw a long workbench pushed up against the outside wall. Set beneath the cluttered top were several deep drawers made from scrap wood that was smudged with paint. Below them was a shelf packed with old wooden crates. Hand tools hung on the wall in makeshift wooden racks, and high above them, running the length of the workbench, was a narrow shelf littered with old tobacco tins, bottles, and other curious artifacts that had been unearthed from the fields throughout the years.

From that room on, running all the way up the left side of the barn to the front wall, were a number of wooden pallets stacked high with bags of organic fertilizer, mulch, and manure.

"What do you think?" Nathan asked.

"He wouldn't have hidden it up there," she said, pointing her flashlight up at the empty hay loft. "And he wouldn't have left it in one of the stalls. That leaves either the tool room we passed, or that," she said, shining her light into the workshop.

"Agreed," Nathan said. "Let's start with the workshop."

She stepped back and gestured politely with both hands. "After you."

Beck sat on the back porch with Sayers, sipping coffee and listening to him recount the history of the property dating all the way back to colonial times. Through the screen, Beck had a commanding view of the field, allowing him to track Nathan and Gina as they walked along the wood line.

He lost sight of them when they disappeared into the old barn in the back corner of the field. That was 15 minutes ago. As the seconds ticked away, his curiosity surged higher. He took another sip of coffee and checked his watch. If he didn't see them emerge from the barn in the next 10 minutes, he'd go check on them.

They started with the workbench. One by one, Gina pulled out the heavy drawers and examined their contents. She found hand tools, rolls of twine, tags, stakes, flagging tape, deer repellant, spare work gloves, and an infestation of mouse nests.

While she was doing that, Nathan was pulling the wooden crates off the lower shelf and inspecting the assortment of junk stashed in each one. When they were done, they pointed their flashlights at the opposite wall, where an old table saw sat next to a pile of loose boards. In the corner, a collection of long wooden stakes were propped up against the wall. Other than that, there was nothing.

"We're doing this all wrong," Gina said, running her flashlight around the room. "We need to think like an archeologist."

Nathan had turned and was pointing the beam of his flashlight at the shelf of old bottles and tobacco tins. "You mean, think like an archeologist who just returned from Mexico."

"Huh?"

He climbed up on the bench so he could reach the shelf, then removed a handful of old pill bottles sitting atop an old wooden cigar box that was covered with a thick layer of dust. Burnt into the wood and set inside an oval was the name Te-Amo and the image of a bull and a matador. Below that were three lines of text printed in Spanish.

He slid the box off the shelf and climbed down. In the beam of Gina's flashlight, he used his thumbnail to pry open the small brass latch holding the box shut, then slowly opened it. Inside was a long strip of linen cloth approximately 14" wide that had been folded over several times. When Nathan pulled it from the box, it felt heavy in his hands.

With his heart racing, he set the cloth on the bench and carefully unwrapped it. As he pulled back the last fold of cloth, Gina gasped when she saw the tear-shaped pieces of gold, each one a quarter of an inch thick, strung on a hair-thin strand of spun gold.

"Lágrimas de la Emperadora," Nathan said, just above a whisper.

As Gina ran her fingers over the gold pieces, she imagined the Mayan warrior queen, Lady Six Sky, doing the same thing when it was first presented to her over 1,200 years earlier. "We did it," she said, awestruck. "We found it."

"Yeah, we did," he said, his feelings of anger churning anew. Seeing the necklace firsthand, holding the tear-shaped pieces of gold in his hand, each one worth tens of thousands of dollars, was a cruel reminder of the tragedy the necklace had caused, a result of the greed of one person.

And now they were going to expose him for his heinous crime.

"Let's go," Nathan said, as he rewrapped the necklace. "Beck's probably going out of his mind."

He laid the bundled cloth back in the cigar box and then slid it into the center compartment of his backpack.

They left the workshop and were walking toward the front of the barn when a shadowy figure stepped out from between the tractor and the hay wagon.

"Well, well…what do we have here?"

19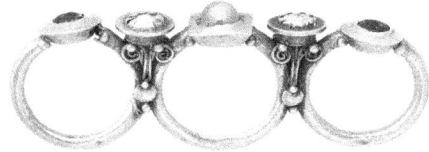

Five Minutes

"You," Nathan growled.

"Yes, me," Frank Sobol replied. He raised the Glock 42 pistol he'd been holding down at his side. "It looks like you have something for me."

"I don't know what you're talking about," Nathan said,

"Just give it to him," Gina whispered.

"You should listen to her," Sobol told him. "She's a smart girl."

"How did you know we'd be here?" Nathan asked, taking a quick inventory of his surroundings. To his right was the hay wagon. On his left, five feet away, a pallet loaded with bags of fertilizer. Next to it was a thick wooden post with a narrow ladder that extended up to the hay loft.

"How did I know? I've known exactly where you are for some time now."

"What are you talking about?"

"He had my help," came a voice from the other side of the hay wagon.

Nathan spun around, shining his flashlight in that direction. "Brandt?" he said, shocked.

"Go ahead, Frank. Tell him," Brandt said. "He deserves to know."

Sobol wasn't sure why Brandt was there, but it didn't matter. His plan had worked to perfection, and now he was on his way to a colossal payday, one he'd been dreaming about for the past seven years. "Well, if you insist," he said. Then, to Nathan, "You see, after you and your large friend came to see me at the dealership I did some checking. Turns out I did know your grandfather after all. Of course, I had no idea he had a grandson who was so clever. This whole plan was your idea."

"What plan," Nathan asked, buying time. He turned off his flashlight, then, using the darkness like a shield, eased the backpack off his shoulder and set it down on the plank floor next to his right foot.

"It all started when you tried to get Brandt, here, to put a tracker on my car. After you left his shop, he called me and told me what you were planning to do. By the way, that little show you put on for the receptionist? I have to admit, that was very clever. Ineffective, but clever. You see, the whole time you thought you were tracking me? I was tracking you!"

"What are you talking about?" Nathan asked.

"Brandt never put the tracker on my car. He put it on your friend's truck. All those coordinates he gave you were phony. The whole time you thought I was moving the notebook to a different location, I was sitting at my desk at the dealership."

"Why'd you do it?" Nathan ask. "Why'd you steal the notebook? My grandfather *trusted* you!"

"Stealing it was never the plan. I was just going to borrow it for a bit, then put it back."

"Once you found Ballard's hidden code."

"That was the general idea, yes."

"And the poison?" Nathan asked.

"Again, not part of the plan," Sobol admitted. "But, hey, sometimes you have to improvise."

At the opposite end of the barn, Nathan saw Beck's head inch around the edge of the door then quickly pull back.

"But, back to your original question," Sobol said. "How did I know you'd be here? Simple. Brandt called me this morning and told me you were in Lexington, at a *tree farm* of all places. I asked myself: what's a kid your age doing at a tree farm on a Saturday? Looking for a hidden gold necklace, perhaps? I jumped into my car and drove right over here, found on an old cart path right down the road, cut through the woods, and what do I see? You and your friend slipping into this old barn."

"Well, it looks like everything turned out just like you planned," Nathan said. As he spoke he nudged the backpack under the hay wagon with his foot. In the muddy darkness, the black cloth was completely invisible.

"Yes, I'd say our efforts are going to pay off quite nicely, not that it didn't require some deception along the way. But story time is over." He aimed the pistol at Nathan and said, "I'll take that backpack now."

"You want the backpack? You can have it. But you won't find the necklace in it," Nathan lied. "It's right here in my back pocket. You want it? Come and get it."

"How about I just shoot you instead and be done with it?"

"You want to shoot me? Go ahead," Nathan said. "Let's see how good a shot you are."

Sobol extended his arm, taking aim, when Nathan dove to his left, tucking and rolling in a tight ball just like he'd practiced at home. But instead of springing to his feet and running, he stopped himself behind the pallet.

Sobol tracked him across the floor and fired, the bullet striking the bags of fertilizer.

Nathan stayed low and scrambled to the next pallet when Sobol fired again. This time the bullet grazed a bag of organic seed starter. He made it as far as the last pallet and stopped. The barn doors were less than 10 feet away, close enough to run outside. But then what? Would Frank go after Gina? *Of course he would.*

From where he was hiding he couldn't see if she was still in the barn or if she'd used his distraction to slip out the back. And what about Brandt? What was he doing? What if he grabbed Gina as insurance? What then? *No time to think about that now,* he told himself.

Sobol was 10 feet away and getting closer, grunting as he ducked around each of the pallets, his search becoming more frantic. He stepped out from behind the row of pallets and moved laterally, keeping his back to the tractor, the Glock pointed straight ahead, ready to fire.

As he approached the last pallet, Nathan jumped out and grabbed his gun hand, jerking it up toward the roof. Sobol fired, but the angle of the gun sent the bullet up into the empty hay loft where it hit high up on the wall. What happened next was a blur.

Beck appeared, seemingly out of nowhere. He grabbed Sobol's forearm with one hand, the gun with his other hand, and brought it down hard against his knee, snapping Frank's wrist downward in a way wrists aren't meant to bend. There was a sickening sound of breaking bones as Frank cried out in pain and the gun fell harmlessly to the floor.

"Go," Beck told Nathan. "I'll take it from here"

"No," Nathan said, pushing Beck away. "I need to finish this."

Beck stepped back and watched as Nathan went to work.

First, a left jab to the face.

"He *trusted* you."

WHAM!

Then, a jarring right cross.

"And you *betrayed* him."

WHAM!

Frank's head jerked back with each blow but he didn't go down. Nathan set his feet and attacked again, this time with a blinding flurry of jab-cross, jab-cross combinations.

"You took him away from us!"

WHAM! WHAM!...WHAM! WHAM!

"And now he's gone!"

WHAM! WHAM!...WHAM! WHAM!

Frank wobbled, blood gushing from his nose and mouth. But Nathan wasn't done yet. Consumed by the rage he was feeling, he fired off a volley of piston-like jabs.

"Now…"

WHAM!

"You're…

WHAM!

"History!"

WHAM!

Frank's eyes rolled back in his head and he fell backward over the front tire of the tractor.

Nathan looked at Beck, out of breath, but confident as his cloak of anger lifted.

"Feel better?" asked Beck.

"I feel great," Nathan said.

"We need to go," Beck said, "And I mean *now*. If this clown figured out we were here, there's no telling who else knows, or if he brought more of his thugs with him."

Nathan scanned the back half of the barn. "What happened to Gina?"

"She snuck out the back while you were playing hide and seek with Frank," Beck said. "I sent her back to the truck to wait for us."

"Please tell me she grabbed the backpack."

"She did."

"What about Brandt?"

"What about him?"

"He was here," Nathan said.

"Brandt was *here*?" Beck exclaimed.

"Yeah, you didn't see him?"

"No, I was out front."

"He must've slipped out the back when the shooting started," Nathan said.

"Whatever," Beck said. "Come on, we need to leave."

"What about him?" Nathan asked, pointing at Sobol's prone body.

Beck surveyed the barn, turning in a slow circle as he considered the options. "There," he said, pointing at an old grain box sitting in the front corner.

"Are you serious?" Nathan asked.

"Uh-huh," Beck replied. "Where he's going, he'll need to get used to tight living quarters. May as well get started now."

They each grabbed a foot and hauled Frank's body over to the grain box. Then, with considerable effort, they hoisted him up and dropped him inside. Eight bags of fertilizer, and 400 lbs. later, the lid of the grain box was effectively sealed shut. The only way Frank would be leaving the barn was when the police removed the bags of fertilizer and pulled him out.

Nathan and Beck jogged across the field and were passing the house when Everett emerged from the back porch.

"Were those gunshots I heard?" he shouted.

"Go! Now!" Beck told Nathan, pointing at the truck. As Nathan hurried away, Beck walked over to the stairs. Everett was standing at the top, throwing glances at the old barn. "Everett, everything is fine," Beck told him. "There was an incident in the barn but it's been handled." He didn't mention Walter Ballard, or the role he had played in the fracas. "The police are going to come very shortly to inspect the scene," Beck said. "They may ask you some questions, but the bulk of what they'll need to know will come from Nathan, Gina, and myself. Until they get here I need you to steer clear of the barn. It's a crime scene and it's absolutely vital that nothing be disturbed."

"A crime scene? What's this all about?"

"I'll let you know when I figure it out," Beck said.

"Very well, I'll keep to the porch until the police arrive. Is everyone all right? Was anyone hurt?"

"Everyone's fine, except the guy with the gun. But you don't have to worry about him. When this is all over, I promise I'll come back and explain everything. But it's going to cost you another cup of your fresh-brewed coffee."

"Deal," said Everett.

Beck pulled out of the driveway and drove north, heading toward Lexington center. He had one hand on the wheel and was using his other hand to call Jameson.

"Hello, this is Jameson," he said, answering right away.

"It's Beck. I need you to work your magic and get a team of detectives over to Waltham Street in Lexington right away. The property in question is a tree farm owned by Harvard University. It's about a mile from Rt. 2."

"I'm familiar with it," Jameson said. "What happened?"

"It's a long story. We're on our way back to Nathan's house and we'll explain everything when we get there, but I will tell you this: there's a barn behind the house. It's down in the back corner of the field. It needs to be locked down at once and there are a number of bullets the police will want to recover."

"Bullets?" Jameson repeated.

"Hold on Jameson," Beck said. "How many shots did he fire?" he asked Nathan.

"Uh…let me think," Nathan said, counting them off in his head. "Just three."

"Three bullets," Beck told Jameson.

"Is that Nathan?" he exclaimed.

"Yes." Beck replied.

"Please tell me he's alright."

"He's fine," Beck assured him. "It's been a wild day and he's got quite a story to tell."

"I can't wait to hear it," Jameson said.

"You'll get some detectives to the scene?"

"Yes, I'll take care of it."

"Good…and Jameson?"

"Yes?"

"There's an old grain box in the front corner of the barn. It's impossible to miss because it has 400 pounds of fertilizer piled on top of it. There's a guy inside. He needs to be taken into custody—"

"Wait," Jameson cut in. "There's a man inside the box?"

"Yes."

"Let me talk to him," Nathan said, gesturing with his hand.

"Hold on Jameson. Nathan has something he wants to say to you." He handed the phone to Nathan and then looked at Gina in the rearview mirror. "You all right back there?"

Gina had the cigar box open on her lap and was staring at the necklace, unable to take her eyes from it. "Well, I didn't get shot," she said, "so there's that."

Nathan jammed the phone against his ear. "Jameson? You have to make sure the police arrest the guy in the box. Do *not* let him get away. Promise me you'll tell them that!"

"Arrest him? On what charge?"

"Murder."

"Murder?" Jameson repeated, louder.

"I'll explain everything when I get home." He disconnected the call and put Beck's phone back in the cupholder. "We need to pull over," he said.

"Yes!" Gina said. "Preferably someplace with a bathroom." She wrapped the necklace in the linen cloth, tucked it back in the cigar box, and slipped it back in Nathan's backpack.

"Pull over? Why?" Beck asked.

"Brandt never put the tracker on Sobol's car," Nathan said. "He put it on your truck, instead."

"Why would he do that?"

"You heard me say I need to use the bathroom, right?" Gina said.

"It was a ploy, designed by Sobol to get me to find the notebook. All those coordinates Brandt gave us? They were fake. Sobol was at the dealership the whole time. He never left."

"Uh, guys?" Gina said. "A *bathroom?*"

Beck hated being played. He clenched his teeth and said, "If I ever see Brandt again, I'll make him *eat* that tracker."

He drove another 500 feet and pulled into a Denny's-style family restaurant. The parking lot was full and he circled it twice before falling in behind an older couple walking back to their car.

As he watched them back out of their parking space, Gina grew impatient. "Sorry, can't hold it," she said, then pushed the door open and climbed out.

"Go with her," Beck said, watching her hurry toward the front door of the restaurant.

"Why?" Nathan asked.

"Just do it, and make it quick."

"You really think somebody's following us?" Nathan asked.

"Go."

"All right, all right. I'm going, I'm going."

After he parked, Beck cursed Brandt's name and grabbed a flashlight from the glove box. He knew the GPS tracker had to be the magnetic kind, which Brandt would've hidden somewhere beneath the truck. Wherever it was, Beck would recognize it right away, having used trackers of that sort on several occasions. What he'd do with it once he found it was another matter. He could always put it on the restaurant's delivery vehicle, but beating Brandt senseless with it felt like a more appropriate form of payback.

Nathan cut through the sea of parked cars and went into the restaurant through the side entrance. There was a narrow hallway that led to the front lobby, and when he got there he saw padded benches lining the outside wall, packed with families waiting for a table. To his right, the dining room was filled to capacity, the ceaseless chatter of the crowd creating a solid wall of sound.

He went to the hostess station positioned just inside the front door where two young woman were standing. One had the phone pressed to her ear taking a reservation; the other one was gathering laminated menus for the party she was about to seat.

"Excuse me," he said to menu girl. He had to speak up to be heard. "Where are the bathrooms?"

"The bathrooms?" she said, over the clamor. "Back corner of the dining room." She pointed in that direction, then stepped out from behind the station. "Cavanaugh? Party of eight?"

Nathan zig-zagged through the crowded dining room until he reached the far corner. There, he saw another narrow hallway. Mounted on the wall next to the opening was a long vertical sign with the word "RESTROOMS." Set at the top was a Victorian-style drawing of a hand, pointing.

He followed the hallway to a raised-panel door painted a curious shade of red. Affixed to the middle of it was another restroom sign, this one horizontal and without the hand. He pulled it open just in time to see a man at the opposite end of the hallway hustling Gina out the back door. "HEY! WHAT ARE YOU DOING? STOP!" he shouted as he broke into a full-out run.

He raced past the bathrooms and a door that led to the kitchen. He was almost to the end of the hallway when Campbell stepped out from a small storage room, grabbed him with both hands, and marched him across the hall, pinning him to the wall.

"LET GO OF ME!" Nathan shouted, fighting to break free.

Campbell took one look at Nathan's face and recoiled in shock. "No way!" he said. The sight of Nathan's facial features, which matched Asher's in every way, was something right out of a carnival nightmare.

Nathan kept struggling.

"Hey! Kid!" Campbell shouted, shaking Nathan to get his

attention.

Nathan fought harder.

Campbell pulled him forward and slammed him hard against the wall, once, then twice. "Listen to me," he shouted.

Nathan stopped resisting.

"This is very simple," Campbell said. "You get the girl back when I get the necklace."

"What necklace?" Nathan asked.

"Don't get cute. We know you have it. The necklace for the girl. Refuse, and you'll never see her again."

"I-I don't have it with me," Nathan stammered. "It's in the truck."

"Okay, here's what you're going to do," Campbell said calmly. "You're going to go get it and bring it to me. I'll be in a van parked behind the restaurant."

"What van?"

Campbell dragged Nathan over to the door and pushed it open. "Guess," he said.

A row of angled parking spaces ran along the chain-link fence that marked the back of the property. Parked in one of them was the Bickford Electric van. D-Mack was standing next to the side door, one hand gripping Gina's arm, the other hand clamped over her mouth.

When she saw Nathan, her eyes went wide and she tried to scream.

Campbell yanked him back from the door and pulled it shut. "You got five minutes, kid. Bring me the necklace and this whole thing ends peacefully. We both get what we want. But if I catch one *glimpse* of your oversized friend, things are going to end very badly for the girl."

He released Nathan and shoved him down the hallway toward the dining room. "Five minutes starts right now. And remember what I said: if I see the big man, it's lights out for the girl."

Priya sat on her motorcycle at the far end of the restaurant parking lot, watching Gargantuan Man crawl around on the pavement, checking the underside of his truck with a flashlight. She'd been trailing him ever since he backed out of Nathan's driveway at 11 o'clock that morning. When he pulled into the tree farm's driveway, she drove past it and turned down the next street. Parked a few feet back from the corner, she watched Beck and the two kids talking to a man she assumed was the owner. She was mildly curious when she saw Nathan and Gina walk past the house and disappear into the field. But when she heard gunshots a short time later, she pulled the phone from her pocket and called Asher.

"You are *not* going to believe this," she'd said when he answered. What followed was a detailed recap of the day, starting with their arrival at the tree farm, the kids vanishing into the field out back, and ending with Gina racing back to the truck, visibly shaken, clutching a backpack to her chest with both hands. Priya knew that look.

The girl was scared.

Afraid of anyone seeing what she had inside the backpack.

Or taking it away from her.

As Asher was listening, he had taken a burner phone from his desk drawer and sent Campbell a text message, giving him the address of the tree farm. When Priya called again with an update from the restaurant parking lot, Asher sent a follow-up text.

By that time, Campbell and D-Mack were already in the area. They pulled into the restaurant parking lot seconds after Beck, then drove around to the back of the building as any legitimate service provider would do.

Nathan raced through the dining room and exploded out the front door. When he got back to the truck, Beck was lying flat on the pavement underneath the bed examining every inch of metal that would accommodate a magnetic tracker.

Nathan pulled the back door open, grabbed his backpack, then checked the time. Two minutes gone—three to go.

"What's up?" Beck asked.

"Nothing," Nathan said. He slammed the door shut and started to leave.

"Wait!" said Beck. He climbed out from under the truck and brushed his palms together, shaking loose some dirt and debris. "Where's Gina?"

"Uh...she's fine..." Nathan blurted out.

"That's not what I asked you."

Nathan checked his watch again. Three minutes gone—two to go. He had no time for this.

"What are you doing with that?" Beck said, pointing at the backpack.

"Uh, nothing...just...uh...nothing."

Beck saw the panic in his eyes. "Tell me what's wrong." he said calmly, an undercurrent of anger brewing inside him.

316

"I can't…I mean…there's no time."

"What do you mean, no time?"

Nathan checked his watch for a third time. Four minutes gone—one to go. He was almost out of time. "I'm going to get Gina," he said, like a coach outlining the next play. "I need you to stay here. Do not follow me."

Beck opened his mouth to respond when Nathan took off running. He made it to the side door of the restaurant and then veered right, running along the side of the building before racing around the back corner.

Campbell was standing at the back bumper of the van keeping a close eye on the parking lot. When Nathan ran up to him, clutching the backpack, he tapped the face of his watch and said, "Look at that, 30 seconds to spare."

"Where is she?" Nathan demanded, out of breath.

Campbell pounded on the back door of the van with his fist. Two times. *Boom, boom.*

The door swung open and Nathan saw Gina sitting on the floor, her arms wrapped around her knees that were drawn up to her chest. D-Mack was sitting next to her atop a large contractor's toolbox. He took one look at Nathan and did a double take. "What the…?"

"Freaky, right?" Campbell said. "He's like a carbon copy, only younger."

Suddenly, Nathan knew who had sent them. The question was, how did Asher know they'd be here, at this restaurant, at this precise time? Now wasn't the time to dwell on it; he had to get

Gina out of there. He looked at her and said, "Are you all right?"

She was staring at the floor, too angry to speak, and could only manage a nod.

"Thank Perseus," he said, hoping she'd pick up on his subtle cue.

Which she did.

She turned her head and looked at him, confused, and that's when he did a thing with his eyes. He glanced quickly to his right…*that way*…then back at her again.

"All right, all right, you've seen her," Campbell said impatiently. "Now give me the necklace."

Nathan unzipped his backpack and was about to reach in when Campbell grabbed his arm.

"Uh, uh, uh…not so fast," he said. He leaned forward and pulled open the pack. When he saw the cigar box tucked inside, he let go of Nathan's arm and stepped back. "Continue."

Nathan pulled the box out and turned it so Campbell would be able to see what was inside. Then he opened it and pulled back the folds of linen cloth, exposing a section of the necklace. "Whoa," Campbell said, recalling Asher's words.

"When you see the item in question, you'll understand why I want it."

Nathan closed the box, then slid it back into his pack and zipped it shut. "You get this, when I get her," he said, holding it up in the air.

"Dee, bring her out here," Campbell said.

When D-Mack heard that, he quickly jumped out of the van and stood at the bumper.

"You see how easy this was, kid?" Campbell said. "We all got what we wanted, and no one got hurt."

D-mack grabbed Gina's elbow and pulled her up, then guided her forward.

Nathan stepped closer and offered her a hand. "Easy does it," he said.

"No, it's okay, I got it," she said.

Their eyes met and he nodded his head. *Now.*

"PERSEUS!"

20

The Repository

Gina jumped off the back of the van and landed on top of D-Mack, sending him crashing to the ground. As she climbed to her feet, Nathan tossed her the backpack and then launched himself at Campbell, hitting him square in the face with a vicious right elbow. Campbell staggered backward, off balance, and grabbed the edge of the door to keep from falling.

By that time Gina was already running. With the backpack in hand, she bolted toward the main parking lot where she knew Beck would be waiting in the truck.

Nathan, by design, ran in the opposite direction. He darted past Campbell, giving him a hard shot to his right eye, with his elbow, then ran toward the chain-link fence. With one leap he was half-way up it. Then, hand over hand, he scrabbled over it.

"You get him!" Campbell shouted, pointing at the fence. "I'm going after her."

D-Mack, furious at being taken down by a school girl, ran to the fence and scaled it with relative ease. When he landed on the other side, he was standing on an access road that skirted a big box store. He looked to his left and saw Nathan sprinting away. As he took off after him, Nathan suddenly changed direction and ran behind the store.

Gina sprinted into the parking lot when she heard a sharp, shrill whistle. She looked back over her shoulder and saw Beck standing with his back to the building, just inches from the corner. "Beck?" she muttered, then doubled back and ran to him.

"Are you all right?" he asked.

She nodded her head as she tried to catch her breath. "One of them…the leader, I think…he's coming after me…"

"Oh, goodie," Beck said, rubbing his hands together. "You wait here. I'm going to go say hello." He stepped around the corner and saw Campbell charging directly at him, 15 feet away and closing fast. His face was smeared with blood and his right eye was nearly swollen shut. When he saw Beck, he tried to stop.

Too late.

Beck pivoted on the balls of his left foot and swung his right leg through the air with blazing speed, delivering a spinning back kick that hit Campbell in the side of the head like a 50-pound cinder block. Campbell teetered momentarily, the entire universe spinning before his eyes, then everything went dark and his legs buckled, dropping him to the pavement like a bag of rocks.

Nathan darted behind the box store, ran for several feet, then stopped. "Enough!" he shouted. He was tired of being chased. Tired of people trying to hurt him. Trying to hurt Gina. His earlier bouts with Frank Sobol and then Campbell had energized him. He turned and waited for D-Mack to catch up with him, thinking of the things Beck had taught him about adversaries: about not hitting them, but evading them; using their own energy against them to frustrate them and tire them out.

D-Mack came running around the corner of the building and saw Nathan standing perfectly still like he was waiting for the bus. It only made him run faster.

Nathan held his position, unaffected, like D-Mack was a gust of wind that he couldn't see.

With full force, D-Mack lowered his shoulder and drove it into Nathan's midsection.

Only, Nathan wasn't there.

He had waited until the very last second, then dropped into a squatting position. D-Mack sailed over him, unable to stop his forward momentum, and that's when Nathan stood up, launching his adversary into the air, arms flailing, before crashing hard on the pavement.

D-mack got up on all fours, momentarily stunned, then stood, anger consuming him, and faced Nathan, who had resumed his earlier pose.

You want me? Come and get me.

D-Mack exhaled angrily and charged again.

This time, Nathan braced for the collision, then took a step to his left at the last moment and extended his right leg outward, sending D-Mack sprawling headlong onto the ground for a second time.

D-Mack's fury surged. He pushed himself up off the ground and faced Nathan yet again. This time, he hunched down, his arms up and fingers hooked like claws as he slowly circled his target like a predator waiting for the right moment to move in for the kill.

Nathan decided to feed the beast. "Uh, do you think we could speed this up?" he said. "It's getting late and I have a few chores I need to get done before my folks get home."

The beast in D-Mack erupted and he flew at Nathan in a mad rage.

Once again, Nathan waited. As Beck had taught him, timing can be a powerful ally. With D-Mack bearing down on him, he waited…waited…waited, and then took a short step to his right and delivered a powerful right cross to D-Mack's jaw, who stumbled forward wildly and collided face first with the back wall of the box store.

Flesh vs. cinder block.

Not a fair fight.

D-Mack turned, wobbly, and saw Nathan's left fist sailing at him.

Left jab. *POW!*

"That was for Gina. This one's for me."

Right cross. *POW!*

Then he did it again for good measure.

Left jab. *POW!*

Right hook. *POW!*

"Excuse me. Are we done here?" came an impatient voice from 20 feet behind him.

He turned and saw Beck standing there. Gina was at his side, looking very pleased after witnessing Nathan's brutal treatment of D-Mack.

"Yeah, we're done here," Nathan said. He gave D-Mack a shove and watched him topple over and land in a heap on the ground.

When they were back in the truck, the first thing Beck did was call Jameson. With the phone sitting on the center console, the speakerphone on, he gave Jameson a full rundown of the events of the past hour. After Jameson's initial shock at Gina's abduction, albeit short lived, Beck explained that the culprits were only using her to get the necklace.

"Do we know who these two men were?" Jameson asked. "I mean, were they acting alone? If not, then —"

"Asher sent them," Nathan cut in.

"How do you know that?" Jameson asked.

"When they saw my face they both had the same reaction. I heard the one in charge say something about me being a carbon copy."

"Where are these men now?" Jameson asked.

"In the back of my truck," said Beck.

"Well, we can't have that, now, can we? Let me make a call. You three sit tight until someone comes. It won't be long. The person I'm sending will be from the Repository. When you hear that name, you know you can trust him."

"The Repository? He's one of yours I take it," said Beck.

"Yes."

"Interesting name. I'd love to hear more."

"And perhaps one day you will. Sit tight. Help is on the way."

Fifteen minutes later, a gray commercial van pulled into the parking lot. The driver paused briefly to scan the lot, then drove to the back corner where Beck had moved his truck. The last thing they needed was for a restaurant customer to walk by and see two men tied up in the back, flopping around like a pair of freshly caught sea bass.

The van stopped in front of the truck and a young man got out. His height and muscular build suggested he was a blocking tight end for a Big-10 university, taking the summer off to earn a few extra dollars. He was dressed in crisp gray slacks with a blue corporate-style polo shirt and matching ballcap. Not a company logo in sight. He walked up to the driver's window and said to Beck, "Good afternoon sir. I'm here to pick up two items for the Repository. Where might I find the merchandise?"

Beck hitched his thumb over his shoulder. "They're in the back," he said, opening the door. "Here, let me give you a hand with them."

"No, that's quite all right, I'll take care of it, sir," the driver said. "You sit right there and enjoy this beautiful summer day."

He walked to the back of the truck and lowered the tailgate. After a brief visual inspection of "the merchandise," he went back to the van, opened the sliding door, and removed two nine-foot Christmas tree storage bags. Red polyester, with heavy duty canvas handles.

"Huh. Never thought of using *those*." Beck said under his breath, as the driver carried them past the open window.

"Using them for what?" Nathan asked.

"Clean up."

Nathan wrinkled his brow, then looked at Beck.

"What?" Beck asked.

"You're not talking about leaves and sticks are you?"

"No, I use a garden cart for that."

Nathan had no reply. Obviously there was still much he didn't know about Beck.

The driver hopped up into the back of the truck and got right to work. In a matter of minutes he had both bags packed and zipped shut. One by one he carried them back to the van, making it look painfully easy, and slid them inside. Then, he stepped into the van, pulled the door shut behind him, and left. No toot of the horn. No goodbye wave. He just drove away, pulling out of the lot as unobtrusively as he had pulled in.

"Well, that's not something you see every day," Gina said.

"Hey, are you guys hungry?" Beck asked, trying to lighten the mood. "We could go back inside and have lunch. I hear their pizza is really good."

"NO!" they both shouted.

"Yeah, I didn't think so," Beck said, grinning.

As they drove away, Nathan couldn't let go of the fact that Asher had somehow learned of their presence at the restaurant, and that he'd sent men there to ambush him and Gina and steal the necklace. But now that his first two goons had failed, would he send more? *Yeah, he will*, Nathan told himself…*and more, and more, until he gets the necklace.* The glaring truth was: the necklace would continue to be a threat for as long as Asher Rickman believed he still had it.

"This was just the beginning," he muttered.

"What was that?" Beck asked.

"Asher Rickman is not going to stop until he gets the necklace."

"I still want to know how he knew you'd be here," Beck said.

"Maybe he bugged your truck, just like Brandt did," Gina

suggested.

"Maybe," Beck replied. "But my gut tells me it's something else." He checked the rearview mirror, making a mental note of the vehicles he saw, then turned into a convenience store parking lot, drove past the gas pumps, and stopped at the second entrance like he was reversing direction.

As he watched the long line of vehicles approaching from the left, he spotted a silver and black Yamaha SR400. The driver was wearing a black touring jacket and matching helmet, and was crouched down like a Supersport World Championship racer. Something about it was eerily familiar. "Huh," he said, "I think we just found our answer."

"What are you talking about?" Nathan asked, checking the traffic in both directions.

"See this motorcycle?" Beck said, pointing it out as it passed by. "It was following us when we left the Auto Barn."

"I saw a bike just like that when Kendra was driving me to work. It pulled up next to us at an intersection. I only remember because the rider was staring at me. He was either checking me out, or he likes beat-up old Volvos. And then, I saw him again, when my dad was driving me home later that day."

"Must be working for Rickman," Beck said. "Let's find out." He saw a break in the line of cars and pulled out. The motorcycle was five cars ahead of him.

One of them signaled, then turned into a drug store parking

lot.

Four cars.

Another car slowed, then cut across the oncoming lane into the entrance for an outdoor furniture store.

Three cars.

Beck accelerated and the driver of the next car pulled over to let him pass.

Two cars.

When Priya saw that, she revved the engine and screamed past the next three cars, riding down the solid yellow centerline.

Beck lost sight of her when she cut back into the right lane ahead of a small red convertible, then raced down a narrow side street. "I think we've seen the last of that guy," he said.

Nathan looked over at the side street as they passed it. The motorcycle was nowhere to be seen. With that question answered, one detail remained. They had just turned onto the Alewife Brook Parkway when he said, "Hey, can we make a quick detour?"

"Sure, what's up?" Beck asked.

"I'll explain on the way. Take your next right."

By the time they made it back to Nathan's house, it was almost 2:30 p.m. Jameson and Kendra were sitting on the front porch waiting for them. Elizabeth and David had yet to return from their trip into Cambridge with Gina's parents.

"Good, your parents aren't back yet," Gina said, seeing the

empty driveway.

Beck pulled in, then backed out and parked at the curb behind Kendra's Volvo.

That's when Gina opened the door. "Well, gentlemen," she said. "I'd say it's been fun…but—"

"Wait," Nathan said, cutting her off. "I want you to be here when we tell everyone what happened."

"Yeah, right. Like that could happen," she said. "You know once my parents get home I'm stuck there."

"So, write them a note," he said. "Do it now. Hurry, before they get back."

"Write them a note?," she repeated. "Is that supposed to be a joke?"

"I'm serious. Make it two lines. Short and sweet. I went for a walk. Be back soon."

"Went for a walk? Since when do I do that?"

"You did it today," he said. "At the tree farm. You walked from the driveway to the barn. Then you walked back. Or did you run?"

"Okay, okay, I get it," she said. "I'll go write a note. But if they pull in before I'm done, I'll see you when I see you."

"Why are you still sitting here?" Nathan asked.

She mumbled something he couldn't decipher, then ran over to her house. In the kitchen, she tore a piece of notepaper off the cube on the counter and scribbled a short message. When it came to writing a note to throw off your parents, Nathan had an advanced degree, so she used his exact words.

Went for a walk
Be back soon
-G

When she walked back into Nathan's house, she found Jameson and Kendra sitting on the living room couch. Beck was over in the corner, examining the books in the ladder-style bookcase. Nathan was at the opposite end of the room, standing at the front window, watching the street through the open curtain.

"You're back," Jameson said, surprised, when she walked into the room.

"I'm back," she replied tentatively, unsure why Nathan insisted she be there.

Kendra got up and gave her a fist bump. "Good to see you, sister."

"Likewise," Gina said. "We sure could've used you today."

"Why? What happened?" Kendra asked, like she was ready to jump into action.

"You're about to find out," Gina said. She looked at Nathan and said, "Any word from your parents?"

"They just called," he replied, keeping his eyes trained on the street. "They'll be home any minute."

"I see. Well, in that case, do you mind if I use the bathroom?"

"Be my guest," he said. Normally, this would call for one of his clever comebacks, but his days of teasing her about the bathroom came to a permanent end in the back hallway of the restaurant.

She had just gone upstairs when Nathan saw his father's car pass the house and pull into the driveway. "They're here," he said. He let go of the curtain and stood motionless, gripped by the enormity of what was about to happen.

When Jameson saw that, he got up from the couch and crossed the room. "Are you all right?" he asked Nathan, who still hadn't moved.

"Yes and no," Nathan replied. "Mostly no."

From the kitchen came the sound of Elizabeth and David, laughing and joking as they walked up the back stairway, their voices carrying all the way down the hallway.

"Well, *you're* the one who said it," Elizabeth said, teasing.

"Yes, but I had no idea that…you know…" David replied, in his own defense.

"Why do you think I left to use the lady's room?" Elizabeth said. "It was everything I could to keep from laughing out loud."

They walked through the kitchen and made their way down the hallway. When they entered the living room, Elizabeth immediately sensed something was amiss. There was palpable silence, as if someone had died, and people were scattered about the room. Nathan and Jameson were at one end, Beck was standing at the other, and Kendra was sitting alone on the couch.

David looked at Jameson and shrugged. *What's going on?*

Jameson shook his head…*don't know*…then nodded at Nathan, indicating he was the one who had called the meeting.

"Uh, honey," David said to Elizabeth, "I think maybe we should sit down."

"Yes, let's all sit," Jameson said, putting on an upbeat face.

"Go ahead," Nathan told him. "I'd rather stand."

Jameson's worry meter clicked up another notch.

Just then, Gina came down the front hall stairs. She paused at the arched entryway to the living room when she saw Elizabeth and David sitting on the couch, unsure how they were going to react when they heard the news of the day.

"Gina?" Elizabeth said, surprised. "I didn't know you were here. What about…?"

"My parents?" Gina said, as she walked into the room. "They don't know I'm here." She looked at Nathan and said, "They think I'm taking a *walk*."

Nathan had no snappy reply. The time he dreaded had finally come, the moment when he would utter the most difficult words to ever cross his lips—possibly the toughest words he would *ever* say. He felt like he was standing before a great abyss, being pulled forward by an invisible force from which he was powerless to break free.

He walked over and stood next to Gina, who was seated in one of the red overstuffed chairs. From that vantage point he could see everyone and they could see him.

"Jameson? Kendra? Thank you for meeting us here on such short notice," he said, easing into the conversation. "Mom, Dad, I know you're wondering what this is all about. The truth is," he said, pausing for a beat, "Beck, Gina, and I had a very difficult day today. There's really no easy way for me to tell you what I'm about to say."

From outside came the sound of footsteps racing up the porch steps. Seconds later the front door flew open and Julie Nichols ran into the room, followed by Jordan Prescott and Connie Freeman. Julie went to Nathan and grabbed his shoulders with both hands. "Is it true?" she said. "You found it?"

Jameson stood at once. "What are you doing here?" he asked. In all the time he'd known them, the facilitators never travelled together in public.

"Yes," Elizabeth said, getting to her feet. "Who are you and what are you doing in my house? And you, take your hands off my son!" she told Julie.

Jordan raised both hands in a calming gesture. "Elizabeth, we can explain," she said.

"How do you know my name?" Elizabeth demanded.

"Uh…Jameson?" Jordan said. *A little help here?*

"Everyone, please, take a deep breath and calm yourself," he said. His eyes settled on Nathan. "I believe Nathan is about to clear up this matter for us. Isn't that right, Nathan?"

Reluctantly, Nathan nodded his head.

Elizabeth stepped closer and gently cradled his face in her

hands. "What is it?" she asked. "What is it that you're afraid to tell me?"

Before he could answer, the front door opened again. Everyone turned to look as Donald Brandt walked into the room.

"YOU!" Beck growled through clenched teeth. He stormed across the room toward Brandt, his face a mask of fury.

He almost made it.

Julie Nichols stepped into his path, raising both hands to stop him. "Don't," she said.

"Out of my way," Beck growled.

"Not until you hear what he has to say."

"I'm done listening to him. The last time I did, he double crossed us."

"No," Julie said. "He didn't double cross you."

"What are you talking about?"

"He double crossed the person who killed Henry Hammond."

21

Revelations

"WHAT DID YOU SAY?" Elizabeth yelled.

Jameson looked at Brandt. "Is this true?"

"Yeah, what are you talking about?" Beck said. He was still inclined to push past Julie Nichols and plant his fist in the center of Brandt's face.

"EVERYBODY JUST *STOP!*" Nathan shouted.

The room went silent.

He had too much anger, brought on by the lies, the denials, and the physical pain he and Gina had endured. Most of all, he had too much respect for the man who had chosen him to carry on the legacy of the Hammond bookcase, only to have his life savagely taken from him.

He looked at his mother and said, "You don't know these people?"

"No," she replied, casting a hostile look at the group.

"*You* do," he said to Jameson.

"Yes," Jameson said, nodding.

To his mother, Nathan said, "You know that your father helped people in need, as others in our family have done for generations."

"Yes," she said.

"What you don't know is that he assembled a special team of people, five in all, each with a specific skill that he needed to better serve those who came to him for help."

Elizabeth listened in rapt silence, shocked that her father had done this without her knowledge. Why would he keep such a thing from her?

"One of those five people, the one they call Pennyman, put the poison in your father's water bottle," Nathan said. "Today, Beck, Gina, and I apprehended him. As we speak, he's sitting behind bars. Isn't that right, Jameson?" he said, louder, not breaking eye contact with his mother.

"Yes, that's correct," Jameson replied.

Elizabeth took Nathan in her arms and hugged him tightly, tears flooding from her eyes. David appeared at her side and joined the embrace. A gut-wrenching silence filled the room as the others stood motionless, watching them join together in a moment of profound sadness and relief.

Elizabeth stepped back, wiping her eyes. "Why?" she asked. "Why would someone my father *trusted* do such a thing?"

"For a gold necklace worth untold millions," Nathan said.

"Wait a minute," she said. "Are you telling me that my father had a million-dollar gold necklace? Where would he get such a thing?"

"He never had it," Nathan explained. "The necklace was hidden. No one knew where."

"Hidden? That makes no sense."

"Elizabeth? If I may..." Julie said.

"Yes! Please!" Elizabeth blurted out. "Say something, anything, to help me understand this."

"The necklace belonged to a Mayan warrior queen named Lady Six Sky. It was discovered during an archeological dig in Guatemala, and for reasons unknown to us, the archeologist who found it returned home and subsequently hid it. According to his daughter, he put a clue to its whereabouts in his field notebook, which she gave to your father the day before he died."

Elizabeth turned to Jameson, outraged. "Did you know about this?"

"No," Jameson replied. "I was away at an estate sale in Vermont. When I returned home the next day, Henry was already suffering from the effects of the poison."

"The notebook was taken from your father's desk the night before he died," Julie said. "We had it on good authority that Pennyman stole it, and as Nathan said, he was the one who poisoned your father's water bottle. But to prove it, we needed to catch him with the notebook in his possession. Finding the notebook was key, and for the past seven years, the three of us...(gesturing at Jordan and Connie)...have attempted to do just that."

"Why?" Elizabeth said, anger charging her words. "So you could use it to find the necklace, then sell it? How does that make you any different than this *Pennyman* character?"

"Oh, we had no intention of selling it," Julie said. "Quite the opposite."

"Your father's goal was to find the necklace and return it to the Mexican government," Jordan said. "After his passing, our sole mission was to fulfill that wish, and by doing so we'd be honoring him as well."

"As I'm sure you know," Julie said to Nathan. "Your grandfather had a profound effect on a great many people."

"Including us," Connie said. "As I told you before, he was like a father to me."

"This still doesn't get *you* off the hook," Beck said, pointing an angry finger at Brandt.

"Go ahead, tell him," Julie said.

"I knew that Pennyman stole the notebook," Brandt said.

"You might as well use his real name," Connie mumbled. "By this time tomorrow, the whole world is going to know it."

"Right. Like I said, I knew Frank stole the notebook. He knew that, and he promised me that if I ever breathed a word of it to anyone, the authorities would never find my body. For years he tormented me, stopping by my shop every few months to make sure I didn't forget his promise. On Thursday, when you came back to my shop and told me what you wanted me to do, I devised a plan that would expose him and put him away for the rest of his life."

"What plan?" Beck snapped. "You played us, plain and simple."

"Yes, I did, or so it appeared to Frank."

"What's that supposed to mean?"

"After you left, I called him and told him that you wanted me to bug his car with a GPS tracker; that you were going to trick him into thinking you knew where the notebook was so he'd go get it and move it to another location."

"But you never bugged his car," Nathan said. "You bugged Beck's truck instead, then fed us phony coordinates that led us straight to the notebook."

"That's right," Brandt said. "Frank wanted you to have it, but he couldn't just walk up and hand it to you. He was convinced that if you had the notebook, you'd find the clue, and eventually, the necklace. As it turns out, he was right, which is why I showed up at the tree farm this morning."

"You expect us to believe that?" Beck said. "Admit it, you were there for the necklace and nothing else."

"No," Brandt said calmly. "I was there for this."

From the pocket of his jeans he pulled out a small digital voice recorder no bigger than an art eraser. He held it up in the air, pushed the play button, and Nathan's voice instantly filled the room.

"Why'd you do it? Why'd you steal the notebook? My grandfather trusted you!"

"Stealing it was never the plan. I was just going to borrow it for a bit, then put it back."

"Once you found Ballard's hidden code."

"That was the general idea, yes."

"And the poison?"

"Again, not part of the plan…but, hey, sometimes you have to improvise."

Brandt hit the stop button.

"Huh," Beck said, realizing he had Brandt figured all wrong. The man was both cunning and resourceful—two qualities he admired. Part of him wanted to shake Brandt's hand. Another part wanted to slug him for not telling them his plan.

Brandt walked over to Elizabeth and handed her the recorder. "For your father," he said. Then, sadly, "I'm very sorry for your loss. We all are."

Elizabeth took the recorder, considered it briefly, then said, "I don't know you, but clearly my father saw something good in you. I'd say this recording is proof of that."

A moment of silence followed.

"Which brings us back to the necklace," Connie said.

"Yes, the necklace!" Julie said, excitedly. "Where is it? Can we see it?"

"How did you know I found it?" Nathan asked her.

She nodded at Brandt. "Wroth called us after he left the barn."

"Who's Wroth?" Elizabeth asked.

"They all have code names, Mom. He's Wroth," he said, pointing at Brandt.

"Fane," Julie said.

"Sidney," Jordan said, raising her hand.

Connie tapped her chest. "I'm Finch."

"Those are very unusual names," Elizabeth said.

"Your father's idea," Jameson told her.

"My *father* gave you those names?" she said to the group.

"They were theologians and writers from the 17th century," Julie replied.

"Leave it to my dad," Elizabeth said, showing the hint of a

smile.

"About the necklace," Nathan said. "There's something you need to know."

"What is it?" Julie asked, when she saw his troubled expression. "You do have it, right?"

"Yes, but there's another person who wants it. Someone with vast resources who will stop at nothing to get it."

"You don't mean Asher Rickman, do you?" Jameson asked. *Please say no.*

"Yes, that's exactly who I mean."

"But, how did he find out about it?"

"He's had someone tailing us all week, probably waiting for us to find it," Nathan said. "He sent a pair of his goons to ambush us this afternoon, shortly after we left the tree farm. Sadly, for them, it didn't work out the way they planned."

Beck looked at over at Jameson and nodded once. *Thank you.*

Jameson nodded in return. *Anytime.*

Campbell and D-Mack were currently at an undisclosed location, undergoing an in-depth "interview," as Jameson like to call it, with two very persuasive associates, both former Delta Rangers whom he used for such matters. Once their statements were "taken," they'd be turned over to the Lexington police, along with a recorded confession that would include how they assaulted Nathan and Gina, the name of their employer, and any other details the Rangers deemed pertinent.

"Asher Rickman is a phantom," Nathan told Julie. "He operates under the radar of law enforcement, orchestrating thefts of high-end artwork, jewelry, you name it. If it has a six-figure price tag or higher, he'll try to steal it…and he usually succeeds."

"An ancient gold necklace worth millions is just his cup of tea," Jameson added.

"A week ago he stole a necklace from an auction house in Brookline worth close to a million dollars," Nathan said. "That may sound like a lot to you and me, but to Rickman, it's pocket change. The necklace, on the other hand, would be a major score. He's got the desire and the resources to find it, and I know for a fact that he won't stop until he lays his hands on it. For that reason, I hid the necklace someplace where he won't think to look for it."

"Oh, okay," Gina said, grinning. "I was wondering why we stopped there." Then, in a lower voice, "Did you tell Richard?"

Nathan frowned and waved it off. *Not now.*

"You didn't tell him?" she exclaimed.

Nathan glared at her. *Quiet!*

She grabbed his arm and pulled him down to chair level. "You don't think Rickman has contacts in North Cambridge? Of course he does! And they're sure to know who Richard Abbott is. Everyone does. What if they show up at his house? You don't think they'll search the barn?"

"You worry too much," he said. "I'm telling you, nothing's going to happen. Now, can we talk about this later?" He pushed her hand away and stood up. "Sorry about that," he told Julie. "As I was saying, the necklace is in a safe place. If you want to come back tomorrow morning at, say, 10 o'clock, I'll be sure to have it here by the time you arrive. It's caused my family enough pain, and as far as I'm concerned the Mexican government can have it. I never want to see it again, ever!"

"Well, I suppose one more day won't hurt," Jordan said. She looked at Julie, then Connie. "Right?"

"Make it two days, three if you like," Connie said. "I'm just relieved you weren't hurt while trying to find it. This Rickman thug sounds dangerous. And Frank Sobol? Anyone who's capable of taking a life is seriously unhinged."

"Tell me about it," Brandt said. "I've been living in fear for years."

Julie walked over to Nathan and shook his hand. "Nathan, thank you," she said. "I know this wasn't easy on you: tracking down the person who killed your grandfather; fearing that he might come after you; finding the hidden clue in Walter Ballard's notebook, then risking your life to retrieve the necklace. I had a good feeling about you. Your detective skills are nothing short of amazing."

"Well, I had excellent help," Nathan said. "It was Gina who found the hidden clue."

"Why does everyone keep calling it a hidden clue?" she crabbed. "Seriously. It was right there in black and white. Anyone could've found it. All they had to do was *look!*"

"My girl does it again!" Kendra crowed. She leaned across the coffee table and gave Gina another fist bump.

"You both did a remarkable job," Julie said. "That goes for you too, Beck. We're all thankful you were there to watch over these two."

"Yes," Elizabeth said. "Thank you."

"You should've seen Nathan," Gina said, excitedly. She punched the air with her fists as she spoke. "He was like Rocky Balboa…

pow-pow! pow-pow!"

"Will you stop?" Nathan said, slapping at her hands.

"We should probably go," Jordan told Julie.

"Yes, I think these kids have earned some extended relaxation time," Julie said. "But before we go, Elizabeth and David, I know the past seven years have been very hard on the both of you. Secrets are a dangerous thing. They can be destructive and hurtful, but they can be a good thing, too, as Henry Hammond taught us all. If he kept the existence of our group from you, it was done for your own protection. He loved you, Elizabeth, *and* your sister, more than life itself. Whenever he mentioned the two of you, it was always with a glint in his eye and joy in his heart. I hope you can find peace now, knowing that his killer has been caught and will spend his remaining days behind bars."

"Thank you," Elizabeth said. She and Julie exchanged a hug, then it was Jordan's turn, followed by Connie.

Brandt shook David's hand, gave Elizabeth a hug, then went over to Beck and extended his hand. "No hard feelings?"

Beck took his hand and they shook. "No hard feelings. But I do have a question."

"Shoot."

"Where did you hide that GPS tracker?"

"Sorry," Brandt said, shaking his head. "Can't tell you. Trade secret."

"Fair enough," Beck said. "Maybe one day our paths will cross again. I can always use a good electronics guy."

"Well, you know where to find me," Brandt said. "Just don't touch the glass."

345

After the four facilitators left, Gina snuck out the back door and cut through the lilac hedge that ran along the side of the house. From there, she zig-zagged through the neighbor's yard, hopped over a fence, cut through another yard, and ended up one street over from her house. Then, in keeping with the note she'd left her parents, she took a walk. With every step, the trying events of the day slowly wafted away like morning mist.

Nathan left the living room and went outside to clear his head and process the startling truths revealed by Julie Nichols and Donald Brandt. He was sitting at the picnic table rewriting the timeline of the past seven years when Jameson appeared at his side.

"Do you mind if I sit?" he asked.

"Go right ahead," Nathan told him.

"There's something I'm curious about and I didn't want to ask you in front of the group," he said, as he took a seat across from Nathan.

"Ask away."

"The facilitators," Jameson said. "How did you find them? Your grandfather took great pains to keep their identities a secret. No one, not even me, knew their real names."

"He gave them to me."

"He?"

"My grandfather."

Jameson stared at him, thinking. Then he grinned. "Devereux."

"Uh-huh," Nathan replied. He didn't mention the bookcase, or the curious light that appeared out of nowhere and crawled slowly across one of the shelves, making the letters in Devereux's name glow like phosphorous rock.

"That doesn't surprise me in the least," Jameson said. "Nor should it surprise you. It speaks to the incredible foresight that your grandfather had. At a very early age, you were already his choice to be the next keeper of the bookcase. He knew then, as the events of this week have clearly shown, that a time would come when you'd need the help of someone you could trust without question."

"You knew Devereux?"

"Yes."

"But, I thought he kept his identity a secret. From everyone except his clients, that is."

"That's correct," Jameson said, giving Nathan a knowing look.

"Wait, *you* were one of his clients?"

"Oh yes," Jameson said, emphatically.

The inflection in his voice suggested he was a repeat customer, prompting Nathan to wonder what items he could've had that required Devereux's unique service.

"These revelations, from Fane and from Wroth," Jameson said. "They're startling. I can't imagine why Pennyman would do such a thing."

"You never heard the whole story, did you?"

"No. The first I heard of Lía Ballard was 45 minutes ago," Jameson said.

"Well, the night before my grandfather died…" Nathan began. For the next 10 minutes he detailed everything Jordan Prescott had told him, starting with Lía Ballard's arrival in the bookshop and ending with their visit to Connie Freeman's house where she revealed how she'd seen Frank Sobol standing alone at Henry's desk. When he was done, Jameson sat there, mortified.

"Henry never told me about Lía Ballard, or the notebook," he said. "Why would he keep that from me?"

"He was protecting you," Nathan said.

"By not telling me the truth?" Jameson exclaimed, his frustration making a rare appearance.

"That's right. When Lía Ballard came into the shop that day, she told him dangerous men were chasing her, trying to get their hands on her father's notebook. I think my grandfather didn't want you to get pulled into it. When you think about it, he probably saved your life."

"By sacrificing his own as it turns out," Jameson said sadly. He shook his head at the inequity of life, and the great sacrifices people make to protect the ones for which they care the most.

"YOU HAVE A HEAVY BAG? THAT IS SO COOL!" Kendra shouted, breaking the grief of the moment. She was standing outside the garage door, staring in through the glass.

"Beck got it for me," Nathan yelled back.

She walked over to the picnic table. "From what Gina said, it sounds like you've been using it."

"It helps me relax," Nathan said. "Plus, I'm getting stronger."

"Oh yeah?" Kendra said. "Let's see."

"Huh?"

"Stand up."

He threw his legs over the bench and stood up across from her.

She squeezed his left bicep, then his right. "Eh, you might make a tough guy someday."

He slapped her hand away. Hard.

"What? You wanna go?" she said. "Right here? Right now?"

"I wouldn't want to hurt you."

"Ohhhh, okay, Mr. Attitude," she said. She nodding her head like she was willing to let it slide, then threw a quick jab at his stomach. With equal speed, he jumped back and her fist never touched the fabric of his shirt.

"Ooh, that was good," she said, impressed. She took a boxing stance and launched a shot at his chin.

He swayed to his right and her fist flew past his head. Not even close.

She tried again with her left hand, but he squatted and watched her fist sail overhead.

She was getting steamed now. She walked away, turned, and then exploded at him. He waited for the right moment, then dove on the grass at a 45° angle, tucked and rolled, and sprung up on his feet again—just like he'd practiced over and over.

She stumbled forward several feet then stopped and spun around, her face flushed red. "Oh, you've *had it* now!" She charged again, but instead of the tuck-and-roll maneuver, Nathan decided to give his legs a stretch. He raced around the corner of the house, then cut right and slipped through the lilac hedge.

Several feet back Kendra did the same thing. But when she came out the other side, he was nowhere to be seen. She ducked back through the hedge, into his yard. "Where is he?" she shouted.

"Beats me," Jameson said.

She ran to the front of the house. Nothing,

She continued up the driveway. Nothing.

She was standing in front of the garage, baffled, when she

heard the blaring peal of a car horn. "NO!" she shouted, then took off running down the driveway. She cut across the lawn and stopped short when she saw him sitting behind the wheel of the Volvo.

"Get out of my car, *NOW!*" she shouted.

He waved, gave her a big smile, and honked again.

After dinner, Nathan sat in the living room with his parents, listening to them reminisce about Henry Hammond, the man and the father. There were smiles. There were tears. There were fond memories and funny stories. Before long, the smiles began to outnumber the tears.

Elizabeth spoke of interesting places her father had taken her and her sister throughout New England and beyond. Magical places. Historical places. Each one tucked away in a remote village, or sewn into the fabric of the scenic countryside, often requiring a long trek through the woods or along a lazy river—every step an adventure to be cherished.

It was a fitting tribute to the man who had touched so many lives from the confines of his bookshop, feeding the literary appetites of his devoted customers, while furthering a legacy that had begun five generations earlier with their ancestor, David Hammond, who had arrived in America with a bookcase and a dream.

Minutes turned into hours, and with each story Nathan was more energized than ever before to carry on the Hammond legacy, entrusted to him by a man he'd known for only a few short years. Would it be a gift or a curse? He'd already dodged bullets, and endured physical abuse from hoodlums and their hired thugs.

Would the satisfaction he got from helping people in need outweigh new dangers he was sure to face?

Only time would tell.

22

Deception

The door slid open just after 9:30 p.m. It was heavier than they thought, and it took some effort. There was a partial moon hanging over the trees, and as they eased the door back, a soft column of light fell across the old plank floor. Once inside, they turned on their flashlights, sending narrow beams of light slicing through the darkness like a pair of Jedi light sabers.

They were creeping forward, moving deeper and deeper into the room, when a lone figure stepped out from behind the row of pallets that were lined up against the outer wall.

"Looking for this, Connie?" Nathan said, holding up the cigar box. "Or would you prefer I call you Finch?"

Connie spun around and pointed her flashlight at him, lighting up his face and the cigar box at the same time. "Well, how do you like that?" she said, in a snide voice. "This was a set up."

"What can I say?" Nathan replied. "My friend Gina can be very convincing when she wants to be."

They'd practiced her scolding routine in Beck's truck on the way home, after Nathan detailed his plan to trap Connie Freeman, who he'd figured out was the true architect of his grandfather's death, not Frank Sobol, as he'd originally thought. As part of their ploy, Gina would drop Richard's name, his town, and the fact that he had a barn, implying that's where Nathan had stashed the necklace. The thought of publicly scolding Nathan was a role she accepted with great excitement, and anticipation.

The person standing beside Connie was more interested in the cigar box.

"So that's where he kept it," Lía Ballard said.

"But you'll never lay a hand on it," Julie Nichols called out as she emerged from the darkness just beyond Nathan.

Lía hit her with the beam of her flashlight. "Oh, look! It's the infamous *Fane.*"

Jordan Prescott was hiding behind the first pallet that sat several feet inside the door. She stood and flicked on the lights, then walked between the row of pallets and the outer wall, taking a position behind Nathan—just as they had planned when he called her before dinner to tell her and Fane about the trap he had set into motion.

"And there's Sidney!" Lía announced. "Who else do we have?" She looked around the room, calling, "Come out, come out, wherever you are."

Elizabeth and David were standing in the front corner with Jameson. They stepped forward and walked as far as the end of the farmer's table.

"Oh, hello," Lía said, smiling. "And just who might you be?"

"Allow me to introduce myself. I'm Jameson. And you are?"

"Lía Ballard," she said. "By now I'm sure you've heard of my father, Walter?"

"I'm familiar with his work," Jameson replied. "Especially the contents of that cigar box."

"You mean, the gold necklace he hid from me after he came back from Guatemala?"

"Hid from *you?*" Nathan asked. "Why would he do that?"

"He thought his darling daughter would steal it and sell it for millions of dollars," she said in a spoiled, child-like voice. "Which, by the way, I fully intended to do," she added, spitefully. "If he'd told me where it was, maybe he wouldn't have died so painfully."

"You had his notebook," Nathan countered. "Why didn't you just use the clue hidden inside it to find the necklace." *Like we did, Gina would tell you if she was here right now,* he was tempted to say.

"Use the clue? I did everything but tear that stupid notebook apart looking for it. Then I had an idea. Why not have the famous Henry Hammond find it for me? The word on the street was that he liked helping people who were down on their luck."

"So, you went to his shop that day, acting distraught, claiming that dangerous men were chasing you, trying to get his notebook," Nathan said.

"Worked like a charm," Lía gloated. "And speaking of those dangerous men, would you like to meet one of them?"

No one replied.

Lía looked back at the open door and shouted "JAKOB,

COME AND SAY HELLO!" Then, in a normal voice, she said, "I'd have Viktor join us too, but he's on lookout duty tonight. I think we've had enough surprises for one night, don't you?"

From out in the driveway came the sound of a car door closing. Seconds later, Jakob came walking into the barn. Like an obedient dog, he walked as far as Lía and stopped slightly behind and just to the left of her. He was well over six feet tall and muscular, with a military style buzz cut. He had a narrow face, and clearly visible between his small almond-shaped eyes was a 2" scar that angled downward from his forehead to the bridge of his nose.

"Everyone, this is Jakob," Lía said. "Jakob, these are the people I was telling you about. That's Nathan," she said, pointing. "He's the one who found the necklace. Standing behind him is Sidney. To the left is Fane. And over there is Jameson. I'm sorry," she said to Elizabeth and David, "I didn't catch your names."

"This is Henry Hammond's daughter," David said, angrily. "It's because of you that her father is dead."

"Because of me? No, no, no. That was Pennyman's doing," Lía insisted. "He poisoned Henry Hammond, not me. It was because of him that it took seven years, and the help of wonder boy here, to find the necklace."

"Is that what Finch told you?" Nathan asked.

"What on Earth are you implying?" Lía asked, playfully.

"Do *you* want to tell her or should I?" Nathan asked Connie.

"Whatever he says, don't believe it," Connie told Lía. "He's just a kid."

"You don't have to believe *me*," Nathan told Lía. "But the medical examiner? Him you should definitely believe."

355

"You lost me," Lía said.

"The medical examiner who examined my grandfather determined that the poison he was given entered his bloodstream approximately 20-24 hours before he died. Isn't that right Dad?"

"That's right," David replied.

"That puts it right around the time he was meeting with Finch and the other four members of the team."

"This is nonsense!" Connie said. "Let's just take the necklace and go."

"Wait! I love science," Lía said. "Go on, kid. You were saying?"

"One of the five people at that meeting put the poison in my grandfather's water bottle. That's not a theory, it's a fact. The medical examiner's report proves it. So you have to ask yourself, which one in the group would have poison with them? I mean, it's not exactly the kind of thing you carry around with you…"

"Unless it's part of your job," Julie said, eyeing Connie as she spoke.

"When we came to your house on Thursday, I looked in the back of your car," Nathan told Connie. "You have a very unusual assortment of cleaners. I noticed one of them had a warning label. You know, the big skull and crossbones? There was name on it but I couldn't make it out. What does 1080 mean?"

"Sodium Fluoroacetate," Jameson said. "Also known as Compound 1080. It's what they refer to as a rodenticide. It's used to kill rodents."

"*YOU* poisoned Henry Hammond?" Lía asked Connie.

"I can explain—"

"You told me Pennyman did it," Lía said, cutting her off. "Why would you lie about that?"

"It's like I told you at the start," Connie said. "After Henry showed us the notebook, he told us he was going to find the necklace and return it to the Mexican government. We had no way of knowing when or how that was going to happen, so we had to find a way to stop him. If we didn't do *something*, we'd never get the necklace."

"Yes, I remember you telling me that," Lía said impatiently. "But you still haven't answered my question. Why did you lie?"

"What was I supposed to do?" Connie fired back. "At the time, I'd only known you for what…a week? I still wasn't sure if I could even trust you."

"What else did you lie about?"

"Nothing!" Connie barked, offended by the question. "Pennyman took the notebook and I did what needed to be done. Yes, it took us longer to find the necklace, but here we are. Let's just take it and get out of here."

"Let me get this straight," Jordan said. "You and Frank conspired to steal the notebook and then, together, the two of you were going to look for the necklace?"

"Since we're not going to see each again after tonight, yes, that's exactly what we planned to do," Connie spat.

"So then, why did you implicate Frank when all along you were working with him?"

"Because I knew you'd try to find the notebook. By naming Frank, you'd focus all your attention on him, which would allow me, the last person you'd ever suspect of having it, to search for the clue."

"*You* had the notebook?" Nathan asked.

"Who do you think hid it in the gazebo at Breakheart Reservation?"

"And how did *she* come into the picture?" Jordan asked, pointing at Lía.

"We met. We talked. She claimed the necklace was rightfully hers, and because of that she was due a stake in any monies we received once we sold it. I agreed with her and that was that," Connie said. "End of story."

Lía smiled at Jakob and patted his shoulder. "We were very insistent, weren't we Jakob?"

He didn't smile. Didn't try to bump fists. He just looked at her and tensed his shoulders in what could best be described as a fractional shrug. Not a full shrug. Not half. Not even a quarter shrug. It was like he was trying it out for the first time and had yet to perfect it.

"And when did this happen?" Julie asked.

"Three days after Henry died, all right?" Connie said, growing tired of all the questions. "She called me to see how Henry was making out with the search for the necklace."

"And that's when you lied about Pennyman."

"I think we already covered that," Connie sniped.

"So, all this time, Frank believed that the two of you were looking for the necklace when it was really you and Lía," Jordan said.

"Yeah? What of it?"

"That's a lie," Nathan said. "You made Lía believe you were working with her, but in reality, you and Frank were still working your original plan."

During the meeting at the house, Brandt had played only part of Sobol's confession. There was more, and when Nathan first heard it, he misunderstood what Frank meant. But only after he pieced together Connie's role in the scheme, and listened to the recording again, did he realize the charade they were playing.

Connie turned to Lía and said, "I think this little circus show has gone on long enough."

"Is it true?" Lía said.

"Oh, it's true," Elizabeth said. "Frank admitted it." She took Brandt's digital recorder from her pocket and showed it to Lía. "Would you like to hear it?"

"Oh for crying out loud," Connie groaned. "Enough of this garbage!"

"Garbage, huh?" Elizabeth said. "Listen to this." She adjusted the volume on the recorder, then hit play.

"Well, it looks like everything turned out just like you planned."

"Yes, I'd say our efforts are going to pay off quite nicely, not that it didn't require some deception along the way."

Elizabeth hit the stop button.

"Looks like she's been stringing you along from the start," Nathan told Lía.

"Don't listen to them," Connie said. "There's a perfectly reasonable explanation—"

"Is it true?" Lía said, before she could finish.

"Lía, listen to me, I can— "

"Is it true?" Lía cut in again, louder.

Nathan looked across the room and called out, "Did we get it?"

Brandt came halfway down the stairs leading to the second floor, the old wooden treads creaking beneath his feet, and flashed two thumbs up. "We got it," he said.

Earlier that day, when Nathan was stashing the necklace in Richard Abbott's barn, he called Brandt to see if he had a digital recorder that could be fitted with a wireless microphone to capture and save a conversation. Brandt, as it turned out, had several. They even had wireless earbuds. On the way to the meeting at Nathan's house, Brandt stopped by the barn and hid the microphone atop a beam that ran directly over the farmer's table.

With the recording confirmed, Nathan looked up at the beam overhead and shouted,
"WE'RE GOOD!"

Lía had no idea who he was talking to or what his words meant, but it was clearly time to go. She reached out her hand and said, "Give me the box."

Nathan pulled it to his side. "No."

"You can hand it over," she said, "or I can have Jakob take it from you."

"Well," Nathan said, smirking. "He's welcome to try."

Lía exhaled, showing mild irritation, then turned to Jakob and smiled. "Jakob?" she said calmly, "would you be so kind as to retrieve my father's box from our brazen young guest?"

Like a robot being activated by remote control, Jakob stepped forward and walked dutifully toward Nathan. What was wrong with American children, he wondered. This boy was nothing like the kids in Gdańsk, the port city on the Baltic coast where he spent his youth. Didn't parents in this country teach their children respect? Yes, he would do as he was asked and take the box, but what he really wanted to do was beat some manners into the boy. Not unlike the treatment he'd received in his earliest years.

As he closed the span between them, Nathan backed up, then turned and darted between the pallets. With the tall cube of shrink-wrapped boxes blocking his view, Jakob never saw Nathan slip Jordan the box as he squeezed past her. She held it against her stomach, using her body to shield it from Jakob as he shoved her aside and chased Nathan along the outer wall.

Nathan raced past more shrink-wrapped pallets, and more than a few mountainous boxes of books he'd sorted, to the back corner of the barn. There, he jumped down the old grain chute and disappeared in the black void below.

Viktor was sitting behind the wheel of a black Cadillac CTS, parked several feet from the barn door. Several minutes earlier, Jakob had been called inside. For what reason, Viktor didn't know, nor did he care; he wasn't paid to think about such things. He tapped his fingers on the center console, humming a tune by the popular German rock band, Rammstein, when he felt someone tap his shoulder through the open window.

He turned at once and saw a figure standing next to the car. The person was so close that all he could see was their midsection. Thinking it might be Connie, he said, "Yes?"

Kendra leaned down and said, "You need to move your car. This space is reserved."

"Who are you?" Viktor asked, easing the pistol from his shoulder holster.

His accent was definitely foreign.

"Are you deaf, or just stupid?" Kendra asked. "I said, this spot is *reserved!*"

He pushed the pistol through the open window at her. "Leave now or I shoot."

The way he ran the words together—*leavenoworishoot*—made it sound like a delicacy at the Csabai Sausage Festival in his home country of Hungary.

"That's what I was hoping you'd say," Kendra replied. She stepped back like she was going to comply, then took a vicious rip with her bat.

Right to left.

Homerun swing.

The bat hit the handle of the gun with a sharp crack, which was the sound of Viktor's middle, ring, and pinky finger snapping. The pistol flew from his hand, arcing through the air before landing in a hedge of flowering quince that lined the outer edge of the driveway. Grunting and cursing in pain, he pushed the door open and took several swipes at her with his good hand, but she stepped back and watched him paw harmlessly at the cool night air.

He muttered something in a language she didn't understand, then wriggled his Pillsbury Dough Boy frame out from behind the steering wheel. His feet had just touched the gravel when he pushed off the door frame and launched his 300-pound body at her. She ducked right, set her feet, and brought the bat down on the back of his neck with both hands. He made a sound like a spouting whale and fell face-first on the ground.

"I *love* this bat!" she said as she closed the car door. Viktor's body was as big as a park bench, and when she sat down on him, she tapped the back of his head several times with the end of the bat. "Hey, you still with me?"

He managed a low moan.

"I'll take that as a yes," she said. "Since we have this time together, there's something I want to explain to you. I think you might actually find it interesting. When you pointed your gun at me just now? I was presented with a difficult choice: do I take level swing or a home run swing? It's a harder decision than you might think, trust me. You see, the level swing uses an attack angle that coincides with the descent angle of the ball. We're talking, maybe, I don't know, six degrees?"

Viktor grunted and tried to stand.

"Hey, I wasn't finished!" she said. She rapped the back of his skull with the end of the bat and he collapsed on the ground again. "That's better. Now, as I was about to explain, the home run swing is completely different. It uses an attack angle that maximizes the probability of actually hitting a home run, which is somewhere between 20°-24°. So, knowing that, and taking into consideration the position of your gun, in relation to the pitch of the driveway, I chose the home run swing. Truth be told, I hooked it, so my calculation may have been off a bit."

Viktor moaned again but didn't try to get up.

Jakob dropped down though the opening in the floor and landed on the packed dirt below. He blinked hard several times as his eyes adjusted to the dark, then turned and took stock of his surroundings.

He was in some sort of root cellar or crude storage room. Probably used for old tires, defunct lawn equipment, and rusty patio furniture, he figured. Through the thin band of light coming from the hole in the floor overhead, he saw a wooden door on the outer wall to his left. It was partially open. Assuming the boy must've used it to get away, he pushed it all the way open and stepped outside, where his face met Beck's right fist.

Brandt had outfitted Beck and Kendra with wireless earbuds that allowed them to monitor the conversation being transmitted by the GSM microphone inside the barn. Because of that, they knew that the man in the car was named Viktor; they knew the man who'd been called into the barn was Jakob; they heard Lía's demand and Nathan's subsequent rebuke, and they heard the shuffling of feet as he ran to the back of the barn with Jakob in hot pursuit.

Beck's potent right jab hit Jakob like an anvil and sent him stumbling backward through the open doorway. Just as quickly, he stood, shook it off, and charged, thundering into the darkness with his shoulder lowered, intending to drive it into his attacker's stomach and bulldoze him to the ground.

But using the darkness to mask his movements, Beck had shifted his position and was standing at the side of the door. He watched Jakob run past, lunge at the shadows, and trip on the exposed root of a nearby oak tree. He hit the ground hard and Beck pounced on him, just as the first of two police cruisers tore up the driveway, their lightbars flashing and their tires spitting gravel.

Thirty minutes later, Jakob and Viktor were handcuffed in the back seat of cruiser #1.

It was a tight fit.

Connie Freeman and Lía Ballard were likewise restrained in cruiser #2.

Not talking.

Kendra and Beck were leaning against his truck, watching four officers take statements from the assembled group inside the barn.

"That must've been some hit," Beck said. "Viktor's a big boy."

"Well, you know what they say," Kendra replied. "The bigger they come…"

"The more fun it is to watch 'em drop," Beck said.

David and Elizabeth emerged from the barn. When they saw Beck and Kendra, they walked over to talk to them.

"It's over," Kendra said, giving Elizabeth a hug.

"I never thought this day would come," she said, fighting back tears.

Kendra pulled back. "Tell me, when you played that recording, what was it like to watch their reaction?"

"That was pretty special, I must admit," Elizabeth said, smiling. She looked back at the barn and saw Nathan being questioned by two officers. He was pointing at the beam overhead, explaining how they were able to capture Connie Freeman's confession. Lía Ballard's cryptic comment about the timing and severity of her father's death would launch a separate and immediate investigation.

"He's going to be awhile," Beck told her.

"Yeah, why don't you and David go home," Kendra said. "One of us can drive Nathan back."

"Thank you," Elizabeth said, physically and emotionally weary. After she and David left, Jameson walked out of the barn with

Julie Nichols and Jordan Prescott. "Nice takedowns," he said to Kendra and Beck.

"Nah, it was too quick," Kendra said. "We've got a big tournament next week. I could've used some extra batting practice."

Nathan appeared moments later.

"Ahh, the hero of the hour," Jordan quipped. "Or should I say, of the century."

"There's something I've been meaning to ask you," Julie said.

"What's that?"

"How did you figure out that Finch was the killer?"

"A few things tipped me off," Nathan said. "The first was something she told us at her house. She said she went back to my grandfather's office to get her jacket and she saw Frank standing alone at the desk. To me, that suggested Frank's plan to steal the notebook was already set in motion. I mean, why else would he be hanging around reading an old book he found on my grandfather's desk? Then, when he cornered us in the barn, I asked him about the poison. He said it was never part of the plan. What he meant was, it was never part of *his* plan. In other words, someone else put the poison in the water bottle. Then I remembered seeing the poison in Finch's car and…well…you heard that part already."

"Incredible," Julie said.

"There's something I've been meaning to ask you, too," Nathan said. "Back at my house, you told me you had a good feeling about me. What did you mean by that?"

"I knew from the very first time I saw you that you weren't a quitter. It was when you were visiting your grandfather's bookstore with your parents. I think you were maybe four years old at the time. You were sitting on the bench seat near the front window, struggling with one of those metal ring puzzles."

Nathan remembered the bench seat but he had no recollection of that specific day.

"Your mother told you to leave it, that there was a book she wanted to show you, but you didn't listen; you continued working the metal pieces until you removed the ring. It was that unwavering determination that made us want to recruit you."

"Recruit me?"

"I knew how much your grandfather meant to you, based on our previous meetings," Jordan said.

"So I instructed her to stop by here last Sunday and explain the circumstances surrounding his death—information I was sure you'd never been told."

"Including details about the facilitators' group." Nathan said.

"Yes, *especially* that."

"But at your office, you told me to destroy the list and forget the whole thing."

"That's right. I knew the more I pushed you to quit, the harder you'd work to uncover the truth. It was the kid with the ring puzzle I was trying to reach."

"Your grandfather displayed the same quality whenever I tried to dissuade him," Jameson noted.

"Finch tried to warn me off, too," Nathan said, "but that was different."

"She was afraid that if you continued, you'd eventually figure out she was the killer," said Beck.

"So, you guys *used* me!" Nathan said.

"Do you blame us?" Julie asked. "At this point, your detective skills are pretty much known the world over."

"Once you were fully on board, we needed a way to monitor your progress without arousing suspicion," Jordan explained. "So we arranged for someone to sort of…keep an eye on you."

"You!" Nathan said, pointing a finger at Jordan. "You sent Zee to remove the cardboard."

"It was her idea," Jordan said, pointing at Julie.

"It was her *friend*," Julie countered, pointing back at her.

Nathan gave them both a pathetic look. "I can't believe it. You got me a babysitter."

"Oh, come on, he's harmless," Jordan said.

"Yeah, man…he's totally, like, you know, *righteous!*" Nathan said, in his best hipster voice. "Dude is seriously engaged with the cosmic *oneness* of the universe. You dig what I'm sayin'?"

"What can I tell you?" Julie said, trying not to laugh. "We made a judgement call and it worked out." Then she got serious. "I say this with heartfelt sincerity: what you were able to accomplish is simply amazing. You are, in every way, the living embodiment of your grandfather, although, I'm not sure he would've left the necklace in the barn."

"Not without a pair of armed guards at the door," Jordan quipped.

"Did you open the box?" Nathan asked her.

"Actually no," Jordan said. "In all the confusion, it never occurred to me."

"You still have it, right?" Nathan asked Beck.

"Yup," he replied. He opened the driver-side door of his truck and grabbed the cigar box from the footwell.

Nathan took it from him and handed it to Jordan. When she opened it and pulled back the linen cloth, she saw an old bike chain lock with a scrolling combination padlock.

"Oh, you little sneak!" Julie said. "You never left it here."

"Nope. It's like I told you at my house. I left it someplace where no one, including Asher Rickman, would ever think to look for it."

They stared at him, confused.

Beck opened the door of his truck again. This time, he reached into the center console and pulled out a hefty roll of bubble wrap.

Nathan peeled off the tape keeping it sealed and passed it to Julie. With great reverence she slowly unwrapped it. When she took her first look at the necklace she'd been pursuing for the past seven years, and held the wedges of pure gold that glowed softly in the moonlight, her jaw fell open in utter astonishment.

"It's magnificent," Jordan murmured.

"And absolutely frightening," Julie said. "People we trusted were willing to kill to get this."

"I don't know about you," Jordan said, "but I won't relax until that's locked in a vault."

"We have a vault at the office," Julie said. "We can drive there right now. In the morning I'll call the National Institute of Anthropology and History in Mexico City and arrange for them to come and get it."

Julie removed it from the bubble wrap and covered it in the linen cloth.

"Who gets this?" Jordan said, holding up the bike chain.

"Right here," Beck said, reaching out his hand. "I keep it in the toolbox for special occasions."

They all looked at him, eyebrows raised. *Special occasions?*

"You don't want to know," he said.

Julie tucked the necklace back in the cigar box and closed it. Then it was time to go.

"I'll drive you to the office," Beck said. "I think we've had enough surprises for one night, don't you?"

"Well then, Nathan, this is goodbye," Julie said. "But only for a short while. Something tells me our paths will cross again, and I want you to know that we're here for you whenever you need us."

"Just as my grandfather intended."

"Yes, just as your grandfather intended," she replied. "The note he gave you is proof of that."

"You do realize that we're going to need a driver, right?" Nathan said. "And someone to stock the safehouses."

Kendra raised her hand. "I'll do it."

"You?" Nathan exclaimed.

"Why not?" she replied. "I already know where they are."

"That's true. Okay, you're hired," he said. "Wait, does she get paid?"

Julie gave him a look. *Excuse me?*

"I'm joking!" he said.

"Kid's got a sense of humor," Jordan said.

"Good," Julie told her. "He's going to need it."

Afterword

It was well after midnight when Kendra dropped Nathan off at home. He walked up the driveway and was rounding the back corner of the house when he heard someone call to him.

"Nathan!"

He stopped walking and looked over at the tree line that marked the back of the property. In the thin light cast by the moon, the trees were nothing more than soft shadows.

Again, he heard the voice.

Louder this time.

"Over here!"

He knew that voice. "Gina?" he said, walking over to the garage. When he got to the side door, he saw her standing inside, the door open just enough to allow her to look out at the back yard.

"What are you doing?" he asked.

"I need your help," she told him. There was fear in her voice.

"*My* help? Right now? It's 12:30 in the morning."

She grabbed his arm and yanked him through the doorway.

"Hey! What are you doing?" he said as he stumbled forward.

She let go of his arm and closed the door.

He was reaching for the light switch when she grabbed his arm. "No lights."

A soft shuffling sound in the corner made him turn and look. In the murky shadows he saw the rough outline of a person. "Uh, Gina?" he said. "Who is *that?*"

"She's nobody you know."

"Then, what's she doing in my garage in the middle of the

371

night?"

"You're going to help me save her life."

Provenience

WILLOW & VINE AUCTIONS is a fictional business.

THE 7-10 SPLIT, also known as "bedposts," is considered one of the most formidable shots in bowling. It occurs when the bowler has knocked down every pin except those in the opposing rear corners (the number 7 and 10 pins).

BENNET WINCH are purveyors of British-made luxury luggage and accessories. Founded in the UK in 2014 by Robin Bennett and Robin Winch, each of their products are handmade in England using traditional skills and materials.

THE LEATHER DISTRICT is a neighborhood of Boston, MA, located between the Financial District and Chinatown. It was first developed as a residential area but soon became the center of the city's leather industry, giving way to its name. Many of the buildings were designed by architects, including Peabody and Stearns and Willard T. Sears, and reflected a strong Richardsonian Romanesque style. It was listed on the National Register of Historic Places in 1983.

PASSIVE VENTILATION systems have been documented as far back as Classical times (the period of cultural history between the 8th century BC and the 5th century AD, comprising the civilizations of ancient Greece and ancient Rome) and are intended to supply and remove air in an enclosed space. The passive flow of outdoor air does not require mechanical systems and is achieved through fixed or adjustable openings such as louvers, doors, and windows. Almost all historic buildings were ventilated naturally.

A DAVENPORT DESK has an inclined lifting desktop attached with hinges to the back of the body, and drawers on one of its sides. The center compartment features storage space for paper and other writing implements, and smaller spaces in the form of small drawers and pigeonholes. The desk is credited to Captain Josiah Davenport (1771-1836) who commissioned the design from English furniture maker Gillows of Lancaster near the end of the 18th century.

THE PEMBROKE TABLE most likely derived its name from Henry Herbert, 9th Earl of Pembroke (1693–1751). The useful and versatile style that could be easily store or tucked into the corner of a room emerged on the market during the last quarter of the 18th century. It features a central drawer and flaps on either side, which, when raised, are supported by hinged brackets known as "elbows" to increase its size. They were traditionally crafted of mahogany and featured slim tapered legs. With a set of casters at its base, its uses included dining, writing, serving tea, or for taking a bedside meal.

A WOODEN BOOKBINDING PLOUGH consisted of two pieces of wood joined together by a central wooden screw, with the "plough" having a metal groove that held the blade. They were traditionally used for cutting the edges of books in the 15th century and were a mainstay of binderies until the second quarter of the 19th century when they were replaced by guillotines that offered greater output, speed, and accuracy of the cut.

GRATTOIR is an 18th century French bookbinding tool, or "scraper," used to aid in backing and smoothing the spine linings.

FRATTOIR is also an 18th century French bookbinding tool used to scratch up the spine to get better adhesion of the transverse vellum lining.

THE FIRESIDE POETS were a group of 19th century American poets mostly situated in the Northeast United States. They wrote in conventional poetic forms to present domestic themes and moral issues. The poets often included in this group were Henry Wadsworth Longfellow, John Greenleaf Whittier, James Russell Lowell, William Cullen Bryant, Oliver Wendell Holmes, Sr., and occasionally, Ralph Waldo Emerson. The "fireside" moniker arose out of their popularity, as families would read their books by the fire in their homes.

PERSEUS is a name from Greek mythology. Alongside Cadmus and Bellerophon, he was the greatest Greek hero and slayer of monsters before the days of Heracles. The Perseus constellation is located in the north sky and is one of the 48 ancient constellations listed by 2nd century astronomer Ptolemy, and among the 88 constellations defined by the International Astronomical Union. The Perseid meteor shower starts in July and peaks in August and is caused by Earth's passage though debris left over from the Comet Swift-Tuttle in 1992.

THE "SUBWAY DRESS" refers to the pleated ivory dress worn by Marilyn Monroe in the 1955 movie "The Seven Year Itch." In the scene, Monroe is standing on a subway grate in New York City fighting an upward draft caused by a passing train. It went on to become one of the most iconic moments in movie history. The dress eventually sold for 4.6 million dollars at a Beverly Hills auction of Hollywood costumes. Along with an additional one-million-dollar auction company commission, the anonymous phone buyer paid a total of 5.6 million dollars.

POMMEL HORSE is a gymnastics apparatus with a metal body covered with foam rubber and leather, with plastic handles (or pommels). It dates back to Alexander the Great, whose Macedonian soldiers used an early version of the pommel horse (a simple wooden structure modeled after a horse's back) to practice mounting and dismounting. This practice was repeated by the Romans and was later added to the ancient Olympic Games.

PARKOUR, also known as "free running," is a movement technique of efficient running, jumping, vaulting and climbing using real-life objects as an obstacle course. Not limited to physical training, it conditions the mind to see possibilities where none seem to exist.

MINDSET TRAINING is designed to improve confidence, mental sharpness and stability by improving reaction time and decision-making under pressure. It can also include functional fitness techniques to help build a strong core and develop quick movements. Having a tactical mindset puts training to use by thinking about all possible outcomes.

A MNEMONIC PHONE NUMBER is an alphanumeric equivalent of a telephone number.

T-MINUS is a sequence of counting backward, generally during countdowns to space launches. It was adopted by NASA for the space program in the 1960s. During a rocket launch, T-minus translates to "time minus," with the "T" representing the exact time that the rocket will be launched into orbit.

THE TROUT QUINTET is the popular name for the Piano Quintet in A Major, D. 667, by Franz Schubert. It was composed in 1819, when Schubert was 22 years old, but wasn't published until 1829, a year after his death. The piece is known as the Trout because the fourth movement is a set of variations on Schubert's earlier Lied "Die Forelle" ("The Trout").

BRICE MARDEN is a contemporary American artist often labeled a Minimalist and an Abstract Expressionist. His works are derived from highly specific personal experiences and his paintings of the 1960s helped to define minimalist painting.

CRUISE SHIP ANCHORS are used to keep the cruise ship in a stationary position, generally, when they stop out at sea. The anchors are usually between 10-20 feet in length and weigh between 10 and 20 US tons. Most modern cruise ships have more than one anchor (one on the port side and one on the starboard side of the ship).

"FLY THE COOP" is a metaphor for departing suddenly or escaping from confinement. It is American in origin and dates back to the early 20th century. At the time, "coop" was slang for jail or prison.

THE GLOBAL POSITIONING SYSTEM, or GPS, is powered by a global radio navigation system comprised of 24 operational satellites that orbit the Earth. The Global Navigation Satellite System (GNSS) network emits radio signals from medium Earth orbit to communicate with GPS devices. GPS operation is based on trilateration, which uses the position of three or more satellites and their distance from the GPS device to determine latitude, longitude, elevation and time. Information about the satellite location and signal travel time of at least four satellites will quickly and accurately calculate a vehicle's travel route, speed and more.

BREAKHEART RESERVATION is a public recreation area covering 652 acres in the towns of Saugus and Wakefield, Massachusetts. In addition to a hardwood forest, it includes two freshwater lakes, a winding section of the Saugus River, a series of 11 interconnecting trails, and scenic views of Boston and rural New England from rocky hilltops. In 1706 it was referred to as "The Six Hundred Acres." Today, it offers swimming, hiking, biking, trail running, cross-country skiing, fishing, orienteering and a play area for dogs called "Bark Park."

NATIONAL INSTITUTE OF ANTHROPOLOGY AND HISTORY (INAH), is a federal government organization founded in 1939 to guarantee the research, conservation, protection and spreading of pre-historic, archeological, historical and paleontological heritage of Mexico.

PAUL BUNYAN is a fictional lumberjack and enduring folk hero in American and Canadian folklore. Many tall tales were based on his larger-than-life character, including the creation of the Grand Canyon with one drag of his massive axe and the creation of Minnesota's 10,000 lakes by the footprints of his trusty companion Babe the Blue Ox. Historians believe he was based in large part on the real-life lumberjack Fabian Fournier, a French-Canadian timberman who moved south after the Civil War and got a job as the foreman of a logging crew in Michigan. The first Paul Bunyan story, "Round River," made it into print in 1906, penned by journalist James Mac-Gillivray for a local newspaper in Oscoda, Michigan.

SUPERSPORT WORLD CHAMPIONSHIP RACING is a motorcycle racing competition on hard-surfaced circuits. The championship runs as a support class to the Superbike World Championship.

GSM stands for Global System for Mobile communication and is a standard digital cellular network used in Europe and much of the world. A GSM bug is a wireless listening device fitted with a SIM card (Subscriber Identity Module) using the GSM network, and can be accessed and controlled anywhere by a telephone call. They are inexpensive and easy to acquire, and are popular for their simple design, made to be conveniently concealed in cars or buildings, and their range (up to 30-50 feet).

CSABAI SAUSAGE FESTIVAL, or "Csabai Kolbászfesztivál" is an annual celebration of Csabai sausage held since 1997 in the small Hungarian town of Békéscsaba. This four-day sausage festival attracts thousands of visitors with delicious sausages, fun competitions, folk music, and an accompanying wine festival. A highlight of the event is the sausage-making contest comprised of more than 500 teams from all around the globe. Csabai sausage has protected geographical indications (PGI), which identify an agricultural product, raw or processed, whose quality, reputation or other characteristics link it to its geographical origin.

Illustrations

The chapter page illustrations are used with permission from the Metropolitan Museum of Art in New York City. Founded in 1870, the museum features over 5,000 years of art from around the world at The Met Fifth Avenue and The Met Cloisters.

Chapter 1   Silver bracelet, 304 BC – A.D. 364 (Egypt)

Chapter 2   Claw Anklet, ca. 1887-1813 BC (Egypt)

Chapter 3   Gold armband with Herakles knot, 3rd-2nd century (Greece)

Chapter 4   Three Rings:
Wrapped Gold & Agate Scarab Ring, 4th century BCE (Etruscan)
Ring of Hanefer, ca. 1492-1473 BC (Upper Egypt, Thebes)
Scarab Finger Ring, ca. 1279-1213 BC (Egypt)

Chapter 5   Gold Pendant and glass bead necklace, 2nd half 6th century-1st half 7th century (Belgium)

Chapter 6   Bronze bracelet with four rings, 9th-8th century BCE (Italy)

Chapter 7   Maenad-head earrings, 1st century BC (Egypt)

Chapter 8   Gold arm band with man's head, 1st quarter 10th century (Indonesia)

Chapter 9   Scarab, ca. 1635-1458 BC (Egypt)

Chapter 10   Gold and glass necklace, early 5th century BCE (Italy)

Acknowledgements

One of the most important aspects of creating a truly engaging story is to "keep it real." Be it character-centric actions and dialogue or something as unique as the contents of an archeologist's backpack, getting it right not only serves as an educational tool, it helps to make the story come alive in the reader's mind. As a writer, I find sifting through descriptions, gathering historical facts, and adding critical details that help give the story and its characters depth to be one of the best parts of the journey. To those experts who shared their wisdom so readily, I offer my heartfelt thanks.

Nathan Cole's training regimen was written with the help of George Amaru, 4th degree black belt instructor. George also lent a helping hand with the front cover graphic. Beth Selig, from Hudson Cultural Services (HCS), was a wealth of information regarding archeological processes. John Boudreau, U.S. Army Sergeant, Retired, provided valuable knowledge about firearms, police and military equipment and practices, and physical combat, drawing from his many years of dedicated service. Tristen Deutsaw, U.S. Navy, Retired, continues to be my eyes into the world of the U.S. Marshals Service, and Brad Reisfeld, in the Chemical and Biological Engineering Department at Colorado State University, helped sort out the source and effects of various poisons. Tambien, a mi hermano de armas, José Merced, que ayudo con el titulo, le digo muchas gracias!

Once written, the job of preparing the manuscript wouldn't be possible without the superb editing of Karen Struthers, the layout skill of Laura Borden, and the graphics help from the good folks at Gem Graphics. To the shopkeepers that share my books with readers of every age, including Paul Connolly, Steve Levy, and the staff at the Toadstool Bookshops, just to name a few, I thank you. To teachers and librarians worldwide, the real superheroes, without your dedication to literacy, words would be nothing more than a series of curious shapes with no form or meaning.

And to the dedicated followers of the Third Floor Mystery Series, may the intrigue of an old bookcase, hidden in a dark and dusty attic and filled with countless unsolved mysteries, continue to keep you turning pages late into the night.

About the Author

Alfred M. Struthers lives in Peterborough, New Hampshire with his wife Karen. In addition to crafting books that inspire, teach, entertain and make a difference in the lives of readers both young and old, he is a singer/songwriter, woodworker, photographer, and avid collector of fossils that line the streambeds in and around Cooperstown, New York.

To find out what he's been up to lately, visit:
thirdfloorbooksllc.com.

Coming Soon!

The Shadows Grieve

(The Helen Bainbridge Chronicles, Book 2)

Nathan raced up the center stairway to a tiled landing that was roughly 10' square. There, he saw Gina standing at a window, peering out at the parking lot below. "What are doing?" he asked, urgency in his voice. "And where's Rachel?"

"What are you talking about?" she asked, quickly turning from the window. "I thought she was with you."

The sound of shuffling feet erupted from the first floor as someone exploded through the front door. That was followed by a second person, then a third.

Nathan looked down into the foyer and saw the same three men from earlier: the leader, in a thin black-leather coat; the other two clad in olive-green British commando sweaters. All three were holding a handgun at their sides.

He backed away from the top step and hurried over to Gina. "They found us," he said, keeping his voice low. He looked to his left and saw a long hallway that stretched past a row of offices. To his right, another stairway led back downstairs to a rear emergency exit.

A voice echoed through the foyer. "You," one of the men said. "Check that end of the building." Then to the other man, "And you check that end. I'll look upstairs. Remember, I want all three of them and I want them alive!"

Nathan took Gina by the shoulder and pointed at the back stairway. You take the stairs. He tapped his chest and then hitched his thumb over his shoulder at the hallway. I'll go that way.

"What about Rachel?" she whispered, a look of desperation on her face.

The sound of heavy boots scuffing the polished marble steps filled the air, getting louder with each passing second.

"We need to save ourselves first," Nathan said. "Then we can worry about her. Now, GO!"

As she disappeared down the back stairway, he sprinted into the hallway, passing office doors, all closed. He was approaching the end of the hall, where it made a 90° turn to the left, when Rachel stepped out from behind the corner. The resulting collision stunned them both and sent them tumbling to the floor just as the man in the black leather coat appeared at the mouth of the hallway.

When he saw Nathan and Rachel laying in a heap on the floor, he turned toward the stairway and shouted, "THEY'RE UP HERE!"

Nathan, groggy from the collision, scrambled uneasily to his feet. He shook Rachel's shoulder and said, "Get up!"

She didn't move.

The sound of heavy boots pounding the linoleum thundered down the hallway. Nathan shook Rachel's shoulder again, harder. "Come on! Get up!"

She made a soft murmuring sound but remained prone on the floor.

Just then, the sound of footsteps stopped and the hallway grew quiet. Nathan looked up and saw a Beretta M9 pistol pointed directly at his head.

www.ingramcontent.com/pod-product-compliance
Lightning Source LLC
Chambersburg PA
CBHW060150260626
47160CB00001B/206